John Malcolm was born in Salisbury in 1929 and was educated at the Cathedral School, Salisbury and then King's College, Taunton. He has been a practising solicitor in London since 1954. He has written scripts for television; theme music for films and television (he wrote the music used as ITN News's theme for the first twenty-five years); revue songs and satirical sketches. As well as being a competent jazz pianist, John Malcolm plays tennis and drives the most elegant Bentley ever made. He now spends most of his time writing, and is working on the sequel to *The Tesla Trinity*.

By the same author

Let's Make it Legal

JOHN MALCOLM

The Tesla Trinity

GRAFTON BOOKS
A Division of the Collins Publishing Group

LONDON GLASGOW
TORONTO SYDNEY AUCKLAND

Grafton Books
A Division of the Collins Publishing Group
8 Grafton Street, London W1X 3LA

A Grafton Paperback Original 1987

ISBN 0-586-06957-7

Printed and bound in Great Britain by
Collins, Glasgow

Set in Times

For Jane

Author's Note
The Facts

Nikola Tesla was born in what is now Yugoslavia in 1856. He died in New York in 1943. He was possibly the greatest scientist who ever lived, yet few people have heard of him.

Tesla delivered alternating current to the world producing electric power and all its consequent marvels. He invented radio twenty years before Marconi lodged his patents. He designed the bladeless turbine. He devised the system which made computers possible. He demonstrated radio-controlled boats to a disbelieving U.S. Navy Department at the turn of the century. He drew the blueprints for vertical take-off aircraft fifty years before the scientific establishment made them a practical reality in 1952. He designed remote-control rockets which even now are on the secret list.

The history books do not do justice to Tesla's genius. If they did the free world might not be facing the little-known threat presently posed by Russian advances with Tesla's most astounding discovery: an invisible electro-magnetic shield which no bullet, shell, aircraft or missile can penetrate. Any city or country which possesses it will be inviolate from any form of attack, conventional or nuclear.

The following pages describe – as fiction – the search for the secret of the Tesla Shield. Some readers may feel that the very idea that Tesla made a model of his invention, to be found after his death, absurd. Consider then that Margaret Cheney in her 1981 biography, 'Tesla: Man out of Time' (Laurel Edition) records that Tesla made such a model and left it in the safe of the Governor Clinton Hotel. It was found after his death.

What is beyond dispute is that the American and Russian

Governments have poured billions of dollars and roubles into this hunt. This was confirmed by the U.S. Government in 1981 under the Freedom of Information Act.

Whoever first unravels this technology – assuming that it exists – will control the world. The intelligence services of the West admit that the Russians are in the lead.

* * *

The characters in this book, with the exceptions noted in the following paragraph, are fictious. Any resemblances to actual people, living or dead, are purely coincidental. Without prejudice to the generality of this statement I wish to emphasize that no member of the Westinghouse family lives in New York; Christopher Hackett is a product of my imagination and is not intended to represent any scientist, living or dead, in California, or anywhere else; neither Officer Pierce nor any other officer said to be working out of the police precinct in Flushing Meadow Park is intended to represent any actual officer, living or dead; Professor Rex Hirshfield is imaginary and not intended to represent any past present or future member of the temporary or permanent staff of MIT or any other university or college; Maurice Gilbert is fictitious and not intended to represent any scientist in Belgium, at CERN or anywhere else.

Nikola Tesla is real, as is Kolman Czito and his son Julius although not the manner or the date of Julius's death. Kolman's grand-daughter, Sarah, is imaginary as is Emanuel Yatanabron. Tesla's friends and associates mentioned on pages 192 and 193 are real. The donation ascribed to Fritz Lowenstein on page 211 is imaginary.

The action, attitudes and opinions of the Soviet, British, American, Yugoslav, Swiss and French governments are figments of the author's imagination.

Contents

ACKNOWLEDGEMENTS

I am indebted to many people for reading the whole or parts of the manuscript of this book. I extend my sincere thanks to them all.

I must mention especially: the help given by Edmund Ward, his much-needed encouragement and expertise on construction; Dr Dennis Rosen, a true polymath, for his help not only with the more arcane reaches of physics, and the relevance of CERN, but also for his literary counsel; Lt-Col. Thomas Bearden (USAF Retired) a leading world authority on Tesla, and whose publication 'Solutions to Tesla's Secrets and the Soviet Tesla Weapons' (Tesla Book Company, Milbrae, California) was of immense help; John Ratzlaff whose knowledge of Tesla is encyclopaedic; Charles Ruch of the Westinghouse Historical Society, Pittsburgh, who spent many hours researching Tesla's time with his company for me, and for suggestions concerning the Westinghouse Time Capsules; consulting engineer Malcolm Tappin and his partners in Kenchington Little, London, who provided the mechanics for the underground boring in Flushing Meadow Park; Air Chief Marshal Sir Christopher Foxley-Norris who guided me through the air sequences in Book III; Ed Hudson who could never have had a dumber student in the intricacies of computers; the late Professor Hugh Seton Watson for help with the language of Yugoslavia; Vizyan Ekkel for his knowledge of Russia and its *mores*; Mike Herbison and Therea Lubar of the University of Colorado in Colorado Springs for arrangements made for me in that city; Charlotte Muzar of Michigan for personal recollections of Tesla, and William Terbo, of New York, Tesla's nephew, for much help on many subjects to do with this book.

My friend Nat Solomon gamely carted the 6 kg weight of the first draft of the book round an Italian holiday to give me an invaluable reader's reaction. Alma Corry typed the first 900 pages and gave many helpful suggestions. Iris Searle typed the final draft with unfailing courtesy and accuracy. My agents, Roger and Tim Hanock, and Brian Codd maintained my spirits when they reached low ebbs. The girls at the Daily Telegraph information desk are wonderful. I also thank those who kindly showed me round CERN and hope they will forgive the liberties I have taken with their incredible accelerator.

Nick Sayers at Grafton was the sort of editor authors pray for but rarely find.

Foremost and finally my love and thanks go out to my wife and family. It took me a year to write the first draft and another four months to complete the editing. Most of that time I was so engrossed as to be a zombie and they understood.

John Malcolm

BOOK I
The Nuclear Shield

'Human history becomes more and more a race between education and catastrophe.'

H.G. Wells
(*Outline of History*)

1

Date: 24 September 1981
Nizhnii Uspensk, Nr. Varaslav, USSR

He was a trained, adept and disciplined liar, and took great pride in that skill. Today that devious artistry would be tested, and to the limit. The stakes would be the highest he had ever risked: the love of the few and only people he loved. Lifeline!

He had arrived at the station barely half an hour ago, fifteen minutes after dawn. He had slept fitfully on the uncomfortable, crowded journey. What was exhausting him now was the walk.

People in the West knew that there were shortages even in Moscow, but apartments had reasonable plumbing, hot water and heat – too much of it in many buildings. The streets were thronged with trucks for many hours of the day. Cars, while not abounding, as in London or New York, were there in their thousands, and there were roads to cope with them. In the rural districts, three hundred miles from Moscow, where Rakov was walking, life was different.

He had packed his boots, without which his present journey would have been impossible. He wore his oldest clothes. He carried few personal possessions, the weight of his old suitcase was accounted for by the gifts he brought. Yuri Rakov was going to spend a few days' leave with his family.

It was not a long walk by their standards, just twelve miles. As a boy he had thought nothing of it. Now, after years as a city dweller, and with official cars to take the strain, his legs felt as though they had atrophied.

The track that led to the peasant village where his family lived was inches thick in mud from early rains. Horse drawn farm carts, tractors, and the occasional truck or car had turned what was baked hard in summer into a quagmire. There had been no point in asking his family to meet him; they owned no transport. There was one telephone in the village. It would have been unwise to trouble the minor official in whose home it was; it would have raised awkward questions.

He had written a letter, so that, given the vagaries of the Soviet postal system, they might or might not be expecting him.

As he trudged and heaved his way through the mud, he regretted the deception he was forced to practise on them; on his mother in particular. He had always been closest to her. She probably guessed, but so long as he did not actually tell her, she would keep her guesses to herself.

His older brother Dmitri was the strong man of the family; no physical effort would defeat him. He was not clever. He could barely read; lessons at the local school consisted of teachers reading to the children, not the other way round.

Yuri had been fortunate. A young graduate, who had offended authority with some persistently original but unorthodox work, had been punished. Her *napravleniye* – her work assignment after graduation – was a dreaded rural school. Big city teaching had its problems; but in the villages, the lack of recreation – outside a vodka bottle – and the monotony of a vegetarian diet with meat a once-a-week phenomenon, made life an endless boredom. In her case the worst deprivation was lack of cultural conversation. There were others. The children, for instance, were sons and daughters of peasants, most of whom could neither read nor write, and – whether through genes or environment – lacked any thirst for knowledge, a daunting task for any teacher.

For Irina Gusev, Yuri was a godsend, the first pupil who showed any sign of wanting to learn. As time went by he exceeded her every expectation and became the focal point of her life. She spent hours with him in extra coaching, and experienced real joy when he did well. And that was how Yuri was able to break the mould. It was a bitter-sweet moment for Irina Gusev; a vocational success, but she lost the one person who made her life bearable, to a high school in Moscow.

Yuri's sister showed no such talent. He loved her. He tried to help her. She wasn't interested. He couldn't understand why. In many ways she was brighter and quicker than he. But whenever he encouraged her to read, she would reverse the order of the letters. Dyslexia was an unknown word then, and there. Everybody gave up on Nadya, including Yuri. He remembered her as a constant source of fun, and a marvellous mimic. He wondered how he would find her now, married and with a daughter of her own, a niece he had never seen.

And what of his parents? How would they be? His father could not read, but he did not conform to the clichéd picture of the peasant husband who regularly beat his wife. He had the strength, and he got drunk. There had been times when Yuri, as a child, had been frightened as his father impotently raged at what the Bolsheviks had done to Yuri's grandparents. But usually, just as the child feared his father would break out into violence, he collapsed dead drunk.

Pyotr Illyich Rakov worked in the cotton fields, and Yuri was sure that no thought of any better life had entered his head. His father knew his strengths and limitations. That was the way it was. That was the order of things.

His mother, of course, also worked the fields, as every peasant woman did. Perhaps she could not heave the sort of back-breaking load his father could manage, but only perhaps. Her hands were one of his first memories of life, hands that treated him so gently, yet were gnarled and calloused. How would she be now? He had not seen them for three years.

His life as a child had been happy. As with all Russian children, he was pampered and petted by his parents and all adults.

He was never hungry, although looking back on it, he realized there must have been times when his mother and father had gone without so that he, his brother and sister could have the best. It happened in every family, all the time.

At last he came within sight of the village, the clutch of timber shacks called *izbas*, and in the distance the turnip domes of the church. The landscape held few trees. The fields were bare earth, a rich red colour. The grass was superbly green. Yuri Rakov was coming home, to those he loved, and that was pure excitement for any Russian.

A dog barked, ears pricked. It bounded towards the stranger to the village. Faces appeared, questioning, from all the *izbas*; they all knew who was expected. With confirmation that the visitor was one of their own, they spilled out of their homes to greet Yuri Illyich.

They waited respectfully, smiling, approving, as the family greeted their son. Yuri's brother was first. Hardly giving him time to put down his case he grabbed Yuri by the shoulders, a stream of welcoming endearments accompanying his bear hug. His father was next, in his best suit – his only suit – proudly displaying his war medal, in honour of his military son. There were tears in his eyes as he kissed his son on the lips. His mother also cried, when she held him as if he was still in the cradle. His sister was last. Almost shyly she went to him, kissed his lips and held him. Yuri was shocked. Somebody had put out the light in her soul. She had aged ten years in three, coarsened, her hair grey, eyes that had danced in fun seemed dimmed as if by old age. Then they hugged him again; each in turn. Then they all held each other.

They were interrupted by the shy complaining voice of the one who had been left out in the excitement, Rina, his nearly two-year-old niece. Her uncle swept her off her feet. She squealed, half in fright. He hugged her, and kissed her, several times. She struggled, not knowing what to make of this stranger, but soon relaxed and giggled with him. He held her at arm's length, loved what he saw, and kissed her again.

Next, Yuri was hugged, less emotionally this time, by Nadya's husband, Vasily. Yuri had known him all his life. He lived only a couple of kilometres down the track in the next village.

His mother produced a metal keg containing *kvas*, and glass mugs all round, and they all drank the bitter, muddy fermented liquid, saluting Yuri's return. It had lost none of its earthy appeal for Yuri. He held out his glass for a refill, and they all laughed. Rina laughed a few seconds after the adults, and they all laughed again.

Now came the difficult part for Yuri. They wanted to know what he had been doing, and he was not prepared to tell them. He hid behind the not-complete-fiction that his work was secret, and he was not allowed to talk about it. That was true in itself, but what he was allowed to tell them, but dare not, was that he was a member of the dreaded *Cheka*, the *Komitet Gosudarstvennoe Bezopasnosti* – the KGB. During the war – the Great Patriotic War as his father called it – ordinary people had a different attitude. The secret police were helping win the war, and were one with the masses. A knock on the door in the middle of the night then, did not signal terror, but a call for help; the Motherland needed help, and it was freely given. When the war was over, and Stalin resumed the purges begun in the thirties, fear returned. It was strongest in Yuri's father's generation. There was hardly a man past the age of sixty who did not have a relation or friend who had suffered the labour camps or worse. After Stalin's death the purges stopped, and the terror abated, but the KGB was still the hated enforcer of state will which provided the network of informers who reported every deviation from the rigid norm of accepted behaviour. It threatened every person, every family. It was the reason why nobody trusted strangers, and no one spoke their real thoughts to any but the family circle or the closest of friends. It was not that people feared being sent to the *gulags* – that was reserved for the likes of dissidents, protestors, those against the Motherland, they deserved to be sent to Siberia – but all aspects of life, residence, job, privileges if any, depended on *spravkas* – permits – and the KGB had power to withdraw such permits and so make the already-difficult path of life impossible.

Yuri knew that if his family ever found out his true job they would never trust him again; they would have to guard their tongues; he would become a stranger in his own home. The thought was unbearable.

'Do you have a woman? When are you going to be married? You are already forty. You should have a family by now.' It was his mother talking, on her favourite subject.

Yuri dissembled. 'I need to make my way in the army first. It is a full time job. They send me everywhere, at a minute's notice. That's no life for a woman.' But that was not the real reason.

'Excuses. Excuses. Other soldiers marry and have children. Do you want me to die before I see my grandson?'

'There is nobody suitable . . . '

'In all of Moscow! Nonsense. You're not trying,' she said as she tended the pots containing her 'secret' recipe for *bortsch* and the special stuffed and boiled dumplings, *pelmeni*.

They plied him with questions about his job. At first he refused to discuss it, pleading state secrets. But they pressed him about the people he worked with, and what sort of secret work. It was exhausting. He told lie after evasion after white lie. The more he told the more he had to remember for the next question. It was difficult and tiring. But when they got on to the subject of Moscow, he felt safe. He spoke amusingly and with gathering confidence. There was a strange reaction. They didn't believe him and yet he was telling the simple truth, the sort of places he visited in Moscow, his daily life, without any reference to work, just the social side of his day. Too late he realized that such peasants as went from the villages to Moscow to sell the produce from their private plots, had a different perspective from the privileged *Cheka* officer. What he told them didn't fit the experience of their friends. As a major in the KGB he had the use of special shops. He lived in accommodation luxurious by ordinary standards. His mother's eyes were fixed on the floor. He began to tone it down. He mentioned an imaginary person he had met in a queue for some underpants from East Germany – a luxury to most Muscovites – and there were glances of recognition; that rang true! He expanded on what he knew to be the daily drudgery of the endless search for everything from meat to ties.

His mother and sister cleared the table. His father produced another bottle of vodka, and the three men got down to the serious business of the evening, talk, between men; and drinking; the women were ignored. At first they talked of sport, a safe area where all opinions were valid and they could be as outspoken as they wished; nothing to fear. Yuri relaxed and thought the going was getting easier. But as Dmitri produced the third bottle of vodka the conversation turned to the subject of domestic passports, and when, if ever, the Kremlin would make the Chairman of Corrections release them to their workers so that they were no longer tied to the land like serfs of the Czar. From there it was a short step to a full-blown political debate, with a frankness and degree of criticism that appalled the KGB officer. Of course he had taken part in many similar and equally damning charges against authority, but it had always been with brother officers; within the service it was commonplace, one of the privileges that went with the job. For civilians it was forbidden. What was worse, it was Yuri's duty to report the conversation. As he listened to their words he thanked God they did not know he was one of those they hated, and who put their jobs at risk, lost them important permits, had entries made in personal files to destroy their prospects whenever a *kharakteristika* – an official reference – was required.

These thoughts coursed through Yuri's head, mixing with the vodka, the emotional joy of being with his family, the grim satisfaction that he was among those he could trust, even if they weren't.

Yuri produced his own special bottle of vodka, vintage, unobtainable; even his father had never seen such a bottle, let alone tasted it. He explained that it was *defitsytny* goods, under the counter, obtained through the influence of a friend who worked in the state shop, and they understood that; everybody had such a friend. With the downing of the first shot of the smoothly burning liquid, tears came to Yuri's eyes. His father and brother quite understood. It was a wonderfully moving experience coming home after three years to the bosom of the family. They all cried, all three men. They tried to put their arms round each other's shoulders while still sitting at the table. Dmitri fell off his chair. They laughed.

By three a.m. they were all dead drunk, sleeping on the floor. Aleksandra Nikolayeuna Rakova appeared. She looked down at her prostrate menfolk and smiled. She wondered if she should do anything to make them more comfortable, but it seemed pointless. They would be unconscious for hours. As she looked at the face of her favourite, Yuri, her breath caught in her throat; he was the most loved and she saw him so seldom. How long would it be to their next meeting? Another three years!

'Yuri Illyich . . . ' she sighed, 'what are you hiding?' Nobody heard her.

Mother and daughter were up at first light because Rina was stumbling about the *izba*. The women kicked and dragged and cajoled the men from the floor on to the big bed in the corner, where they resumed their chorus of snoring. Any thought of father or Dmitri going to work was out of the question. There would be no consequences. They were good workers with good records; the occasional 'illness' was acceptable in circumstances like these.

But they were not to sleep out the morning in peace. The first they knew of trouble was a noise in the sky. Not an aeroplane, a helicopter, and that was a rarity. Every head in the village peered upwards as the pilot sought a suitable landing place in the quagmire of mud. Eventually a field seemed to satisfy him and he eased down his noisy machine. For a while he let the engine run and lifted just off the ground a time or two to make sure he was not stuck in a mud patch.

The plastic door slipped open and out stepped a young man in uniform, with the tell-tale *Golubye Forazhki*, the distinctive blue cap-band of the KGB. It was a familiar figure; Lieutenant Vesnavich was the local supervisor. There was an almost audible collective grunt. He was arrogant, small-minded, officious and ineffective. He was the nearest thing the community had to a common enemy and village idiot. But there was also fear. What brought him to their village? Who had erred from the path of strict conformity? Who had said too much, or sold the right thing to the wrong person?

Vesnavich made his way straight to the Rakov cabin. Mother and daughter stood on the step, outwardly stern, but inwardly alarmed. Never had he arrived in the village by helicopter. Aleksandra Nikolayeuna suddenly knew he had come for her 'baby,' Yuri, and she was afraid.

As it became clear where he was headed, people emerged from other *izbas* to watch.

'I must see the Comrade Major Rakov.' There was no

word of greeting, just the simple officious statement.

'Wait!' Yuri's mother was equally imperious. Nadya stood her ground as her mother went inside.

Yuri felt sick and his stomach burned. He turned away from his mother's urgings, not listening to what she was saying, wanting only oblivion. The woman had dealt with this situation many times in her life; not only for her husband and sons as they grew up, but also for her father and brothers. She knew that time was the only answer. She looked fondly at her son, and decided to let him sleep.

'He is not well. I may have to send for the ambulance.' (A cumbersome procedure that could take several hours.)

'It is forbidden!' The standard official response came automatically to Vesnavich's lips. 'Bring him out to me, or take me to him.'

'Why? What is so important it cannot wait a few hours until he is better?' Nadya looked sharply at her mother, surprised that she should question the man with the hated blue cap band.

'Who are you to question orders from Moscow, woman?'

Aleksandra Nikolayeuna blanched as did her daughter. She turned and entered the room again. This time Yuri's eyes were open. He had heard the magic word Moscow. 'Tell him . . . a few minutes. And please bring me some water.'

She filled a battered tin bowl with cold water from a standing jug, and gave it to her son before returning to the arrogant officer.

'Well?' said the lieutenant.

'Wait,' she said. 'He will come; in his time. My son is a major in the army. You are a lieutenant in the . . . ' She could not bring herself to say the word her family had such cause to dread. 'You are not!'

His eyebrows inched up. Before he could express his surprise, Rakov emerged wearily, nursing his hurting head. The arrogant lieutenant changed chameleon-like into the fawning sycophant. 'Comrade Major, good-morning. I am so sorry to trouble you at such a time, and may I say I am privileged to make your . . . '

It was the mother's turn to show astonishment.

'What is it?' Rakov was abrupt.

'I'm sorry to bring bad news, but Moscow Centre want you to return.'

'I only arrived yesterday, on ten days' leave. I haven't seen my family for . . . '

'My sympathies, Yuri Illyich, but the orders are to bring you with me in the helicopter. There is a plane waiting to take you to Moscow.'

A personal helicopter, and charter plane required the sort of senior signature Rakov would have been unwise to question. He didn't like the sound of any of it. 'Wait for me.'

As Yuri turned, his father's figure stood in the doorway, behind him, Dmitri. Rakov senior seemed about to speak, then abruptly stood aside to let his son pass.

As Yuri began to dress, the older man spoke, coldly. 'What branch of army are you in that you are treated with such reverence by him?'

'I told you father, it's secret. I'm not allowed . . . '

'We're not that out of touch. We know the KGB have no respect for army.'

'I'm a major; he's a lieutenant. That's all there is . . . '

'You're one of them, aren't you. One of the *Golubye Forazhki*!'

Yuri struggled to find any lie to avoid his father knowing the truth. 'He's acting on orders. You were in the army. You know how they screw up even the simplest of . . . '

'They make all sorts of mistakes, but not about who their fellow thugs are!' Yuri stubbornly refused to admit it. His brother broke his will.

'Look at your mother, your sister . . . ' They were gazing at the imitation Persian rug on the floor, shocked.

'Transistor radios, foreign clothes . . . these can't be bought by army . . . by ordinary people. You're a major in the KGB. Admit it!'

Yuri nodded.

'For how long?' demanded his father. 'How long have you been deceiving your family?'

Yuri felt wretched. 'We each serve the Motherland as we can. I'm on the technical side . . . '

'You're not a torturer, or a professional rapist, you mean?' pressed his father. 'You don't report people's private conversations so that they lose their *spravkas*. What is your technical side? Did you put bullets in the heads of Soviet soldiers who refused to kill their Czech comrades?' Rakov was shocked less by the venom in his father's voice as by what was supposed to have been the most secret of field punishments during the invasion of Czechoslovakia.

'I know nothing of those things, and neither should you.'

'Some of those soldiers came from this farm. Those who did kill their comrades told us the truth of the hundreds buried in the fields outside Prague.'

'It's a long story, father. I didn't join for fun.'

'There's always a choice, my son. You took the easy way!'

'It wasn't like that!'

'That's what they always say!'

'In my case it . . . '

'Did I teach you nothing?'

'Pyotr, please . . . ' His mother interceded for Yuri.

'Be quiet, woman. This is serious business.' He turned back to Yuri. 'Don't right and wrong mean anything to you any more? What the *Cheka* do is disgusting.'

'You're talking about years ago!'

'It is enough, is it, my son, that you turn your unseeing eye to those who do these things?'

'It's not simple, father. I am a Party member . . . '

That too came as a shock. 'We are a difficult people. We

need strong, very strong hands even to hold us together, as one nation, let alone protect us from our enemies, of whom there are many. It's necessary to be strong to survive. Things happen that should not happen. That's life!'

Yuri had never seen his father in such a rage.

'Don't you know what the Bolsheviks did to your own family? Your *Cheka* comrades were the ones who carried out their orders. They butchered anybody who opposed them, and they enjoyed it. I saw one of your *Cheka* comrades take his sword to your grandfather when he tried to stop a *Chekist* raping your grandmother. He made a bit of a mess of it, but eventually your grandfather died. Then he too pleasured himself with your grandmother, and so did several other . . . comrades. They didn't kill her; she died of shame.'

Yuri Rakov had heard it all before. He had no words to offer. His father strode from the room.

Nadya was frightened. Dmitri was disgusted at his brother's excuses. Pyotr Illyich Rakov confronted the lieutenant.

'Get off my land. Your business is not with any member of my family.' Vesnavich recoiled from the other man's anger. Rakov senior walked past him.

Nadya shepherded her daughter through the door. Dmitri stood guard over his mother. Yuri went to her. Brother took a step to stop brother and then saw the anguish in his mother's eyes. He turned his head. She knew she wouldn't see her son again. She held him close, and the tears coursed down her face.

'Yuri Illyich, my son, my son,' she sobbed.

Yuri too was crying.

'I'll write . . . I'll be back . . . '

They both knew he wouldn't. Gently, Yuri eased his mother's grasp of his body. He kissed her on both cheeks, and on the lips. He wiped his eyes, picked up his bag and walked out of the *izba*.

Date: May 1922
Astoria, Long Island, New York
The noise was considerable, but there was an order about Czito's machine tool shop in Long Island. The building was not much more than a timber shed, but there was a professionalism about the way the men applied themselves to their screaming machines. Julius Czito was huddled over an oil-stained blueprint with two other mechanics.

Frankly, I was not feeling at my best. I expect it showed in my face. Kolman Czito should have been there. I was faced with the son, Julius.

'Hello, Mr Tesla. Nice to see you again.' He held out his hand. I appraised the fresh-faced American thirty-five-year old son of my former assistant.

'Julius . . .'

'I'm afraid father's not here. He retired you know . . .'

'Oh!' I nearly left.

Julius was solicitous. 'Come into the office.'

That was nothing special either; a corner of the shed held temporary partitioning which barely blunted the decibel count.

'Do you have some ground here?' I asked.

Julius had no idea what I was talking about.

'Ground?'

'Land, earth.'

'There's a yard out back. We junk stuff there.'

'This is Sarah,' I said, indicating the box. 'Sarah, my friend. She's been with me three years. I had to stay up with her the last two nights. She passed away this morning. Could you find a patch for her? Clean it up a little. Bury her. Look after the grave.'

I had been a good customer, and a good friend of his father. I felt I could ask this small service.

'Sure, Mr Tesla . . .' Julius held out his hand for the box, which reluctantly I handed over.

Sarah was a pigeon, not just any pigeon. She was special.

When I tell you that at times a piercing white light shone from her eyes, almost blinding me, you may think I imagined it. If I did, the experience at the time seemed real.

I made myself a promise at the beginning of my career, my life's work was too important to be sidetracked by close relationships. So I eliminated emotion from my life. I had almost succeeded when the forward Miss Sarah had come calling. She tapped imperiously on my hotel window one morning, demanding breakfast. I was ensnared.

Julius did not bury Sarah. I came to my senses later, and reclaimed her body. The backyard of an engineering shed was no proper resting place for one who had meant so much to me. She lies in an unmarked grave where I fed so many of her kin, in Central Park.

I went back a few days later.

'Father finally gave up,' said Czito the son.

'You told me,' I said.

I had liked what I'd seen of the young Julius and now had serious business with him.

'I'm on my own. I'll get this place fixed up soon . . .'

'I wonder if you're ready for your first Tesla assignment.'

'Ready and eager.' Julius was entitled to feel pleased. Wait till the customers heard about this! 'What's it to be, Mr Tesla?'

'What's your usual fee, Julius? Twenty-five dollars?'

'Depends what it is.'

'Your father and I worked on some interesting ideas . . .'

'I did a few weekends straight through without overtime. Your Nobel Prize didn't do the business any harm.'

I soon disposed of that one. 'I did not accept the award. It was never formally offered.'

Julius was unrepentant. 'Sure, Mr Tesla. I just wanted you to know how grateful we were all the same. The publicity brought us a lotta business.'

'I would have expected your father to have taught you the difference between discovery and mere invention. I am a

pioneer. I discover new fields of knowledge which make invention possible. To ask me to share the Nobel Prize with an inventor . . .'

'Mr Edison is a great man.'

' . . . is a complete misunderstanding of the forces of progress. I make no secret of my work. I need no prizes to tell me what I've done.'

'I'm sorry, Mr Tesla. I didn't realize you felt like that about it.'

'You didn't think, young man, and that is more serious than lack of tact.'

'It won't happen again.' Julius looked contrite. I doubt he felt it.

'I've never believed in secrets,' I said. 'Mr Westinghouse was of the opinion that if I had, I'd be worth several fortunes by now. I daresay, but I intend to keep one secret, perhaps the only one, who knows? I'll give you a hundred dollars now, another hundred on completion of the work, but for that price I insist on absolute secrecy.' I cast a glance round the dilapidated premises. 'By the look of things, you need the money.'

'A lot of our work is confidential.'

I smiled. 'Not as this is confidential. You will make me a model.'

Julius was eager. 'Give me the drawings. I'll have the men start on it right away.'

I shook my head. 'Not the men. Just you.'

Julius was puzzled. 'I don't understand. My men have been with me years, some of them joined before I was old enough to talk.'

I was firm. 'This is not like other assignments. There are no drawings.'

'Then how . . . ?'

'Did your father never tell you? I have this . . . gift. It's a form of photographic memory. My mother who could neither read nor write, had a similar skill. Once heard, she

could memorize pages of poetry without a fault. Mine is a little different. I work out the detail in my head, as though there's a working model there. I alter, adjust, modify, until I know it works. My memory files it. I can call it up at will. Exact. No drawings!'

'Why, Mr Tesla?'

I took my time about replying. 'Many, who should know better, scorn my ideas. They demand practical demonstrations to back up the theory. Schoolboys!'

'So what do you want me for?'

'This is not a working model. It's a three-dimensional record of an entirely new principle.'

'What is it? A secret weapon?' The young man was joking.

'It's more dangerous than any weapon.'

'Dangerous to handle?'

'No, no. I've already said too much. It'll take about fifty hours of your time. Just you and me.'

'I must know what it is.'

He sought to prise more information from me. I don't think it was perverseness. He probably didn't like being asked to make something not knowing what it was. Nor would I in his shoes.

I changed tactics. I knew nobody else I could trust. 'Call your father. Take his advice.'

Julius Czito picked up the telephone. His father was a long time answering.

'Probably in the garden,' explained the son.

Julius repeated my request and listened.

'Very well, Papa.' He replaced the earpiece in its cradle. 'My father says the decision must be mine. You have never asked him to make a dangerous unknown something. But he trusts you. I will ask you one more time. What is it I am to make?'

I smiled. 'If you won't make the model for me, I'll abandon it. I can't take the chance it will fall into the wrong hands. I love this country. When I got off the ship from

Europe I had the price of a bed and food for one night. I survived. I prospered. This is for America. If ever it's at real risk from an enemy – and I don't mean some remote war politicians want to dabble in – it will have a real defence.'

Julius was moved, I could see that, but would he do what I wanted? Had I convinced him that if he said no, I meant what I said; the secret would go with me to the grave.

A look flickered across the young face. His eyes told me what he was thinking. Perhaps it's just another Tesla pipe-dream. I didn't mind that. I was used to scepticism.

'When do we start, professor?'

* * *

2

British Army of the Rhine
West Germany
September 1981

The train slid off the rails, out of control, careering towards its appointment with disaster. It soared through space and crashed on to its side in a cascade of lethal splintering glass. Soon, seeping dark red liquid oozed from the wreckage.

'I think it's about time we left,' said the colonel.

His middle-aged guest felt for the knot at his civilian tie. It was, as usual, awry. He straightened it, rose and followed his host.

There was a momentary pause in the chaos as the important people left the scene. Then a loud, laid-back Etonian voice drawled: 'Richard, you're a prat!'

The president of the mess committee was a major in his late forties, passed over for promotion a dozen times.

'That port decanter has been part of the regimental silver for a hundred years. The damage'll be on your mess bill at the end of the month.'

The young uniformed officers uttered their automatic chorus of respect for the oldest man present: 'Fuck off, sir.'

Richard Lloyd, instead of trundling the miniature silver train bearing the crystal decanter of port sedately to the diner next to him, had uttered a piercing whistle, cried 'Stand back for the Advanced Port Train' and sent it the length of the mahogany. Lloyd was 32, his craggy features were not particularly good-looking. He had a lot of dark hair over a fresh-complexioned face. He looked more like a farmer than a soldier. There was intelligence behind the dark eyes but something else smouldered, more than impulsive, less than fanatical. And he was drunk, as were the remaining officers of the Regiment of Royal Electrical and Mechanical Engineers, that warm evening near Hanover.

'Who's got the ball, then?' Richard Lloyd was determined to go all-the-way with the evening's entertainment – rugby football in the anteroom, with the stakes a little higher – two huge, crystal chandeliers.

The officers crowded through the door, and shoved the leather armchairs and chesterfields to the wall! The colonel touched Lloyd on the arm.

'Can I have a word with you, Richard. Just a few moments before the game begins.' It was a statement, not a question.

The commanding officer was in a different league from the PMC. Tall, patrician, he might have been mistaken for a blimp, with his white hair and ruddy cheeks, until one encountered the toughness and intelligence in the eyes. Lloyd struggled to clear the excitement and fuddle from his brain. He made a poor attempt to bring himself to attention, he even remembered not to salute (as he was not wearing his cap), but he lost his balance and would have fallen had not his senior officer grasped him firmly at the elbow and propelled him from the room. The man in civilian clothes followed.

'I want you to meet Arthur Forbes. He'd like to ask you some questions.'

'But shir . . .' protested Lloyd, 'it's dining-in night . . .'

'There'll be others,' said the colonel.

Richard Lloyd was not pleased to be dragged from what promised to be a few hours of violent action followed by merciful oblivion. He didn't want to face the problem he was beginning to think was insoluble. To disappear down the neck of a scotch bottle in company with brother officers, was a good way of avoiding decisions. But even Richard, even in his present mood, was no match for

'Oliver,' as his colonel was nicknamed.

Richard took the civilian to his private club, intending to continue his drinking, if more expensively. If the man in mufti had anything interesting to say – which Lloyd doubted – to hell with it.

Richard's club was private in the sense that those under the age of 18 were not admitted, unaccompanied females encouraged, and the cabaret funny and original.

It was not the sort of venue Forbes had in mind.

'If you want to talk to me tonight, mate, it's here or nowhere,' said Lloyd, shouting for attention.

Forbes had his orders.

The waiter threaded his way to a table. Stage curtains parted to reveal a nuptial bower; raked bed, draped in lacy fringes, suggestions of a four-poster and large overhead mirror.

'Champagne,' commanded Lloyd. 'And not the German muck. My guest is paying.' Forbes shrugged.

'You should ease up, Richard,' said the civilian. 'You're going the right way to work your passage right out of this man's army.'

Richard had difficulty in focusing.

'Who gave you permission to use the patrion . . . imic!' He should never have attempted the Russian thought. 'To you my name is . . . captain!' He thought he had scored a point.

Forbes tasted the Moet et Chandon, and nodded. The waiter poured.

'If that's all you've come to say . . . message received, strength five, understood. So now let's get on with the piss-up.'

The cabaret artists appeared. He in white tie and black tail suit, carried her in bridal white, to the fortissimo organ accompaniment of Widor's Toccata. Gradually the volume abated.

Forbes usually spoke quietly when he was angry.

'You're idle, motiveless, irresponsible, unpredictable, and quite possibly dangerous.'

'Hear, hear!' said Lloyd. 'You want to watch these two . . . ' He waved expansively towards the stage. Forbes grabbed the neck of the bottle as it disappeared over the side of the table. '. . . They're not what they seem.'

Live musicians took over from the taped organ. An excruciating violin meandered round 'Smoke gets in your eyes.' Each artist, taking turns, undressed the other.

'You seem to have a death wish. Under-achievement in all your exams, bad reports from headmasters . . . '

'Hear, hear,' said Lloyd again, slurping champagne over his blue tunic.

'And you would have flunked Sandhurst if you hadn't helped defeat the Navy at rugby football. Now you've got yourself mixed up with an Iron Curtain national in flagrant disobedience of NATO standing orders, not to mention . . . '

'Leave her out of it.'

'I wish I could.'

'Who the hell are you?'

'Does it matter. Your colonel's introduction will have confirmed my bona fides.'

'A Whitehall wallah sent to give me the hard word. Behave or I'm out of the army. Queen and country. All that crap.'

'I wish it were that simple.'

Forbes' attention was momentarily diverted to the stage, where it was becoming clear that the bride had a flat chest, while behind the stiffened shirt-front of the 'groom' a pair of splendid mammary glands were struggling free. Forbes brought his mind back to his task.

'Tell me about Marta Gracanica.'

'Piss off!' Lloyd leaned back nonchalantly, and just beyond the point of balance and gracefully the chair took him crashing backwards to the floor, leaving his feet either side of his champagne glass. He made no attempt to get up. Forbes and the waiter wrestled him upright.

'I'm taking you home,' said Forbes.

'Gotta finish the bottle.'

'Sooner or later, sober or pissed, you're going to talk to me about the Yugoslav woman.'

The mess corporal struggled to hear the foreign voice at the other end of the telephone connection, above the din made by the junior officers' rugger match. Eventually he managed to understand that the caller was asking for Captain Lloyd. He tried to make her call back in the morning, but she persisted. He knew exactly where Lloyd had gone, but thought he would be too drunk to understand the foreigner. But she said it was an emergency.

Lloyd seemed sober enough as he held Forbes' gaze for a moment.

'What the hell's it got to do with you?'

'Yugoslavia's communist. That means enemy. Who is she? What does she do?'

'She's a chemist; wants to work with glass. Vases and things. Put Pilkingtons out of business. Is that a threat to the military security of the West?'

'You work on military hardware.'

'In charge of vehicle maintenance. Big deal.'

'Mobile missile launchers.'

'We don't even talk about what we do. We are two people in love. But I don't suppose that figures in the cloak and dagger vocabulary of MI5 or 6 or whatever. You're wasting time and the taxpayer's money trying to turn a lovesick bull – I recognize myself O.K. – into an international in . . . shi . . . dent!'

'What are you going to do about her?'

'Get married.'

'Permission won't be granted.'

'I couldn't give a fish's tit.'

'You'll be court-martialled.'

Lloyd laughed.

'What a prat mission you're on! She won't have me.'

'So the bull's attentions are not welcomed!'

'She won't give up her fucking glass, or her fucking Yugoslavia.'

'What are you going to do about that?'

'Try not to think about it.'

This was a development Forbes had not expected.

'We have reason to believe that Miss Gracanica is working on a top secret project for the Yugoslav government.'

'Balls!'

'Have you ever heard of Nikola Tesla?'

'You can't avoid him in Belgrade. Museum. Face on banknotes. Fucking Leonardo.'

'Gracanica's special subject is electricity. That's where she got her qualifications. Do you know what Tesla achieved in Colorado Springs in 1900?'

Lloyd didn't care.

'He made fifty lamps, twenty-five miles away light up without any intervening wires. He sent power . . . not wireless waves . . . actual electric current in significant surges through the atmosphere. NASA has spent a billion dollars and can barely do it over a mile.'

'No shit!'

'Tesla used similar principles to make a weapon, a defensive screen of power. It can stop anything.'

'Sounds like we just won the war.'

'Nobody knows how he did it. Your girlfriend may be working on this. We want you to find out.'

'So it's spy time in Hanover! Double O six-and-seven-eighth's! Christ you must be scraping the bottom of the barrel if you'll take on my impressive list of character defects!'

'I wouldn't have touched you,' replied Forbes mildly, 'but Warsaw Pact is making more progress than the good guys. You're what's called a target of opportunity.'

Lloyd felt unclean.

A waiter whispered in Richard's ear and pointed to the rear of the room. Lloyd rose, steadied himself on the edge of the table.

'Where're you going?' asked the major from London.

'Telephone . . . lady . . . foreign accent. I shall tell her all about you and . . . '

'I wouldn't advise it,' said Forbes crisply. 'She might not appreciate it!' That sobered Richard a little.

He picked up the instrument and struggled to clear his head. 'Hello . . . Is that you Marta?'

The voice that answered was deeper. It belonged to a stranger. 'It's Greta. You remember.' He didn't. 'I'm Marta's sister.' He vaguely recalled somebody older, shorter, but he couldn't put a face to the sound. And suddenly he was afraid. He knew what was coming. The advance shock waves cleared his swimming head.

'Yes, Greta . . . ' He heard the sound of her sobbing. It confirmed his premonition.

'I don't know how to say this, Richard . . . How to tell you . . . Marta's dead.' His body went numb. His brain stopped. He was catatonic. 'Richard! Richard! Are you there? Did you hear me?' It was impossible as well as unacceptable. They were so close their relationship was telepathic. If the current had been turned off the other end, one of his senses would have got the message. 'Richard . . .'

'No! . . . No! . . . ' he shouted the words. 'It's not true.'

'Yes. They went to see Momma and Pappa. It was an accident.'

'Accident? What accident?'

'She drowned.'

'Impossible. Marta swims like a dolphin!'

'It was a power boat, travelling very fast. They never saw her. Never even stopped.'

Richard began to think more rationally. 'You don't believe this ridiculous story?'

'Yes, Richard. I do.' Greta's words were calm and final.

'Have you seen her body?'

Greta hesitated. 'No . . . '

'I thought as much! Have your parents seen . . . ?'

'It's not allowed.'

Richard relaxed. 'Lies! A hoax! Official games!'

'She was badly injured. The propellers. Terrible injuries. They say it's better not to look.'

'So who identified her? How do they know it's Marta?'

'Her boss. Her employer. He spoke to Mamma and Pappa. There's no mistake.'

His emotions went through phases. Absolute denial, rejecting the obscene idea. Doubt. What if it was true? Panic and the beginnings of desperation.

'Richard. Are you all right?'

Finally the rejected fact insisted its way into his conscious mind. It overwhelmed him.

'Richard . . . Oh Richard . . . '

His voice became quiet, controlled. 'Thank you for telephoning, Greta. Goodbye.'

'Richard, are you . . . ' But he had replaced the receiver.

He returned to the darkened room. An unseen hand held open the curtain. The two artists appeared, like opera stars, to take their applause. Both were naked. His penis was limp, used.

Forbes' face was flushed.

'This cabaret's a bit much. Do you know that . . . '

'This is your doing,' raged Lloyd. 'Your flat-footed Bonds wreaking their usual cock-ups, and the answer is, Marta's dead.'

It was news to Forbes.

'Who says so?'

'Run down by a powerboat. Your idea was it? To stop me leaking the secret of our latest back-axle.'

'We'd have no motive.'

'But they would. If they found out your clumsy goons were after her.'

'You're not thinking straight.'

'I'm going now,' said Lloyd, quietly, absent-mindedly, 'because if I don't I'll probably kill you, and we wouldn't want that on my record would we!'

Impulse took Lloyd to the Yugoslav border; that, desperation and rage. More experienced minds would have called it grief. He knew Marta's sister wouldn't lie. He knew he should accept the fact. Doctors were everywhere, and communist or capitalist, they knew how to diagnose death. He had to see Marta for himself. Until he did, he would never believe she was dead. Simple proposition, and something positive to do. Action. He moved the TR7 three places forward.

Why hadn't she told him that she'd changed job? At least given him a clue; warned him? If she was doing something secret, commie police would go spare if they knew about him! Did they know? A sliver of fear entered the emotional equation. He flipped over the title page of his passport. 'Occupation: Engineer.' True, if misleading. Would they have his name on a list at the border? If so, what would they do? He had to take that risk. Had to.

The suspicions of the border guard were aroused by the absence of luggage.

'You go on holiday, and you have no change of clothes?'

'I'll buy whatever I need.'

'You have money?'

He did. Sterling travellers' cheques left over from his last week on Porec with Marta. The guard inspected the car, then, he opened the passport.

'Is this you?'

'Four years ago!' Lloyd was beginning to sweat.

'What does this mean? En . . . gi . . . neer?'

'Mechanic.' Lloyd pointed to the bonnet of the car and mimed using a wrench.

'And what business do you have in Yugoslavia?'

'None. It's a holiday.'

'With no change of clothes!'

'Yes.'

'Wait!' He conferred with his sergeant. For several minutes the serious soldier sought to persuade his superior there was something wrong.

Lloyd suddenly realized the construction 'Oliver' might put on his sudden appearance at the communist border, without permission, absent without leave. Court-martial? For desertion? He put the thought out of mind. He still had to know the truth about Marta.

The sergeant picked up the telephone. The young communist casually unslung the Kalashnikov rifle.

'Don't you know it's rude to point guns at people?' Lloyd sounded more confident than he felt. The elderly English couple in the shining Morris Marina behind Lloyd looked apprehensive. She pointed at Lloyd's number plates. The man laboriously completed a U-turn and drove back to safety.

The sergeant spoke.

'Come with me, Mr Lloyd.'

'What for? What have I done? Is my passport out-of-date?'

'We don't want trouble. Please come with me.'

The young guard drove Lloyd's car away.

The windowless room smelled of stale tobacco. There was an ancient wooden table and two chairs. A single light fixed to the wall behind reinforced glass emphasized the bareness of the room. The inside of a coffin, Lloyd thought.

'Take off your clothes.'

'Why?'

'Take off your clothes or we'll do it for you.'

The temperature in the room was over ninety degrees Fahrenheit. Lloyd was scared. His clothes had gone two hours ago.

He told himself not to worry. It would all sort itself out. This was Yugoslavia, not Albania.

He'd attended courses on interrogation; how to conduct them, what to do if he found himself on the receiving end of intimidation techniques. He consoled himself with the fact that he didn't have any sensitive knowledge. Then he remembered what one cool lecturer had said: 'If, by any chance, you really don't have anything to tell them, make something up. They hate admitting mistakes.'

A Yugoslav captain entered and threw up a friendly salute. The other officer was in his late forties. A major. Russian, with a blue cap-band. He leaned in a corner and lit a Kazbek *papiros*, the hollow-tubed cigarette, pinching its end erect. He let the match burn, looking at the naked Lloyd through the flame. The Yugoslav spoke.

'My name is Zykic; Captain Zykic. I've been assigned to your case by higher authority.'

'What case? What am I supposed to have done?'

The captain was quietly firm in his reply. 'I will ask the questions. You will answer. What is your name?'

'You know that. You have my passport.'

'A passport is pages of paper. It can be stolen . . . forged. What is your name?'

'Richard Lloyd.'

Again Zykic was reasonable in his tone.

'Mr Lloyd?'

'Look at my passport, the photograph. It is me.'

'What is your rank or title?'

So that was it.

'My name is Richard Lloyd. That's not a lie. My rank was mister when my passport was issued.'

Zykic was more insistent.

'My patience is not without limit, and my friend here' –

he glanced at the Russian – 'has none at all.'

'Captain in the Royal Electrical and Mechanical Engineers.'

'Why are you trying to enter my country illegally?'

'I'm on holiday. There's nothing illegal in that.'

'Attempting to enter the country without properly identifying yourself is a crime, as no doubt it is in yours. Tell me the truth.'

'It's personal. A few days' leave. A break.'

'You are lying. NATO officers are forbidden to enter communist countries.'

'Everybody does it.'

'Why have you no luggage?'

'I decided on the spur of the moment. It's just a weekend. I can buy what I need.'

'Or will you be meeting somebody who will supply you with what you want?'

Lloyd tried anger, to keep the fear out of his voice.

'I've had bad news from home. Broke up with the lady friend. I need a couple of days on the beach, and a skinful of booze.'

The Yugoslav looked as if he might even believe the story. Not so the Russian. He leaned off the wall and walked a circle round the chair. Lloyd turned in his seat.

'Sit still.' The Russian's voice was harsh. Lloyd looked to the front. The Russian looked into Lloyd's eyes. He took the cheroot from his lips and tapped the ash on to Lloyd's naked thighs.

'He's lying,' he said. He put the smoking butt on the edge of the table. 'I can always tell.'

Without warning he swung his arm in a wide backhand slash across Lloyd's face sending him crashing to the floor. Lloyd's reaction was reflex. He sprang at the Russian who side-stepped and kicked Lloyd's testicles. It wasn't a hard blow, just accurate, and Lloyd collapsed on the floor, doubled up.

Gregorev's glance suggested the treatment was a bit harsh.

Through gritted teeth, Lloyd managed to say, 'What the hell did you do that for?'

The Russian spoke casually to the Yugoslav, in English. 'I think we keep this one incommunicado for a few weeks. No announcement. He just disappears.'

* * *

Date: May 1922
Astoria, New York

It was the first hot day of summer, the temperature in the factory over a hundred degrees. The door and windows of the office were shut, and brown paper pinned over every aperture. No prying eyes would see the object on the table.

Julius Czito had worked on the model with me for three weeks. Apart from time spent buying materials, most of the work was done after six o'clock when staff had gone home. Julius was a conscientious worker, even if he didn't have his father's flair. The model was about three feet square. It had the shape of an irregular prism. I showed my appreciation.

'You have done a good job. Your father taught you well. I did not think we could finish it so soon.' I counted out two hundred dollars. 'A bonus! Three hundred in all. Satisfied?'

'You're very generous.' But Julius was obviously not satisfied.

'Are you still trying to work it out?'

'You mean have I guessed?'

'You should have some ideas. What area of science have we been working in?'

'I don't even know that. I haven't the slightest clue.'

I was delighted.

'That is eminently satisfactory. Now if you will kindly call me a taxicab, and give me newspaper and string with which to wrap it up, I will leave you to your business.'

As Julius picked up the telephone and dialled, I said:
'One more thing. Do you know anybody who could cut the model into three separate pieces, artistically and without loss of definition? And of course a person of discretion?'
Julius spoke into the telephone. 'This is Mr Czito. I need a taxi right away. Name of Tesla.'
He replaced the instrument and pondered a moment.
'There is a man. He's a jeweller. I don't know if he would . . .'
'Can I rely on his discretion?' I repeated.
'I would say so.'
'Please be kind enough to write down his name and address.'
Julius Czito cast about the cluttered desk for paper and writing materials.
'I cannot conceive that we shall need to talk of this matter again,' I said, 'but in case we do, let us agree on a name for it. Something innocuous and preferably misleading. I know. We shall call it the Trinity. Three in one. Father, Son and Ghost.'
Czito was shocked. 'I am surprised, Mr Tesla. Your father being a priest.'
'Do, you accuse me of blasphemy!' I suppose I was angry. 'Those who understand this will be able to make peace on earth; and make it stick. I see no sacrilege in that.'

* * *

Date: Classified
Akademgorodok, Novosibirsk, Siberia

Approximately 2,000 miles due East of Moscow is the city of Novosibirsk. It is the area headquarters of the Soviet Academy of Science. Within the city is the closed town of Akademgorodok where research for scientific warfare is carried out. One department contains experts from a wide spectrum of scientific disciplines whose function is unusual. Theirs is a think-tank, with sophisticated laboratory equipment and an unlimited budget. Their function is both offensive and defensive. They are expected to let their scientific imaginations run riot. No thought is too wild to be dismissed. They acknowledge no conventional mathematical, physical or chemical boundaries. They question every scientific assumption. Theirs is a never-ending search for new methods of attack, while at the same time finding counter measures to defeat the use of those weapons in case the West has already got there first.

The head of this department is given no personal publicity. He is referred to in all official documents – and the references are few – as 'Y'.

The section is known as the Department for Continuous Research into New Procedures for Peaceful Co-Existence – PPC.

At this time 'Y' was Boris Yakushenko, a major general in the KGB. He had direct access to the Politburo and, if necessary, to Brezhnev personally.

Yakushenko was interviewing Yuri Rakov. The general left his subordinate standing to attention for several minutes. He believed discipline was the key to survival of the Party; that every opportunity should be seized to impress it on junior officers.

'Stand up straight. Do they teach you no respect for senior officers in the lax life of Moscow?'

'Yes, Comrade General.'

'Did I give you permission to speak?'

Rakov snapped his mouth shut.

'That's better.' He looked down at the papers in his file on Major Rakov. 'Somebody appears to think you are an exceptional officer. So you have influence; family in high places?'

Rakov said nothing.

'I want names. I want to know who you are.'

Rakov still said nothing.

'Insolence is a serious offence.'

'Permission to speak, sir.'

'So is sarcasm.'

'No influence, Comrade General. No family or friends in . . . '

'Don't lie to me.'

'My parents work on a collective. I am the first to make officer grade.'

'Party, then?'

'I am a member. Nobody else.'

'I shall have a thorough investigation made into your background. This . . . rubbish . . . ' He threw the file of papers on the floor in disgust, ' . . . was prepared by an incompetent. Superficial. Lies. I'll find them . . . your . . . friends! I shall take steps to . . . neutralize your influence. Understand?'

Rakov said nothing.

'Sit down.' The general even smiled. He enjoyed watching them tremble.

'My standards are high. I use the American carrot-and-stick principle. The stick is fear. Loss of promotion. Execution is not unheard of. The carrots – for the few who make it – are sweet. Virtually any luxury you would like, Western or home produced, male or female, and for the exceptional officer, I have been known to recommend promotion of one rank. On any officer's *kharakteristika* that means a lot.'

'Yes, sir.'

'I asked Moscow to send me their best man, somebody with that rare and usually discouraged quality, an enquiring mind. Your mission is probably impossible, but failure will not be tolerated.'

Rakov did not know what to make of 'Y'. He seemed interested only in such intimidation that any effort would be too tentative to be effective.

'What do you know about physics?'

'I have my degree. I came out with the best marks from my university . . . '

'I know all that . . . ' The older man said tetchily. 'Are you interested? Really interested?'

'Yes, Comrade General, but I have made my career in KGB.'

The general spoke under his breath.

'They send me an amateur.' Out loud he added, 'What about electricity? Electronics?'

'I did some experiments . . . '

'Tell me about them.'

'I tried to reproduce some of Tesla's early work in the laboratory. My professor was not an admirer of Tesla. Said his best work was well documented and had been overtaken.'

'He should be shot,' said 'Y' mildly.

'I thought it was true of certain of his inventions, but there were others which had not been fully tested or documented by Tesla, on which I wanted to work.'

'And you got permission to do some testing?' Yakushenko's eagerness made Rakov wary.

'No, Comrade General. My professor was called away before I could finish telling him what I wanted to do.'

'Which was?'

'Tesla claimed he had produced electricity developing potentials of 50,000,000 volts. I tried to repeat the experiment.'

'Without permission!'

'My professor had not forbidden it, sir.'

'Sly disobedience! Don't try it with me!'

'When I switched on the apparatus, a piece of metal fell off a shelf and produced a short circuit. I got an electric shock which knocked me out, and my experiment got out of control. It blacked out the science wing, and set fire to the laboratory.'

'You were disciplined, of course.'

'I was put back a year. My punishment was to repeat a whole year's work, Comrade General.'
'And did you?'
'Yes, Comrade General.' Rakov said meekly.
The general grunted. He got up and began to pace the room. 'You will spend two days here in our special department. On Tesla's work. We've invested a lot of resources on a project in Riga, Latvia. We are about to have a test run. You will come with me.'
'In what capacity?'
'The security officer. To make sure nothing goes wrong.'
'Are you expecting trouble, Comrade General?'
'Of course.'

* * *

Date: June 1922
New York, N.Y.

I peeled away the pages of the New York Times in which the model was wrapped. It was made of quartz, big, solid, translucent. Using both arms, I lifted it on to the chest of drawers by the window. Emanuel Yatanabron, the Jewish jeweller was skilful. No, that was ungenerous. He was an artist. He had made each part of the Trinity a thing of beauty.

It was barely nine in the morning, and signs indicated another hot day. The fire hydrants would be cooling. So far the heat hadn't baked the sidewalks, the sun was still low in the sky. My room faced almost due east. The sun shone through the window on to the Trinity; a silent explosion, a kaleidoscope of refracted colour. There was a depth I did not remember from the making process. There were indentations on the top which could have been the miniature tracks of wheeled carts of thousands of years ago.

The Jew had made weight and counterweight interact by gravity to hold the three parts together. I gently pulled each end. 'Father' did not move, but 'Son' and 'Ghost' parted smoothly, silently. I looked at each in turn. On the left, 'Son' had a distinct list to starboard; sparish in shape, it had a masculine strength. On its own, divorced from the other pieces, what was it? A paper weight? Too big for that. A door stop? That was blasphemy! How about the centrepiece? 'Father'? On its left side were the serrations which joined it to 'Son'; on its right a concave curve. I looked from a different angle. The lines and patterns seemed to weave under my gaze. What was 'Father' on its own? An abstract sculpture? Perhaps. I turned it concave side down. It was an old bridge, its underside smoothed by a hundred years of river race.

No matter what I did with 'Ghost' it resembled nothing I could think of. It was abstract. It had a bulge on one side and the other three were straight, more or less. I layed it on each side in turn. No familiar shape emerged. Perhaps that was the essence of the Holy Ghost. It had no form of its own. It was spirit not substance. I slid the pieces together, making them one again. Trinity, I decided, was the right name; the only name. Each part existed in its own right, but was not complete without the other two. Together the three were one, and the whole made perfect sense. I am not a religious man, father and upbringing notwithstanding. But even if I were, I would have had no sense of unease at the title. The Trinity was but another manifestation of the harmonics of the number three. That was the way of the Universe. Orderly. In threes.

Those who looked at Tesla's Trinity would say I had made a riddle, a puzzle to be solved. But anybody who understood my new physics – and I knew nobody then who even began to appreciate the principle – would know immediately what it meant and what had to be done to make it work. More had been learned in the last twenty years than in the previous four million. At some point any scientist would be able to put the three pieces of the Trinity together and know its secret. When would that be?

The World War to end all wars was barely four years in history. Although the conflict had not touched American soil, millions of families still mourned their dead. I was not fooled that there would never be another war. The Bolsheviks in Russia had been in power five years, but even a superficial reading of Karl Marx showed that they would not be content to keep that revolution behind their own borders. Those who did not subscribe to communist beliefs might have to fight for their own. There had always been wars, and there would always be those who would provoke them. The victors would not necessarily be those in the right, but those with the most power. My shield was a match for the biggest gun, and no matter how many of them, but in the wrong hands it was also a devastating weapon. A nation protected by the Trinity could attack others with impunity. That was why there were three parts. If one piece fell into the wrong hands at least there was a chance they would be denied the other two, and therefore the secret itself. Could the shield be built with only two parts of the model? Possibly. It would depend on the state of the art at the time of their discovery, and on the skill of those who worked on them. If I was still alive there would be no problem; Governments would come to me as a suppliant for my knowledge. I would not deny them, in spite of their historic short-sightedness.

My next task was to decide what to do with the three parts of the Trinity to ensure their survival. On what principles should I make that decision? Who could I trust? If I was dead, anybody I trusted would probably also be six foot under. That ruled out any personal custodian. Should I bury them? Childish! A treasure hunt, no less! It debased the invention! Besides, the most ingeniously chosen spot could become the foundation for a skyscraper. People die and institutions don't accept gifts without knowing what they are.

When would America need them? Really need them? Impossible to answer. Twenty, forty, a hundred years? Not a hundred years. It wouldn't take other scientists that long to make the discoveries I had made. It would probably happen in the lifetime of somebody now alive. Young, probably very young. That was a thought, but one with a new set of problems. I would not decide immediately. There was no rush.

I needed time, and yes, I admitted it, inspiration to decide where to hide 'Father', 'Son' and 'Ghost.' Then I could work out the signposts.

Meanwhile I needed something in which to wrap the Trinity. In a bottom drawer I found a piece of my mother's needlework, a parting present when I left for Paris. On black velvet she had worked a picture of my father's church in Smiljan. It was appropriate that the Trinity should be wrapped up in the church. I tied it with string.

* * *

Date: September 1981
Clear, Alaska

The white polar world was a still calm fairyland in the cold light of a bleak sun, the only movement an occasional lazy flurry of surface snow from a five knot breeze. But it was a barren place, inhospitable to most forms of animal life, particularly human. In a storm, five minutes without felt overboots would mean the amputation of both feet. Another three minutes without full protective outer garments could mean a wooden overcoat. And yet it had proved possible to extract oil and pipe it thousands of miles. Heavy civil engineering works were executed, building materials flown in, houses and offices built. An early warning station for the North Atlantic Treaty Organization had been built, thirty feet underground, and layers of specially reinforced concrete poured on top. The radar antennae were indistinguishable, at a distance, from the myriad of strange Arctic shapes.

Lieutenant Charles Tyson didn't personally register the cold. He was in shirtsleeves and officer-issue gabardine, and his legs were wrapped round the wings of his chair. He was in an air-conditioned seventy degrees wondering how the hell the graduate from West Point with the sort of Washington connections his family had, got elected to this cold hell.

Sure, he'd done a deal with his men over a load of blue jeans. He *was* doing them a favour. Designer pants at twenty bucks a pair! He'd only paid $10, and if the seams came apart that wasn't his fault. He'd get that s.o.b. of a C.O. one of these days!

They said he was in the front line of the next world war; that the lives of two hundred million Americans depended on his vigilance; his radar screens were the eyes and ears of NATO. The first person to know that Brezhnev had decided to heave the big bang at New York or L.A. was likely to be good old Chuck Tyson. Good for a laugh for the first couple of days, but soon you got to thinking of all the sun and partying you were missing.

His men watched their video display units, alert, noting the appearance and disappearance of the blips on the screens. There was British Airways flight 282 to London passing out of range now, its place taken by another image – what was it, Freddie Laker or an F.111?

There were two problems; the cold and the boredom. They had the best equipped gymnasium this side of the Rockies, and the camp theatre showed 'X' movies twice a week, with Valium tablets.

First day men looked at the radar screens with awe; realizing the enormity of the responsibility, terrified an intercontinental ballistic missile was about to be launched in Siberia or wherever. Satellites, aircraft, ground radar would plot the trajectory waiting for the moment the computer would predict which city's million souls would reach eternity that day.

The boredom factor was it never happened.

Life only became interesting when something went wrong, and given the age of computer hardware such events were becoming more frequent. The trick was to distinguish between computer malfunction, Pentagonal cock-up and the beginning of the end of the world.

Date: Classified
Riga, Latvia, U.S.S.R.

It was hot in Riga. Its latitude is similar to Edinburgh, and in mid-summer it occasionally hits the high eighties, as it had this day.

Yuri Rakov was an unhappy man. In spite of the high priority his mission had been given, the plane sent to fetch them arrived late, developed engine trouble thirty minutes out of Moscow and had to return to a four hour layover. The general said he had appointed him to make sure such things did not happen.

The scientists resented him as much on the journey as they had in Novosibirsk. His questions were 'childish.' He was an 'amateur' who only hindered their work. As tempers frayed, their jokes against authority and the Party increased in savage parody. His duty was to report their deviationist talk. More than likely he himself would be in trouble for letting it happen! He made a mental note that one day he would do his duty by these casual subversives.

The apparatus that housed the 'experiment' was a metal sphere, ninety feet in diameter. The engineers making last-minute checks on the top of it, looked like midgets.

The team leader told Rakov that the steel casing contained plasma, the substance in which nuclear explosions happened.

'Shouldn't we be using geiger counters?' asked Rakov.

'There's no radiation.'

'I thought you said that plasma . . . '

The leader was impatient. 'I don't have the time or the inclination to give you a lecture in physics. Take it from me the whole area has been swept.'

'Is it safe? When you turn on or whatever you do?' Rakov pressed the scientist. He did not immediately answer.

'I shall be here and so will all my colleagues. If you're too scared, go away.'

The control room was a concrete bunker projecting a few feet above ground level and about a kilometre from the sphere.

Rakov gave his general a slightly different version.

'The plasma is thought to be stable but they can give no guarantees. In the unlikely event of an explosion, the calculations show that the bunker is almost certainly safe.'

He didn't know why he told the lie. Probably just superstition (in which he did not believe), but so many things had already gone wrong. There was also a familiar tell-tale of danger: a stirring of the hairs on the nape of his neck.

The general had no doubts.

'If you think I'm going to be around when they let off the contents of that oversized football . . . We'll observe it from that hill top. Better view!'

In retrospect, Rakov found it difficult to describe what happened. One moment they had been standing beside the mobile control vehicle, hearing the voices from the command centre:

' . . . three, two, one . . . '

And then the sphere disappeared, swallowed up by the ground. Within a second there was a ghostly whooshing noise and Rakov, his general and the control vehicle were sucked into the air towards the site of the sphere. Rakov landed on the slope of the hill sixty feet from where he'd been standing, and began to somersault down the hill. Then came the counteraction, an explosion, a brief flash of brilliant white, followed by a buffeting of shock waves which pounded at Rakov's body. A huge cloud of debris was hurled into the air. Screams came from inside the van which was slowly tumbling over and over.

'Help me up!' shouted the general.

He was not a pretty sight. His uniform hung about him in shreds. He was clutching a broken ankle.

'Get me out of here,' he commanded.
'But there are men in the van. We must help them.'
'Fall-out! Radiation!' 'Y' gasped.

Date: September 1981
Clear, Alaska

Tyson decided to think about matters of real importance; his up-coming fourteen day 'liberty.' He'd stand in the yard of the family pad in Georgetown and watch the sun from rise to setting. He wondered whether he'd see Susie or Marsha first, or would it be Sasha; hell no, she'd married that Madison Avenue jerk. But that wasn't all bad. He had put $250,000 into a real estate deal in Baltimore and when that came good, Chuck would make half-a-million, without risking a cent of his own money.

Tyson wasn't sure what it was that interrupted his day-dreaming, possibly just a change in the atmosphere and slight straightening in the seat by the screen-watchers.

'Status report, Meadows!'

The top-sergeant punched his computer console buttons, stared at his master screen.

'Everything normal lieutenant!' he cried in his Georgia sing-song drawl.

But that was the last moment everything was normal.

The first problem was that B.A. 283 Los Angeles to London was wiped from the screen; then other aircraft went. The missile prediction computer decided to list every major Western city as about to be nuked; that had to be a technical malfunction because the alarm of carefully calibrated musical gongs that heralded enemy missile launches was silent; but only for a moment. And instead of a steady escalation of tonal signals there was a zany imitation of 'Jingle Bells'.

Tyson was already gripping his red hotline to NORAD, the Command Centre in the Cheyenne Mountains, at Colorado Springs. 'Alpha One to Control . . .'

'Go ahead, Alpha One . . .'

'All our alarms are sounding but there's no track on launches'. Pause.

'We have it, Alpha One. Stand by . . .'

The wait seemed like hours. It was twenty two seconds. Tyson wondered how many more he had left on this earth. Pity about Marsha! And then all his screens went out 'Alpha One to Control. I'm blind. All my sensors are out. I'm blind. Repeat, blind!'

Control answered immediately; not cool. 'Alpha One. We need the source and we need it now. Throw in everything. Satellites, radar, AWACS, infra red, beams!'

The years of rote training and rigid discipline paid off. The men and women responded. The complex array of sensors went through a million permutations in seconds to avoid the interference and came up with the answer. 'Alpha One to Control. Source: Riga, Latvia. Ivanland!'

'Other sources confirm, Alpha one. Stand-by . . . '

Tyson needed no encouraging to keep alert now.

The voice of Control deepened a shade, trying not to be too pompous about the portentous announcement. 'Prepare for "State of military vigilance," Alpha one. Acknowledge time 1351.'

Tyson echoed the order. 'Preparing for State of military vigilance. Acknowledge time 1351, sir.' This was the first stage of NATO alert. It would be followed by 'Simple alert;' then 'Reinforced alert.' The fourth stage, 'General alert,' was the Third World War.

Colonel Jim Masters was a Texan whose only regret about joining Uncle Sam's Army was that he had to give up his stetson, without which he found it difficult to get through the day.

'Sit down, boy. Now hear this,' he said laconically, 'the official line on that . . . incident yesterday.'

'Is it war, colonel?'

Masters quoted. '"A combination of sunspots and erratic polar electromagnetic activity" . . .'

'Bull!' The lieutenant's comment was just audible.

As the colonel's private opinion coincided with that of his junior officer, he did not administer a reprimand.

'There is no damage to our installations. No aircraft were hit. Communications were out but secondary systems took over without problem. And I have a couple of satellite shots.'

He flung one at Tyson with the comment, 'Before . . . Riga, Latvia, from one hundred and eleven miles up. No cloud cover. Perfect definition. High resolution. A group of buildings giving strange readings to our satellites. Heat, some gamma rays. Low frequency electrical discharges. Here's the second.' He flipped another photograph at Tyson, who caught it in flight.

'Wipe out. All buildings flattened.'

'What caused the explosion?'

'Boffins say it could have been an implosion. Certain detail of the debris doesn't make much sense to the intelligence weirdos.'

'What's the press release say?'

'Nix.'

'News blackout? That'll create more interest than . . .'

'No official statement. What's there to say? If anybody asks: yes there was some electromagnetic interference with our equipment that day, but nothing we couldn't handle.'

There was a knock at the door.

'Come,' yelled the colonel.

A uniformed admin. sergeant entered, saluted and approached the desk.

'Signal from Headquarters for the colonel.'

Masters ripped open the envelope, dismissing the sergeant.

'Waddya know! We have an apology on our hands from the Ruskies. More gobbledygook. "A low frequency experiment for the development of new communications system suffered accidental damage. Before the equipment could be brought under control certain powerful frequency emissions escaped and may have caused temporary malfunction of American monitoring devices. These could have no harmful effect. The Government of the Union of Soviet Socialist Republics apologizes to the United States Government. Such incidents can, unfortunately occur while a nation is testing the boundaries of scientific knowledge in the cause of peace for all peoples of the world." Shit!'

'Why give so much information? They never do that!'

'I ain't falling for that crap.' Masters chewed heavily on the cigar. 'They've got something hot goin' down in Latvia that we sure as hell don't have, and we don't even know what it is. Get your ass back to your post. Double your vigilance. Treble emergency drills.'

* * *

Date: July 1931
New York, N.Y.

I must confess that I was not as diligent about placing the parts of the Trinity as I had intended. I had thought of many possibilities, but rejected each, in turn, for valid reasons. I had placed 'Ghost' only five years after we made the model. Its obvious destination had been staring me in the face.

Of the possible candidates, the second favourite had to be my Westinghouse connection. They paid me a million dollars for my alternating current patent. With my help wholetime for a year they developed it successfully. It established my reputation as the foremost electrical engineer. (Edison did some good work but he was distracted by his love of wheeling and dealing.) My good friend George Westinghouse had bailed me out of a difficult situation when an oscillator caused an earthquake in Lower Manhattan.

(People say it didn't happen. So-called scientists claim it can't be done, but the records of Mulbery Street Police Station for 21st July 1896 tell a different story.) That settled 'Father.' What about 'Son,' I had no inspiration. Something else worried me. If I was too eliptical nobody would know what the Trinity was. If I was too specific unscrupulous people might get their hands on it. I needed to leave a clue as to what I had done, to get the scientific community thinking in terms of a model of my shield. That was when the idea of using the safe at the Governor Clinton Hotel first occurred.

* * *

Date: September 1981
Zagreb, Yugoslavia

Lloyd's presence in Zagreb was a testament to Winston Churchill's theory that the only thing communists respect is strength. Richard had finally lost his temper, mainly with the Russian, but he'd aimed it at the Yugoslav captain. He'd threatened him with the prediction that if he was not released, the Western press would make it headlines and thousands of British and other tourists would take their desperately needed currency to other balmy climes if harmless holiday makers were to be arrested and beaten up. It should not have worked. It was almost a cliché, but the man was Yugoslav and not Russian. He'd believed it. They threw his clothes at him. His car was a mess, carpets ripped up, and the upholstery systematically slashed.

The church of St Sophia is ornate baroque, its icons a wondrous reminder of the heyday of the Serbian-Orthodox faith. A smattering of locals was sitting, some praying. Tourists circulated, gawping at the visually indigestible splurge of gold.

Mary's stocky figure soon appeared, the muted flower pattern of her dress contrasting with the garish informality of the foreigners. Marta's childhood friend knelt. After a moment, Richard took to his knees. Through tented fingers he whispered: 'Why the secrecy?' He'd tried accosting her in the street as she left the office for lunch but she'd brushed past him and then dropped her handbag and muttered the time and place as he helped her pick up her things.

'I'm being watched. We all are.'

'Why?'

'Because of Marta.'

'I don't understand?' said Richard too loudly, and quickly glanced to see if anybody had heard him.

'Three weeks ago Marta told me she was going away. She couldn't tell me where, but she was excited. Then, last Wednesday, our director told us she'd been killed in an accident. As what she'd been working on was classified we were forbidden to talk about it or Marta's death to anybody.'

'It doesn't make any sense. Don't you have any idea what she was doing?' Mary shook her head. 'Or where she went?'

'This morning,' said Mary, lowering her voice another pitch, 'I was sent for. There was a secret service colonel – not the usual idiot, a rather frightening man – he knew about you. He kept asking questions about you and Marta. How you'd met. Where you'd been together. How long. What you talked about. I've only met you twice so I could tell him very little. He was not pleased about that. I have to telephone him immediately if you try to contact me.'

'Have you? . . . ' She shook her head again. Lloyd was worried not only for himself, but also for Mary. 'You're in danger coming to see me.'

'Maybe. The important thing is for you to know they're looking for you. You must get away, out of the country.'

'Not until I see Marta.'

It was Mary's turn to scan the church for signs of a watcher. She seemed to be satisfied. She continued: 'You can't see her. She's dead.'

'I don't believe she is.'

Mary was so surprised she turned her head and looked straight at him. 'But that's silly. Why would they say she's dead if she isn't?'

'Why all the fuss if she is?'

'Because they think you're a spy and they're terrified she told you what she was working on.'

It was obvious but the thought hadn't occurred to Lloyd. 'But that's ridiculous. We never talked about work; hers or mine. I didn't even know she'd been moved.'

'You must get away. They'll arrest you and I hate to think what they might do to you.'

Lloyd persisted. 'If she is dead, where will they have taken her?'

'Her body? Dubrovnik, I suppose, where her parents live. She called me once from there.'

'After she left Zagreb?'

'Yes. Just to say she was all right and the job was wonderful.'

'Where will they have taken her?'

Mary felt sorry for the grief-stricken figure. She didn't know how to answer. She said the obvious. 'At the funeral home . . .'

'In Dubrovnik?'

'I suppose so, yes.'

'Will you be sending flowers, if Marta is . . . dead?'

'Yes.'

'Where?'

'To her parents' home I expect. Now please go . . . I feel very sorry for you, Richard, and of course about Marta . . . but please don't try and see me again. I'm not very good at this sort of thing.'

Date: September 1981
Dubrovnik, Yugoslavia

It is two hundred and forty miles in a straight line from Zagreb to Dubrovnik, but there aren't too many straight roads in Yugoslavia. After six hours' driving, through the night, through the mountains at Karlovac, and then along the coast road from Split, Lloyd arrived at the well-known tourist resort in the lee of the towering Mount Srdj with the dawn, exhausted.

He parked the car by a small bay just north of the town where he'd swum off the rocks with Marta. More memories!

He stripped and dived in, the cold water bringing stinging stimulation to aching muscles. He lay on his back savouring the early sun. He swam all the strokes he knew, exercising each set of muscles in turn. At last he'd had enough. He did a fast crawl to the shore. He stood and shook the water from his eyes. His heart lurched at the sight of a uniform. This time the person wearing it was female, about twenty-five, dark, olive skinned.

'English?' she asked, in English. Lloyd nodded. 'Your car?' She continued, indicating the Triumph.

Could he have been traced this far this soon? Would they have phoned ahead the number of his car! Would the border guards have notified anybody? A thousand questions and not an answer in sight.

'Is that your car?' She insisted.

'Yes.'

'Your clothes?'

Lloyd nodded again.

'Get out of the water.'

'I'm naked.'

'I know that.'

'I have no towel.'

'So?'

'There's a travelling rug in my car. I could at least dry myself.'

The officer considered the request. She shook the dirt loose from the rug and laid it on a sandstone rock about ten feet from Lloyd. She sat down.

'Would you mind turning your back?'

'I have four brothers. Do you have something I haven't seen before?'

Lloyd climbed from the water and began to dry himself.

'We have naked beaches in our country. I have seen many naked men.'

'Bully for you, dear.' Lloyd dressed quickly. The hint of a smile crossed the girl's face.

'What happened to your car?'

'I beg your pardon?'

'The seats are damaged, torn.'

Lloyd had forgotten what they'd done at the border.

'Vandals,' he improvized.

'You have reported it, of course.'

'Yes . . . No . . . It happened in Austria. I didn't want any hassle. Insurance will pay.'

'You have a good figure. For a man.'

Lloyd pulled his shoes on.

'What are you doing here? At this time of the morning?' she asked.

'Having a swim.'

'Where did you get the bruises?'

Always stay as close to the truth as possible, they had said.

'I got drunk last night.'

The familiar story appeared to satisfy her.

'Your papers, please.'

Lloyd could not risk being identified. His connection with Marta might be known in Dubrovnik.

'My passport's at the hotel.'

'Everybody must carry papers.'

'I'm sorry. I couldn't sleep. Spur-of-the-moment.'

'I do not understand.'

'I didn't think there would be anybody about at this hour.'

'What hotel?'

'Dubrovnik Palace.' She had expected that.

'Your name?'

'Smith.' There was bound to be one Smith at that huge impersonal barn of a hotel.

'First name?'

'John.'

'I shall check with the hotel?'

'Be my guest.'

'You're inviting me to dinner with you?' It was not what he had in mind.

'Why not.'

'Good morning, Mr Smith. You are lucky I am going off duty now. I shall not be checking your story until . . . seven o'clock tonight.'

Lloyd didn't know what to make of that. Was she serious? Would she really check up on him? She had made no notes. Would she expect him to take her to dinner? What would she do if he stood her up? Forget it, or make trouble by doing a double check on him? The breaks were not going his way.

* * *

Date: August 1931
Governor Clinton Hotel, New York

I sent for the hotel manager, a thin stalk of a man, balding, his complexion the colour of underdone pastry.

'I want you to keep something for me. Somewhere very secure.'

'There's a small safe in my office, or there's the vault.'

'Perhaps that would be best. I wouldn't want this to fall out accidentally.'

'Let me have it and I'll give you a formal receipt,' he said primly.

'I shall need your personal guarantee that it will be

released to no one but me, and if anything should happen to me . . .'

'I know. Your legal representative . . .'

'No. This is secret and of national importance. You must not allow anybody but an authorized officer of government research to even touch it.' That should make an impression on even this dullard. 'Take me to the vault.'

I felt rather pleased with myself. The little message I had left on the wrapping would keep prying fingers away.

*   *   *

3

Date: September 1981
Georgetown, Washington, D.C.

Most people called Ruth beautiful, a reflex reaction to personality, but not strictly accurate. She was tall, at five foot nine; her hair was dark and seemed unfashionably long. Her eyes were clear-sky blue, quite wide apart, the nose in reasonable proportion, but the jaw was squared, giving her face a pugnacious set. She was certainly not bandbox pretty, nor did she have high cheekbones, so often the telltales of beauty. It was the confidence she radiated that gave off her magic, part heritage, part environment of wealth and power; it was as individual as a Goya. The eyes were intelligently knowing, the glint of earthy humour never far away, but the capacity for anger was signposted by a sudden shift of shoulders and a slight shake – almost tick – of the head. Those who didn't know her well called her arrogant. She was never that, but on sure ground or confronted with fools, she was certain and powerful. One had to look hard, or be one of a very small circle, to glimpse her vulnerability.

Where had she gone wrong? What had she done or left undone? Was her thinking basically faulty? She was a mature thirty-six and no tyro at the business of love. Apart from instinct, which she knew could be a hopelessly inaccurate guide in things emotional, she had used her not inconsiderable intellect on the relationship, and all the answers had come up right. She hadn't dived headlong into male arms. That was an ever-possible temptation but she hadn't fallen for it this time. She had in the past, several times, and she'd found a formula for dealing with it. She let the initial emotion rip, soaked herself in his company, saturated her thoughts with him, saw him every day and nightly. It always paid off: time worked its usual marvel and showed the situation for what it usually was, exciting but temporary. She hadn't tried that this time, but then Frederick – no middle name – Coverdale was no ordinary pair of arms.

His technique was clichéd but effective; he ignored her. She knew he was doing it deliberately. Others had tried that gambit. The trouble with Frederick was that he seemed to mean it. When he maintained the pretence long past its effective time-span, Ruth became irritated. When he still kept it up she was forced to the conclusion that he was a one-off who didn't care what she thought, was obviously not after her money and therefore a suitable candidate for her short-list of possible husbands. A very short list; it contained only one name. The fact that he hadn't proposed and showed no sign of doing so was not important.

Frederick Coverdale was fifty. He had an agreeably rugged face, Valentino eyebrows and cold grey eyes. He was fourteen years older than Ruth. Since the death of his first wife Karen, a year earlier, he'd been the most eligible bachelor on either coast.

Frederick made his first million, effortlessly, on Madison Avenue, New York. Not that he was in any way creative, or had imagination, just a flair for recognizing talent in others. He was also ruthless in his pursuit of excellence and profitability. Shrewd investments in real estate and Silicon Valley had turned a small fortune into a financial statement variously estimated at five, ten or even twenty 'mill'.

Ruth had picked her way through the clutch of aspirants for a permanent post at her bedside slowly. She had 'swung' briefly at Berkeley but found it sordid. She was fêted at Harvard Law School as much for her straight 'A's' as for her feminine graces. In a two-year stint at a prestigious Washington law firm she'd learned the tricks of the politico-legal lobbycat and how to turn off importuning hands-under-table without losing the firm clients. She satisfied her appetites selectively, and without acquiring a reputation for promiscuity, lesbianism or frigidity; quite a feat in that gossip city.

At last she had arrived at the end of her carefully planned scenario – so she thought – as the day had dawned on the portable altar at the Beverly Hills Hotel where Frederick awaited his – as he thought – carefully chosen (and intensely privately vetted) mate. And so the brilliant and beautiful daughter of the nation's number one senator said 'I will' to the man most likely to be the next Secretary of State. The event neither of them had planned occurred as they were leaving the hotel in the Rolls Royce Camargue: the senator's fatal coronary thrombosis which left Ruth the presidency of the family business and control of the power base it represented.

The marriage might have been different if she'd been able to call him Freddie. Frederick was such a clumsy name. He was not a Freddie, never would be. Freddie was another person. There was no point in anguishing over what she had done five years ago; she had the present to cope with.

It was not unbearable. Her marriage was one that millions would envy. He was too old, but not senile. He was good-looking but not pretty. He was strong – maybe that was it, was he overpowering? No, not that. She had neither the need to dominate nor be dominated. She had worked that one out when she was younger, and would not fall into a relationship where that was a hang-up. He was intelligent, he was considerate; yes, there was that. That was something else. Was it *the* problem? Was it the cause? He treated her with altogether too much respect, there was no doubt about that, but that too was only symptomatic; but of what? What was she moaning about? It amounted to his privacy. There was a corner of the real man that was concealed from her. His insistence on separate bedrooms was another symptom. That was it! She felt better. She had identified the thing that was at the heart of her disquiet. He would not reveal himself. He would never tell her what he really thought and that made a mockery of her idea of marriage. Did that help? If she knew the cause she ought to be able to do something about it.

There was too, the sex problem. He always had an excuse. He did work long hours. He was the sort of person who was consumed by his challenges. Maybe it did take him longer to enjoy relaxation than other men. Even so, it hardly explained one trip to the passion field every six months. He was not gay. She had wondered. It would have explained a lot. She was frightened of that. She didn't think she could handle it in the civilized way of her generation. She could never share his anatomy with a man. She was not disgusted; she was even – at a technical level – interested, in the emotional and biological detail of such encounters, but it was prohibited emotional territory. She had looked for clues, sure that if another relationship did exist she would spot it. There were none. Conclusion? He was undersexed. Big deal! When they did make love, he was – what was the right word for it? Thorough. How did she know he indulged her with such calculation? She lost patience with herself. She knew! That was good enough!

Were those her only complaints? That he kept part of himself private and wasn't a sex maniac? What did she expect? He had been married to Karen for twenty years; it took time to adjust to the ways of a new partner. But it was five years. She should not be complaining. She should be grateful she had a husband who was not interested in her money, treated her well and didn't sleep around. But she was not satisfied, and there was no point in pretending that this was a marriage that she could live with indefinitely unless things changed – no, not things, him; he would have to change. He would have to reveal what was in that private corner. Then it would work, she was sure of that. No matter what was in that hidden recess she could cope, if only he would bring it out.

What had he been like with Karen? She had avoided asking herself that question before. Jealousy she could do without. But now she needed to think about it; she needed answers for her marriage.

Karen was different; that much was sure. She was the product of Frederick's thinking at age thirty. Why did she say thinking, and not taste? Because that was the way Frederick would have thought of it. Karen was an intellectual. Some would have called her a blue stocking. She looked quite good, wore reasonable clothes, smart even, but had no interest in them; her mind had a different focus of attention. There had been no children, which suggested a form of trauma, or sterility. Had they made a conscious decision to avoid a family? If true, what did that tell her about Frederick? That he had rejoiced in his terminal communion with Karen. She could have been one of those. Frederick? Certainly, he now felt too old. Ruth had not demurred on the basis that she would change his mind for him, in due course. Had the time now come? At thirty-six she didn't want to leave it much longer. She was not certain she wanted to bear his children; not without finding out what occupied that hidden corner.

It was eight o'clock on a sunny Fall morning and she felt like shrugging off the depression and immersing herself in a day devoted to 'favourite' things. Before she could put the thought into effect there was the familiar light tap on her door.

Frederick was one of the few men who made a vest or waistcoat look good. Most men were too fat or too thin, the vest emphasized the paunch or hung loose on a void. Frederick was as flat and muscle-hard there at fifty-five as he had been thirty years earlier. Was he too immaculate? If only . . . she abandoned the criticism. It would get her nowhere, as usual. Frederick approached the bed. She offered up her cheek for the usual peck of a kiss. It did not come. She opened her eyes. He was smiling; that in itself was unusual. At this hour he reserved his facial muscles for a frown at the prospect of the day's work. He gently pulled the sheet away from her body. She was, as usual, naked. Frederick admired her body. This too was unusual, in fact, Ruth decided, unique. She wondered what would happen next. She did not have long to wait.

'A very beautiful body, my dear,' he said as he bent over and kissed each nipple in turn. It was no peck, but a soft, warm caress, his tongue gently lapping until each reacted to his stimulation. Ruth let her eyes close, and kept her tiny moan of pleasure to herself. She felt his lips on hers; they were hard and dry, neither full nor thin, about half an inch each, sensuous only occasionally, as now. She opened her mouth. He bit her upper lip; another first, she thought. Was this to be the prelude to a revelation of the part of him he had always kept so private? He stood back, his eyes smilingly admired her body, her eyes, her lips, then her breasts. They travelled down her tanned downy skin to the bush of raven hair, which he gently parted, and then probed with his tongue. It was as if another person was making love to her. Oral sex had never been on the menu before.

'I thought I might be a little late for the office today, if you have no other pressing engagements.' And he took off his jacket.

He was as immaculate about his undressing as he was about his appearance. Normally it irritated her, today it excited her as she watched him hang first his vest then his coat on the chair. Next he took off his trousers, and gave another hint of a smile as he saw her react to the straightness at the front of his jockey shorts. Naked he was quite a sight, she decided. Many of her friends would have been proud of a husband who could show such physique, such a figure, such even muscle control, and such a strong throbbing erection as her fifty-five-year-old presented for her consideration. She put out her left hand and touched its tip, lightly. It was smooth and dry. She drew him towards her, slowly closing her hand around it. She looked into his eyes for a sign that he would give her what she most wanted, a glimpse of the hidden man who was her lover. She saw only that he was still in total control, and even his moment of passion would be calculated to the split timing any actor would envy. She took the reddened extremity into her mouth and sucked, urgently and hard. He gasped. For a fraction of a second he lost control. His eyes gave away the hidden man. She saw, not ecstacy or even lust, but panic. It was a start. Perhaps a little more of the unexpected could tell her who he really was.

She stroked his stem slowly as she took his testicles into her mouth and tossed them from side-to-side and round-and-around, allowing her saliva to add warm sensation. She paused and looked again into his eyes; they were hard, as if he appreciated the tactics she was employing and even her goal. He climbed on the bed and sat astride her. She opened her legs as he bent down and let his nose touch her hair, teasing her lower lip. Then he traced the cleft to its terminus, and then followed it onward to her other cheeks, which he also parted. He probed with delicate fingers, and then drew a circle stimulating the sensitive surface of the other exit until she began to lose control, when he abruptly stopped. He grasped her thighs and with an athletic, smoothly-executed lift, turned her through one hundred and eighty degrees until she was perched athwart him. He eased her down, enveloping his vibrant undry shaft.

Ruth was confused. He had never used such techniques before; in five years nothing quite like this had happened. But, she decided without too much difficulty, the whys would have to wait, there were more insistent demands on her powers of concentration. She did not believe in counting climaxes; it was a biological inexactitude even to pretend it was possible; at best it spoke poorly of the quality of the orgasms. She could not do it today; she was drowning in them. They engulfed her. Her mind blotted out everything else. When she thought she had reached the limits of her capacity for sensation, she realized Frederick was still there, and holding on. With a thrust that travelled up from the basement he exploded and she reached another dizzier, undreamed-of peak and the breath broke from her lungs. She shuddered. She held him.

She stayed like that while the energy subsided, and her emotions returned to some semblance of normality. She did not know what was going on inside Frederick. His eyes were closed, his face a mass of perspiration, his chest heaving. There was no doubt about his physical prowess; as to the rest, it would have to wait for another time and place. She'd had enough for one day.

Date: September 1981
Dubrovnik, Yugoslavia

Richard Lloyd was in a musty bar near the base of the mountain, a hundred yards from the funeral parlour. He ordered a hamburger and potatoes, and a lager. Time was running out, fast. The funeral was at nine o'clock tomorrow. He'd rejected an open approach, assuming his name would raise an immediate alarm. He peered carefully out of the window. He could just see the undertaker's front door. It would be lunchtime soon. Ideal.

A desultory stream of visitors went in and out. He thought he recognized Marta's mother from photographs. She was in tears. The director was apologizing. By three o'clock, Lloyd knew there would be no lunchtime opportunity.

He walked back to his car. Nobody, apparently, was watching it. He sat there for two hours, dozing, trying not to think of all the things that could go wrong.

At five o'clock he was back in the bar, with two screwdrivers from his tool kit. At five-thirty precisely, a tall figure emerged from the funeral parlour. Another man was with him. Lloyd waited for them to pass. Instead they entered the bar. The barman poured two drinks without comment. A casual inspection suggested one was the manager, the other a carpenter, the foreman perhaps. Lloyd waited another thirty-five minutes.

He began with a reconnaissance, through 360 degrees. The building was detached, its front set back from the road up seven wide stone steps flanked by short pillars crowned with urns spilling bougainvillaea. The double doors were oak, the lock substantial. The side windows were solid heavy glass, plain alternating with bottle green. At the back was the workshop, a barn-like structure of old beams and brick, built at the turn of the century. The screwdrivers were not man enough for the lock. His Diner's Card wouldn't open the Yale-type latch. Using the larger screwdriver as a jemmy had no effect except to make a mess of the woodwork.

A few feet from the back door was a small window of obscured glass. He held a soggy newspaper against the glass and hefted the screwdriver by its point. Nothing! The second blow from a jagged piece of marble broke the glass. He lost his grip on the stone, which crashed against the lavatory bowl. The steeply rising cliffs behind the building produced an amplifying echo. Lloyd held his breath.

He climbed on to the sill, and then eased his head and shoulders through the frame. His hips stuck. The brass pin of the lever penetrated his crutch. He heaved, and landed on the floor with his trousers torn and round his feet. A bruise spread across his left hip.

Two teenagers heard the noise. The advantage of the missionary position is that the supine party can take in what is going on elsewhere. Thus a seventeen year-old Croat observed Lloyd minus his trousers. She laughed. Her companion mistook this for passion, and pressed on with increasing vigour.

Lloyd twisted the handle of the inner door. In a coffin on well-worn trestles was an old man in his best blue suit. A two-day growth bearded his face. The manner of his passing was written large on his face; not peaceful, agonizing. Lloyd shuddered.

He had to move several pine boxes before he found the brass plate with the name Gracanica M. The lid was screwed down, brass clasps had lead seals bearing an impressed coat of arms. After ten minutes he had the last screw removed. He broke the seals and lifted the panel.

The teenagers uncoupled. He wanted to forget it. She sensed a mystery, saw herself as a leading witness. She ran off.

Lloyd had heard of *risus sardonicus*, the death grin; he had not expected a snarling scowl from beyond the grave by the woman he loved. He told himself that it was involuntary, an anatomical reflex, long after death, that had no meaning.

He wanted to be sick. This was no cover up. Marta was dead. Grief finally had its way with him. The tears flowed. One part of his brain had told him that even if she was dead, he would be able to say goodbye; that bearing the loss would ease if he had one last sight of her at rest. Instead here was a caricature, a poster for a Dracula movie, the stuff of nightmares.

He tried to put the pine panel back in its place. It slipped and landed on his foot. He had been so certain she was still alive, so sure the secret police were making it up. But this was Yugoslavia, not the USSR. For once the police had been thinking of the family. Who would want to see a body looking like that?

But wait a minute, what had they said? A power boat? So badly injured as to be unrecognizable. That wasn't so. Anybody would have recognized her. And she wasn't hurt. She was dead, but there were no injuries.

He steeled himself to look again; not at her face, her body. She was naked. This was the woman he had made love to. This lifeless snarling . . . thing. But there wasn't a blemish on it. No bruises, no cuts, no abrasions. The fingers were semi-clenched. She still wore the single sapphire he had bought her last summer. Marta had been in no accident. There was a pattern on her body, from just below the waist to a semi-circle below the neck. It was as though she had been sun-bathing through trellis-work. No, that was wrong. The faint sunburn was not where the holes would be, it followed the lines of the struts. No, not struts, something thinner; wires . . . string. A string vest was half hidden among the clothes carelessly tossed in with her body. It made no sense. She must have been wearing it when she died, but what manner of death could have made that checker board on her body?

Somebody unlocked the front doors. He left by the back.

The only way was up. He reached the flattened grass where the teenagers had been. The girl appeared.

His clothes torn, his emotions destroyed, he ran for town. He ran among the high walls and narrow streets of the old city, twisted, turned, doubled back, and found himself in a crowd of sightseers, and eventually he reached the harbour, and the ferry at the quay.

He took a seat on the far side of the wheelhouse and gazed at Lokrum. The owner shouted for more customers. A man in the stern swore at him. The boat set off. As the mainland receded more uniforms appeared on the quay gazing at the ferry.

Date: Classified
Akademgorodok, Novosibirsk

Major General Yakushenko was venting his wrath on what was left of the committee of senior academics.

'What about the American Satellite sensors you destroyed in 1976?'

'What about them?' replied Professor Vilkov.

'Are you telling me that you can build a death ray that

destroys targets in outer space and you can't even complete your present programme of research?'

The senior academic was Professor Anton Vilkov. His sister was rumoured to be the most influential politburo mistress. Vilkov was not intimidated; he considered Yakushenko an ignorant bully, and had recently told him so as they demolished two litres of special vodka. 'Yes!' said Vilkov.

The general was enjoying a bad temper. 'What's the problem?'

'Do you know what a scalar wave is?'

'Y' was silent.

'You don't surprise me. It's at the heart of the Tesla weapon, an extra-low frequency wave on the borders of space and time. It may travel faster than the speed of light . . .'

'Nothing can do that,' said the general smugly. 'Any schoolboy knows that'.

There was a pained look on the professor's face. 'That's what we all thought until we began taking Tesla's claims more seriously. That's why I say the wave exists on the borders of space and time. Anything that travels faster than light would, almost by definition, cease to exist, which is one of the effects of scalar waves. A scalar wave is a conduit without any resistance. Unlimited energy can be transmitted through it. In one mode it can be used as a weapon. Two scalar waves are beamed at a target; where the waves meet the energy transmitted causes an explosion. In the continuous mode the waves can be fired to create a thin impenetrable hemispherical shield of intense electromagnetic energy, in which the air is ionized. It gives off intense glowing light. Anything physical which hits the shield receives a huge electrical charge and disintegrates. Stack these shields, one above the other, and not even gamma radiation from a nuclear explosion will get through; it will be re-radiated and made harmless.'

'If what you say is true, what the hell's the problem?'

'The generator,' said the professor laconically. His colleagues nodded in sympathy.

'We've got generators everywhere,' exploded Yakushenko. 'What's so special about . . . '

The professor continued, patiently, as if talking to a child. 'It's a case of criminal negligence by your illustrious service!'

And it was. It didn't achieve the media space it deserved in 1939 when the KGB mounted a robbery at the laboratory of one T Henry Moray, because the only thing stolen was a bunch of plans which this lone secretive and some said barmy scientist had lovingly worked on for forty years. His generator, which he had at last persuaded to tap the zero-point energy of vacuum – spacetime itself – was hacked to pieces by the raiders. Most respected scientists of the day regarded Moray's claims as fantasy, but those in the USSR took him seriously. They had agents close to Moray, reporting on his progress. When he was ready to prove his claims, they alerted Moscow, and elaborate plans to snatch the generator itself were launched. They had transport, heavy trucks, and plenty of men. 'The Cheka was given authority and, for once, all the facilities it needed to get that generator for Rodina.'

'So what was the negligence?' asked the impatient general.

'Some bright spark thought he knew better than his superiors. When he saw the plans, he decided it would be easier and safer to get them out of the country than a rather bulky shipload of mechanical equipment.'

'What's wrong with that?'

'Only one thing,' said the professor resignedly. 'Moray had given up noting every change he made to the machine on the drawings months, if not years, earlier. Your Cheka mates destroyed the only positive and undoubted clue to making the generator work; the generator itself.'

The general was dismissive. 'Excuses for incompetence by your people. 1939! You've had those drawings for more than forty years. Science is light years ahead of what Moray knew, and you mean to tell me you still can't make it work?'

'No. That's the nature of genius, and that's what Moray was. It takes an original mind to make the quantum leap that's the hallmark of most strides in scientific knowledge. Tesla was another.'

'I wouldn't have accepted such failures from any of my people. Heads would have rolled.'

'They did,' said Vilkov quietly. 'At Riga the best brains on this subject in the whole of Mother Russia were blown apart, along with the latest version of the T. Henry Moray generator.'

'And I suppose you didn't put the modifications on the drawings either?' said the general sarcastically. 'And you talk of negligence.'

'We have the drawings, but scientifically, with people, we're back to the beginning. That's why we need Tesla's research.'

'Surely there's an alternative method of generating the power for the . . . scalar waves?' said 'Y'.

'There is. A series of controlled and contained nuclear explosions. And they, if they can be contained, which is by no means certain or reliable, will only allow the weapon to be used in the pulse mode, as a gun; Tesla called it a howitzer. It won't work as a shield.'

The general tried another track. 'You brought the weather to a stop along our border with Poland, and the East Coast of the U.S. How did you do that?'

'Layers of electromagnetic energy with the Moray generator in the continuous mode.'

'So you have made the generator work in the continuous mode!' pressed 'Y'.

'It cut out. That's why the weather went back to normal. We thought we had cured the fault. Riga came next.'

'What now?'

The professor was frustrated, tired and irritable.

'If we go on trying for another ten years we may still not succeed. We need more information about the Tesla physics.'

'You've had the entire contents of the Belgrade Museum. God knows that was difficult enough to get. What more do you want?'

'Tesla never gave a technical explanation of how the device works. His writing is all . . . generalities. There must be a record somewhere, and we have to have it.'

'Where do you suggest we look? What are we looking for?'

'I do wish you'd stop shouting, general. It doesn't help the thought processes.'

Rakov for one happy moment thought 'Y' might die on the spot of a heart attack. He did not. With a massive effort of will, he brought himself under control, and spoke with a quiet hiss.

'I shall conduct these fucking meetings however I please, and if you don't afford me the respect due to my rank I will personally give the order for something unpleasant to happen to you, female friends in high places or no.'

And all the professor did was sigh, 'If you say so general. I shall of course make it plain in my regular private report to the Kremlin, that I am not being adequately supported by military intelligence, and that your continued presence here is not conducive to achieving the objective.'

The confrontation was now complete. It was clear from the ashen look on 'Y's' face that it was the first he knew of confidential communications. His second reaction was to doubt its truth. It was a bluff. The scientist was a past master at it. On the other hand if it was true, and if those in high places thought the professor's importance to the party was greater than his own, or even – perish the thought – that he was hindering the work to discover the greatest weapon in the history of warfare, he could end up before a firing squad.

'My dear professor, I do believe that in our mutual zeal to serve Rodina, Mother Russia, we are in danger of letting our personal opinions as to method obscure the merits of close co-operation. I will report our difficulties to the Kremlin personally . . . ' The professor was now the one to feel disquiet. 'Your failure means the directorate must take over. Major Rakov, who I am sure shares your disappointment at failure . . . ' – and there was no doubt that 'Y' meant Rakov to understand that 'failure' was the word that would go into his file – ' . . . will be in charge of that team. You, Professor Vilkov, with your colleagues, will brief them in perfect detail as to what they are seeking. Now, where do we begin?'

The professor was laconic. 'America, of course.'

For Rakov, who did not believe in such things, it was dawn on the Day of Judgement. He found himself in a vice. He had sworn that it would never happen to him. He had always been certain he had the skill to see such a situation coming and avoid it. But it had descended out of nowhere. No warning. No preparation had been possible. The spotlight would now be on him. What was worse, his name would be coupled with an important – maybe impossible – assignment. Failure would mean a personal disaster from which he could not recover. Success, on the other hand, would be more richly rewarded than it was possible to contemplate. Unless . . . Unless somebody else wanted to claim the credit. Unless the Party decided to expunge all record that they had the knowledge, in which case even success might lead to his own eclipse. He would put that thought out of mind. Failure was the thing to be avoided – at all costs. That meant he would be given authority to do . . . anything. No rules. Dangerous; possibly deadly, but definitely interesting.

4

Date: November 1940
New York, N.Y.
There are two hundred thousand more bodies buried in the borough of Queens than live there. The reason is simple. The granite of Manhattan Island makes it hard to earn a living grave-digging, and you can build a skyscraper on a few burial plots.

The black Buick hearse wound its slow way into the cemetery. I joined the family and mourners at the graveside. Julius Czito did not notice me until his father's coffin had been lowered into the ground. His eyes caught mine. He gave a faint smile of surprise. I had not seen him since we made the model.

I had put on my black three-piece suit, white shirt and black tie. Julius greeted me.

'Thank you for coming, professor.'

'I'm eighty-three,' I replied. 'I shall be joining him soon.'

'Nonsense,' replied Julius. 'You look very fit.' But he lied. I looked terrible. I was thinner than ever, a husk of my former self.

'We had good years together, exciting times.'

The day was not kind to old bones. The wind chill penetrated to the marrow.

'I've taken a room. You'll join us for refreshments?'

I had no pressing engagements. The over-heated limousine was welcome.

I took a tot of whiskey in the steaming black tea. I relaxed. I remembered the day in Colorado Springs. Kolman Czito manned the switchboard while I did the experiment. A copper ball crowned the two-hundred foot mast. The setting could not have been better: desert and towering rockfaces. They thought it was all about making ball lightning. I produced a few thunder claps and some pretty blue flashes. But that wasn't what blacked out Colorado Springs. The Trinity did that. First time! They sued me for it! Little did they know what I had done.

My reminiscences were interrupted.

'What with Hitler rapidly becoming the master of all Europe, I was wondering if you'd make your secret available to defeat the Nazis,' said Julius.

It was eighteen years since we'd made the model. I'd hoped he'd forgotten about it.

'Secret? What secret?' I said.

'The model. The Trinity.'

'My memory's not as good as it used to be.' I had never been a good liar. I'm not sure why I dissembled then. I'd written about it in 'Century' and again in 'Electrical World and Engineer,' but I hadn't told them how to make it.

Fortunately young Julius was called away.

The rest of the company were strangers to me. I decided to leave, but something tugged at my coat. A voice said:

'What do dead people look like?'

It was a child aged about six or seven. Female, with blonde, almost white hair. I didn't have much experience of children. I took the question seriously.

'Human beings look as if they're asleep.'

The girl nodded. 'And not human beings?'

'Animals . . .' I felt pain. Memories of my beautiful bird, Sarah. She had not looked asleep. She became a . . . carcase. I couldn't bear it. That's why I tried to get somebody else to bury her.

'I'm sorry.' I must have allowed my distress to show.

'Did I say something wrong?' she asked.

I smiled. 'Of course not. You must tell me your name, and who you are.'

'Sarah . . .'

And I remembered that piercing white light. So vivid.

'Sarah Czito and I live at . . . '

I heard no more. She was the grandchild or perhaps great-grandchild of Kolman. But why the name? Why Sarah? I had not told anybody the name I had given the gentle white bird with the grey tips to her wings, but wait: yes I had. I told Julius. Had he named her because of that fleeting incident? Too far-fetched. It must be coincidence. Perhaps an omen.

Date: September 1981
Clear, Alaska and Washington D.C.

Charles Tyson's colonel was pointed.

'That's what's wrong with this country; too many playboys with political daddies pulling strings to drag them up the ladder faster than their talents allow.'

Chuck protested, 'I dunno what you're on about, colonel.'

'My ass! You're bored to death and I'm cramping your wheeler-dealing! You ain't learned the difference between a missile and a penguin, and you get the sort of easy number reserved for heroes.'

'Doing what, colonel?'

'You've been posted! Washington! You're here to kiss my ass. Good riddance, Tyson.' He said it without malice, acknowledging an unalterable fact of American life. Know the right people and life was sweet.

Chuck drew his arm up in his smartest salute. His superior officer's acknowledgement was a wiggle of the stockinged right foot on top of the desk.

'And by the way, Lieutenant . . . ' Tyson stopped and turned at the door. 'I just promoted you Captain.'

'Thank you, SIR!'

'Not merit. Orders. Clout.'

Chuck closed the door quietly behind him and wondered what was going on. The orders were clear enough. He was to report a.s.a.p. if not sooner, in civilian clothes, informal, in fact, specifically jeans and 'T' shirt. And under no circumstances was he to mention the new appointment to anybody, unless such person produced unimpeachable authority. What the hell was it about?

He took the daily flight to Andrews Air Force Base and a taxi just short of his destination. It was an office building in the 600 block on 7th Street on the borders of Chinatown. It had seen better days. The list of names in the tacky entrance lobby suggested anything from door-to-door salesmen to Mafioso cover companies importing Afghan heroin. The sign on the second floor glass door read 'Enterprise for Industry Inc.' The small room contained a typewriter, telex machine, two wooden chairs and magazines on a cigarette-burnt coffee table that had been made in the First World War. There was no bell, and no sign of an occupant. He was about to rap on the door of the inner room when he spotted a hand-written note propped up on the typist's desk. 'Back in 30 seconds.'

The room told him nothing. There was a battered filing cabinet in one corner and a table in the other bearing electric kettle and coffee making equipment. A certificate on the wall said EFI Inc. had been registered in Delaware as an incorporated company with limited liability.

The inner door opened and a woman in her late twenties appeared. She would never make the cover of Vogue, thought Tyson, but she had an interesting face. She was tall, dark, and had an alert sexiness that contained no hint of coquetry. Some secretary!

'Yes?' The tone would not have melted the polar ice cap. He turned on the smile.

'Captain Charles Tyson. Reporting as ordered, Ma'am.'

'Captain . . . who?'

'Tyson, Ma'am. I've been posted here from Clear, Alaska, and I sure am glad to get in out of the cold.'

'I think you've made a mistake, Captain. This is a civilian organization.'

There was something odd about the girl's behaviour. She was giving him the hard word, but her eyes seemed to be saying something else. What the hell was going on?

'My mistake, Ma'am.' He turned to leave. At the door he glanced back over his shoulder. 'The only bar in Washington with Marc Chagall murals is right round the corner. How about joining me there at happy hour?'

'Not tonight, soldier. I'm busy.'

The inner door opened again. In the doorway stood a man in his shirtsleeves, his tired grey trousers suggested low-pay government and little interest in appearances. The crew-cut hair style was well out of fashion. Tyson put his age in the early thirties. He had a folder in his hand. He looked at it, then at Tyson.

'They must be desperate,' he sighed.

'You talking to me?' Tyson enquired politely.

'It says here you were given orders not to disclose your assignment to anybody who did not first give you credentials. Right?'

Tyson's brain engaged. He had goofed off with the girl, better not repeat the error with this smart ass.

'Who's asking?'

'I am.' Hard.

'Who are you?'

'My name's Rogers. Pete Rogers. CIA.'

'I'm Santa Claus.'

Rogers flipped his warrant card at Tyson, who compared the photograph with the craggy original.

Tyson handed it back with a nod. Rogers reached round the door and pulled his jacket off the hook.

'Shut up the shop, Heidi.' He turned his attention to Tyson. 'I thought I knew every bar within five miles of this place. Where's these Chagalls?'

Chuck doubted that Marc Chagall had painted the murals himself, but somebody who knew his work had done a fair imitation. Each wall was part of a continuous pattern of blue fantasy. Some fairy figures were complete to the last detail, others merely suggestions of movement. The setting was sylvan, and somehow brooding, seeming to evoke a spirit that was at once Russian and Jewish.

The girl in charge of the desk wore the white highly-patterned blouse of the Ukraine. She guided them past the zakusi – herrings in sour cream, caviar, gherkins, kolbasa sausage – to a dimly-lit table.

'How did you find this place, Chuck?' said Rogers as they sat.

'An aunt thought it was a sign the Russians are taking over America. I think it's neat.'

The waitress who took their order was conventionally American. A white scooped neckline barely covered the nipples and the skirt was six inches long, exposing well-formed legs on high-heeled shoes.

'Why the rigmarole in the office just now?' Chuck enquired.

Rogers was laconic. 'Security, and find out about you and orders.'

'And you deduce from the fact that I reported for duty at exactly the time and place stipulated, disclosing my name and rank in the process, as evidence that I . . . '

'Something like that.'

The returning waitress filled the steely silence with six tall ice-filled glasses with generous measures of amber liquid in the bottom of each.

'Happy hour,' she explained. 'Two for the price of one. Enjoy!'

Tyson drank deep. 'That's a load of shit.'

'You sure don't waste breath trying to impress your superiors,' commented Rogers.

'This posting wasn't my idea. O.K. I goofed with Heidi. It won't happen again.'

Rogers raised his eyebrows at the girl.

'What do you think?'

She gave Tyson a frank assessment.

'He's good-looking. He takes care with his shaving – a girl appreciates that sort of thing. His duds cost a month of my salary. He's clumsy, spoilt, rich. Who isn't?'

Rogers gave a wintry smile.

'Would somebody please tell me what the hell this is all about?' asked Tyson.

'We're CIA.'

'Oh!' said Tyson, uncomprehending. 'Why? Why me?'

'We thought you could tell us.'

Tyson shook his head. 'My colonel bawled me out for using clout to get out of Arctic boredom.'

'Did you?' asked Rogers.

'No!'

Rogers continued. 'There's two ways of playing this. I can give you an errand a day and the rest of the time is your own, in which case if it's your clout calling the shots, you can screw around the social whirl with no problem; or you can do the job for real, in which case I'll chase your ass. What's it to be?'

Tyson shrugged. 'How about a little of each?'

Date: 30 September 1981
Georgetown, Washington D.C.

There was no fat on the spare figure of the man leaning over Ruth Coverdale's walnut dining table. His crew-cut hair gave his well-known head an obscenely nude appearance. The media had given him thousands of column inches, ever since his first storming of a Vietcong machine gun post in which he had personally slaughtered ten of the enemy. Thereafter he kept popping up in front line situations that quickly made him the soldier's general, officer's pain in the ass and televiewer's hero. He also had a knack of articulating exactly what the man in Council Bluffs, Iowa was thinking. Three years into his retirement he was putting that talent to practical use.

Popular General Jack Lubbock was fed up, like millions of Americans, with the provocations of Uncle Sam by third world midget powers who were allowed by the politicians to get away with their murderous activities unpunished. Most shrugged and said there was nothing anybody outside government could do about it. Lubbock did not agree with that. His plan was simple: to form a group of the very rich – a technical description of those worth more than fifteen million dollars, and not to be confused with the merely rich, those worth five to fifteen – which would have two functions: fund an extra-governmental intelligence force, and then use the group's political clout to make the president take the appropriate action. They'd put agents into the field, at home and abroad. They'd tackle what is regarded as one of the most sinister of the Soviet covert operations against the West, the hundreds of Russian moles, usually of American nationality, and with impeccable qualifications, who've been infiltrated into sensitive areas of government, defence, scientific research. They don't steal secrets. They never blow their cover. Intense personal vetting would not reveal a single flaw in their behaviour. Their job is to obstruct any promising new development. There are always valid arguments against anything. The value of these moles is that they've achieved respect through talent and seniority, and they use both to undermine the United States.

General Jack knew that if the group ever became overtly political, it would be strangled at birth. So the focus of the role would be intelligence. The political lobbying to force action was, by comparison, simple. Politicians are the most voracious devourers of dollar bills ever devised. Without money they can never get elected. The main source of the heavy donations is those who've got it. And the biggest bucks come from the very rich.

'Whaddya think?' said Lubbock.

Ruth gave him one of her quizzical looks. 'Sounds to me

like a typical case of old soldieritis; yearning for the days of personal power over thousands of troops.'

'You don't believe me?' Jack was incredulous. 'Everybody knows we go weak at the knees . . . '

'It's not that, Jack. I agree with your diagnosis. I'm not convinced we'd achieve anything.' Ruth did not tell him there was already such a group in place, who did exactly what he proposed, but in a commercial and industrial context. It had a remarkable record in eliminating opposition to its interests.

'Let me give you a for instance?' said Lubbock, warming to his pet topic. 'You've heard of General George J. Keegan, former head of Air Force Intelligence?'

'He's pretty visible.'

'He says there are two Soviet research facilities, one thirty miles south of Seminpalatinsk, the other at Azgir, near the Caspian. They have fission-explosive generators producing unheard-of power stored in huge steel spheres. The power is fed through an accelerator into an electron injection particle beam gun.'

'I read it in Science magazine three years ago! Nobody I talked to believed it.'

'The Pentagon does now.'

'So what are you worried about?'

'The sceptics are in the majority. So no action.'

Ruth was cool. 'What's got you all fired up?'

'The Soviets zapped our radar . . . '

'They apologized.'

'It was a similar sphere, but much bigger, which blew up in Riga. But only after it had demonstrated its power.'

'They explained all that. Low frequency experiments . . .'

'Ruth. Listen to me. They blacked out the whole NATO defence radar. We don't know how the hell they did it, and the Pentagon isn't even interested.'

'What do you want me to do? Lobby the President?'

'He'll only fall back on his advisers. We already know what they're telling him. We need direct action.'

'What the hell does that mean?'

'I've got friends in the service who're worried sick. They want private capital in on this act.'

'Defence projects cost billions. Only government has that sort of money.'

'Not to build military hardware. Not even research. What I'm on about is intelligence. That won't cost the earth, and when we get it, use political muscle to make the Man listen.'

'You want me to put up money to back a private army in competition with Uncle Sam?'

'Working with and for. And not you alone. You know all the big hitters, the patriots. We need a group formed. A plan of action.'

'They'd need some convincing!'

'There's another ex-officer of Air Force intelligence, with a Ph.D in nuclear engineering, name of Bearden. Lieutenant-Colonel Tom Bearden. He's convinced the biggest threat to our security is the Russian advances on the Tesla Shield. That's what Riga, Seminpalatinsk and Azgir is all about. Tesla invented it here, not in Russia. We've got to find out how he did it and . . .'

They were interrupted by the mutter of voices from the hall.

'Frederick's home earlier than I expected,' said Ruth.

'Tell him!' urged Lubbock. 'He's on our side. Hell, he'll be our next secretary of state.'

Ruth was not enthusiastic. 'At the right time.'

General Lubbock wondered what that meant.

Ruth reassured him. 'Politicians and secrets make unhappy bedfellows.'

'You should know.'

Ruth took the general's arm, and guided him to the circular white-painted hall, its double winding staircase a fair attempt at Adam elegance.

'Look who's dropped in, darling.'

Frederick Coverdale handed his hat, gloves and coat to the manservant, kissed his wife on the cheek, and shook hands with Lubbock.

'Welcome to our home, Jack. What do you think of the new place, aside from the fact that it was built two hundred years ago?'

'Is that right! I must tell you, Fred . . . ' Coverdale winced. 'A soldier's a bit of a gipsy. A blanket and three inches of dried leaves is my idea of home. I guess you gotta have something like this in . . . politics.' He made it sound dirty.

Ruth sued for peace. 'I'd like the two men I most admire to stop sparring and buy me a drink.'

Coverdale said, 'I'll ring for Jennings.'

Lubbock interjected:

'I make the meanest martini this side of West Point, ma'am. Fred, what about you? Sherry?'

'A martini'd be fine, Jack.'

Lubbock opened the refrigerator in the wetbar.

'This is the home of somebody who really cares. Gin in the refrigerator . . . '

Ruth completed the sentence. 'And vodka in the ice compartment.'

'That's civilization.' Lubbock eyed the Waterford crystal with suspicion, but finally poured gin to the brim. He dribbled a minute quantity of vermouth into the cap of its bottle, and then allowed one drop into each glass.

'I propose a toast – Mr and Mrs America!'

Ruth and Frederick were puzzled.

'OK. God Bless America, if you'd rather.'

They all drank to that.

'Why the rash of patriotic fervour, Jack?'

'We all need reminding. We didn't build our heritage sitting on our asses, and we won't keep it that way either.'

Date: September 1981
REME Workshops, Hanover, BAOR, West Germany

The colonel sat at his desk, his adjutant stood alongside. The regimental sergeant major stood by the door, his pacing stick gripped tightly under his left arm.

Outside the door, Richard Lloyd waited, his friend Lewis Calshott, another captain of the corps, his escort. Lewis glanced anxiously at his brother officer. It was plain he didn't care what they did to him.

Calshott had tried to prepare his friend for something unpleasant, but got no reaction.

The sergeant major shouted 'Sir!' and opened the door.

'Captain Lloyd, sir. Commanding Officer's orders.'

The two friends marched forward, saluted.

The colonel was formal.

'Captain Lloyd, you absented yourself from your unit for four days in circumstances that strongly suggest an intention to desert . . . '

'That's not true, sir.' His voice was toneless, a token correction.

'You'll have an opportunity to speak. You entered Yugoslav territory without permission and as a result found yourself in a situation of potential embarrassment to the army and your corps, not to mention your country. What is worse, you did so in pursuit of a relationship which you'd been told to terminate. I am sending the papers to the Director of Army Legal Services for consideration of your court-martial. Have you anything to say?'

Richard Lloyd permitted himself a thin smile. It was ludicrous for them to think they could inflict a meaningful punishment.

'I admit to being absent without leave. I had to go. They

said she was dead. I didn't believe them. They said it was an accident. Lie!'

Calshott intervened:

'Colonel, I don't think Captain Lloyd is in a fit state to . . .'

'I don't need your help in conducting these orders!' was the CO's peremptory reply.

'I'm prepared to accept your punishment . . .' Richard recited the well-known formula as though his colonel had never mentioned the words court-martial.

'D'you need a doctor, Captain Lloyd?'

That seemed to register.

'No, sir.'

The colonel measured his words.

'I might be willing to consider another course . . .'

If he had expected a sign of relief from Lloyd he was disappointed.

'I'll give you twenty-four hours to resign your commission.'

Calshott gasped.

'Twenty-four hours, Captain Lloyd. You are dismissed.'

Lloyd and his escort marched out.

The colonel took off his cap and laid it wearily on the desk. The adjutant was puzzled.

'Why so quizzical Jeremy?' asked the senior man.

'Richard'll get over this, sir. He's basically a good officer. Impulsive. But he'll settle down. Now!'

'The army can do without officers who can't obey orders.'

'I thought you liked Richard, sir.'

'Subject closed, Jeremy. What else is there for this morning?'

Lewis Calshott lit his friend a cigarette.

'I tried to warn you.'

'There was a time when I'd have been a bit upset, but now . . . What's the point.'

'Did you hear what the colonel said?'

'Look at it from their point of view,' said Lloyd. 'Marta is . . . was Iron Curtain.'

'Yugoslavia, not Russia! Whose side are you on?'

'Good question, Lewis. That was my problem.'

A uniformed corporal approached Lloyd.

'Message from the mess, sir. Somebody to see you.'

Forbes was in the anteroom, nondescript, diffident; the eyes drooped, suggesting he was having trouble keeping awake.

Lloyd was in no mood for more probing.

'What do you want this time?'

'Are we likely to be overheard here?'

'Why?'

'Do they sweep the mess regularly?'

'I need rest. Can't we make this another time.'

''Fraid not. We'll go outside.'

Forbes headed for open space, eyes agog.

'What are you looking for?' Lloyd was irritated.

'Long range mikes. Parked cars. Static listening devices.' He shrugged. 'It's hopeless really. If they get on to you . . . to me, say . . . I probably won't spot them, and the technology . . . theirs and ours . . . is so good . . . they could be half a mile away and pick up every comma.'

'Well?' said Lloyd.

'I know how you're feeling, and if there weren't a certain urgency I'd leave you to get on with your life and choices, but it isn't like that,' said Forbes. Be considerate, his brigadier had said!

'What isn't?'

'You're wanted. God knows why. Everything I've turned up on you suggests you're a liability . . .'

'I agree with you.'

'I'm supposed to offer you a job in military intelligence, give you a load of crap about the security of the country et cetera. You'll probably spend six months learning Arabic and get posted to Ulster.'

'Your timing's spot on!'

The major nodded.

'Was it your idea. Resigning my commission?'

'They don't tell me such things.'

'What happens if I say no?'

'To me or them?'

'Resigning.'

'Court-martial. Cashiered, I'd say.' That wasn't being considerate.

'My brother officer says I'm not fit to decide anything!'

'What do you say?' asked Forbes.

Lloyd didn't answer.

'Why must I resign?'

'Confusion to the enemy! They wouldn't expect you to get a job with us after that.'

'I don't believe this,' said Lloyd. 'I don't believe any of it.'

'What happened in Yugoslavia?'

Richard didn't want to talk about Marta to this scruffy stranger from London, but he answered.

'The border's normally no greater hassle than Spain or France, but I was shaken down by two sinister goons, one a Russian.'

'Ex-pats were supposed to be infiltrating a team to spring Milovan Djilas,' said the London major. 'Barmy rumour, but they get hyped up at mention of his name. You were unlucky.'

True, thought Lloyd. The words were hesitant at first, difficult to find. He told Forbes everything. Facts, feelings, the lot. It took an hour.

Forbes heard him out in silence. Only once did he seem about to interrupt, and that was when Lloyd told of the marks on Marta's body.

The day turned overcast, loweringly humid.

'How did you get out?' enquired the major.

'I stayed the night on the Island.'

'Alone?'

'I had a bottle of vinjak – local firewater – for company. Passed out. In the morning I latched on to a bunch of Tyneside boilermakers. They gave me a lift in their coach.'

A clap of thunder coincided with a blinding zig-zag of lightning. No rain. Eerie.

'Memories,' said Richard in disgust. 'Who needs them.'

'You will,' was the older man's answer.

5

Date: September 1981
New York, N.Y.

Rakov was no stranger to New York. This was his third visit. On previous trips he had had time to taste the American way of life. He could not deny the excitement. Maybe New York was not America, but there was a hustle, an energy abroad on the streets that was not there in Moscow, or Leningrad. The material prosperity was greater. The shops had produced a profound sense of shock. He couldn't believe such a wide range of choice in clothing, food – especially food – consumer hardware, no queues of any sort; unimaginable to Soviets. He had heard stories from returning colleagues that for their first few days they'd gone into shop after shop trying suits, pants, jackets, overcoats, with no intention of buying, for the sheer luxury of wallowing in the surfeit of choice. He had known he would never do anything so superficial. He was wrong. He had done as had so many before him, and as would many thereafter.

Later, he had begun to examine the lifestyle more carefully, and realized it was not heaven. The price paid for such luxuries was, he was sure, a grinding poverty for millions kept out of sight by the authorities, probably in South and middle America, and for the others – those he saw walking the streets of Manhattan Island – there was an awesome competitiveness about ordinary working lives. At home, once a qualification had been obtained, professional, scientific, manual or secretarial, the system provided a job; it was automatic. Unemployment was the result of misbehaviour, not, as in the United States, misfortune. In the Motherland you were thrown out of a job only for betraying your trust; punishment, severe but just. The fact that comparable crimes did not exist here did not interest Rakov. Slandering the state, dissidence – which seemed to excite the media so much in the West where anybody could denegrate his homeland with impunity – betraying the system that fed, clothed, educated and then provided guaranteed employment, was treason. The writer who slandered his Motherland should be thrown out of the Writers' Union; Sakharov should lose his membership of the Academy of Sciences. Anything less would encourage others to do the same. Too much of that and even Rakov's job could be in jeopardy!

That millions of his fellow countrymen did not see it in that light bothered him not at all; that was their problem.

His family was another matter. He tried not to think about that last day with them. He did not blame his father for never wanting to see him again. But it could not alter the direction of his life. The system existed and could not be changed. Nobody in any position of power or responsibility believed there was ideological justification for what was done. The only philosophy was to use the system for personal advantage, as everybody else did. Rakov was good at it. One day, when his skill got him where he wanted, he would provide a dacha, servants and all the trimmings for his family. Then they would understand!

The immigration officer checked his name against her file of undesirables. Whether she found Rakov's name there, he did not know, but his appointment was for two years, and that was the exact period for which his visa was marked valid.

The customs officer searched each bag thoroughly. He did not bother to ask Rakov if he had brought in any gifts worth more than $100; the chance of any Soviet citizen doing so was remote. The procedure took a quarter the time it did in Moscow; another example of the complacency of Yanks.

He was not met. He approved. He carefully scanned the arrivals hall. Nobody was taking any interest in him. Good. Some thousand people thronged the building, searching for relatives, friends, lost children.

Had Rakov stayed behind in the immigration hall, he would have seen his interviewing officer pick up a telephone.

The tourist in the gaudy Miami shirt photographing his newly arrived girlfriend in between hugs and kisses that would not have been untypical at a Russian railway station, did not interest Rakov. They should have done. The 'tourist' took Yuri's photograph several times.

Nobody followed him. They knew where he was going. It was part of the routine. They had no reason to suspect the true nature of Rakov's assignment.

Yuri took the bus to Manhattan. It was not an inspiring journey. The scenery was flat, the freeway a repeat of any wide-lane highway anywhere in the world, but it gave him a chance to breathe the air of New York, to begin the process of acclimatization.

* * *

Date: 2 January 1943
New Yorker Hotel, New York, N.Y.

I was ill, no doubt about it. And so tired. At eighty-six I suppose I should expect some degree of incapacity, as I told my old friend Samuel Clemens – popularly known as Mark Twain – last night. It was kind of Samuel to call. I enjoyed his reminiscences of the Far East, a place I wish I had visited. He had seen things on his travels for which the only explanation was the existence of a spirit world with which some people could communicate. This led me to thinking about my problem. I still had not decided what to do with the third piece of the Trinity. Then the obvious solution occurred. I took up pen and paper.

'Please call on me this evening. I
have a present for you. Speak of this
to nobody until we meet.'

I gave the bellboy two dollars, with promise of a further dollar when he returned with the answer.

Later I was woken from a fitful sleep.

'Come in. Come in.' I said.

Eugene Jackson was no youngster. He had worked as a bellboy at the New Yorker for forty years. He was over sixty, a spare athletic figure but just five feet two inches in height. He let the younger men carry the big bags now, but he still took all the important messages. He looked embarrassed.

'I'm sorry, sir. I wasn't able to deliver your letter.'

'Was Mr Clemens not at home?'

'You could say that, professor.'

'What do you mean?'

'You sure you have the right address?'

'Show me!' I said. The writing was not as good as it might have been but it was correct.

'Houston Street?' asked Jackson. 'Isn't that where you had your laboratory, a few years back, sir?'

Was it? I really must shake away the cobwebs infesting my memory.

'What if it was?'

The bellboy had something on his mind.

'There's nobody named Samuel Clemens at that address, professor.'

'Nonsense. Mr Twain . . . ah that's the trouble. I should have used his nom-de-plume. Then you would have found him all right.'

'Professor . . . Mr Mark Twain has been dead these twenty-five years.'

'Nonsense. Mr Clemens talked to me, in this very room for over an hour last night. You probably saw him arrive. About five o'clock it was.'

'I was off duty yesterday.'

'Give me back the letter.'

I gave Jackson a five dollar bill.

'Can we keep this . . . just between us?'

'Sure, professor. Anything you say.'

If Mark Twain had died twenty-five years ago, I must be in a bad way! So what do I do with the third piece of the Trinity? I became aware of another knocking, different in quality from Jackson's knuckles on the wooden door. This was a tap, tap, tap. I traced the sound to the window. It was a white pigeon, a beautiful bird with grey tips to her wings. I hurried out of bed and fumbled with the latch.

An undistinguished bird with dirty grey feathers flapped down the side of the stone building. Memory playing tricks again! I thought my beloved Sarah had come back to me. And then I remembered something else. I'd already placed the last part of the Trinity. What a relief! Now perhaps I could sleep.

* * *

Date: September 1981
Near Guildford, England

He didn't look like a brigadier. He was wearing a faded Ralph Lauren 'T' shirt in a dirty blue colour and casual cream slacks that might have been fashionable circa 1920. He was forty-five and looked younger, with a shock of dark hair, no hint of grey. He leaned back, hands behind his neck as Lloyd approached the huge partner's desk, littered with paper.

Richard wore an old blue mohair from Simpson's Daks range. His suit collar was frayed and regimental tie twisted.

'I'm Richard Lloyd, sir.'

The brigadier looked him over.

'I suppose the first thing to say is that we prefer volunteers. And we don't normally take people with discipline problems.'

The thing that impressed Lloyd was the lack of sympathy. He'd had enough of condolence. The brigadier continued:

'You're here because of an accident, the coincidence of relationship and timing. Normally your association with a Yugoslav, plus forbidden trips behind the Iron Curtain would be the end of you . . . '

Lloyd had heard it all before. The brigadier sensed this.

'And you don't give a bugger?'

Lloyd answered carefully. 'You get to the point where you want to say, "OK. We both know what I've done. Do something about it, but don't keep on telling me" . . . sir!'

The brigadier's eyes widened.

'You could turn out to be quite difficult.'

Lloyd braced himself, a slight gesture to regimental bearing. The brigadier changed the subject.

'We don't actually like a lot of formality. Agents are better off if they break the habit. It can be embarrassing if you're in the Lubjanka pretending to be a peasant farmer, and throw up a regulation salute!'

He dialled four telephone digits.

'Max? . . . This is Julian. I think we have a problem child. He's not too reliable at the moment. Maybe a few weeks' leave and then we see what he's like . . . '

Lloyd was not bothered, either way.

The brigadier continued:

'It's the damage he could do if we let him loose on this, and he goes bad on us for whatever reason . . . '

Still staring ahead, Lloyd spoke quietly.

'I don't do things like that.'

The brigadier spoke equally quietly.

'Shut up, Lloyd . . . ' He listened for a few more minutes.

'If you say so.' He replaced the receiver.

'My superiors want me to give you a try.'

'I'm not normally bloody-minded,' said Lloyd. 'I wouldn't have joined the army if I was. But this thing's got me in a bit of a state . . . I've never wanted anything so bad

. . . and suddenly she's dead. What would you have done?'

The brigadier was unsympathetic.

'You've got to get a grip on your life, Lloyd.'

'I've accepted the fact that she's dead. I had to believe the evidence of my eyes . . . but still think about her . . . At first she was there all the time . . . I mean . . . nothing stopped the process . . . I've got it down to about once an hour . . . but I still expect her to . . . every time the phone rings I think I'll hear her voice on the other end.'

'You were in love. These things pass.' And that was the personal issue done with.

The brigadier closed Lloyd's file.

'Sit down. Take off your jacket. Loosen the tie.'

Lloyd complied.

'Forget all you've read about James Bond. Are you hearing me?'

Lloyd nodded.

'We can't afford 'em. Individualists are a menace, and not only to themselves; they put others at risk. Intelligence is teamwork. Most of it's technological. Satellite cameras that can read a newspaper headline from a hundred and ten miles up, monitoring equipment that can analyse fine details of weapons performance by just focusing on ships in an exercise. But that only gets us so far. There's always information that can only be obtained by personal contact. That requires initiative but precise execution of orders. You may have the former but you're not exactly A1 in the other . . .'

'I need something to occupy the mind. I'll give you no trouble, sir.'

The brigadier smiled.

'The normal training period before anybody's let loose in an active situation is one year – and that's intensive. That's just the basic. If you're needed somewhere special – say Yugoslavia, for instance – you would have another four to twelve weeks learning the lingo and something about the *mores*.'

'I didn't ask for this, sir!'

The brigadier was patient.

'Don't add stupidity to the list. You're needed. You've got to understand what's involved if you're to be of any use. If you go in as a love sick mourner you'll wind up dead or worse.'

'How many others are working on . . . this whatever it is?'

'We've had all the pros we can spare on it for months. The scanners and satellites are going round the clock . . .'

'And you're still getting nowhere?'

'I wouldn't say that, but if we'd solved the problem, I wouldn't be talking to you.'

'So why exactly am I here?'

'Because you knew Marta Gracanica, and we think she was working on the Tesla Shield!'

'What's so special about it when we've got nuclear superiority?'

'Missiles break up when they hit it.'

'Why not up and over?'

The brigadier sighed. 'The Shield can be shaped like an umbrella.'

Lloyd was sceptical. 'I used to be quite useful at physics. You can focus something like a laser great distances, but anything more diffuse . . . its energy simply dissipates the further it gets from the power source.'

'Most of the scientific establishment agrees with you. The only trouble is the Russians seem to have turned that particular trick; twice, maybe three times.'

Lloyd persisted. 'How do we know?'

The brigadier told him.

'What do you want me to do?'

'Find out what your girlfriend was working on, bring me back a sample or two.'

'Would I have been asked to do this if Marta was still alive?'

'Even better chance of getting the information.'

'She would not have betrayed her country.'
'Maybe.'

The training camp was a Georgian mansion in Surrey. In spring and summer it was idyllic. The lawns that surrounded the mellow two-hundred year old brickwork of the main house were regularly manicured to an even cut, free of moss and weeds. The remaining timber and gorse of some sixty acres were criss-crossed with rough paths, which provided the physical training area.

The sergeant PT instructor who ran with Lloyd regularly increased the length of his stride in an effort to break the young captain. To his surprise Lloyd was still with him after twelve miles, only a little more out-of-breath than the expert.

The sergeant reported to Major Forbes:

'He's in quite good shape. Physically. As to mental attitude. Not good.'

'Do your best.'

'It'll take weeks to bring him to peak condition and get the psychology right.'

'How long?'

'I can do something with him in a month instead of three.'

'No chance. He has to go in tomorrow.'

'Apart from being a mental case at the moment, he won't have learned any self defence, specialist weapons drill, signals, languages, codes . . . '

'If this oddball is to be of any use to us, we've got to put him to work right away.'

'How long have I got?' The sergeant was frequently asked to do the impossible.

'Forty-eight hours – maybe.'

The track-suited sergeant brought his heels to attention, went up on his toes, and smartly jogged away. Forbes looked at the running figure, the fittest man he had known, and contemplated the fate of Richard Lloyd. He would not survive, Forbes was sure of that. On this sort of mission, even the best trained agent usually succumbed to the battery of technological counter-espionage equipment, let along the huge manpower resources the communists deployed. In Russia, Forbes would give Lloyd two days, maybe less, before discovery. He would disappear; by a bullet in the nether reaches of the Lubjanka, or, if it happened to suit them at the time, a show trial, followed by thirty years somewhere cold. A swop might eventually take place, but only after Lloyd had been neutralized, mentally and physically. In Yugoslavia, where things were slacker he could last out the week.

The brigadier talked to Forbes.

'I find that young man an enigma. Allowing for the fact he's upset about the girl, he still seems to have an attitude of . . . there's an arabic word for it – *alacefic* – not caring, too casual. What's his background?'

'Minor public school, Kings, Taunton. Good home life. Father runs a shop, newsagent, tobacco, sweets; successful. They've taken over the two shops next door in the High Street. Mother taught science at a private girls' school, had a difficult time when he was born, couldn't have any more children.'

'Normal happy home life?'

'Yes . . . '

'Why the hesitation?'

'The "trick-cyclist" reckons there could be an explanation to this tilting at authority bit . . . '

'Psychiatry's here to stay Arthur!'

'The newsagent business is usually a family affair. It has to be if it's to make money . . . '

'And mother thought it was a bit beneath a public school boy to serve behind the counter?' enquired the brigadier.

'Something like that.'

The sergeant took Lloyd to the gymnasium. He put him through a punishing work-out at which Lloyd acquitted himself reasonably well. The concentrated physical effort drove all other thoughts from his mind. For the final test the sergeant threw him eight ounce boxing gloves, and invited Richard to share the ring with him for three rounds. The brigadier wandered in to watch. Lloyd enjoyed the noble sport as a spectator, but had never been any good at it, and reckoned he was in for a pounding.

He climbed through the ropes. It began in a fairly civilized fashion, Lloyd back-pedalling and throwing out the odd left and clumsy right while the sergeant was the aggressor, pushing out a straight left which increasingly penetrated Lloyd's guard making him steadily angrier. The injustice of all that had happened to him reached a climax. The focus of his pent-up rage became the man in the other corner.

'One minute,' called the sergeant, and retired to his corner. He jogged on the spot psyching Lloyd who was fighting for breath. For the first time in a while Richard Lloyd was motivated and he intended to do something about it. He remembered an early school boxing lesson: he who loses his temper loses the fight.

The sergeant bided his time, jabbing out his left, saving the right for the next test of the officer's character. Lloyd kept his eyes fixed firmly on those of his opponent, not on the gloves; the eyes telegraph intention. The sergeant's concentration lapsed; a fleeting moment. Lloyd feinted with a feeble left, which the sergeant absent-mindedly parried, and then brought across a short angry right. It was not on target, nowhere near the jaw. It landed between the cheekbone and the ear, but it had sufficient force, and surprise to knock the sergeant to the canvas. Richard bent down to help his opponent to his feet. The thanks were curt.

'Get to a neutral corner.'

The brigadier, on the point of departure, changed his mind and dragged a chair to the ringside.

Sergeant Maxwell was a model of self-control. An all-round athlete, he taught everything from javelin to the dirty tricks of unarmed combat. He was a well-qualified non-commissioned officer who had passed every test the army put in front of him; all but one. He regularly failed Officer Selection Board. He resented this. His job was to teach mainly officers. To do this he had to test them to the limit. It's a strange relationship, the sergeant punishing the officer, using foul offensive language to encourage greater effort, suffixed always with the soubriquet of 'sir.' But Maxwell went one step beyond the reasonable in the physical department, knowing he could never be found out. It was his job. It was compensation of a sort.

The brigadier knew his sergeant. He had marked the application for officer training 'Not recommended.'

The sergeant's usual drill was to deliver a foul blow, not to incapacitate, but to see how the trainee reacted. Fight or flight! Would his character make him more aggressive, or would he retreat? Maxwell's undignified trip to the canvas changed his strategy. He would give the captain a boxing lesson, a painful one.

Lloyd saw the glint in the sergeant's eyes. OK, so he was in a fight. He had no chance in a fair fight. Maxwell was fitter, stronger and a better technician. Lloyd searched for a chink in the fit man's armour. He saw it in the eyes. Maxwell was losing his temper. He had a chance.

Lloyd took some punishment. The left leads were getting through his guard repeatedly, jarring his head back, splitting his lips, pulping his nose, closing his eyes. His own blows were not accurate and often delivered without the fist clenched, doing little damage. Lloyd grabbed his opponent, smothering his punches, taking a breather. His solar plexus was tender and vulnerable. Maxwell drove him into a corner and was about to administer the knock-out drop when the brigadier's voice ordered 'Stop boxing!'

Four arms fell.

'One minute, gentlemen.'

They went to their corners, wondering why the brigadier had joined in. Maxwell continued his jogging, his face impassive, but the determination to humiliate the officer implacable. The brigadier's intervention to save 'one of his own getting hurt' added fuel to his seething resentment.

Lloyd's face hurt. He thought his nose was broken. His arms were aching agonies. His legs shivered.

The brigadier shouted, 'Bell. Box on.'

Maxwell strode in for the kill. The brigadier closed his eyes against the inevitable. There was little Lloyd could do. He did not have the strength. He decided to look even worse than he felt, if that was possible. As Maxwell came in Richard dropped his lower jaw and let his rasping throat and chest be heard. The sergeant's arms were at his waist, Mohammed Ali style. Lloyd posed no threat.

Richard planned his last hope. He lurched late off the ropes. The sergeant drew back his right hand to finish his man. Lloyd waited an age for Maxwell to get close. He knew he would only have one shot. If that failed his blood would be all over the canvas. It had to be a perfect blow, of which he was probably incapable, fresh, and twice as fit. He let his eyelids droop, he struggled to lift his arms. He was waiting for the slight relaxation that was bound to come as the sergeant savoured his coming victory. He saw it!

Lloyd's clumsily lifted left foot changed direction nine inches. Not a lot, but it meant Maxwell had to shift the aim of his right, and adjust his stance. Lloyd knew that the rest depended on aim. There was little power left in any part of his body, let alone his right arm. He had no time to take a swing. It would have to be an upper cut, and it had to hit the point of the jaw with the weight of Richard's body, and the forward motion of the instructor perfecting the collision.

It wasn't elegant. It wasn't in any manual on how to deliver correct punches. An experienced boxer, mind not clouded by resentment, would have seen it. The sergeant did not. Lloyd heaved the blow at him. It landed on the point of the jaw.

Unconsciousness was immediate. The sergeant's body straightened, his left leg twitched upward in a strange reflex action, and he fell rigid, a tree sawn at the base. His head met the canvas. Lloyd heard it with some satisfaction.

The brigadier clambered into the ring, and bent over the sergeant. He was still unconscious.

'Throw me that towel.'

Lloyd did so. The brigadier put it under Maxwell's head. His pulse was erratic. He looked laconically at the exhausted Lloyd.

'Next time take on somebody your own size.'

Before Richard had a chance to protest at the injustice of the remark he added, 'And see if you can raise the doc. You could have given him concussion.'

Richard Lloyd's face was a bruised, bleeding mess. Every part of his body cried out for analgesic. He felt good. The cloud was beginning to lift.

* * *

Date: 6 January 1943
New Yorker Hotel, New York, N.Y.

I dreamed I was inside a huge turbine, spreadeagled across the face of the disc as it began to spin, welded to it at ankles and wrists. Giant may bugs wired to my extremities provided the power. I squeezed my eyes shut. The buzzing was replaced by the soothing sound of trickling water. I was on the bank of the river at Smiljan. The sparkling flow hit a primitive water-wheel. I blinked. The sound continued, but the scene had changed. The water was coursing off the brow of a baby as my father baptized her at the font of the church in Smiljan. I looked past them to the altar. The simple gilt cross was missing. I couldn't understand it. Could it have been stolen? I knew I would be blamed for its theft. Fear drenched me. I pleaded to be allowed to make a replace-

ment. Jeering laughter. Feverishly I began drawing the shape in my head. The crowd pinioned me against the west door of the church. A burnished bright fire engine arrived. I was sentenced to be hosed to death.

I woke. My nightshirt was sodden. The New York night was still and humid. My dream was still vivid, the trauma lingered. I tried to recall what the cross looked like. But I could not fill the gap. Even my photographic memory would not replace the centrepiece of the altar. I recognized the incidents, distorted though they were, as episodes in my childhood. I remembered making the water-wheel. It was the inspiration for my smooth-disc turbine. I remembered glueing may bugs to the four points of a wooden windmill and watching as the beating wings drove the sails. My friend had eaten the insects live. I felt sick. I smashed my creation. I remembered the fire and being the only one to spot the kink that prevented water flowing through the hose. I remembered the applause of the crowd. Everything had a reasoned explanation; all except the missing cross. What was the significance of that? Maybe it was not in the past, but in the future. There had been times when I had 'seen' what would be. This usually took the form of some technical innovation in my mind's eye. But this was not invention. It was my subconscious trying to tell me something. But what? It had to be connected with church. But what? What was it about a church that was important that I had forgotten? At last a chink of memory filtered through. It was about Smiljan. Yes. What about it? Suddenly I knew. It wasn't a church any more, but a ruin. That was it! I felt better immediately. What a shame. It reminded me of childhood, of father and mother, and brilliant brother Dane. But there was something else. Something I had to do. What was it? But I was too tired. I would remember in the morning.

* * *

At 10.30 p.m. on 7th January 1943, Nikola Tesla died in his sleep of a coronary thrombosis. The New York Times called him 'One of the world's greatest electrical inventors and designers.'

6

Date: September 1981
Georgetown, Washington

Ruth Coverdale thought marriage to the next secretary of state would add a new dimension in her life. She thought the man himself would ignite a fresh spark. Power is supposed to be an aphrodisiac. Why didn't it work that way on her?

She had nearly everything about Frederick Coverdale wrong. He was not interested in women. He had explained his avoidance of the bedroom before marriage on the basis that he was 'rather old-fashioned about some things.' On the first night of the honeymoon he behaved so correctly – but with such calculation – that she nearly screamed aloud with frustration. Only as the days and nights wore on and his technique began to look as if he had learned it from a medical dictionary did she realize he had a profound disinterest in women, in sex and, more than likely, in her.

He was interested in her money. Not that he wanted to write cheques on her account. He had plenty of touching money of his own. He married her for the influence, the political connections, to be accepted by the elders of the Grand Old Party. Ruth could have kicked herself for not seeing it all in advance. All the signs were there. He let them 'hang out' for everybody to see, judging, with searing accuracy, that Ruth would never believe the obvious.

Ruth had not yet made up her mind what to do about it. She would not rush anything. She never had. She knew he would never give her conventional grounds for divorce. He would not womanize, get drunk, knock her about. If only he would. It would make a change, and he might even reveal something of his true character which, Ruth ruefully thought, might not be worth knowing anyway. She would await the turn of events.

Ruth heard a taxi draw into the driveway. She was not expecting guests. She drew aside the curtain and sighed in pleasure at the sight of her favourite nephew.

'Charles! What's happened to you?'

'Me?'

'You're ill!'

'I'm fine.'

'Your skin is . . . deathlike. You've got consumption.'

'Balls, Mrs Coverdale. Gimme a kiss.' She let him hug her, glad to have him, somebody nearer her own age in the house. 'You sunworshippers can't even recognize a white man when you see one. I'm suffering from an overdose of air-conditioning.'

'Lieutenant Charles Tyson! You know something. You look cute in uniform. You should always wear it.'

'Always?'

'All women fantasize about uniformed men. You ought to have a splurge of gold braid, a cockade in the helmet . . . '

'And to think I gave my sword to left luggage!'

They entered the living room. Charles went straight to the window. 'There's nowhere quite like it. I dreamed of this place. It's crazy, but we had a bit of a panic. I thought maybe the big bang had started – turned out to be . . . "electro-magnetic interference" – I didn't see my previous life flash in front of my eyes, I saw Georgetown, decked out in magnolia . . . '

'Charles Tyson it's fall!'

'You know what I mean.'

'We heard about your problem.'

'D'you have a beer?'

'Help yourself.'

'How about you?'

'Perhaps a sherry.'
'How come you heard about our . . . incident?'
Ruth dissembled. 'People talk. And Frederick is . . .'
'He told you?' asked Tyson.
'Is it classified?'
'Not really . . .'
'Well then . . .'
'You sound as if you're making it your business to know.'
'The dutiful wife can't host political soirées if she don't know what to say to all those important gen'lm'n.' Ruth laid on the Southern Belle drawl.
'Why d'you marry the bastard anyway? There's no way he's good enough for you. We all thought you'd go for Dick Harman.'
'None of your business.' Ruth was sharp.
Charles was contrite. 'Gee Ruth. If you're still googoo-eyed for the creep, I'm sorry. I thought by now you'd have found out what a shmuck he is and . . .'
'Shut up, damn, you, and make me a martini.'
Charles made her drink.
'Tell me about it,' said Ruth.
'About what?'
'What happened out there? On the ice.'
'Hey, Ma'am. I'm a soldier boy. I'm not supposed to talk about these things.'
'First off I'm not just anybody, I'm family, and the motto of our clan as you well know is "above all discretion." Next, if you want to get anywhere in that goddamn uniform, you gotta learn to recognize influence when you see it. Political clout . . .'
'So it was you,' said Tyson.
'What was me?'
'My new posting to Washington.'
'I had nothing to do with that.' But the answer was too quick. 'Tell me what happened in Alaska.'
Tyson contemplated his favourite aunt and wondered

what was going on in her beautiful head. Ruth continued, serious, persuasive.

'Some people . . . important people, are worried that the Russians may have a lead over us in new weapons technology. Is it true? Is that what they did?'

'Nothing to tell. One minute everything was normal, the next the screens went out. Black out. Later it all came good again.'

'And the explanation?'

'There isn't one, and my colonel, for one, is furious. He reckons the Ruskies can do something we can't do and nobody on our team seems to care.'

It was confirmation enough for Ruth.

* * *

Date: January 1943
New York, N.Y.

Tesla's death produced a flurry of official activity. Mrs Roosevelt had been promoting the idea of a Tesla medal with the President only days earlier. The FBI took possession of Tesla's effects. The Vice-President, Henry Wallace, said the government had a vital interest. The Alien Property Custodian flexed his muscles. Doctor John G. Trump, an aide to the Defence Research Committee, was despatched to examine Tesla's papers.

When the manager of the Hotel Governor Clinton remembered the package left in the vault by the great man he was shocked to see Tesla's written warning:

> *'Enclosed within is a secret weapon. It will detonate if opened by an unauthorized person.'*

The sirens echoed through the man-made corridors of Manhattan Island, leading some New Yorkers to think Hitler was about to bomb the Big Apple.

Dr Trump, alone, opened the package. His official report

claimed that it contained only a multi-decade resistance box; the type customarily used for Wheatstone bridge measurements. An everyday piece of laboratory equipment.

Cynics did not believe it. Others were prepared to accept that Tesla had perpetrated his final practical joke. Nobody guessed the real significance of the legacy.

* * *

Date: 2 October 1981
New York, N.Y.

Colonel Aleksei Telinger did not look like a Soviet spy. His tall lithe figure, his Brooks Brothers suit and Gucci shoes, were set off by high slav cheekbones and an elegant, courteous mein. An aristo! His desk was in the Ethiopian aid section of the United Nations building. He was, of course, KGB.

He greeted Major Yuri Rakov warily. The messages that had preceded him left no doubt as to the scope of his authority, but had given no indication of what sort of man he was. That was all-important to Telinger's continued enjoyment of the decadent pleasures of capitalist New York. With such high-powered orders he could make or mar Aleksei's future. He prayed he was not a Party dogmatist, or that if he was, he could be persuaded to get drunk once in a while, and enjoy another sort of partying. He spoke with pointed irony. 'Welcome to the land of worker slaves, privilege and decadence, rapidly disintegrating as the forces of greed destroy the capitalist system.'

Rakov was deadpan.

'It will destroy itself as Lenin and Marx predicted. Neither of them said how long it would take, or how high they would ride before their fall.' Rakov was not about to give a hostage to fortune by allowing this sybarite to share his private thoughts.

Telinger was suave in his reassurance.

'Nothing is more certain, comrade. Forgive me for sounding you out in such an obvious way, but since the old days, there's no knowing what type of person will be sent out from Moscow Centre. I'm delighted to have somebody who respects true values.'

Rakov knew exactly what sort of officer Telinger was; he hoped it would not prove significant.

'What do you have for me, Comrade Colonel?'

That was easier ground. Telinger relaxed.

'Not a lot.'

Rakov was tense.

'You've had instructions about my visit?'

'Certainly, major.'

'Then why have you not acted upon them? Moscow will not be pleased.'

'The signal was received exactly four hours ago. There has hardly been time to mount a new intelligence initiative. I have briefed all section heads. Research is being undertaken. I have alerted the embassy in Washington. They have somebody at the Library of Congress today taking copies of everything on record and available for public inspection.'

Rakov was worried.

'A Russian. So openly!' The colonel said irritably:

'I am not stupid, major. The woman is American; a much-respected schoolteacher doing research for a new project.'

Rakov grunted. 'That will take forever, and probably produce nothing. What else?'

'Our own records contain some information. We have press cuttings of NATO reaction to Riga, and the weather incident.'

'They won't tell me anything.'

'Then there are the records of certain specific tasks we were assigned by Moscow Centre at various times. A great deal of resources were devoted to finding living contacts of

Tesla. Most were dead. Then decisions had to be made as to whether there was any point in getting close to immediate relatives. That was only done in a few cases. There was a lead out in Colorado Springs; a man called . . .' Telinger flipped open a file and soon found the name, '. . . Hubert Wiseman.'

'What was his connection?'

'He was a caretaker at the Colorado Springs Electric Company.'

'How can he be of any use?'

'He was there while Tesla was working on electrical experiments; a junior grade engineer.'

'It sounds pretty hopeless.'

'We're following every lead.'

'What else?'

'I have a man in Lower Manhattan trying to dig up old police files. Tesla is supposed to have caused an earthquake with an experiment in a laboratory in Huston Street. Our man is a "journalist" doing a story for Saturday Evening Post.'

'That doesn't sound too promising either.'

'A man called Kolman Czito worked closely with Tesla. He's been dead many years, but his son also did some work for the old man, at least we think he did. We can't be certain. In 1962 we had Julius Czito under observation when he was killed in a car accident.'

'Are you sure it was an accident?'

'We didn't arrange it. Why should they!'

Rakov grunted.

'Czito was also under observation by the US Secret Service at the time.'

'Why?'

'We don't know. It was one of the reasons we thought it might have been set up.'

'It doesn't make sense. This is their country. If government wanted anything from Czito all they had to do was bring him in for questioning and sweat it out of him. They wouldn't even have to do that. Why would anybody refuse to co-operate . . . unless Czito was one of ours.'

'Definitely not.'

'Why this interest in Czito?'

'He had a small workshop at Astoria on Long Island. His father used to make models for Tesla.'

'What else?'

'We have all the scientific papers, magazine articles, we even have *New York Times, Washington Post* obituaries, other stories over the years . . . '

'Our scientists have worked over all the published material.'

'Tell me where to look, major!'

Rakov paced the room. 'How much do the CIA know of our interest in Tesla?'

'Interesting question. Our agents have heard no word. We have some people inside government . . . '

Rakov was impatient. 'I'm not a novice at this work, colonel.'

'The newspapers were the first to tell us that KGB was following up Tesla leads in America.'

Rakov was amazed.

'I don't understand how a government can allow newspapers to publish such intelligence. How can they run a country . . . '

Telinger smiled. 'I used to feel the same. At home everything is ordered. American democracy is a licence for chaos!'

'We need to know where the Yanks are looking, what they find, and we need to keep them off our backs while we're looking.'

Telinger was thoughtful. 'We have some sympathizers in the CIA, and one committed agent, but she is a low grade worker. She does not have authority to search records. The others . . . are not ready for such an assignment.'

'Ready or not, we may have to use them.'

'By not ready, I mean would not obey such orders; might even betray us.'

'We can't risk that. At least not yet. What about computers?'

'I don't follow . . . '

'The government must have the really important stuff on computer.'

Telinger suppressed his cynicism. 'What a pity Stalin was so certain computers were a waste of time. Kruschev wasn't much better. We're years behind . . . '

'I need solutions, colonel, not a recital of age-old problems. We need to find that computer and access it.'

'How would a good-looking young mathematician suit you?'

Yuri Rakov's eyes narrowed.

'Russian, of course,' added Telinger. 'Moscow Centre was prompt for once. His name is Anton. The Americans call him Tony. I do not discourage the idea that he and I have a homosexual relationship.'

'Do you?' asked Rakov mildly.

'No, major.'

Rakov wondered.

Telinger continued. 'He's at Columbus. Doing economics. That's a front. The Yanks don't like us getting too close to their computer expertise. Next year he'll switch to something more important. Meanwhile he plays with the university computers, like many youngsters. Anton's excuse – not that he needs one – is that he gets so little pocket money from Mother Russia he has to supplement his income by writing programs for computer games.'

'Very American, colonel. What is it the poet says about the love of money?'

'Timothy. The New Testament.' The colonel could not resist correcting his junior comrade. 'It's the root of all evil.'

The doorbell rang.

'Don't go, major.'

Rakov rose.

'And don't alarm yourself. This person is expected.'

Date: September 1981
Near Charlottsville, VA.

Eustace Vanderpage, with white hair and a neat comfortable figure was one of the very rich. The white posts and rails round his colonnaded mansion in Virginia, stretched several miles. His was old money from the industrial belt of the east coast, steel and mining.

'You delight and annoy me, Ruth,' he said as he kissed her on both cheeks. 'Your sexy good looks tell me that you've stolen a generation's march on me, so why don't my eighty-year-old eyes show me a dimmer vision?'

'Eustace, you're begging for compliments, as usual, and I won't oblige.'

He replied in kind. 'How is that odious husband of yours?'

Ruth didn't think Frederick unattractive at the moment. 'When he drove me to the airport . . . '

Vanderpage was incredulous. 'I can't imagine him taking time off for such a mundane pursuit.'

'You misjudge him, Eustace.'

Ruth had used the influence she'd inherited, first to identify those of the very rich who had the right attitudes, another intensely private vetting operation by a very expensive agency. She'd then sounded them out with a series of carefully worked out set-piece questions, prepared by and subsequently analysed by one of New York's leading psychiatrists. The entry on Vanderpage had read: 'Sound for the purpose but watch out for signs of senility'. There was no sign of it as his eyes glittered expectantly and he said: 'All your vigilantes are gathered!'

It had not been easy. The guts to take risks was only one

of the qualifications. Patriotism was so often the refuge of the knave. Candidates had to believe the problem existed and that their money and influence could make a difference. Discretion was easy; those who couldn't keep their mouths shut were well-known and avoided. Stamina to stay the course and go on putting up cash when no results were coming in was another essential. As a final test Ruth gave Jack a veto, and vice-versa on every name that passed the tests. The task they set themselves was probably impossible, even in the United States; in any other country it would have been out of the question. What gave it even an outside chance was that there was intense interest in the political process in America. Because democracy was so widespread, elections created power bases at every level; every citizen had a vested interest in the results of the many ballot boxes; his business, his federal and property taxes, his subsidies, his competition were all affected by elected politicians. The whole economy worked that way from the motor industry's fight for sanctions against the Japanese, through defence contracts and their employment consequences, to the choice of Jimmy Carter's Atlanta for the South-Eastern gateway airport over Birmingham, which had the geographical edge.

Senator Seth Stallybrass was a wheat baron from the Middle West. A photographer had to climb to twenty thousand feet to 'shoot' all his acres in one frame. His strongest motive for joining the group was very personal; he'd been bested when the Russians surreptitiously bought up a whole year's supply of grain before anybody in or out of government caught on what they were doing. It had cost him dear. But what hurt him almost more was the humiliation of his industry and country, the heartland of capitalism being beaten to its knees by heretics.

Jerry Brand was the least likely candidate. At forty five she had the build of a football player, six foot of heavy elegance without a wrinkle on her face. Her self-made fortune was in cosmetics. Her hobby was politicians, as husbands. She'd just fired number four and was in the marketplace again. She believed in the system and the psychiatrist rated her with the highest stamina: her file read 'dependable'; it was a bit like her bank reference 'undoubted'.

Marjorie Swanson was the female reply to Gore Vidal; a raunchy writer of complex relationships in contemporary and historical politics, lust, power and violence. Her happy right-wing endings sent surges of hope through the gun-toting, property-owning middle classes. She was totally committed to the belief that democracy was doomed if present trends continued. She was talking to Marvin Bennet as Ruth entered the room. 'If I was supposed to float I'd have been born with waterproof fucking feathers.'

Bennett was not offended. When his father first threw him into the family swimming pool at age four, he fell in love with water. He preferred the salty variety. His first experience at the tiller of a sailing dinghy was as close as he could imagine to paradise. He was bright enough to major in naval architecture phi beta kappa, and after a few years working with the best boat builders, struck out on his own, and in ten years was top of the private yachting mast. Growing up in Kennedy territory forged his admiration for the political process and gave him entrée to an endless vista of potential clients. 'You don't have to put to sea, Marge. That's not the point. A private yacht's a sign you've arrived.'

She dismissed the very idea. 'I can sign a cheque for six noughts; seven if I have to. I'm there!'

Jerry Brand joined in. 'So could I honey, but I don't know who'd accept it.'

'I would,' said 'Governor' Arthur Wilshire, Washington's leading lawyer, and repository of more personally dangerous secrets than any man alive. He'd never defend a case in court; he'd pull entirely different levers and the case would be mysteriously dropped, at least that was the gossip. It rarely happened but Wilshire fostered the notion; it helped justify his fees.

Jerry smiled: 'Fortunately I've never yet had to pay your exhorbitant rates, Arthur.'

Wilshire was delighted with such remarks. 'If you pay peanuts, you get monkeys. For a king's ransom you get the monarch and all he surveys.'

Ruth took the head of the table. 'I'm not going to run these meetings with too much formality . . . '

'What're you doin' with ma money, ma'am?' Bill Reiman asked in his Tennessee drawl. His reputation for meanness was assiduously promulgated to ward off spongers. His chain of food-processing factories stretched from coast-to-coast. To make and keep it expanding and profitable meant dealing with thousands of elected officials and politicians. Underneath the red-neck voice patterns and the cultivated illiteracy was an intelligent, caring American.

Marvin Bennett was impatient with him. 'If you want your dollars back after five minutes why did you put it there in the . . . '

Reiman was cool. 'All I want to know is what's goin' down, and who's doin' what with ma dough? Now ain't that a reasonable askin' ma'am?'

Ruth answered him: 'We haven't spent too much yet, Bill. We're recruiting carefully, key people. They in turn, will seek out agents. We have to be discreet. It's not as though we could take a full page in the Washington Post.'

Lubbock was brisk. 'I'd like to get right down to business. I take it we all agree that one of the first things we need is a line into the Pentagon . . . ' Nods all round. 'Well you've got it. On the need-to-know principle, I'm not naming names, but he's there and he's with us one hundred per cent.'

'Don't we never get to see this guy?' It was Reiman again.

'Nope,' said Lubbock. 'You just gotta take my word for

what he says. Anybody not inclined to do that?' Silence. 'Good. Now here's the bad news: Pentagon says the Tesla Shield is a load of bullshit.'

'They're not all fools in there,' said Eustace Vanderpage. 'How do we know they're not right?'

Lubbock answered:

'The Soviets used it to stop all movements of weather along the Russo Polish border.'

'What does that prove!' said Hale.

'We can't do it,' replied the general. 'Tesla's the only possible explanation.'

'I've dropped the idea round the boys in my labs.' This was Jerry Brand. 'They laughed.'

'How would they know?' Bennett argued. 'They make powder and lipstick.'

Jerry replied acidly:

'I get better people than government. I pay more.'

Vanderpage continued. 'Evidence. I want some evidence we're not throwing our money away.'

Lubbock got angry.

'The Russians have 2,000 scientists in 350 laboratories working flat out. What more do you want?'

'Could be anything,' said old Eustace.

'They're working on Tesla,' said Lubbock. 'They've put our satellites out of action, blinded our radar and stopped the weather. You sound like the assholes in the Pentagon who said the Russians didn't have the technology to put a man in space before we did.'

Wilshire put the lawyer's view. 'I propose a scientific panel – think-tank if you will – to do a proper evaluation . . . '

'Where do we get the brains?' Henry Hale again.

'Universities,' said Wilshire. 'Ex-army intelligence scientists . . . '

'What does your husband think about this, Ruth?' It was Eustace 'stirring the pot.'

'I won't involve him,' said Ruth. There was all round surprise.

'That's the reason you're sitting at the head of the table.' Bennett.

The truth was she didn't trust Frederick. She was not about to say so.

'Think about it. He's not the secretary of state yet . . . '

'His involvement made me put up ma dollars!' Reiman said.

Jerry Brand asked Ruth mildly:

'Don't you trust the son-of-a-bitch?'

Lubbock rebuked her. 'There's no need for that language!'

Bennett interrupted.

'Every need. I've got my ass on the line. I thought they both had theirs out there.'

Ruth tried to soothe the fears.

'He doesn't need to know; yet. He'd just be another head, helper. We've enough. When he's the Secretary . . . when we've done our job . . . . When we've come up with the hard facts, that's when we use Frederick. He'll be able to make it happen.'

7

Date: September 1981
Dubrovnik, Yugoslavia

It was dark. Lloyd couldn't remember where he was. He couldn't find the light. He found the telephone.

'Richard?' said an unfamiliar voice.

'Yes . . .'

'Richard Lloyd?'

'Who's that?'

'It's Bunjy.'

The brigadier had mentioned the name. The embassy man from Belgrade. Lloyd's contact.

'Sorry about the middle of the night and all that, but I'm en route, as they say, back to the old shop, and if, by any mischance you needed a chat, I could change direction south, and look you up for brekkers. What d'you say?'

Lloyd looked at his watch. It was 3.30 a.m.

'At this hour, normally, fuck off.'

'Quite. Seven-thirty OK?'

'All right.'

'Give me a tenner either way old chap. Traffic, don't you know . . .'

When Lloyd woke again light was streaming into the room.

He was in the Villa Dubrovnik, a five-star hotel on the edge of a calm deep blue Adriatic. Fishing boats bustled in and out of the quay. There was a good view of the Island of Lokrum.

Bunjy was about fifty, with salt-and-pepper hair. He had a chubby face, and easy smile. He was not tall, perhaps five foot seven, with a stocky figure emphasized by a double-breasted navy blazer with regimental buttons. The old school tie completed the caricature. He squeezed the morning paper like a swagger stick.

Lloyd didn't know what to make of Bunjy, a nickname he'd acquired at school. Lloyd had said he should have left it there.

'Everybody says that,' was Bunjy's laughing answer. He seemed to be a buffoon, his language out-of-date twenty years ago. His juvenile humour and apparent inability to grasp simple propositions was irritating. But when he talked business he shook off the fool's habit, and donned a quiet, intelligent authority. Lloyd didn't understand why people played such games.

'Care for a walk-about?' asked Bunjy.

'Worried about bugs?'

'The Russians line the walls of every new hotel with 'em don't you know. The Yugos are a bit more selective. The Serbs and Croats don't make good policemen . . .'

They were out of the hotel, heading toward the city wall.

'It's rather charming . . . secret polizei making a balls of things. Trouble is you can't rely on them to be stupid all the time. Occasionally they get an injection of Russian muscle, and that puts the fear of God up everybody.'

'I know,' said Lloyd, with feeling.

Bunjy registered the tone of voice.

'Oh! Really? Good show!'

Lloyd had dreaded his return to Yugoslavia. He had used every excuse to get out of it. The brigadier prevailed. He'd agreed to take one more shot at Marta's friend Mary, in Zagreb. An emotionally exhausting raking over of old fires had elicited one hint of a clue. Marta, phoning Mary from her parents' home had said she only had twenty minutes to get back to work. The slenderest of clues, but it had taken him back to Dubrovnik; the last place he wanted to be.

'Had the devil of a time,' said Bunjy. 'We think it's between Trebinje and Bileca.'

'Think!'

'They don't advertise, you know. We can't find another within fifty miles.'

'How do we confirm it's the right place?'

'Have a look.'

'Knock on the front door? "Please can I look round your secret weapons establishment?"'

Bunjy's face had a pained expression.

'My dear chap you must give us credit for being a bit more on the ball than that. We do have a few . . . ah . . . em agents in place, to use the vernacular. I think I've got somebody reasonably reliable. Don't want to have to send you home in pieces. Apart from anything else the paperwork's simply frightful.' And he laughed again. Lloyd felt a chill in the spinal column. That was a distinct improvement on feeling nothing.

'So how do I get into this place?'

'We're due to meet this chap – haven't used him before – and cross his palm with spondulicks, or rather dinars,' – he pronounced it as in Diners Club – 'he's supposed to do the trick.'

'I thought paid agents were unreliable, only the ideologically committed were safe.'

'Quite right!'

So much for Lloyd's peace of mind!

'We're supposed to take a table near Orlando's Pillar, and have a white handkerchief in the pocket.'

The stone flagged pedestrian square had, as a centrepiece, a statue. Its base was octagonal in shape, with three rows of shallow granite steps. In a niche was a stone-carved figure of a man in armour, with long hair, a shield in his left hand, and an upward pointing sword resting on his stomach. The legend above his head said he lived in the fifteenth century.

When the waiter appeared, Bunjy made no attempt to speak the language.

'Coffee, buns and *vinjak*, dear boy!' Lloyd cringed as people at nearby tables turned and grinned at the imperious command of this Englishman abroad.

Lloyd protested. 'We're not here for a bloody feast.'

'Never miss food, fuck or fart. Never know when you'll get the next.'

A lost-looking man wandered into the square.

'I wonder if this is Raffles.'

The man stared at them. He consulted his tourist guide, his lips moving as he struggled with the words.

'I don't think so,' said Bunjy.

The waiter returned with tiny cups of black Turkish coffee, two balloon glasses of *vinjak* filled to the brim, and pastries overflowing with *kamjak* cream. Lloyd was agreeably surprised by the brandy; he left the cake alone. Bunjy took enormous mouthfuls of first one pastry – and when he saw that Richard had no intention of eating his – the second. He knocked back the coffee in one gulp, saying:

'Only way to get the bloody stuff down,' and then addressed himself to the *vinjak*, treating it with vintage deference.

'What does he do? This Raffles?'

'He's a cleaner.'

'Good God Almighty!' exploded Lloyd; 'Am I supposed to put my life in the hands of a . . . '

'Simmer down, old chap. You'll only draw attention to us, and we don't want that, do we?'

The effrontery of the remark made Richard Lloyd speechless.

Bunjy added quietly, allowing a glimpse of the intelligence to show through:

'Trust me. Not that you have much choice. Now I wonder if this is he for whom we have been waiting.'

He was a small man, about sixty years old, Lloyd judged, and not impressive.

Bunjy murmured:

'Perfect. Once seen never remembered.'

He leaned back in his chair and his right hand lightly brushed Lloyd's handkerchief.

The walk was hard to describe. There was no up-and-down from heel to toe, nor was it a shuffle; more a glide. He had innocent, baby-blue eyes, which asked if the seat was taken. Bunjy held out his hands.

'Good-morning. Lovely day!' said the inimitable Bunjy.

'Ja,' said the man. He ordered *slivovitz*.

'Do you come here often, friend?'

Lloyd had difficulty in not laughing aloud.

The man answered in halting English,

'Only on Wednesday.' He pronounced it Ved-es-day. 'My day off.'

Bunjy was brisk and to the point.

'That's got recognition signals out of the way. This is chummy,' he said, pointing at Lloyd. 'You can call him James.' It was news to Richard.

The man repeated, 'Yames.'

'Have you been able to make any arrangements?'

For answer he handed Bunjy a typed note.

'What's this?'

The man smiled. 'My wife . . . is English. Secretary for travel company. She type. Very good.'

'Hope you didn't tell too many people what's up.'

Bunjy spoke so quietly Lloyd barely caught it. The Yugoslav heard. He laughed.

'Mum's the word,' he said.

The embassy man read the sheet and passed it to Lloyd.

> At five-thirty p.m. take the bus from the main terminal to Bileca. Get off at the second stop after Trebinje. Nikki will meet you. Wear only clothes bought in Yugoslavia, blue denim overalls. You are replacement for a sick worker. You will do a full night's cleaning work. Nikki will show you what to do. Do

not speak. You've had operation on your throat. Nikki will answer for you. If you are caught we will not be able to help you and you must not implicate us. Destroy this!

Charming, thought Lloyd.

Nikki smiled his pride at his wife's prowess. He held out his hand.

'Money,' he said.

In what Lloyd had read about spies, they were supposed to keep a low profile, to have dead letter drops, cut-outs, and merge into the background. Here all the rules were broken. The idiot from the embassy took every opportunity to draw attention to himself. The vital message was type-written by a stranger – another breach of security – and now the local mole was holding out his hand for his pay-off in full view of hundreds of people.

The waiter brought the liquor. Bunjy handed Nikki the newspaper, money inside.

Nikki took his drink at one gulp, and pocketed the paper.

'Burn it,' he said, indicating his wife's handiwork.

Bunjy nodded.

'Have a nice day,' he said to Nikki, who glided away.

Lloyd found his opinion of the embassy 'idiot' changing. What was done openly usually looked innocent. Anybody watching would have taken the Englishman for a loud idiot, confirmed by Lloyd's embarrassment. Nikki, cunning native, struck up acquaintance with gullible tourist to cadge a drink and a newspaper. Not bad!

Lloyd crumpled his new clothes. The stiff plastic boots foretold blistered feet. The miniature Minolta camera was disguised to look like a Swiss penknife. It would only survive a superficial inspection.

The bus was punctual, the waiting passengers silent. He tried to look like the other men on their way to work.

A gnarled figure sat beside him, unshaven, with a heavy

aura of garlic. Lloyd turned his face to the window. His fellow passenger made one attempt to talk to him. Richard ignored him.

Once away from the sea, the lush foliage gave way to barren rock as the bus wound its way into the lower reaches of the mountains. Civilization fell away. Birds whirled into the dusk sky. Lloyd's mind drifted to memories of a picnic with Marta, and carving their initials on a tree. The bus shuddered to a stop.

Nikki was waiting. He gave Richard a blue peaked cap and pinned a plastic identity card to his jacket. Lloyd wondered where his faded photograph had come from. The inscription said his name was Zarco Venac, and he lived in Slano, a village a few miles up the coast.

An eight-foot chain-link fence topped with outward leaning strands of electrified barbed wire surrounded the building. A small knot of men and women was filing past the armed guard who checked to make sure each person was wearing a badge. Lloyd was passed through.

The building was two storeys high, constructed of massive stone blocks. Each wall was three-hundred feet long. The huge door was large enough to admit an aeroplane.

Lloyd found himself in a galleried walkway looking down three storeys into the well of the building, which had been dug out of the rock; a mammoth task. Lloyd wondered why. There was no natural light. Most of the mass of machinery was unfamiliar, but he thought he recognized a Tesla coil.

The cleaning equipment was sorted out. Nikki pushed an electric polisher at Lloyd and grabbed another for himself. They took a service lift to the main floor.

Ten cleaners were at work. They would take a considerable time to cover the entire floor. Lloyd wondered how long it would be before the night shift arrived. Eight o'clock? When would he get a chance to use the camera? How could he photograph the installation without being seen? He took a good look at his fellow-polishers. They looked docile enough, some of them sullen; none seemed to take any interest in what they were doing. They obviously had no idea what was being done in the building and wouldn't have cared if anybody told them. He was the only one who understood what it was about, and at the moment he couldn't even get a decent shot.

He tried to work out a plan, where who would be and when, and then began altering his own movements so that in ten or fifteen minutes he would be out of sight of all of them except Nikki. He was almost there. Suppose somebody did see him? They might be bored with their jobs but they'd soon yell 'spy!' if they saw the camera. He had one last look round. Nikki stared back at him with a distinct lack of enthusiasm; this was the moment of maximum risk. He glanced upwards and his look changed to alarm. Richard saw it and immediately palmed the camera in his handkerchief and blew his nose. He didn't dare look up himself; he kept his eyes fixed on Nikki, every muscle tense. His experience at the border began to work on his imagination. In no time he'd reached screaming pitch in his mind. He switched off that 'programme'. Nikki nodded the all-clear.

Changing direction again, Lloyd took another four shots. He had photographed about half the workshop. He was about to risk one more shot when Nikki grabbed his arm and began shouting. As Nikki paused for breath, Lloyd whispered:

'What's the fuss about?'

'You're being watched, by a woman. Don't look now. Dark skin and black hair. Tall.' He launched into a final tirade and stomped back to his own polisher.

Lloyd soon spotted her. She was checking the dials on a tall copper cylinder, glancing in his direction. Bad luck, so soon into the operation. She was about forty, nearly six feet, with a big figure under her white coat; formidable.

Lloyd applied himself with more diligence to his task. She took a last reading and walked towards him.

Lloyd knew enough of the language to understand that she was asking him who he was. He pointed to his throat. Nikki told her his name.

'*Zovc se Zarco.*'

Nikki told her he was temporary; that he normally worked as a clerk.

She told him to open his mouth. He understood the gesture. He hoped the overhead lights would cast his throat in shadow. She gave it a long look. She pinched his cheeks, provoking him to use his voice. Nikki told her Lloyd had cancer. She went away, muttering.

In less than half an hour the floor was crowded with engineers and others. At eight o'clock Nikki took him to the gallery. Four of them worked towards each other. There was no chance to use the camera.

By ten they had finished the balcony. Lloyd drank the canteen coffee gratefully.

He had done a few stints cleaning lavatories when he joined the army, but hadn't realized how unpleasant the foreign variety was. His father would have said it was the garlic. It took two hours.

The canteen was laid out on true egalitarian principles; cafeteria service, formica-topped tables and linoleum for the workers; close-carpeted dining room, immaculate tableware, top quality food and waitresses for the bosses.

The sign over the minced meat and *sauerkraut* read *sarma*. Nikki added the ubiquitous *strudel*, and left Lloyd to pay. They ate in silence for fifteen minutes.

The formidable woman had been at the *vinjak* bottle. She swayed as she surveyed the eating hall. Lloyd appealed to Nikki.

'What do I do?'

She stumbled, arresting her fall with an outstretched hand, sending a tray of food skittering across the floor. She swore at the inoffensive engineer whose meal it was.

'Watch me! Nod or shake your head when I say so,' said Nikki.

'*Popij, druze.*' She pumped a half-litre bottle of brandy into Lloyd's hand. He drank. He needed it.

She spoke again.

'*Kad ce touj vad biti sursen?*'

Nikki answered for him, raising six fingers at the same time. So that was when they knocked off.

'*Kuda ces poste vada?*' She had asked what he was doing after work. Nikki launched into a long explanation. Lloyd returned her bottle. She drank deeply and passed it back again. He appeared to take a long swig, but swallowed little.

'*Javi se kod mene u stan u cetizi!*'

That was no question, it was an order. She tilted his head back; opened his mouth. The overhead neon spotlighted his larynx. She looked and blinked, and looked again. She tipped the bottle into his open mouth. He gagged and coughed and said 'Christ,' but she didn't seem to hear. She laughed, mirthlessly. Her mood changed abruptly. She became sullen, morose.

'*Lipravnik je svinja – myzim ga. A ti nisi.*' She staggered away.

Nikki explained: 'She's been sleeping with the director but he doesn't like her any more.'

'I don't blame him,' said Lloyd.

'Very angry woman!' Lloyd nodded.

'She is dangerous. I must tell you bad news, Yames. You are to report to her private flat at 6.30.'

'Just what I needed!'

'Is serious, Yames. You can't keep pointing at your throat. Sooner or later you'll have to say something.'

Lloyd did not need to be told.

A bell sounded a strident call back to work. Nikki said: 'Now we clean this place.'

Lloyd used the vacuum cleaner on the private dining room. He undid every piece of paper he could find. There were no tell-tale doodles of secret weapons. By three he was finished and Nikki told him work was over for the night.

'Then I'm off before the dragon catches me.'

Nikki shook his head. 'Not permitted. Everybody leave at six o'clock. No cleaner go before that.'

'What do we do till then?'

'Sit in here . . . drink coffee.'

'Give me a duster!'

'Why?'

'I'm going to polish the balcony.'

'Nobody does that.'

'Is there a rule against it?'

Lloyd was amazed. Two huge iron girders spanning the building were moving apart, opening the roof.

As the motors clanged to a halt, an extendable meccano-like structure began climbing upward, powered by a whining motor. At its apex was a highly-polished copper sphere. The copper ball eventually stretched two-hundred feet into the night sky.

Lloyd studied the heavy equipment, all manner of electrical gear, Tesla coils, transformers for high frequency current. A circular structure with a circumference of about four-hundred and fifty feet rose from the floor. It stopped at a height of twelve feet. Its black core was covered in shining steel mesh. It was a gigantic electric coil. Inside the circle it made, and directly below the structure pointing through the roof, was another coil, much smaller in size. This was no more than ten feet in diameter. The frame was made of glass; wires tightly bound it in dense snug rows. It was connected to the copper ball by a thick plastic-covered wire.

Those below him were too preoccupied with the machinery to take any notice of a cleaner on the balcony. He pressed the camera's shutter several times.

There was an air of expectancy. All eyes looked up to the control box. The director glanced at the top of the mast. He nodded. At first there was only a crackle. Lloyd followed everybody else's gaze upwards. Frissons of electric current were smothering the ball. The power built up. With it came a low rumble. The volume of sound increased. As it did so the sparks danced higher and higher on the copper sphere. The lights dimmed as the surging power took its toll.

Gashes of zig-zag light shot thirty feet high. As the current increased so did the length of the light, until it stretched a hundred feet above the ball, now crowned with a halo of luminescence.

The assistant looked apprehensive. The director concentrated on the dials.

Lloyd was witnessing a man-made storm. The noise was thunder; the ground was shaking under his feet. The energy surging from the copper ball was creating forked lightning. White coated engineers cast concerned glances at the control box. The director smiled. The violence escalated. The claps of thunder assaulted Richard's eardrums. The whole building became part of the electrical field. Sparks, inches long, were dancing off every metal surface.

Nikki tugged at his sleeve; speech was impossible. Lloyd reluctantly followed him into the cafeteria.

'Where are we going? I need to see what . . .' But Nikki urged him through a door and up steps. On a half landing was a cupboard. Nikki stepped inside and pulled Lloyd after him, closing the door.

'Look through there,' said Nikki.

Nikki pointed to a hole in the brickwork, switched off the light. The noise got worse. In the confined space it felt as if a succession of bombs was exploding round the walls. Lloyd bent down to peer through the hole. He could just make out a number of lights; a hundred, maybe more, a mile away, on another mountain. They glowed, dimly at first, and then with increasing brightness until they illuminated a whole area of the mountainside.

Abruptly the noise ceased; the far mountain went dark. The sudden silence left a bursting sensation in Lloyd's ears.

'What was that? Why did you want me to see those lights?'

Nikki shrugged. 'I don't know what they mean. But they light up when they make the lightning and thunder – not always – just sometimes.'

'So what?' said Lloyd. Nikki shrugged again.

'I want to get back. See what's happening inside.'

The woman was unconscious, her legs drawn up to her chest, her arms flung wide. Two men bent over her. A white-coated man appeared, toting a doctor's bag. He exposed her chest and bent his ear for heartbeat. He plunged a hypodermic needle into the cavity between two ribs. The adrenalin did not work. The doctor shook his head. Why did Lloyd's memory produce an image of the dead Marta? He felt sick.

The motors took up their whining noise again. The aerial began its controlled collapse. The giant coils descended into the floor like a science fiction cinema organ. The workers on the floor broke into desultory groups carefully avoiding the corpse. Lloyd still gazed at it, revolted, mesmerized. Nikki dragged him back to the canteen and plied him with more coffee.

Lloyd did not know what he had witnessed. It was an electrical experiment of some sort, but what? What did it do? Had the Tesla coils generated the power that caused the lightning and thunder? What was the significance of the lights on the far mountain? He would write it all down. Others would have to decide.

A full-scale search was in progress in the early morning light. Twice the number of the evening guards turned out every pocket, and gave full body searches. The man beside him was sweating. As he was searched a soldering iron dropped down his trouser leg. The guard shouted. The gate was slammed shut on the queue behind Lloyd. His arms were pinned to his side.

'*Poznajes ga. Da li ste drugori*?' Lloyd guessed he was being asked if he knew the man. It was easy to deny. They stripped the frightened worker to his body belt; it contained an assortment of stolen tools. Two guards frog-marched him away.

Every eye focused on Richard. Should he make a run for it? Hopeless. He would be shot. Guards moved in on him. The search began. Armpits to wrists were thoroughly felt. The guard slipped his palms down Richard's chest and then moved in close to repeat the movement on his back, paying particular attention to his waistband, searching for a body belt. Next he crouched and pushed Lloyd's lower limbs apart. His hands encircled each leg in turn feeling all the way to the ankle. He explored the crutch.

'*Svlaci se!*'

The order was accompanied by hand movements to take his clothes off. They would be searched, his camera found and that would be the end of Richard's career as a spy! Maybe the end of Richard.

Date: September 1981
New York, N.Y.

Telinger made the introduction.

He was a good-looking boy in his late teens with a lank lock of silky brown hair with eyes a rather deeper shade. Good-looking was the wrong word, Rakov decided. He was beautiful, and had an elegant, careful walk, almost feline. Rakov was aware of his increasing pulse rate.

'Comrade major . . . '

'Names are not important,' Yuri interjected.

'This is Anton.'

Rakov nodded at the young man, who smiled, shyly. Rakov let Anton introduce himself with enthusiastic references to his progress at university and getting to know the American way of life.

'We will eat,' said Rakov.

'By all means,' began Telinger, 'I know all the best restaurants.'

Rakov was dismissive. 'I'm sure you have more important things to do.'

Something in Rakov's genes had dealt him the homosexual urge and the pleasure it gave him. Although not unknown in the peasant community, it was rare; another aspect of Yuri his father would rage about. His mother would look at the floor, her love undiminished.

Anton – Yuri preferred the Russian to the Americanized version of the boy's name – chose what they would eat: Japanese food. It was bland and insubstantial, not Yuri's taste, but he watched the computer genius suckle the sushi and teriyaki, eyes alight at the flavours. The sake was warm and had little appeal for the KGB major, apart from its potency. He applied liberal quantities to his young guest, whose inhibitions fell away like sheaths of character in a good play.

'Now tell me how we gain access to CIA secrets,' said Rakov.

'How much do you know about computers, Comrade Major?'

'Assume I know nothing. And this is America. Don't call me comrade or major,' replied Yuri Rakov.

'Ten or fifteen years ago it would have been simple,' said Anton. 'A straightforward entry via a public telephone line. Now every computer has its own built-in security. The more sensitive the material the deeper it's buried. Getting through each layer requires an increasing classification of privilege.'

Rakov was impatient.

'What we're looking for will have the highest classification.'

'There's no point in trying direct access. We'd never make it.'

'Can you access the CIA computer?'

'I've made friends with a man. He's a field service engineer. One of Greg's jobs is maintenance on the mainframe computer at the United Nations.'

'I said CIA, not the UN.'

'CIA has a direct link from Langley to the UN computer.'

'Why? What for?'

'Maybe they're checking out our *Golubye Furazhki*,' said Anton, precociously using the KGB nickname. It had unhappy associations for Rakov. He scowled.

'Don't get to know too much for your own good!'

Anton paled.

'An open line? For everybody to see?'

'Of course not,' said Anton. 'They use a front. Institute for the Study of World Surplus Food.'

'I still don't understand. Why would the CIA . . . perhaps the reason is unimportant. Does this mean you can use the link to call up information in the CIA computer?'

'That's where my friend comes in. We meet to discuss new programs, play games . . . ' Rakov wondered what sort of games. 'I go to Greg's apartment. He comes to mine. There's equipment all over the place. It wasn't difficult to borrow one of his diagnostic tapes, without his knowledge.'

'How does that help?'

'I inserted some new code after the header of the hardware diagnostic tape. I slipped it back among his things. He never suspected a thing.'

'What does that achieve?'

'Greg will have made his usual preventative maintenance call on the UN computer. He will have used the diagnostic tape to gain access. My new code will have given the computer a virus, right into the heart, the patch area which requires the highest privilege to access it.'

'Virus?'

'Not literally; not a medical bug, but an electronic one. It behaves just like the animal variety. Once planted it can makes copies of itself. So it can move around in the memory, copying itself in a new location, and erasing all trace of its existence in the former place.'

'How does it get what I want?'

'It doesn't. I've programmed it to monitor all passwords used on the private data link, and store them in the system's patch memory. Whenever you're ready, I'll go down to the UN building, activate my virus and the computer's memory will yield up all the passwords it's intercepted and hidden in the system's patch area.'

'It's as simple as that!' Rakov was incredulous. 'I can't believe even stupid Americans . . . '

'It's not at all simple, Comrade Major. It may all go wrong. The theory's right, and there is no other way, except bribing somebody rather important.'

'Out of the question!' said Rakov immediately.

'There is another problem. I can't access it using a terminal. It only works via the main console. I'll have to do it on a weekend.'

'They must never know we've gained access!'

'Don't worry. My virus will keep moving, destroying all evidence of its existence as it goes.'

'You mean we could use it again, and again?'

'Sooner or later it'll reveal itself, probably by accident. But even when they know it's there they'll have one hell of a job finding it.' Anton laughed. 'Eventually they'll have to cut off the power.'

Rakov was impressed. He hoped the boy was as good as his confidence. 'How old are you, Anton?'

'Seventeen years and three months, Comrade Major.'

'How do you know so much in such a short life?'

'It's like an ear for music. There are thousands like me.'

It was not false modesty; just true.

They had their coffee and cognac in Harry's bar at the Waldorf Hotel. Yuri gave the young man a hundred dollars. He booked them a room.

Later, Rakov paid off his taxi a few blocks from his apartment. He hoped Anton was more proficient with his computers than he was in bedroom skills. Not that Yuri was complaining. What he lacked in technique, he made up for in enthusiasm. It was Rakov's first homosexual encounter since he'd said goodbye to his family.

Anton's first problem was security at the UN building. He showed the pass Telinger had given him. His name was logged. He was conscious of watching eyes as he crossed the main concourse. He pressed the elevator button for Telinger's floor. He sat at the colonel's desk, doodling, for twenty minutes.

He walked down three floors, then took the elevator to the first basement car park. In the back seat of a green Plymouth was a head. Part of Anton's mind asked if it was a 'hit' man about to take aim. The hair was black and crinkled, so was the face underneath. The eyes were closed. On the back ledge was a peaked cap. A chauffeur!

He returned to the stairwell. He walked the remaining flights to the computer section. His luck held; no security! He took his seat at the console. Nervously, he switched on.

The screen began the 'conversation.' 'User name?'

He tapped out ANTON.

'Password?' was the reply.

The next part was tricky. The hatched rectangle on the screen would not show what letters he keyed in. This was the first test of his clandestine program. He keyed in the words 'EXECUTE VIRAL 1'.

After a few moments information began to appear on the screen. Even Anton was amazed. Every password appeared at every level of privilege. He concentrated, committing each to memory.

He cleared the screen and logged off as Anton. A new 'conversation' began.

'User name?'

Anton tapped out the letters 'EARLYBIRD,' the top security password of the CIA computer. He prayed no other password was needed. If there was and he didn't have it, its absence would trigger an alarm at the CIA, inaudible, invisible, enabling security to catch him without warning. It was the worst risk, but there was nothing he could do to avoid taking it. He typed the word 'DIRECTORY.' Then he made a general enquiry into the program library. He found 'Database.' He tapped out the word and was told to state the subject matter of his enquiry. He used the word 'TESLA,' and was dismayed. There were two hundred pages of entries under that name. Most of them were obvious and well-known. Newspaper and magazine articles, references and quotations, excerpts from O'Neill's biography of the great man. Anton qualified Tesla with 'WESTINGHOUSE.' The entry was even longer, with details of family as well as corporate information worldwide.

The air-conditioning was working perfectly but Anton was sweating. He knew that the longer he stayed, the greater was the chance of discovery. He had no diplomatic immunity, and could expect no mercy from an American jury on a charge of espionage. He qualified Tesla again. He typed in 'CZITO JULIUS.' The machine told him Czito was knocked down by a taxi in Astoria, New York on 29th October 1962. The CIA agent's report continued:

> 'Czito was lying on the ground, badly hurt, dying. I identified myself as a government employee. Czito said "Tell them they need the Trinity. The Tesla Trinity. Father, Son and Ghost," and then he lost consciousness. He died in the ambulance en route to hospital. Known associates: Czito, Kolman – father/employer . . . '

There followed a list of names and addresses, the last of which was Yatanabron, Emanuel, jeweller.

Anton decided not to use the computer's printer; it could contain a record of whatever it printed. Instead he felt for the miniature flash camera.

He qualified Tesla with one more entry: 'DEATH BEAM.' The short directory contained the headings: 'History. Political evaluation. Scientific developments. Military potential.' In his excitement, as he tapped out the last two words, his elbow knocked the camera. It fell into the shredder basket.

He keyed in the letters 'MILITARY POTENTIAL.'

At Langley, Virginia, the headquarters of the CIA, a duty officer glanced casually at the screens monitoring the activity on various computers. There was something unusual going on. What was it? A pattern. That was it. But what was wrong with the pattern. He searched the familiar battery of screens. It told him nothing. He leaned back in his chair and looked at the VD units through half-closed lids. Then he had it. One of the screens was not normally in use on a Sunday. Which one? It did not take long to identify the active screen. He wondered why an important agent would need to access highly classified information on Tesla on a weekend. He reached for the phone.

Anton always marvelled at the way a computer paused after a question was keyed in, as though it was, humanlike, mustering its thoughts before committing to an answer. The other side of his brain told him it took time for the right place to be found in the memory. Seconds, sometimes minutes. And sometimes, one had to wait in line, like a traffic jam. Very human. Anton smiled. The screen began filling with line after line of detailed appraisal of the state of research, the names of scientists, the locations of their laboratories. A new paragraph began with the caption: 'Latest assessment of the state of Russian research into

Tesla Shield/Weapon.' Anton was excited. It was the jackpot.

The door opened quietly. Two soberly-dressed young men entered the room. They looked quizzically at the young Russian at the console.

'Good afternoon, sir. Do you have some identification?' It was quiet and so polite.

The one with the handgun tilted its barrel upwards.

Yuri Rakov had seen the anonymous black Chevrolet arrive. He couldn't help it. Its speed and the lurching of the body against the suspension as it cornered into the driveway was quite unlike any diplomat's limousine. He was not surprised when Anton emerged in handcuffs.

He reached for his umbrella, and joined the fringe of a conducted tour. The three men had to wait while it passed. Anton saw Rakov and gave a very slight nod in the direction of the building he had just left. Full marks, thought Rakov. Pity I can't give you more of a reward than this, and he pressed the button on the underside of the umbrella. He was about ten feet from Anton when the compressed air gun shot the tiny deadly pellet into that beautiful body. Anton scratched his thigh.

The black car moved out of sight. Rakov stayed with the group as it entered the building. It was a pity he could not have got within range to use one of the faster acting weapons in his briefcase. It would be three or four hours before the wax seal on the pellet melted, and the poison was released into Anton's system. In another hour he would lose consciousness. After that it didn't really matter when he died.

Rakov wondered at the idealistic clap-trap spouted by the guide, and the gullibility of Americans who believed any international institution could function impartially. Telinger used the UN for covert KGB activities. Rakov was sure the CIA, British Intelligence and everybody else did the same.

He stayed with the group until it had passed security clearance, and then slipped away to the console room. In the glow from the glass in the door his eyes scanned the room. He looked for drawers. There were none. Shelves contained only paper. He dismissed the waste bin and went on searching. He looked under every desk, machine and cupboard. He found nothing. He sat where Anton had sat, trying to get inside his mind. Where would he have hidden – whatever it was? What was it? Paper? Unlikely. The printer hadn't been used. The camera? Yes. It must have been the camera. But where? Where could one hide a camera in a room like this?

There was a noise like a pistol shot. Rakov whirled. Nobody. His umbrella handle had fallen on the hard floor. As he bent down to retrieve it he saw the camera lying snugly under the shredded paper in the waste bin.

The film was developed in the projection room of a theatre off Times Square. He was disappointed there was only one exposure.

'That'll be twenty dollars,' said the bored technician.

Rakov was angry. 'For one print!'

The reply was cool: 'For speed and discretion.'

Rakov broke the news about Anton to Telinger.

The colonel was furious.

'You've blown my cover. I sponsored him.'

'Fortunately, there's no connection to me,' said Rakov coolly.

'I've spent years gaining the confidence of people from the Third World, Japan, Britain, Europe. It'll take years to make up the lost ground. You've put back our foreign policy gains by ten years.'

Rakov laughed. 'Nothing takes precedence over my mission.'

Telinger shook his head. Rakov continued:

'A CIA agent followed Julius Czito in October 1962 when he had his accident. He recorded his dying words:

"Tell them they need the Trinity. Father, Son and Ghost." What do you suppose that meant?'

'A dying man . . . perhaps it was a prayer,' offered Telinger.

'"Tell them *they* need," not *I* need,' pressed Rakov. 'And Father, Son and *Ghost* – not *Holy Ghost*, which most people say.'

'I bow to your superior knowledge of religious custom,' said Telinger sarcastically.

'No jokes, colonel. What happened in October 1962?'

'What do you mean?'

'What historical event? Day of infamy in the annals of Mother Rodina, if you like?'

'I don't know what you're talking about.'

'The Cuban missile crisis! Why should Czito think "they" would "need the Trinity" to combat our missiles?'

'You're making a great logistic leap on very slender evidence, comrade!'

'Czito was an engineer. His father was Tesla's trusted model maker. The son was also a maker of models. Did he make models for Tesla?'

'Tesla's father was a priest . . . ' mused Telinger.

'Father Son and Ghost. What does that sound like to you?'

'To be honest, a prayer. Any other meaning is too far-fetched . . . '

Rakov was excited but angry.

'You've gone soft, Telinger. Soft hands, soft brains, soft options. This is it, I tell you. Tesla got Czito to make him a model and he named it for your Holy Trinity!'

BOOK II
Separation

'All our ancient history . . .
is no more than accepted fiction.'

Voltaire.
(*Jeannot et Colin*)

8

Date: 10 October 1981
Georgetown, D.C.
He'd done it again!

The sun was already high into the morning sky heralding another beautiful fall day. Most of Washington had been at their desks for three hours or more, yet two of its more illustrious citizens were still in bed.

Ruth was determined, this time, to ask why; determined that Frederick would not steal into his clothes and away about his commercial occasions before she had returned 'to earth.' She tried to bring her emotional pulse to normality. She breathed deeply. That only made matters worse. She lay quite still. Eyes still shut. That seemed to work. But where was Frederick? There was not a sound in the room. Oh! Damn! He'd beaten her again!

A small, satisfied growl at the back of Frederick's throat told her she was wrong; again! He was still there, on his back, naked, the rise and fall of his chest a mere ripple. How did he do it? But at least his eyes were shut and he had the decency to show some sign of being spent.

'Frederick . . . ' She had intended it to be a formal request. It came out as a gooey sigh. She cleared her throat. 'Frederick . . . ' It didn't help much. 'Can I ask you something?'

He didn't open his eyes.

'Why? You want to know why?'

That was exactly what she wanted to know, but she wasn't prepared to express it so bluntly.

'Frederick . . . I know you have trouble with endearments, showing emotion . . . but even so, for the last five years, the first five years of our marriage you've . . .'

'I thought you would know. You're so perceptive.'

'Frederick. You don't even know my question!'

'Why have I suddenly started behaving with unaccustomed passion, using techniques never before celebrated in our union? I'm surprised the obvious never occurred to you.'

'The obvious?' Ruth began to feel like a parrot.

'I've fallen in love with my wife.'

That begged more questions than it answered. It also made Ruth's heart lurch, her breath stop. Frederick continued with the revelation.

'For the first time in my life! I had no idea what I'd been missing!' As though he'd suddenly discovered the taste of papaya!

'I thought you loved me when we got married.'

'Come on, my darling! You can't fool me with that one. And you didn't love me. It was . . . curiosity . . . maybe a certain respect. If I was pompous I'd call it a form of hero-worship. The older man, successful, most sought-after bachelor . . .'

'You didn't love me? Not even when you asked me to marry you?'

He leaned across and kissed each nipple, warmly, caressing.

Ruth didn't want to moan, she was too interested in what he was saying.

'Don't be silly.' Even his chiding was a caress. 'You captured me. You wanted me. You needed to satisfy your curiosity about this strange man, impervious to your attractions. It suited me. You were the perfect wife for somebody like me. A marriage of powerful common interests.'

'That's disgusting!' But she didn't say it in anger.

'Most of the world – the old world – organizes its marriages like that. They wouldn't dream of letting such an unstable commodity as emotion dictate the choice of lifetime companion. What an absurdity!'

'I loved you, Frederick.'

'I doubt it. You preferred me to the other sycophants for your hand or fortune . . . '

'I did!'

'Don't con me, my darling. Women are much more cold-blooded than men, particularly about marriage. They want security and kindness, success, admiration. As for love. For most of you it's simply a bonus.'

'I've been married to you for five years . . . You're a monster. A cold unfeeling monster.' It was said without malice.

'You've known since the day we first met, at that awful film star's party in Laurel Canyon, that I had no interest in women. If that makes me cold, then you've known . . . '

'Did you love Karen?'

'Of course not. And she didn't love me. It wasn't that sort of arrangement. Mutual respect. That's another matter. We liked each other, as I've always liked you . . . '

'Can we go back to the beginning? What exactly is it you feel for me now?'

Ruth was getting angry. Not with Frederick, especially, but with the fates that had dealt her such an incredible hand. Also with the fact that she seemed to be the idiot in the debate.

'Will head-over-heels do? I've always liked and admired you. Those were the basic reasons I married you. You're not beautiful, but you know that. Alluring, compulsive, intelligent: you know that. Tolerant, amusing, cultured, a superb business-woman . . . I don't need to extol your many . . . I'm in love with them.'

'Tell me about the new . . . Have you been going to night school?'

'Don't spoil it by calling it names!'

Ruth's emotions were in turmoil. She didn't know what to think or feel. She needed time. He didn't give her any.

'Now it's your turn. How do you feel about me? You're so much better at expressing your emotions.'

'I was thinking about getting a divorce' didn't seem the right way to begin.

There was a tap-tap on the door. Ruth grabbed the sheet.

'It's eleven o'clock in the morning!' Panic!

Frederick was relaxed.

'Leave it outside the door, Jennings.'

He shrugged into his dressing gown.

'It's eleven o'clock in the morning, Frederick. Exactly eleven o'clock! How did you know to ask Jennings . . . Lover! That's not love. It's calculation! And what have you asked Jennings to bring? Your post? Briefcase? Messages?'

Frederick opened the door, and reached down. He returned with Dom Perignon and glasses on a Tiffany tray. Ruth's mouth dropped open.

'You're making me feel like Doris Day in one of those Rock Hudson films!'

'Who's Doris Day?'

That was more like the Frederick she knew.

'She's the blonde singer who made . . . ' And to her amazement she saw that Frederick was laughing. He'd been teasing her; something he never did.

'I had an appointment this morning . . . '

'You'll be late!'

'At the White House . . . ' He let it hang in the air.

'What are you doing with champagne? Get dressed. Order the car . . . '

'I saw the President at eight o'clock.'

Frederick had strong hands. They opened the cork with ease, the bottle at a forty-five degree angle; not a drop of the golden liquid was spilled. He presented Ruth with her brimming glass. Ruth already knew what came next.

'Here's to the new secretary of state!'

Frederick put his hand over her glass.

'No.'

'No? But everybody knows you're the next . . . '

'Everybody's wrong. I'm the new National Defence Adviser.'

'What does that mean?'

'A new post. The man feels that the secretary of state has enough on his plate. He wants somebody who only looks after our own borders. Star wars is part of it. My role is exclusively the defence of our country.'

'But he's already got . . . '

'It's a new set-up. I get to appoint my own people, from scratch. No inherited attitudes. No entrenched bureaucrats to wear me down. The most important job, after his!'

'Aren't you just a little disappointed, Frederick? After all, everybody . . . '

'You don't understand. I'm my own man, darling. Always have been. I like doing my own thing. At State I'd have to conform, do the right thing, the conservative thing. OK. If I had to. . . But this is much more of a challenge. Drink to me?'

What would have happened, Ruth wondered, if she'd decided on an early morning in her office instead of a lie-in? She raised her glass to this new man, her husband.

Date: 4 October 1981
Trebinje, Yugoslavia

There were a number of ways he could be spotted: sweat, suffused face, nervousness, tic, smell of fear even. Richard convinced himself he betrayed all of them. One of the canteen staff arrived beside him to be searched. In late middle age her girth disclosed that she was a picker at the food she served. She was attractive, out-going, hard-edged and a firm favourite with all the men. Lloyd's searcher was not satisfied. He didn't know what it was, but there was something wrong. He stood back for a hard look at Richard. He circled him.

The woman's guard rapped out an order. She opened her

coat with a leer. He took it as an invitation. Men back in the queue sniggered.

Lloyd's guard signalled for him to take off his coat. This is it! thought Richard.

The other guard stepped in close to the canteen woman, cupped her breast, palpated it and squeezed the nipple. The leer left her face. She stepped back. Those watching held their breath.

Lloyd's guard put his hand in the pocket of the coat.

The woman drew back her arm and took a roundhouse swing at her importuning guard. The slap caught him between face and ear. The noise resounded the length of the queue. He tried to ride the blow, but lost his balance and sprawled on the ground, red-faced, not amused. The line of waiting workers roared its approval. The supine figure began shouting orders as he regained his feet.

Richard's guard stood, motionless, disbelieving, his hand still in the coat pocket.

Uniformed women appeared and subjected their victim to a distinctly unsensual body search.

Lloyd's guard watched, the coat gradually slipping from his grasp. With a shock Richard saw the Swiss-knife camera peeping from the pocket, snagged in the lining.

The crowd began barracking. If Lloyd did nothing the camera would fall out of the pocket and discovery would be inevitable. Richard ran a bluff; he stretched out his hand for the coat. The guard's head shot round expecting trouble from another source. He glared at Lloyd who did his best to look bored and innocent. It worked. The coat was thrust at him, the guard helped his senior to brush down his uniform and was barged angrily away.

Lloyd ambled out of the gate and crossed the road to the bus stop, expecting every moment to be recalled by the suspicious searcher.

Transport was nowhere in sight. The hub-bub over the woman subsided. The senior guard gave her a loud haranguing, and released her. Calm settled into the queue. Still the bus refused to appear. Nikki joined Richard, then the woman. Lloyd didn't smoke but longed for a cigarette. The blessed sound of grinding gears announced the arrival of the bus. Richard's guard remembered his disquiet. He searched for Lloyd, located him and shouted. The woman thought he was shouting at her and returned a loud obscenity. The bus drew to a stop blocking the guard's view. Lloyd and Nikki boarded. The guard left the queue and headed for the road. The woman decided against boarding the bus and peered round the back of it making a rude sign, then boarded rapidly. The guard strode into the road and hastily stepped back to avoid being mown down by a car. The driver shut the doors. The guard shouted again. First gear was noisily engaged. The guard tried to stop the vehicle. The driver shrugged and pressed on.

Date: 13 October 1981
Near Guildford, England

It was too much to expect the brigadier to say 'well done' or even 'good show'. 'What're you doing here, Lloyd?' was the cheering opening gambit. 'I sent you at considerable financial and logistical cost, to do a job. What brings you scuttling back after five minutes?'

'Sir, you don't seem to understand . . . '

'You've survived the worst part, getting in and getting out again, clean. You could have kept it up for weeks, given us real information.'

Lloyd resented the bollocking. He'd photographed the most secret workshop in Serbo-Croatia, got out with the film and without compromising the local agent. He wasn't going to take 'stick' for that.

'You told me to go in and find out what Marta was doing. I did just that.'

'Tell me what was she doing?'

'It's all there. On film. In my report.'

'Tell me what she was working on,' the brigadier insisted.
'It's on film.'
'What's on film?'
'What she was working on.'
'Then tell me what it was.'
Lloyd was annoyed too.
'How do I know what it means? It's there, on film, the whole shebang, sir.'
'You ran like a scared animal with less than five per cent of what you were sent in for.'
'I'm not an expert in electronics . . . '
'Then how the hell did you get into the Royal Electrical and Mechanical Engineers?'
'I know about weapons, missiles . . . army hardware. This was not like anything I'd ever seen. I couldn't evaluate it. It's a job for experts . . . sir!'
'You could have sent out the film, and your written report. We spent a lot of time and cash giving you communications and back-up. You should have stayed put. We need photographs of the paperwork. We need close-ups of those machines. I want tape recordings of what they're talking about . . . '
A lethargic man in a white coat entered the room. In his late twenties, he had a bookish bored appearance. He spread enlargements of Lloyd's photographs on the desk.
'Tell me about them, Butterworth,' said the brigadier.
The young man cleared his throat.
'They are . . . disappointing . . . '
'They're clear enough to me,' said Lloyd. 'Brilliant!'
The technician continued:
'They may look spectacular . . . but it's old hat, just a repetition of what Tesla did seventy-five years ago.'
'I don't believe it.' This was Lloyd's outburst. 'Why should they go to all this trouble to repeat out-of-date experiments. It doesn't make sense. You've missed something!'

The young man was not put out.

'I'm sure you're right. We can't think what it is.'

Lloyd bent down for a closer look. He was impressed with how much he had been able to record under difficult conditions. He picked up an enlargement of a small section of the floor. It was one of his last shots. The definition was perfect. He had been standing on the balcony, and the magnification was twenty or thirty times. One photograph was of the woman, breasts uncovered, her head drooping, eyes staring in death, arms flung wide. What was that? A pattern across her breasts, extending from the waist upward, and stopping in a half moon round the neck; the same marks he had last seen on Marta. He gagged.

'What's up lad?' said the laconic Forbes.

'That's it,' said Lloyd. 'That confirms everything. Those are the same marks that Marta had. That proves what she was working on.' He rounded on the man called Butterworth. 'You may not know what this all means. I can tell you it has to be . . . what I was sent for. That woman died an identical death to Marta. I can't be wrong. Not about that. I shall never forget those marks. Never. Find the answer to that and the whole thing is solved.'

The young man was not impressed.

'That's no big deal. She was electrocuted wearing a string vest. So was your girlfriend. I thought you'd been told.'

The brigadier studied his shoes. Lloyd was nonplussed. He eventually found his voice.

'How? How?'

'A hundred ways. This lady was drunk. That place was live, but live. Millions of volts were flying around looking for some kind soul to give them earth.'

'And Marta? She couldn't have been drunk. She took her work too seriously!'

'Who can say? When you're playing about with this much energy, it only needs a momentary lapse of concentration. This is tens of thousands' times the current they put through the electric chair. It spills over, arcs . . . look what was happening to the copper ball. Think of the amount of power required to make that lightning . . .'

It was so casual. That's what got to Lloyd.

'Bloody goose chase, was it? I went in there with that poor old sod of a Yugoslav, risking his life, my liberty . . . for the sake of . . . nothing.' Nobody was impressed with that outburst. 'What about the lights on the other mountain?'

Butterworth showed faint interest.

'They were trying to transmit power without wires. Another Tesla trick.'

'Isn't that pretty sensational?' Lloyd wanted to know.

'You could say that,' said the boffin. 'NASA in America has done it over a distance of a mile or so. If your Yugoslavs had managed to light the whole of Dubrovnik, now that would be something.'

The brigadier addressed the scientist.

'That's all for now. Ta very much.'

Butterworth gathered the photographs.

'Just a minute,' said Lloyd. 'If my memory's right, Tesla put the whole power supply in Colorado Springs out of action . . .'

'So they say,' replied Butterworth.

'How?'

'Who knows? You saw the sort of power generated . . .'

'All that did was dim the lights. It didn't black out Dubrovnik; not even the workshop.'

'You're talking about eighty years ago. Bad connections, overload. Inadequate equipment . . .'

'Balls! Guesswork!'

'Can't be anything else,' said Forbes.

'Wrong!' said Lloyd. 'You may be prepared to write this off as kindergarten stuff. I was there. These people knew what they were doing. Tesla was their favourite son; their god! And they've got all his paperwork. A country with their economic problems doesn't waste that sort of money on a trip down electrical memory lane.'

'What are you getting at Lloyd?'

'I'm not sure,' said Lloyd. 'I'm feeling for something. They were serious. Forget that stupid woman, but the rest . . . it was professional. And there was something else. I can't put my finger on . . . yes, I can. It wasn't over. They hadn't finished the experiment.'

'What do you mean?' asked Butterworth.

'You're right, sir. I should never have come out. It wasn't over. I suppose I was scared . . . shit scared to be honest . . . It was all too much . . . too much to take in . . . the woman being killed . . . I suppose I wasn't used to the tension . . . I thought I'd got it all; that I had to bring it all back. But I'd forgotten what a feeling of expectation there was in that huge room. But I'd seen only part of it, the beginning. They'd only just started.'

'Does this make any sense to you, Butterworth?' asked the brigadier.

'Not really.'

'I tell you they were going on from there. Don't ask me to what. Suppose . . . just suppose that Tesla's experiment at Colorado Springs . . . No, don't suppose, answer me, Butterworth. Why did Tesla go to Colorado Springs?'

'To conduct experiments in electricity.'

'What experiments?'

'To make lightning. Transmit energy through the air. To plug into what he believed was an atmospheric power source.'

'Nothing else?'

'Who knows!'

'What's the evidence? He knocked out the power supply in the town. That was no accident. Tesla invented the alternating current generator. Vibration, short-circuits were the very things that prevented him perfecting alternating current. He'd mastered the whole of that scene. It was never overload that blacked out Colorado Springs!'

'What was it?' asked Forbes.

'Early experiments with the power source for his Shield.'

Butterworth was looking at Lloyd with renewed interest.

'You've done your homework on Tesla,' said the brigadier.

'I want to go back to Yugoslavia, sir. This thing – whatever it is – killed Marta. I'm going to find out what it is. It won't bring her back, but . . .'

'Butterworth?' said the brigadier.

The young scientist shuffled his feet.

'The official line from my superiors is that this is a load of codswallop. There are screwballs all over the world with labs in their basements making claims to everything from spoon-bending to re-materializing people on Jupiter. Officially the Tesla Shield's in that category.'

'But what do you think, Butterworth?' pressed Lloyd.

'I've got a mate working at CERN Geneva. The nuclear accelerator. They're doing experiments into the origin of matter, the smallest things in the universe. The secret's in the speed at which they do the bombardment, when they catch the infinitessimal fragments breaking up. They've had some weird experiences. Paranormal. He's done some research into Tesla. You could say he's a fan.'

'What are you getting at?'

'Unofficially . . . otherwise I'll get my head eaten off . . . I think it might be worth following up on Trebinje.'

For the first time in weeks, Lloyd felt a sense of achievement, purpose. He'd been able to climb outside the grip of his grief and do something. His dread of being on Marta territory was not borne out. He wanted to go back. He was meant to go back.

'Very interesting. Are you thinking the same as I am, Arthur?'

'Probably. If there is anything in this, there's no point in sending Richard back. We need somebody who knows what they're looking for . . .'

'Christ, sir, that's just not on. This is my baby. I've been there. I sussed it all out.'

'Don't get upset, Lloyd,' said the brigadier. 'You've done splendidly. We're grateful, but you've got to move over now and let the experts have a go, particularly as the men at the top don't seem to rate it.'

'Let me go with him!'

'And try and get two of you into Trebinje? Sorry. Are you game to go in Butterworth?'

'It'll make a change from white coats and NAAFI tea.'

'Where does that leave me, sir?' asked Lloyd icily. 'Having got me kicked out of the army to pursue the Yugoslav connection . . .'

'That's enough of that!' said the brigadier sharply. 'Better start making your arrangements, Butterworth.'

The scientist nodded and ambled out.

'You wanted me for my knowledge of Marta and Yugoslavia,' said Lloyd. 'What're you going to do now? Teach me Arabic and send me to Northern Ireland?'

'Simmer down, Richard,' said Forbes with a smile. 'We do have something else in mind for you.'

The brigadier continued: 'The Central Intelligence Agency has come up with a theory that Tesla may have left a record of the Shield . . .'

'Most of his papers are in the Museum in Belgrade,' said Lloyd.

'Not in writing. A model of some sort, or rather bits of one. Three bits. They want us to see if we can find any of them over here.'

'He didn't work here. All his friends and contacts were in the States,' said Lloyd.

'Exactly,' said Forbes.

'We have an interest in finding those bits, or at least in

making sure the Russians don't. The Prime Minister has vetoed the idea of an undercover team in the US, it doesn't fit with the relationship with Reagan, but we can send in a liaison officer. That's you.'

'I'm not exactly diplomatic material.'

Forbes dealt with that.

'I think you're a lucky bugger, and you know the background. We'll give you stuff to read, bring you up-to-date on what little we do know. And you have shown the sort of . . . I hate to call flagrant disobedience of orders initiative, but frankly we need somebody who's not afraid to break a few rules while ostensibly helping our allies.'

The brigadier, watching Lloyd closely for his reaction, continued:

'Liaison is your title and that's how you'll behave, but you're under our orders and responsible to us. Your allegiance is first and last here. Whatever you find out we're to be the first to know. We'll tell you whether to pass it on to the Yanks.'

'How about it?' asked Arthur Forbes.

Date: 10 October 1981
Astoria, Long Island, N.Y.

What was the Trinity? Rakov was sure his diagnosis was correct but what exactly was it? A model, certainly; both Czito father and son's occupations led to that conclusion, but what was the significance of the name? The Trinity meant three of something, three of a kind. Was the model in three parts? If so, why? To make it difficult for any one person to get the secret? There was a limit to what the deductive processes could do. He needed more facts. Where to find them? The only positive link was Yatanabron. Emanuel Yatanabron, a jeweller. What did a jeweller and a not very successful engineer who made models, have in common? They both made things. That made no sense. Perhaps it was nothing to do with Tesla. They both belonged to the same fishing club! Rakov didn't think so. His intuition told him Yatanabron was a lead. If there was a connection, he would know what it was. Rakov needed help, ideally KGB muscle men who knew their way around. There were none. Instead he was allocated two so-called reliable 'heavies', criminals! The embassy said they had used them before and they performed well for money.

'This is the State Department,' Rakov yelled down the telephone to the nearly deaf Yatanabron. 'I need to see you on a matter of great importance.' He was not sure the jeweller heard him. Rakov gave his name as Ernest Scamelli, and said he would prove his identity on arrival. He had an impressive-looking forged state department pass.

The two heavies were . . . well . . . heavies and they looked it. Rakov would much rather have had men committed to the cause, and to what would happen to their wives and children if they 'screwed up.'

'You do nothing without my order. Understood?' insisted Rakov.

The older man had grey hair and a muscle-bound paunch which made him look twenty years older than his thirty-eight Christmases. He was cleaning out his right ear. He nodded, bored.

His companion was an ex-boxer, and proved it every few seconds by a snort through his flattened nose. He was driving the four-year-old and battered Oldsmobile. His voice was pitched several tones above his grosser colleague's and had an effeminate drawl at odds with his bearing.

'You don't need to worry, man.' Snort. 'For the bread you're paying we can throw in a corpse or two.'

The thirty-eight-year-old protested that a rubbing-out rated a bonus, invariably. It was a new word in Harv Willet's vocabulary.

'Ain't that so, Chile?'

The welterweight was South American.

'Go to sleep, Harv.' Snort. 'Leave the brain power to me, OK?'

Harv nodded. Rakov sighed in dismay, hoping that their talents would be adequate.

The first shock was the Doberman. It growled at them, deep in the throat. The hairs on its back rose two inches. It stopped the itch in Harv's ear.

Yatanabron lived on the second floor of a fifty-year-old brick-built house of six storeys with no elevator; a cold water apartment.

'You from the State Department? Is that what you said? – Down Sergeant' – to the dog – 'Can't stand the telephone. Never could get used to it. Come in, come in.'

Sergeant showed his teeth. The men didn't move.

'Could you call off your dog, Mr Yatanabron . . . please!'

'Funny. He's good with people as a rule. I've only got to tell him once. Sergeant. These men are from the State Department. You mustn't be rude to them.'

And still Sergeant growled. Yatanabron took him by the collar and pulled him back with a jerk.

Yatanabron was a tall, neat man, and fit. His grey hair was sleeked back, and there was a reddish glow to his cheeks. He moved two tennis rackets from a chair and offered it to Rakov.

'Lucky you caught me in. If it hadn't been for the rain I'd have been out on the court. I may be eighty-five but I still play every day. And I smoke fifty cigarettes a day; ever since I was twenty.'

Harv and Chile backed to the window, staring at the dog. Harv fondled the shape of his revolver. Chile felt the throwing knife at the small of his back.

'We're making some enquiries about a Julius Czito . . . ' said Rakov.

'Old Julius is dead. Died years ago.'

'We know that. 1962, but we believe you knew him.'

'We were buddies. Used to play pool together every Saturday night.'

'You mean you were just friends?'

'What else did you expect? He was an engineer. I'm a jeweller. What business could we do together?'

'Is that the only association you had, as friends?'

'Sure.'

Rakov was disappointed. The old man was telling the truth. A false lead.

'Only did business with him once, and that wasn't even for him. Oh . . . he recommended a few friends of his to buy anniversary presents, but real business, something to get the teeth into, only once.'

Harv chose that moment to speak.

'Get rid of the hound, Major, and we'll sweat it out of the old timer.'

Rakov was angry.

'Don't mind Willet. He sees too many gangster movies.' He turned on the two heavies. 'Out! Wait in the car!'

They warily circled Sergeant.

'Just yell, Major,' said Harv, not convincingly.

Yatanabron was not fooled.

'I haven't seen your identification, Major . . . Scamelli, did you say? Sergeant! Heel!' With one bound the doberman was at his master's side, and this time there was no mistaking the growl or who it was aimed at.

As Rakov gingerly felt for his wallet, the old man continued:

'Those two look more like gangsters . . . '

Yuri handed over his forged pass. Yatanabron looked at it and then compared the photograph with Rakov's face. He seemed satisfied as he handed it back. Rakov tried to reassure the jeweller.

'I'm not in charge of the hiring at State. Personnel does it. I've had some complaints about those two, but what can I do? You were talking about business with Czito. Did it have anything to do with Professor Tesla?'

Yatanabron relaxed and smiled.

'So you know about it! Julius made him a model. Beautiful! Didn't know the old fool had it in him. Tesla wanted it cut into three; a precision job, and he wanted it artistic.'

Rakov said, matter-of-factly:

'Ah, the Trinity,' hoping for confirmation of his theory.

'What did you say?'

The telephone rang.

'It's my daughter. She always rings at this time; to make sure I'm all right.'

He found the handset under a blue-striped tracksuit.

'It's OK Ruth. I'm not dead yet . . . ' and there was a pause. It was obviously not the old man's daughter. 'Yes. Emanuel Yatanabron speaking . . . '

Rakov could just hear an excited male voice.

'I don't understand. There's already a man here from the State Department . . . He's a what!'

Yatanabron's face lost its colour. He gasped. The shock was too much for the old heart. The telephone dropped from his fingers. His face went into spasm. Rakov moved to help. The doberman threatened. Rakov stood back.

In a few seconds the seizure completed its work and Yatanabron's face relaxed. His hands dropped and his body slid to the floor . . .

'Mr Yatanabron . . . ' said the voice on the telephone. 'Are you all right? Can you hear me?'

Rakov felt for a weapon. He had none. Even the tennis rackets were beyond reach.

'Mr Yatanabron,' said the telephone voice. 'Are you all right?'

There was a rattle in the old man's throat. The dog's ears went up, and he looked at his master, puzzled. Rakov took the opportunity to leap for the door. He almost made it. His body was into the hallway when the dog's teeth clamped on to his fingers and locked. The pain was intense.

He tried pulling his hand. It was useless, and the pain increased to intolerable levels. He held the door closed with his good hand, preventing any more of the dog getting through. He tensed, waiting for the moment when the dog would try for a better hold, as they always did. Not this doberman. He clung to what he had. Rakov wondered if he could open the door wide enough to kick the dog in the head. He decided the canine would probably have his own throat out first. He yelled:

'Willet . . . Chile . . . Willet . . . Chile Help!'

They heard him at the third shout. They pounded up the stairs. Harv pulled out his automatic. Chile put out his hand to restrain the fat man.

'Watch me.' He moved round to the far side of Rakov.

'When I nod, open the door.' He didn't snort.

Chile put his own hand through the narrow gap in the door and chucked the dog under the chin.

'There's a good boy . . . There's a good boy . . . now get to know my smell, boy . . . that's the ticket, Sergeant.'

The growling lessened. Chile nodded. Rakov let go the door. As it opened Chile brought his right hand round, under the dog's throat and with a strong upward thrust cut deep into the animal's flesh from left ear to right. The dog's jaws opened, fighting for breath. Rakov grabbed his hand back. Chile slammed the door, but not quickly enough to avoid the bloody jet from the severed carotid.

Harv jammed his foot to the floor of the Oldsmobile. The tyres screamed on the wet road, spewing out grit and filth. Pedestrians ducked and cursed.

9

Date: 10 October 1981
Georgetown, D.C.

Ruth was talking to Ed Jamieson, the thirty-five-year-old lanky West Virginian who ran her West Coast real estate developments. The phone rang. Her English secretary used the American phraseology.

'This is Annie Jordan . . . Yes, General. She's in a meeting at the moment. Can I get her to call you?'

Ruth nodded to Jamieson.

'I had to fire the supervisor on that office building on Wilshire. I'm replacing him with the guy we used at Huntington Beach.'

'That was residential!' said Ruth.

'Hold the line please, General. I'll see if I can interrupt her.' Annie punched the mute button. 'He says it's urgent, Mrs Coverdale . . . ' Her training at Pitman's Secretarial College had not taught her how to call her boss by her Christian name.

'Will you excuse me, Ed?' She picked up her extension.

'Yes, Jack . . . '

'I have to see you, Ruth.'

'I have a hell of a morning. Frederick wants me to lunch and then help him choose furnishings for his new office.'

'Ruth, I gotta see you right away, and we need some of the other guys there too.'

'What's happened?'

'Not on the phone.'

'I can give you an hour at eleven.'

Jamieson protested. So did Annie Jordan. Ruth shrugged.

Stallybrass arrived with Lubbock.

'The Russians have a lead on us,' said the general.

'You said that before,' replied Ruth.

' I have proof. A young Russian was caught red-handed accessing the CIA computer on Tesla . . .'

'At last we have a lead,' said Stallybrass.

'He died.'

'How?' asked Ruth.

'Ricin. To stop him talking. Pellet in the thigh. Minute. Coating dissolved with body heat, released the poison. He went into coma after a couple of hours and died the next day.'

'Assassinated by his own side?' Stallybrass was incredulous.

'Not unusual,' was Lubbock's reply.

'What did they get out of him?' asked Ruth.

'Nix.'

'What was he after?'

'Most of what he saw was published material. He was reading our assessment of current Soviet state of Tesla knowledge when the agents arrested him. My friend is trying to get me copies but the security clamp is on hard.'

'I don't have much time, Jack.'

'I've only got one lead. A man called Julius Czito was killed in a road accident in 1962. He knew Tesla and probably worked as a model maker for him.'

'Probably?' said Stallybrass.

'His dying words – to a government man – were: "Tell them they need the Trinity. Father, Son and Ghost."'

'What does that mean?' asked the senator.

'Tesla made a model, broke it into three pieces and called it the Trinity.'

'That's schoolboy talk. Tesla was a serious scientist!'

'That's what the Pentagon thinks. But my friend reckons the Soviets will put men on to it.'

'And you want us to do the same!' The Senator again.

Lubbock seemed to change the subject.

'Heard from your nephew, Chuck, recently, Ruth?'

'How did you know?'

'I got him seconded to the Central Intelligence Agency.'

'Why?'

'We have a friend in the Pentagon but nobody at the sharp end of the CIA.'

'You want to put a mole in that organization?' enquired Stallybrass.

'He'll never do it,' said Ruth.

'He has an interesting record. You could make him an offer he might find difficult to turn down.'

'What do you mean?'

'Money turns him on.'

Voices were heard from the hall.

'That'll be Frederick. I must go.'

Stallybrass stopped her with:

'I have news of the Brits.'

'Can't wait, and don't talk about it in front of my husband. . .'

'They've got a lead in Yugoslavia . . . '

'Where are you, darling?' The excited voice of the 'new' man in Ruth's life was near the head of the stairs.

'Totally different angle.'

'The Brits are a waste of time,' said Lubbock.

Frederick appeared in the doorway, a beaming smile of anticipation on his face. It froze when he saw a worried Ruth in urgent debate with a general and a senator.

'Why are the Brits a waste of time, general?' His voice had lost its warmth.

Ruth and Lubbock spoke together.

'As secretaries, Jack was saying . . . ' said Ruth.

'As soldiers . . . ' said Lubbock.

Ruth was the first to recover. She took Frederick's arm.

'These two old men are boring me to death, just passing the time until you took me to lunch!'

It was a brave try but Frederick was not fooled.

Date: 10 October 1981
New York, N.Y.

The CIA computer connected Yatanabron's name with Tesla. The information was flashed to Rogers' office. The three of them took the shuttle to JFK. It was Tyson's first experience of a corpse. He didn't feel too good.

The doctor, in his late fifties, who had seen every indignity one man could inflict on another, said:

'Heart.'

'Balls,' said Rogers.

'Cyanide?' asked Heidi.

'No way,' said the doctor, bending down for another sniff around the face. 'Natural causes.'

'Never,' said Rogers. 'It's a KGB job. Gas pistol, needle, tiny pellet, pressure point. Undetectable.'

'You write the certificate! Me. I'm a simpleton. I see cardiac arrest brought on by too many years at seventy-six beats a minute.'

'Shock?' Tyson spoke for the first time.

Pete Rogers was not pleased.

'Who asked you?'

The doctor smiled.

'Now there's a thought. Wouldn't rule it out.'

Rogers wasn't having it.

'Strip him, doc. I want the body searched for needle holes, and pellets.'

'I'll do it at the office.'

'This is urgent.'

'Why would the KGB want him dead?' Tyson again.

Heidi joined in. 'Butt out, Tyson, until you know what you're talking about.'

The doctor liked the idea.

'They were only here ten minutes. Why kill him?'

'Look for holes, Jamie. I'm the investigator round here.'

Doctor James Millbank shrugged and began pulling off the old man's clothes. He looked up at Tyson.

'Would you lend a hand here.'

Tyson pulled and pushed and found it all disgusting and a desecration of the man that had inhabited the body that was behaving like a rag doll. After an age, Millbank stood up.

'No holes. No needle. No pellet!'

Rogers was not to be proved wrong. 'Look up his ass.'

The doctor was good-humoured.

'Look up it yourself. I'm going home.' And he put his various instruments back in his bag and snapped it shut.

'Five bucks says it's natural causes.'

'You're on.'

'Witness!' said Tyson.

'Drop dead,' was Rogers' laconic reply.

Rakov's hand was pumping blood when he ordered Harv and Chile out of the car.

He slid to the driving position. The automatic gearbox freed his good hand for the powered steering.

The doctor, just retired, another KGB recruit, was expecting him. The wound was painfully cleaned. Twelve stitches were inserted. Rakov made him tighten the bandage. The doctor gave an anti-tetanus injection. The only conversation was clinical question and answer.

'I'll need to see you again in two days. The hand needs rest and so do you.'

Rakov's base for the visit was an economy apartment in an anonymous block on East 61st Street on the fourth floor of a walk-up. The view from the living room was a panorama of rooftops. The furniture was old but comfortable. The kitchen was well-stocked with the basics. Yuri unscrewed the cap of the Smirnoff vodka. He reviewed progress. He had been in the US barely three days and already a KGB colonel was compromised, a brilliant computer expert was dead, as was the only man who provided a link with the Tesla secret. If he kept up this rate nobody would be left in a week.

He doubted if Anton would have talked before the drug acted. Initially he would have been too scared of Russian consequences to do so, and there wouldn't have been time for them to get to work on him psychologically or chemically. Rakov was reasonably sure he had not been noticed as he joined the party outside the United Nations building. Certainly the two agents who arrested Anton had not given him a second glance. He had been logged as a visitor of Telinger's, but not under his own name. They would have his physical description but that would not necessarily connect him with either Anton's illegal search of the CIA computer memory, or his death.

What about the Yatanabron incident? There had been people in the street on Long Island. Their attention must have been attracted when he yelled for help, although he was in too much pain to notice. The phone call was obviously from CIA and must have been a follow-up to what Anton had unearthed; that gave Rakov another clue; Anton had not had time to erase his work. And Yatanabron was dead. Rakov couldn't help musing on the irony of that situation. He had died of a heart attack, but they'd never believe it, not with the doberman killed.

What had he learned? From Yatanabron? That he had cut a model made by Julius Czito into three, presumably the Trinity, although the old man had not confirmed it. According to Yatanabron it was a thing of beauty. What was it? What did it look like? Where was it? Why did Tesla demand secrecy? He had made no secret of his claim. It was even mentioned in the New York Times obituary. Maybe he was looking at it from the wrong end of the problem. Maybe it wasn't secret at all. Could it be Tesla was fed up with trying to persuade people to back him, he just went ahead and made the model? But why? Why make a model at all? Rakov could think of only one explanation: that a model would be more convincing than something in writing? But the real problem was, was it the model of the Shield? It could be something entirely different, the secret of his vertical take-off plan, a laser, his battery-operated motor that achieved four hundred per cent efficiency – almost perpetual motion! It could be anything, but the only interpretation that fitted all the known facts was that the model contained the process for the Tesla Shield. Until something better came up he would put his resources into that.

Where did that get him? What was it a model of? He didn't know. What was it made of? No idea. How big was it? No clue. He had chosen a jeweller to cut it, and that put an outside limit on its size. If it was ten metres high and wide Tesla would have gone to a sculptor. Tesla wanted it cut artistically; why? That suggested that . . . what did it suggest? Why not simply use a power tool to slice into three pieces? Might that cause damage? Possibly. A jeweller suggested precision, but also . . . a gift?

The events of the last two days caught up with Yuri. He eased off his jacket and lay on the bed.

Date: 12 October 1981
Washington D.C.

Tyson was in the inner office looking over Rogers' shoulder, reading Dr Miller's post mortem report. The telephone rang. Rogers listened and passed the receiver to Tyson.

'Mrs Coverdale.'

Tyson nodded.

'Hi Ruth. What's goin' on?'

Heidi eavesdropped the conversation in the outer office.

'I wondered if you were free for dinner tonight. Jack Lubbock will be here. Frederick's out of town so I thought you might like to barbecue us some beef.'

'Sounds good,' said Chuck.

'Shall we say about six . . . your work permitting, of course . . . '

Tyson asked Rogers if he was needed late. Pete shook his head.

'Great, Ruth.'

'Wife of Frederick Coverdale?' Rogers' enquiry was casual.

'Yeah. Why?'

'That guy draws a lot of water.'

'So?'

'What's he to you?'

'Nothing, as if it was any of your business.'

Rogers was sharp in his retort.

'Anything that concerns you concerns me.'

'I don't go for that. My private life is my own . . . '

'Wrong. In CIA you will be continuously subject to intense personal vetting. Nothing you do will go undiscovered.'

'And if I don't like that?'

'I may not be able to fire you, boy, or get you shifted out of here, but I can sure pass some bad news up the line.'

'No need for that. I just like to know when I'm not getting my constitutional rights.' As Rogers opened his mouth to give Tyson another broadside, Tyson put up his hands in surrender and continued:

'Ruth's my aunt. More like a cousin really. I stay with her when I'm in town. She has a place at Malibu she lets me use. Anything else?'

Rogers turned to the last page of the pathological report on Emanuel Yatanabron.

> ' . . . had a degenerative heart condition. He must have been having regular angina pains, some severe. He could have died at any time, even taking modest exercise. An emotional shock, perhaps even some especially bad news conveyed by telephone would have been enough to stop the heart beat . . . '

Pete didn't bother to read any more. He grimaced at the yellow self-sticking memo slip on which Jamie had written 'You owe me five bucks.'

Heidi put down her receiver slowly. Later she asked Rogers why the wife of the next Secretary of State wanted newly-promoted Chuck Tyson, CIA, to meet General Jack Lubbock, who some saw as an extreme right wing presidential candidate.

Date: 12 October 1981
New York, N.Y.

The bandage snagged the sheet. Pain flooded the hand. Rakov was instantly awake. He wanted to discard the telltale white but remembered the doctor had said three days and even then he risked septicaemia.

He was physically immobilized, depressed, and the quest for the Tesla Trinity model looked hopeless. Tesla died in 1943, aged eighty-six. How many of his contemporaries could be alive now? Yatanabron was probably the last, and now he was dead. Would he have kept a record of what happened to the pieces? Would Tesla have told him what he was going to do with it? This was a problem for a computer. He cursed the necessity to kill Anton. He could have fed the names and information into the electronic brain and it would have identified the best guesses as to the location of the three secrets. Rakov doubted that Russian machines were capable of such sophistication. That left the human brain. He needed help. He needed to talk to Moscow.

Rakov scanned the street from the second floor hall window. No sign of surveillance.

When he left the apartment he took the usual precautions but saw no shadow; the hair at the nape of the neck remained in place.

He was startled by the sales girl on the perfume counter of Saks Department Store.

'Hi!' she said, as to an old friend. 'How're you today?'

It took him a moment to realize that this was not a sign of recognition, but a welcome to a customer, perhaps even an attempted pick up.

'I'm very well, thank you. How are you?' The intrepid undercover killer was ill-at-ease.

'You're cute. Where're you from?'

Rakov would not be drawn.

'I'm late.'

The girl beamed at him.

'Have a nice day! Be sure and come back now.'

At the glove counter Rakov suffered the usual indecision at the profusion of choices. In Leningrad or Kiev, gloves were Russian-made, all one style and shunned. Rakov was angered at this further evidence of the plenty produced by the 'doomed capitalist system.'

'Cut your hand? My husband gave me an electric carver for my birthday. I did the same!'

Would these Americans never learn to keep their counsel, Rakov despaired mildly. This woman was in middle age, striving without success to keep her figure within the confines of her black dress. In view of the paucity of early morning customers she was happy to settle down to a long chat.

'Take my advice. Don't try it on the injured hand at all. It won't tell you nothing. When you get the bandage off they'll be two sizes too big. What am I saying? I could make another sale! I made that mistake once. Of course, I get a discount, not a big one, you understand, but it helps. Not that it makes up for throwing money away. All they're good for now is working in the yard . . . '

'I'll buy these.' Rakov had chosen the ones that fitted the swollen hand. The woman's attitude changed from avuncular to formal at the rejection of her advice.

'Certainly, sir. That'll be twenty-three dollars plus sales tax. Cash or charge?'

'I will pay you cash.'

Using a street payphone he dialled the trade delegation office.

'This is Viktor. Who is that?'

Rakov knew the telephone line was tapped, so did Viktor.

'This is Boris Kliment. I wish to report that I have been quoted three prices . . . ' That meant he wanted a meeting at one o'clock. 'For sixty-eight tons the price was within our limits but not for lesser quantities.' That meant the meeting was to be at 68th Street.

'Where are the goods to be collected?'

'The supplier is in Lexington, Kentucky. Can you confirm that I can place the order?' Each of the street names had a code word. Lexington meant Fifth Avenue.

'Hold the line.'

Rakov waited impatiently.

'The order is confirmed.' Rakov replaced the instrument and looked at his watch. He had fifteen minutes to kill before the pick-up. At precisely one o'clock he stood on the corner of 68th and Fifth Avenue, hard by Central Park. A black Ford Thunderbird drew to the kerb. Rakov climbed in.

Rakov came straight to the point.

'I need to talk to Moscow. Professor Vilkov for one, maybe others.'

'When?'

'As soon as possible.'

Viktor pondered. His name was not Viktor. It was Pyotr Paulovich Liepa. His main claim to fame was his unswerving devotion to Party dogma, his compulsive neatness and time-keeping, and an encyclopaedic memory, particularly for any wrong-doing. Under Stalin he would have prospered briefly, been denounced and shot. In the more tolerant times of Kruschev and Brezhnev his sort was dealt with by promotion. His last, brought about because he had discovered the full extent to which his factory manager was lining his own pocket at the expense of the state, was to the KGB. The manager was dismissed, and moved, to a bigger factory where the opportunities for graft were greater.

Moscow Centre sent 'Viktor' to America for his memory. He knew now every code used by each agent. He could put a face to every one of several hundred names working for the Motherland. He was also the most boringly loyal member of the party. Consequently defection, a constant source of worry with a foreign appointment, was not a risk. Viktor hated America, and could not wait to get back home.

'It will take time,' said Viktor.

'How long?'

'I don't know where Professor Vilkov is. Moscow? Novosibirsk?'

'Track him down.' said Rakov.

'I'll try.'

'And I have to talk to Major-General Yakushenko,' said Rakov.

The general's reputation was well known. Nobody voluntarily brought themselves to his notice.

'You're sure it's the general himself, not one of his subordinates?'

'The general.'

'Who do you wish first?'

'The professor.'

Viktor promised to get Moscow to call direct on one of the payphones at Grand Central Station, and gave Rakov detailed code instructions.

Rakov nodded. He looked at his watch. Viktor compared the time with his own.

'You're two minutes fast.'

Rakov didn't argue. His hand throbbed.

One hour later Rakov was struggling to hear what Professor Vilkov was saying, on a bad line and over the noise and bustle of trains and people.

'I want to know what I'm looking for,' shouted Rakov.

'Impossible to answer.'

'You must have some idea.'

'Not really,' said the professor.

'Tell me what he was working on, what the so-called new physics is.' Rakov was angry. 'You're the scientist. You've done the work on it. You must know what a model might look like. I want to know how big, what it's made of, what colour, what material?'

'I can't even guess without more information,' said Vilkov.

'Read the library material, what he claimed for this thing. The Academy of Sciences must be able to come up with something.'

'Give me a few days.'

'I can't even give you a few hours, professor. The opposition is close on my heels. They may be ahead of me.'

'I'll try to phone you again in two hours. Either that or I'll put a signal through to Washington. Stay on the line. Another caller wants you.'

'Yes, professor.' Rakov waited. A familiar voice spoke, and suddenly, as if in deference to the importance of the general, the interference stopped. 'Y' could have been in the next room.

'You know who this is?'

'Yes, sir.'

'No names. No identification. This is an open line.'

'Indeed sir.'

'First, I don't like being kept waiting while my employees gossip with others . . . '

'I had to speak with Pro . . . ' he stopped himself from identifying Vilkov just in time. ' . . . the other person because I needed his input before I talked to you.'

'I am a busy man.'

'If this wasn't of vital importance I wouldn't be speaking to you direct.'

'Get on with it!'

Rakov hurried on. 'There is some evidence.'

'I would hope so!'

'It seems reasonable to assume that the old man did leave . . . shall I say some bric-a-brac in various places.'

'What's bric-a-brac?'

'He went to a jeweller and had three things made. A jeweller. I think that may be the crucial fact. When the three are put together they make up a whole story. What my other caller needs.'

'What do you want from me?'

'Names. Anybody to whom he could have given each piece.'

'How do you expect me to know?'

'People have studied the old man, his work and background. Somebody could make educated guesses at likely recipients.'

'Why ask me? Ask them?'

'If I were there, sir, I would. Unless the orders come from you it could take months. I need the answers today; tomorrow at the latest. The opposition is working on the same facts.'

'I'll put a signal through to 16th Street.' The Russian Embassy was on 16th Street, Washington. The general broke the connection.

Date: 12 October 1981
Georgetown, D.C.

Tyson was late. Lubbock prepared to give him a lecture about discipline and punctuality. Ruth told him it was not one of those occasions. 'I don't know how he's going to react to this,' she added.

'When a United States general tells a captain what to do, he does it,' asserted Lubbock with confidence.

Ruth was less certain.

'We're asking him to betray a trust.'

'CIA's not army proper.'

There were noises at the front door.

The general was urbane, Ruth edgy, Chuck polite.

'Good evening, sir.' He kissed Ruth's cheek. 'How are you?'

'Get you a drink, son?' Lubbock was trying too hard.

'Thank you, sir. I'll take a beer.' Lubbock produced a can.

'Ruth?' he asked.

'A martini, Jack.'

'When you were told you had an hour to pack your bags, and you were on your way to a new appointment in Washington,' said Lubbock as he poured the gin, 'didn't you wonder what was goin' on?'

'Yes, sir!'

'You had any satisfactory answers yet?'

'No, sir.'

Lubbock warmed to his task.

'Did you see the President on TV this morning, son?'

'I heard about Frederick's appointment.'

'Good,' said the general, 'then I don't need to explain that!'

Tyson looked uncomprehending but kept his mouth shut. Ruth was not happy at mention of her husband.

'I arranged your transfer, Chuck. You may look surprised. Retired generals don't usually get to issue orders. The fact is, I'm only nominally retired. Like your Uncle Frederick, shall we say, I'm still in the service of Uncle Sam; the special service of . . . d'you get my drift, son?'

'No, sir,' said Tyson.

Ruth decided it was time to intervene.

'What Jack's trying to say . . .' but Lubbock interrupted.

'Leave this to me,' he said, the senior officer in command. 'This is army business. Are you a patriot Chuck?'

'I sure hope so, sir.' said Tyson with plastic enthusiasm.

'What I'm about to tell you mustn't go further than this

room. If repeated, it will be denied, by everybody, including the MAN . . . ' he glowered at Tyson, daring him to say he did not know he was referring to the President. 'You were chosen – as was I – because you were known, I say again, known from pedigree, family and background to be trustworthy. Yours is a delicate mission. You won't be allowed to talk about it. There'll be no orders in writing and you won't get no purple heart. But you'll be serving your country.'

Lubbock told him about the Trinity and the Russians. Tyson had heard it all before.

'My new job, and what you're gonna get into, is under-under cover operations. On the technical side the KGB has recruited scientists at all levels. Their brief is to block research projects which conflict with Soviet interests. They never come out into the open, and they're impossible to detect. All they do is put forward well-argued, contrary scientific points of view. Because of position, reputation or sheer persuasion, they get to kill promising projects. They're working to stop Tesla Shield research, and they're doing a fine job.'

'I'm no scientist, general.'

'That's just an example, Chuck. They've got similar people in the CIA. That's where you come in. We've got to flush 'em out.'

'How, general? I'm a new boy. I just about get to make the coffee.'

'You need to change that.'

'How?'

'I've read your reports, Chuck. You need to smarten up. Stop the deals on the side to make a few bucks. You're gonna become the keenest officer ever. Think you can do it?'

'I guess so. What do I do for you?'

'Not for me, son. For the President of the United States. He wants to know every damn thing that goes down, no matter how unimportant. But nothing in writing. All verbal. To me.'

'And if you're not around I tell Frederick. Is that what you're saying?'

'This is strictly one-on-one. You to me. Me to the Man.'

'If that's so, what's Ruth doing here?' It wasn't a smart remark, just puzzlement.

Ruth couldn't think of an answer. After only a moment's hesitation, Lubbock continued:

'She's one of the President's few. She reports to me on her world, social and business.'

Ruth joined in.

'We don't want you to be out-of-pocket on this thing, Chuck. I'll see you get an extra couple of thousand bucks a month into your account.'

'Hey, you don't have to do that Ruth!'

Lubbock's sentiments also! But Ruth knew it was the clincher for the materialistic nephew. She didn't blame him. If you wanted something in the world's bastion of capitalism, you paid for it.

Date: 12 October 1981
Guildford, Surrey

The thing that decided the issue was the letter. It was a normal morning in all other respects. He got out of bed at seven, and was entering the dining room thirty minutes later when Lewis Calshott asked him if he'd picked it up from the hall table.

He recognized the handwriting immediately. His father was sending him one of his occasional epistles, extolling the virtues of hard work in the newsagent's world and no doubt complaining, subtly, of course, about his mother. He put it in his pocket to read when he felt stronger.

He was in the garden when he opened it. His father had written:

'No time for a long chat. The Fleet Street strikes are taking all my time with the customers' accounts. Your mother thought we should tear it up. I didn't agree, so here it is.

Your affectionate Father.'

Richard felt in the envelope and drew out another letter. The handwriting was also familiar. The postmark was Dubrovnik, 20 August. His heart turned through three hundred and sixty degrees.

'My darling Richard, (Marta had written)

The most wonderful thing has happened, but at the same time the saddest. I have a new job. I'm not allowed to tell anybody about it, I'm not even supposed to say where I am. If I wrote to you in Hanover they would throw me in jail, but what is worse I'd lose my lovely new work. So a trusted friend will post it in a few days.

I can't tell you about my work. It's secret, but the most thrilling thing is that I put my training to the test, to the limit. And I'm working for one of my country's favourite heroes.

The sad part is that I could never leave Yugoslavia now, however much I love you, and I do, yes I do. It's not that work is more important to me than loving you. It's much more complicated than that. It's about love of country, fulfilment in my profession, pride in myself and what I am, and in what I hope you love in me, my . . . I think the English word is integrity. It's an awful word to say. I hope it sounds better to you.

I'm not going to ask you to come here and marry me. I know it would destroy many parts of you that I love so much. So this letter is goodbye. Please don't try and see me again. I won't change my mind. I know that. I think I shall always love you.

Marta.'

Lloyd couldn't remember the last time he'd cried. Now, out of sight of the mess and any other eyes, the tears flowed.

Two hours later, he returned to the mess, and rang the brigadier.

Date: 12/13 October 1981
New York, N.Y.

Grand Central Station was thronging with travellers. The shops were crowded with merchandise; newspapers, magazines, flowers, fruit and confectionery were on groaning shelves and spilling on to makeshift displays on the floor. Men and women stood about idly, waiting for trains and lovers. Rakov leaned against the wall beside the bank of telephones, reading the Wall Street Journal; just another businessman trying to outguess the stock market. He looked at his watch. The rule in the dangerous world of espionage and counter intelligence was to leave any venue at one minute past the appointed time. He was fifteen minutes adrift. But it was only a phone call.

After a further five minutes he returned to his apartment.

It was a quiet insistent knocking that woke him. Through the spy hole in the door he saw a young girl in her mid-twenties, in a torn grey tweed jacket and jeans. Her hair was awry, her face smudged with dirt. Rakov slid back the chain.

'Viktor sent me,' she said.

Rakov opened the door wider.

'I don't need to come in . . . '

Rakov pulled her into the apartment.

'I don't talk to contacts in hallways.' He remarked on her dishevelled state. 'What happened to you?'

'It's nothing to worry about . . . ' she panted.

'I'm not worried about you! You've exposed my cover by coming here. What happened!'

'My father had an accident. He can't walk. He said you needed this package urgently. He made me come instead.'

'Your father?'

'Viktor,' she said. 'I am Anna.'

Rakov was exasperated.

'You still haven't answered my question. How did you get into that state?'

'Don't you know anything about New York?' she said defiantly. 'There's policemen in the streets. Doors are locked at night. Bells ring in the janitor's rooms. I climbed up the back. Got in through a second floor window . . .'

Rakov was aghast.

'Into another apartment?'

'I'm not stupid!' she said. 'Landing window.'

'You should have phoned. I would have met you.'

'Phones are tapped!'

'Give me the package, and use the bathroom to clean yourself up.'

He took the envelope and opened it. There were two messages; one from the general, the other from Vilkov. The professor's read:

> 'Assume from fact that jeweller cut the object that it is a solid object and not a moving/working model. Difficult to be precise, but could not be less than half a metre square (when in one piece) and may be made of translucent material. This should not be treated as accurate forecast, merely a best guess. Supply any further facts soonest and we will improve on the guess.'

That was a fat lot of good, thought Rakov. But he supposed it was better than nothing. He read the other signal.

> 'Reference: Telecall 'Y'/Boris
> Date: 12 October 2305 hours
> Subject: T

The name POUSKAS occurs as a well-disposed friend who got T work in Paris. Any person bearing that name is worth pursuing. CHARLES BATCHELOR gave T intro. to Edison. But T left Edison's company when denied promised royalties. T reportedly rejected Nobel Prize because it was to be jointly awarded to him and Edison. Do not pursue any Edison connection. George Westinghouse Jnr, born 1846, ten years before T, had a lifetime association and friendship. Good prospect. HQ of Westinghouse Company is Pittsburgh. Dr CHARLES F. SCOTT, Emeritus Professor of Electrical Engineering at Yale, was a Westinghouse chief engineer and wrote memorial review of T's work. He worked closely with him for the year T was at Pittsburgh. Mutual respect suggests a fruitful lead. CHARLES PROTEUS STEINMETZ, engineer friend of Electric Company was a known T supporter. Samuel Clemens, otherwise 'Mark Twain' was a close friend. One CRAWFORD of the dry goods firm of Simpson & Crawford lent T money, as did Colonel JOHN JACOB ASTOR, owner of the Waldorf Astoria Hotel, New York. Lawyer LEONARD E. CURTIS of Colorado Springs Electric Company arranged T's trip there. FRITZ LOWENSTEIN was an assistant to T in Colorado. In 'Electrical World and Engineer' published on 5th March 1904, T wrote: "For a large part of the work which I have done so far I am indebted to the noble generosity of Mr J PIERPONT MORGAN . . . extended at a time when those who promised most were the greatest doubters." Morgan was a banker but also backed Edison. Architect STANFORD WHITE was close to T and built giant copper electrode transmitter for him at Shoreham, Long Island. GEORGE SCHERFF was T's book-keeper and secretary at Houston Street, New York, later lived at Westchester. He was businesslike (unlike T) and tight-lipped. B. A. BEHREND wrote the standard textbook on alternating current, 'The Induction Motor'; one of few who understood T's work. They were also close. ROBERT UNDERWOOD JOHNSON, poet and editor of Century Magazine, lived on Madison Avenue, at Murray Hill, where T was a frequent guest. Johnson and his wife were close family friends. Mrs J. may have had sexual interest in T yet J. continued T friendship after wife's death. He worked with T on translations of Serbian poetry. JOHNSON and WILLIAM K.VANDERBILT were the only two people known to be on first name terms with T. EDWARD DEAN ADAMS, President of Cataract Construction Company, and organizer of International Niagara Commission, chose T's polyphase system for the Falls. Later formed a $500,000 company for T. SAVA KOSANOVIC, Yugoslav ambassador to America, was T's nephew and administrator of his estate. KENNETH M. SWEZEY, science writer, was a teenager when he first met T, became a close friend in T's last twenty years. KOLMAN CZITO, an engineer with premises at Long Island, made models for T. Son JULIUS may have carried on the tradition. Rear Admiral RICHMOND PEARSON HOBSON, Spanish American War fame, interested T in the movies. JOHN J. O'NEILL, Pulitzer Prize winner, was on intimate terms with T and wrote his biography in 1944.'

Viktor's daughter waited for Rakov to finish reading. Rakov whispered, to himself: 'The bastard! Even when it's critical he won't get off the fence; simply throws in everything. I get the blame if I make the wrong choice. Bastard!'

'Are you talking to me?' Anna asked.

She reminded him of his own sister at that age, tomboyish, ready for anything!

'Come here, *bednyashka*. Are you all right? No broken bones?'

'I'm fine, thank you. You're not a bit like Daddy says.'

'What does Daddy say?' He was teasing her.

'I didn't mean . . . Daddy doesn't talk about work . . . It was just . . . You're very important . . . and important people from Moscow are supposed to frighten us.'

'And I don't?' he said with a mock scowl.

She giggled, shaking her head.

Rakov smiled. It was a relief to relax his guard, if only for a few minutes.

'You need a taxi? Night streets are dangerous.'

'I've got my bicycle, chained to the railing. I'll be OK.'

'You show promise. I wish those who sent me messages were as enterprising.'

As he let Anna into the cold October morning the sign on the Bank of America building told the sleeping New York that it was 4.30 a.m. and the temperature 36 degrees fahrenheit. He wondered if his niece Rina would grow up to be as smart. He hoped not.

Date: 13 October 1981
Georgetown, D.C.

At 5 a.m. both Frederick and Ruth were awake, neither admitting it to the other. Ruth's mind was in turmoil. She had so far avoided the topic of her meeting with Lubbock and Stallybrass, but eventually she would have to find a convincing explanation.

'Are you awake?'

Ruth contemplated denying it, but there was a doziness about Frederick's voice that suggested his senses might not be on full alert. She tried to sound equally sleepy.

'M'mm . . . '

'What were Jack and Ernest doing here?'

She went close to the truth:

'It's all hush-hush. At least Jack says it is. He wants money to start a magazine . . . '

'Jack Lubbock as writer/publisher? That I don't believe.'

'Inside intelligence. Only to big hitters, telling them what the Russians are up to that we're doing nothing about.'

Silence.

'Are you still awake?'

'That could be dangerous. People could wind up before the Grand Jury . . . '

'That's what I told him.'

More silence. Had she convinced him? More silence, then a quiet snore. Ruth didn't feel like sleep.

Date: 13 October 1981
New York, N.Y.

Rakov settled down with the messages. Vilkov's gave him little to work on. He tried to visualize what the Trinity looked like. A block of ice? Ridiculous! What else was translucent? Plastic? But it was in its infancy in the early part of the century. Quartz? Possible. What message did the model contain? Was it a formula? Why hadn't Vilkov given him a clue? It was the Russian obsession with secrecy. The survival of the Motherland was at stake, and they still couldn't bring themselves to give out classified information. Crazy! Three blocks of quartz? Plastic? Glass? How about glass? Why not? It could be made into any shape, contain all sorts of colours, engravings, patterns. Patterns! Was that the secret? T. was working on something that needed fifty million volts. Electricity meant waves . . . bands of frequency perhaps. It wasn't much but it was something. Should he ask Vilkov outright if that was it? Pointless. If Vilkov was authorized to tell him, he would have said so.

Rakov made himself black coffee and turned to the general's ream of information. How was he expected to evaluate these names? There were eighteen of them. They were either dead, or senile! Great! Who were the three most likely recipients of Tesla's trust? But that assumed all three pieces were in America. What basis was there for that? He should have made Anna wait for a message to Moscow Centre. He wrote:

> 'No reason to assume all three pieces in US. Please check out other T connections in other countries and advise. Am working on list of American names and will advise progress.'

What progress? He didn't even know where to start. He looked at the list again. Pouskas. His connection was a hundred years ago. He checked the New York telephone directory anyway. No Pouskas. Forget it. Batchelor? Same time frame, and connected with the hated Edison. He struck his name.

George Westinghouse? He'd paid Tesla a million dollars for his alternating current, and had been a close business associate for years. He'd even bailed him out of the Houston Street earthquake fracas. Rakov put a star against his name; thought better of it, and added two more.

Dr Charles Scott? Scientist in the same discipline as Tesla, chief engineer for Westinghouse, the man who had turned Tesla's patents and holograms into reality. But he was part of the same company. George Westinghouse died in 1914. Anything Tesla had given him was therefore either with a member of the family, maybe somewhere on company premises, possibly with Scott. He put a star against Scott, and wrote 'See Westinghouse.'

Steinmetz, founder of GEC. The professional connection was there all right. GEC worked on defence contracts. A possible. Yuri gave him one asterisk.

Crawford – a dry goods merchant. His only claim to consideration was that he lent Tesla money. Who didn't! He struck Crawford.

Astor. Would Tesla entrust such a secret to a hotelier? However rich? His name was removed.

Leonard Curtis? Rakov gave him three stars, and bracketed Lowenstein's name with him.

J. P. Morgan rated one star solely because of Tesla's own words of praise, but he was unlikely because of his Edison connection.

He gave Stanford White one star.

George Scherff got three stars, for the closeness with which he worked with Tesla, and for his known discretion.

Mark Twain had died twenty-five years before Tesla. He was out!

B. A. Behrend? Three stars.

The telephone rang. It was 4.30 a.m. He picked up the instrument.

'Yes?'

'You know my voice?' It was Viktor.

'I do.'

'Did your order arrive safely?'

'Yes.'

'Both items?'

'Yes.'

'Just checking. Good night.'

Rakov approved. The only unusual thing about that call was its timing. Anybody bugging that conversation would have a hard time making any sense out of it. Back to the list.

Robert Johnson, even if he did call him Nikola, was a poet, and poetry and electronic shields didn't seem to meld. His name disappeared.

Vanderbilt was difficult. Rich and influential, he was interested in education, having endowed the University at Nashville, Tennessee, among other establishments. A possible. Two stars.

Adams? Difficult. Not too close to Tesla in later years but chose Tesla's system for Niagara Falls.

Kosanovic was a relative but he was also ambassador for Tito, a communist. His name went.

Kenneth Swezey was close to the scientist and many

years younger. A journalist would be able to publish the invention. But that was the last thing Tesla wanted. He struck the name.

Kolman and Julius Czito. The father died first. If Julius had kept any part of it, surely he would have said something to the CIA agent. He struck both names.

Admiral Hobson had rank and heroic reputation, but his relationship with Tesla was personal. The movies! Would Tesla put his secret weapon in the same thought process as Hollywood make-believe? On the other hand, an Admiral was well placed to get authority to listen. Two stars, reluctantly.

O'Neill? Three stars for influence as a respected writer on scientific subjects, and knowing Tesla better than anybody else.

At seven-thirty Rakov phoned Viktor. He refused to talk on the telephone and still couldn't leave home. The elaborate code was used. The limousine met Rakov. The driver took his messages. He wanted the starred names checked out, present addresses, occupations, and all known relatives.

He was dropped near a deli. Over smoked fish, cheese and black coffee he thought about the names again. Who was the favourite? There had to be one – somebody who rated an extra star. He liked the look of George Westinghouse.

Date: 13 October 1981
Near Guildford, Surrey

Lloyd lay in bed contemplating his so-called failure. He changed the subject in his mind to more personal matters. It didn't help. Marta had not been a popular subject at home. His father said marrying a foreigner would ruin his army career. His mother's angry retort was that discrimination on grounds of nationality was criminal; what mattered was that Richard had only known her five minutes, and talk of marriage was ridiculous. He would get over her! The comity of view between his parents didn't last long. They soon turned the argument into the familiar sniping about their own marriage.

What of the present? He had a shrewd suspicion that there would have been no court-martial even if he'd turned down the alternative. But it was a bit late for those thoughts. Marta? He'd thought the letter would destroy him, but it had had the opposite effect. In a strange way it helped. The solace he'd sought in opening her coffin which had been so cruelly shattered, he'd found in the words she'd written.

He was not the same man who first met Major Forbes. His character had been through some burnishing. Marta's death, his handling at the Yugoslav border and then spying behind the Iron Curtain, had changed a few attitudes. Was he better for it? He didn't know. He felt different, as though the curtain had come down on the first act of his life; the next would be for real, the test of him as a man, whether he was made of the stuff to justify his existence on this earth. He didn't know how he would meet the test. The only certainty was that before Marta's death the thought would not have occurred to him. If it had, he would have dismissed it.

He wondered when, if ever, he would get the summons to begin his 'liaison' job in America.

10

Date: 13 October 1981
New York, N.Y.

The bar off Times Square was not salubrious. Boarded floor, huge mahogany bar and plenty of Irish accents. Their table was well away from other ears. The single candle, in its squat, glass pot, distorted the features of the two New York 'heavies.' The KGB major produced a slip of paper.

'This is the address.'

'Nob Hill!' said Harv.

'What's the phone number?' asked Chile. 'I'll check if anybody's home.'

The girl serving drinks had legs that would have done credit to a cossack. Yuri ordered two more beers and another vodka. His hand was throbbing again.

Chile returned.

'No answer. So the current Mr Westinghouse is either locked in one of his own refrigerators, or he's taken the family out.'

Rakov nodded. 'I'll pay you one thousand dollars each . . .'

'And all we can carry.'

'No.'

'Could be a fortune in a place like that. Split it three ways.'

Rakov said coldly: 'It's going to look like an ordinary burglary, but I'm not running the risk of being traced through you two. A thousand dollars each and I dispose of everything we take.'

'Fifteen hundred!'

Their attitude was unfortunate; for them. It emphasized

the risk they posed to Rakov. He would have to do something about it. He continued the negotiation. 'One thousand two hundred and fifty dollars; if we get in; if I get what I'm looking for.'

Harv was quickly on to the snag in that arrangement.

'We don't know what you're looking for. You could say anything. Twelve fifty if we get you in. The rest is your problem.'

'I agree.'

Chile added a note of caution.

'We need to pick up our . . . equipment.'

'No guns!'

'I don't use 'em.'

'No guns.' Rakov was looking at Harv, who shrugged.

They stopped at Harv's house, then the apartment building where Chile had his room.

When they reached the brownstone mansion on the East Side, an hour and a half had passed. Rakov insisted on one more phone call, to make sure nobody was at home. While Chile was using the telephone, Rakov found Harv's revolver, which he deftly removed. When Chile returned to say there was no answer, Rakov showed him the gun, and pressed it into the tender skin under Chile's jaw. Chile spread his arms and said:

'Search me. Just the blade. That's all I ever need.' It could have been a threat. Rakov handed Chile a pencil torch.

'When you're in and it's all clear, shine this once.'

'Aren't you joining us, Major?' Chile was sardonic.

'At these prices? Not initially.'

They were fast. In seven minutes there was a brief flash of torchlight from the ground floor.

Harv was perched on the fence. He grabbed Yuri's bad hand and jerked him over into the back yard. Rakov ground his teeth against the pain. The wound began bleeding again.

As soon as he saw the light glint against the opaque objet d'art in the Sheraton glass cabinet, Rakov knew he'd found the first piece of the Trinity. Was this Father, Son or Ghost? He didn't care. It was an omen. His luck was in.

'Fill your pockets. Only small objects. That silver cup, the clock, the two Meissen figures.' Pity about those!

They drove for three-quarters of an hour, and came to the river. The only light was the reflection of Manhattan's street lights from the low, scudding clouds. The dirty water at Brooklyn pier was flecked with jetsam, the short waves chopping at the gnarled timbers. There could have been a thousand eyes hidden in the shadows of the night. The only sounds were the water, and the background growl of New York's traffic. The far side of the river was in total darkness. He nodded at Harv and Chile.

'As far as you can.'

Silver ashtrays skimmed the water. The Meissen figures curved through the night air like grenades. Soon the last piece had gone.

Harv spoke quietly.

'Fucking waste! Could have made another grand on that lot.' He held out his hand to Rakov. 'You have something of mine, Major.'

Chile looked curiously at the KGB man. The criminal fraternity disliked political jobs. The rules were always changing. With the Organization, the game was profit and keeping the lip buttoned. The pay was good and lawyers appeared if things went wrong. If there were problems with a political job, people tended to disappear into the foundations of high rise buildings. So Chile was wary as he waited for the Russian to return Harv's gun.

Rakov used his good hand to draw out the revolver. He turned it over. Chile relaxed, comforted at the sign of the professional checking the safety. But the KGB major released the catch clumsily, with his left hand.

Chile was renowned for his speed with the blade. A firm

upward thrust and a close body was silenced in a second. He could pierce a six inch circle at twenty-five yards. As Rakov squeezed the trigger on Willet, Chile's right hand moved faster than ever before. He knew he was going to be too late. He registered Harv's falling body from the corner of his eye. He knew he shouldn't be looking there, that it was taking his concentration from the urgent job of getting out the knife, and throwing it to deflect Rakov's aim. He also registered the sound of the shot, vaguely surprised that it made so little sound against the background noises. A hundred yards away it would be mistaken for the slap of a boat against the quay.

It was the movement of Chile's body as his left shoulder went down and his right hand snaked behind his back to grip the knife that saved his life. The bullet hit his breast bone and glanced off. The force knocked Chile back, winding him, and pinning his right arm under his right hip, which was as far as he had managed to pull the knife on its journey from the sheath next to his spine.

Rakov thought he'd killed both men, so he now made a mistake. He glanced away to make sure Harv was dead, That gave Chile just enough time to get the knife clear of his body, bring it back over his head, and throw it. The blade entered the right shoulder, twisting as it sheared into the soft sinewy hollow between breast and shoulder joint.

The pain was bad, the arm paralysed. Rakov's left hand was useless for firing the gun. He used it to grip the handle of the knife and yanked it clear of the shoulder. The pain was terrible, but the muscles worked again.

Chile gasping, pushed himself to his feet. He had to make a choice; fight or flight. He chose the latter. Mistake. Rakov had time to take careful aim. He brought Chile down with a bullet in the thigh. He was grasping his shattered leg when Rakov put the third shot into the back of the South American's neck.

Rakov pushed his resources to the limit and managed to

get each body to the edge of the pier. He heaved and kicked Willet until he slid into the water. Then he remembered: the car keys were still in his pocket. Stretching at full length he managed a finger-hold on the collar of the jacket. He pulled the body against the tide. With pain suffusing every muscle he reached the pocket and the keys. Harvey Willet, face down, drifted away on the murky tide.

Rakov lay still, trying to summon seemingly non-existent energy. He began losing consciousness. What woke him was a sharp kick on the kneecap. Adrenalin flooded his system. Fear gripped. Incredibly, Chile had done it. Rakov was near the end. He didn't think he could fight any more. And then he looked into Chile's eyes. The kick had been the reflex of dying nerve ends. Inch by inch, Rakov eased the twitching corpse to the edge of the splintering, disused pier, and ultimately, head-first like a lazy seal, into the water.

The doctor had been recruited at university, at the dawning of his political conscience. At seventy he was still a committed Marxist. The noise of chattering filtered into the hall. He tried to send the KGB major away. Rakov prevented him closing the door in his face by falling full-length on the shaggy, off-white pile of the carpet. It made an interesting backcloth to the blood seeping from Yuri's shoulder.

'Get up!' hissed the doctor.

Rakov did his best. Eventually they reached the office. The doctor left him and returned, moments later, the red-stained rug in his arms. He inspected the wound, probing, ignoring Yuri's grunts of pain. He stood back.

'You need hospitalization.'

Rakov shook his head.

'There could be permanent damage to the arm and shoulder. You could lose the use . . . '

Rakov nodded in acceptance.

'It must have proper repair work under general anaesthetic. I don't have the facilities here.'

Rakov was not interested. He had remembered 'Father.' 'In the car. There's an ornament. On the back seat. Get it!'

The doctor was impatient. 'Forget about ornaments. You could die!'

Rakov was adamant. 'Do it!' The command was a croak, but it conveyed the urgency. 'And do it now!'

The doctor returned with the modern sculpture. To his dismay the major was on the telephone.

'See if you can get hold of the professor,' he gasped. 'I need to see him.'

'You want to talk to him, you mean,' said Viktor.

'No, I must see him.'

'He's not in town right now.'

'Get him to come over.'

Vilkov was in Russia. They both knew this.

'I don't know if I can.'

'Tell him I've made my first purchase.'

'Can't you describe it over the phone?'

'It's not that simple.' Rakov's mind refused to concentrate.

'Are you still there?'

The doctor put out his hand for the receiver.

'Give me that!'

It was enough. Rakov continued:

'Tell him . . . give him this message exactly. Father wants to see him, personally!'

The instrument clattered to the floor as Rakov fainted.

Date: 15 October 1981
Washington, D.C.

Pete Rogers was 'fighting' the telephone when Heidi entered with a sheaf of papers.

'You'd better read these, and quick.'

He glared at her. Ten minutes later he yelled: 'Heidi! Come in here!'

'Where's the fire?' she said, leaning against the architrave.

'They've wished some goddamn limey on us.'

'Why?'

'Liaison!'

'What does that mean?'

'Some asshole told the Brits about the Trinity so they want in on the action!'

'And that's an order?'

'It's not as simple as that. The Man wants to keep in with them. So we appear to co-operate . . . '

'But they don't get any goodies!' Heidi completed the sentence.

'Right on! Where's Tyson?'

'Nursing a sore head, if there's any justice.'

'You went out with him?'

'We painted certain places a nicer shade of pink.'

'What did you find out?'

Heidi reflected on her roisterous night.

'There's plenty of guile there. He means to travel through life in the fast lane. His family's got money, but he doesn't score until a couple of the old folk pass away. He's a good hard lay. He knows how to make a girl feel wanted. If he's being used by Lubbock and his aunt, he doesn't know it, or he's a good liar.'

Rogers made up his mind.

'I don't trust him. He doesn't know intelligence from pastrami pizza and he may have other loyalties. We'll need to put him where he can't do any harm.'

'How about wishing him on the Brit?'

'Now that, young lady, could be the brightest . . . '

The door burst open. Chuck Tyson showed no sign of a hangover, quite the reverse. His cheeks were ruddy with good health, the eyes sparkled, and his clothes . . . well his clothes . . .

Heidi said 'Oh!'

'Sorry I'm late, folks. I needed duds; to go with the image. What d'you think?' It was Ralph Lauren's latest casual look; brown bomber jacket with wide-bottomed cream slacks.

Rogers was not impressed. Heidi came to his rescue.

'Pete's been saving up for one of those outfits for years!'

Rogers was brisk. 'You're on a new assignment, as of this moment. Call the British Embassy. A guy called . . . Captain Richard Lloyd. And get dressed!'

'Jesus! What do I want with a limey?'

'We have orders to liaise with the Brits on Tesla.'

'Why me?'

'Let me tell you about intelligence. Army is all "Do this! Do that!" Intelligence is initiative. Guys who can think for themselves, who don't wait for orders at every intersection. Get out there. Follow up leads. Put your heads together. Come up with joint ideas. All I ask – the only order I'm giving you – is don't give him anything sensitive and keep in touch; once a day. Heidi'll give you a number, and a code name.'

'What do I do about back-up?'

'Are you thinking of starting a war?'

'What if we get into a situation where we need reinforcements?'

'Forget the army. We don't go in for shoot-outs at the KGB Corral!'

'Where do we start?'

'Heidi'll give you some background files. Take it from there. Go call the guy.'

Tyson closed the door behind him. Heidi raised her eyebrows.

'What's with you?' said Rogers.

Heidi was non-commital.

'Nothing . . . I just wondered . . . '

'Wondered what?'

'You just gave a rookie carte blanche. I hope you don't regret it.'

'What can they do? They don't know nothin' and we

won't give 'em nothin'. We got rid of two problems in one.'

Tyson was finishing his call when Heidi returned to her desk.

'Get Richard to give me a call.' He mouthed a kiss at Heidi, watching her open a wall safe. She found a name and lifted the telephone.

'This is one-one zero . . . I need clearance on a name: Capistrano – C.A.P.I.S.T.R.A.N.O. . . . OK. Put that down to one-one-zero . . . No, you don't get to know the name of the agent! Just patch through all messages from Capistrano to one-one-zero. Got it . . . ?'

Date: 15 October 1981
Colorado Springs, Colorado

Ruth closed Margaret Cheney's new biography 'Tesla: Man out of Time.' What it tell her? She gazed, unseeing, into her yard, Georgetown's swath of autumn colours making no impression. Cheney was more objective than earlier writers. She cast doubts. They gave Ruth pause. Had everybody been duped? Was he genius, or laboratory joker? Was the Tesla Trinity a con?

She remembered her father's friend who was something scientific in Colorado Springs. An old address book yielded his number. He confirmed that Tesla had blacked out the city, and was sued for it; also – Cheney's contradiction notwithstanding – that there were still folk who said he'd lit two hundred 50-watt bulbs, wirelessly, at a distance of twenty-six miles. She was wasting her time. Two thousand scientists in Russia, more, probably in the US, would have nailed a hoax years ago. She turned her attention to her business.

But Tesla wouldn't leave her alone. All morning his excursions out west intruded like an irritating melody. She re-read Cheney on 'Blackout in Colorado Springs.' It was 1899. He said he'd send a wireless message to the Paris Exposition. His timing was off but he did invent radio.

He'd conducted at least one experiment entirely alone. Foolhardy! Dangerous! But significant? Not for Ruth. If she'd believed in psychic powers she might have thought she was being sent to Colorado by the spirit of Tesla. Garbage!

But if you're rich – especially if you're very rich – you don't have to believe anything to indulge a whim. That's how Ruth justified it.

Her Learjet began its descent to Petersen Field. The telephone beside her buzzed. 'Darling, where are you?' asked Frederick.

'Oh dear!' thought Ruth. 'Colorado Springs?' she said sweetly, as though that was where everybody spent Thursdays in October.

'Without a word to your ever-loving!' There was a slight smile in his voice which took the romantic curse off the cliché.

'I'm sorry, darling. I tried to reach you but you were closeted with Chairman Mao or somebody, and this couldn't wait.' How, she wondered, was she suddenly able to lie with such glibness.

'What couldn't wait? If it's interesting I'll fly out and join you. I love the Broadmoor.'

That was not a good idea. 'You'd be bored silly. It's just another piece of ground for condos and a shopping strip. Besides you've got to get your show on the road.'

'If you say so.' But he obviously wasn't convinced. 'How long will you be gone?' There was something more than frustrated ardour in his voice.

'Just overnight.'

'I'll miss you?' he whispered. Were her ears deceiving her or had he moued a kiss down the line?

'Me, too. See you in the morning, honey,' and she firmly replaced the handset. If he persisted in hovering over her every step like a lovesick teenager, life was going to get difficult.

The jet banked over the huge expanse of desert and aimed at the foothills of the Cheyenne Mountains in the approach to the Municipal Airport.

The hotel limousine took her to the Broadmoor, not only one of the world's finest hotels with private zoo, it was a self-contained community with its own power station.

Half an hour later the man who was at school with her father joined Ruth in her suite. The now-retired, overweight, much-respected academic, and member of the governing body of Cheyenne College, tried to answer her questions.

'Tesla's not remembered too fondly here. He left a lot of debt. He smashed the main generators of the Electric Utility, with the result that very little remains of Nikola Tesla.'

What about his workshop? I know he built a huge facility. . .'

'We can't even agree where it was located. The best bet is down by the Deaf and Blind School. But there's nothing to see.'

'What happened to it?'

'Who knows! Got torn down for new construction?'

'How did he smash the generators?'

'Overload probably.'

'Only probably?'

The academic was hesitant.

'I'm a scientist by training. I don't like talking about things I can't prove.'

'You interest me.'

'I was afraid of that. You want me to speculate, in the hope it'll turn up some wonder from the past to explain one of his dizzy claims. I would if I could, even though I don't believe a word of it. Tesla was a great man, no doubt about it. Alternating current was a unique contribution. But what is conveniently forgotten is that he had a lot of lousy ideas, that never worked. He admitted as much. As he got older he didn't get wiser, just more stubborn about what he couldn't prove.'

'So you don't believe there ever could be a Tesla Shield?'

'I won't go that far. He may have found a new aspect of physics the rest of us have never dreamed of. Conventional theories are being stood on their ear every day with new discoveries in space, but I don't think you'll find anything in Colorado Springs.'

Ruth was disappointed, and knew she had no right to be. If you threw a million dollar jet and a few thousand bucks worth of fuel at a psychic whim what else should you expect? She was needled at her own stupidity. She went on, praying for any straw to grab at.

'You say there's nothing left of this building, but surely he left something of his work behind; perhaps only a momento,' Ruth persisted.

The laughter-lined, white-haired academic ruminated. 'There was something . . . I'm trying to think . . . to do with the physics laboratory. I remember.' He laughed again. 'You wouldn't be interested.'

'Try me,' said Ruth.

He chuckled.

'Tesla had an assistant, Fritz Lowenstein, a German. Worked with him here. He made a presentation to Cheyenne College, shortly after Tesla died.'

'What was it?'

'Lowenstein claimed it was part of the equipment that knocked out the generators, but I smelled a rat. I checked him out. It seemed Tesla never trusted him. He was supposed to give evidence in the dispute over the Marconi radio patents. At the last minute he switched sides and said Marconi got there first. Our Fritz was livid when Tesla won. I felt certain his gift was a sort of petty revenge.'

'Was it?'

'I couldn't prove it was a deliberate hoax.'

'Have you still got it?'

'I think so . . . We put our best brains on to it. They said it appeared to be a simple oscillator with no connection whatsoever with the Tesla Shield.'

Ruth's hunch was still nudging her.

'I'd like to buy it.'

The fat man's paunch heaved as he laughed again.

'Academic institutions don't sell their heritage!'

'Some heritage! If it'll ease your intellectual conscience, I'll make a donation.'

'On condition that . . . ?'

Ruth smiled.

Date: 15 October 1981
New York, N.Y.

Major Yuri Rakov scanned the newspapers for the second day in succession. There was no mention of the burglary at the Westinghouse home. Perhaps that was not so strange, burglaries were such a commonplace in New York. Yet the Westinghouse name was well-known. He gave up trying to ponder the mysteries of the capitalist press.

He looked through the Daily News. It was at the bottom of page two.

> *BODY RECOVERED* The corpse of a Caucasian male was fished out of the East River early today. Police said bullet wounds were found. Gangland execution?

Rakov shrugged. They had to die. They'd seen 'Father,' the first piece of the Trinity! They'd also shown signs of going into business for themselves; in time there would have been a demand for money, linked to threats. He was glad he'd closed that chink. He wished he knew more about police reaction to the Westinghouse break-in.

Vilkov arrived, officially supporting a communist-inspired peace campaign. He would appear on television, make a few speeches. As cover, it was a bit thin.

The meeting took place in the Waldorf Astoria Hotel. Rakov arrived first. A low level cut-out booked, signed in and left the key in the New York Times in the coffee bar. Rakov picked it up.

He handed Vilkov 'Father' and waited for the congratulations. Vilkov's eyes narrowed. Rakov had seen that look when he was about to tangle with 'Y'.

'What is this? A joke?'

'No professor. It's the first piece of the Trinity.'

'You make me leave important work in Moscow, make a journey of thousands of miles . . . for this!'

'It's exactly as you described. Translucent material. Not a recognized shape. Could be part of a bigger object . . .'

'*Durak neschastnii!* You incompetent idiot. This is nothing. An ornament. A cheap, *bliad* sculpture that was supposed to be a work of art fifty *bliad* years ago.'

Rakov was not used to being the butt of gutter language.

'Where did you get it?'

'In the Westinghouse home.'

'Did you take all their ornaments?'

'Just this one. It fitted your description, professor.'

'Don't put the blame on me. Show me the other pieces.'

'Other pieces?'

'You bring me all this way, just for this!'

Rakov's face said it all. 'How was I to know? I'm not a scientist!'

'They gave you the job because you're supposed to have intelligence. You could have described it over the telephone. I could have told you it was . . . nothing!'

Rakov had never made such a serious mistake. He dared not contemplate the consequences.

'You have other leads?'

Rakov looked away.

'It won't take me long to formulate another plan. The general has given me many names . . . '

'He's a fool, protecting his own arse with every name he could find. You began well; with Westinghouse. But remember, he died in 1914; probably before Tesla even made the model.'

Rakov was frightened. The extent of his failure could not be hidden. Then there were the bodies. Unnecessary murders were frowned on. Two hasty killings to protect a worthless ornament spelled serious trouble.

'Maybe the Westinghouse company has a museum. That's it . . .' Rakov tried to give himself confidence.

'Forget it,' said Vilkov.

'But . . .'

'There's no museum, just a historical society. It won't be there.'

'But you said Westinghouse . . .'

'You told me to check out the leads,' said Vilkov irritably. 'My whole damned department was disrupted trying to track down information KGB should have had on tap for you.' It was getting worse, thought Rakov. 'I told you to concentrate on Westinghouse. If you had . . .'

'I did! That's why . . .'

'Then I presume you know all about their time capsules.' said the professor, his jaw jutting out.

'Time capsules? Er . . . no. I'm afraid . . .'

'Yakushenko is an incompetent, sending you on a mission with no back-up facts! Typical of the military, and he has the nerve to call it intelligence! The time capsules are rocket-shaped containers made by Westinghouse as publicity stunts for the World's Fairs in New York in 1939 and 1963. They contain samples of everything anybody in five thousand years' time might want to know about our civilization.'

'How can they be of significance . . . ?' Rakov interrupted.

'Shut up and listen,' said Vilkov. He rummaged around in his briefcase found a small booklet and flung it at the KGB major. 'Read that. It tells you all about them.' Rakov flipped through the pages registering the diagrams but little else. The professor continued. 'This isn't my idea. It's what you might call a consensus of those who claim to have brains in Akademgorodok.' He told him about Charles F. Scott whose name had rung bells for somebody at

Novosibirsk. Old files were brought from the archives, many memories were checked. Moscow was making great play over its firsts in space ahead of the Americans. In 1963 they held gatherings at which the vodka flowed freely. Scientists from all over the world were invited, especially Yanks. Scott had rather a lot to drink and became indiscreet. 'The tapes were whirling away, of course', the professor continued, 'but the transcript is not too good. He claimed to have put something in one of the capsules.'

Rakov was studying the drawings. 'Not possible. Every inch is full.'

'Not in the nose cones,' said Vilkov.

Yuri looked again. 'True,' he said. 'What was it and what did it have to do with Tesla?'

'Scott worked with the great man for a year at Pittsburgh. Although he was – as he put it – a pain-in-the-ass to nearly everybody, he was a great inventor, and Westinghouse was making a fortune out of many of his patents. It was disgraceful that they didn't put anything of his in either capsule. After all, as he said, Einstein had his finger among the contributors.'

'Do you seriously put Tesla in the same category as Einstein?' Rakov wanted to know.

'Undoubtedly,' said the professor. 'Many would say his work was better.' Rakov was amazed. He knew Tesla was a name in his time, but had assumed because he was unknown to the general public that he would have been regarded as just another inventor.

'Tesla had sent Scott a present?' said Professor Vilkov.

'At first he thought it was a joke. Tesla wrote him a note with the gift; something about if he Scott, couldn't unravel its meaning, it would only be a matter of time before scientific advances caught up with his, Tesla's, invention, and then everybody would know what it was. Scott couldn't fathom it, so he decided to let posterity work it out in the nose cone of the capsule.'

'Are you telling me,' asked Rakov slowly, 'that one part of the Tesla Trinity is in one of those capsules. If so which one?'

'I'm not stupid, Rakov. I don't know where the hell they are. What I've given you is a best scientific guess; a possible lead, and I've no idea which capsule.'

Yuri read the booklet. 'These things are buried fifty feet underground . . .'

'Quite so,' said Vilkov.

'Next to a tidal river, in a swamp, under a public park . . . and within sight of a police precinct.'

'These are technical problems, beyond the scope of my department?' said the professor with disinterest.

'I'll have to see Scott, of course?' said Rakov, 'maybe even sweat him a little.'

'He died in 1944,' said Vilkov.

Rakov read on as he digested that fact. 'It says here they're encased in pitch-lined steel pipes, the voids are filled with concrete and there's a granite monument on top of them!'

'Yes . . . well . . . ' said Professor Vilkov, packing his case. 'You didn't expect it to be easy, did you Comrade Major?'

11

Date: 16 October 1981
Palo Alto, Ca./Washington D.C.

It felt like England. There was a cold snap to the air. The Learjet skimmed a bank of fog. The water below was grey, uninviting, crowned with white wisps. Ocean-going liners, tankers and cargo ships lined up for entry to the port facilities. But when Ruth deplaned the accents were American, the car was Cadillac, the chauffeur laid-back Californian; the city was San Francisco.

It was a boring twenty minute drive along the Bayshore Freeway. She came to the low Altos hills, and drove through the archway of magnolias to the business section of Palo Alto. The city was dominated and virtually owned by Stanford University. The road of waving palms that led to its picturesque chapel was grand enough for any movie setting. She passed white-railed paddocks with grazing horses, low-rise, high-tech buildings each one spawning a millionaire a day.

She had said she wanted the best, but most research was government-funded or carried out in universities. There was a guy, she'd been told. He was a genius. Christopher Hackett. Government had him on a retainer into six figures and he didn't even have to go to an office. He was a one-man problem solver. A maverick.

The sign read: 'Keep Out!' C. Hackett, Pres. It was not an imposing building. The old 'stick' construction badly needed a coat of varnish. Ruth was sure she had the wrong place. She consulted the note. Sombody had screwed up! He would pay! Having come this far she decided to take a look. Inside the lobby, papers were scattered haphazardly across an old oak table and scratched steel desk. Nobody attended the single telephone. Ruth put her parcel on the table and looked for a bell. No luck. There were two doors. The first was the lavatory, the second a sound-proof lobby. When she opened the second door a high-pitched screeching attacked her ear drums. An eighteen-year-old, wearing earphones, waved her away. She retreated, and waited. After several minutes the white-coated boy appeared. He was about five feet ten inches, and fresh-faced; she doubted he shaved yet. He held out a grease-stained hand.

'I'm Chris Hackett . . . '

Ruth looked at his hand and her own.

'Whoops,' he said. 'Sorry about the grease. You must be the lady I had a phone call about. I didn't get the name . . . '

'I don't give it until I see the set-up, and decide if I can do business. I don't think you're quite what I've been looking for . . . '

He laughed.

'Everybody says that.'

'And I need somebody with a little more experience.'

He was not put out.

'The face you mean. You think I'm sixteen. I'm thirty six . . . '

It was hard to credit.

'I had an accident. Gas furnace. Goddamn thing blew up. I lost most of my face. You're looking at a different part of my anatomy.'

His real age was in his eyes.

'Are you a one-man band?' she asked.

'Lunch break,' he answered.

'At four in the afternoon?'

'Sometimes it's midnight. That's how we work.' And his voice said that if she didn't like it, it was fine by him.

'How good are you?' As she said it she realized it was a stupid question. Anybody worth his salt would say he was the best.

'Somebody must have told you we know what we're

doing or you wouldn't be here.' That made a change! Understatement yet! It was getting more like Britsville by the minute.

'How about discreet?' She wondered how he would handle the question; it was the most important of all. He had no trouble. He was straightforward and direct. Then she knew what was different about him – apart from his face; he saw no need to sell himself, or his services. Very English!

'I'm no gossip. I don't talk about my work to people who have no right to know.'

'Right or need?'

'Whatever.'

'I want fast action and total confidence and I'm prepared to pay.' He smiled.

'If I'd taken that at its face value every time, I'd be a millionaire by now.'

'Don't bother,' said Ruth. 'It's over-rated.'

His laugh was an attractive sound. Mr Hackett was bright; relaxed, and confident, and, she guessed, tough. He would keep his client's secrets. She pointed to the brown paper parcel.

'That's what it's about. Take a look.' He lifted it, weighing it. He peeled away the corrugated paper.

'What is it?' he asked.

Ruth was disappointed.

'Don't you know?'

'Once upon a time it was . . . or had pretensions to be an oscillator.'

'Is that all you can tell me?'

'Where did you get it? What's its history?'

'I want to know everything about it. Everything its capable of. If it's broken I want it mended. Whatever it did, I want it to do it again. If it was part of something else, I want to know what. If you can't make that one work I want you to make another that does work.'

'Why?' was all he said.

'For money.'

'Not good enough.' He didn't care whether he got the job or not. Ruth was not used to that.

'I don't have to look for work. It comes to me. Like you. If money turned me on I'd have done something else. Persuade me that box of tricks is worth my time, I may give it a try.'

'With your attitude I'm surprised you get any work.'

'I'm busy, lady!'

'That is part of a machine Professor Nikola Tesla used to smash a whole power station.'

It began silently. The laugh built inside him. Ruth was not amused. That made it worse. The laugh burst out. A gale.

'What's so goddamn funny?' The fury in her voice had some effect.

'I'm sorry. I really am. But after the build-up . . . you're just another Tesla nut!'

Ruth put a thick envelope on the desk.

'Perhaps you'll be able to open that without bursting a blood vessel.'

The shape suggested dollar bills.

'Save it. My advice won't cost you a nickel . . .'

'Count the fucking money, scientist.'

He didn't want to. It was not his scene. But he wondered how much she thought the trinket was worth. Hundred dollar bills! All old notes! None in numerical sequence. A careful client; but she wasn't a client and he wasn't going to take her as a client. He had more important things to do. He gave up counting when he got to a hundred.

'Twenty-five thousand dollars?' he asked. She nodded. 'That changes nothing.'

'You're a goddamn freak! Arrogant to the point of blasphemy. Your disregard of money is an insult to the ethic that makes this country tick, and you're a pig-ignorant half-baked so-called scientist who couldn't tell a retort if it barked at you.'

The inanity of the pun hit them both at the same time, and they both burst into laughter.

Members of staff began trickling back from their break. They looked at their boss and his visitor and smiled at their helpless laughter.

He was the first to speak. 'I don't want your money, lady . . . '

His eyes were definitely not those of a teenager. They were wise windows to an interesting person.

'My name is Ruth.'

'Truly, Ruth. I don't want it. But you make me laugh, and there ain't too many laughs in my business. I'll tell you what I'll do. Because I like you. The craziest reason for doing anything in business.' She smiled in sympathy with the thought. 'There's a piece of equipment I can't afford. I may never use it. But a combination of circumstances could happen when it would avert a disaster and save many lives.'

'What sort of disaster?'

'Now I'm going to talk about discretion and confidence.'

'How much?'

'Seventy-five thousand bucks.'

Ruth didn't hesitate.

'One condition. You start work now!'

'When I get my equipment. I'm busy right now.'

'If I'm right and you're wrong, you realize this could be rather a dangerous item.'

'There's no chance of that.'

'Even so. You tell nobody but me, and that goes for any other wise guy working on it.'

'Anything you say, Ma'am.'

'Ruth!' she said.

'Ruth!' said he. 'How do I get in touch with you?'

'Don't call me . . . as they say . . . ' smiled Ruth.

'I work all hours. D'you wanna know when I crack the dangerous secret, or wait until there's a break in your social calendar?'

'Don't write it down, and don't tell others. My name is

Coverdale. You can always reach me through this number. No elaborate messages. Just leave your number and I'll call you back.'

Date: 16 October 1981
Flushing Meadow, New York

The first problem was getting into Flushing Meadow Park. Rakov had driven under the ELS – the elevated train system – three times. He had passed alongside the park for twenty minutes before he eventually found his way in. There were a number of shocks. The Shea Stadium drew thousands of New York Jet fans on a Sunday. There was a police precinct within five hundred yards of the monument, with blue-and-whites coming and going day and night. The burial site of the Westinghouse Time Capsule was in full view of a hundred foot high restaurant, and the park was the stomping ground for kids with footballs, assorted joggers and dog-lovers.

Viktor's value became apparent when Rakov laid the difficulties before him. In twenty-four hours he'd assembled a team of KGB technicians and equipment.

Within one hundred and twenty feet of the capsules was the only building they might be able to use as cover. It was once a pièce-de-résistance of the World's Fair; a circular open structure, futuristic in design, a mass of interlocking steel tubes with a roof made of open wire strands converging on a centre; the wind whistled through the wires making them sing. At the base was an anular enclosed brick-built service corridor, all its entrances sealed.

It had not taken a KGB technician three minutes to remove the sealing screws and enter the service area. At the point nearest the capsules was a lavatory, with a manhole giving access to a drainage chamber a few feet down. It was enough, said the KGB men; from there a start could be made. Rakov wondered how. He didn't have too long to wait. As darkness fell, a nondescript truck was driven into the car park nearby, over the grass and into the centre of the wire-roofed building. A team of eight manhandled machinery and equipment into the corridor. In just twenty-seven minutes, the task was accomplished, the truck and all but five men gone; all apparently undetected.

The major was nervous. The whole affair was too complicated. He hated having to rely on so many people. Every extra body multiplied the opportunities for things to go wrong. He had to use high technology equipment which could easily break down, and a noisy digger within feet of people and dogs. The capsule was below the level of a tidal river, four hundred feet away, which meant the continual risk of flooding. The recovery of the capsule was estimated to take three to four days; Rakov plus five men would be holed up in the tunnel and had to be fed and watered. A succession of look-outs was posted, round-the-clock; an almost impossible task, as they had no cover. Rakov banned the use of machinery the first night. The men worked with pickaxes and shovels.

The first watchers were a young couple in the back seat of a rented Chevrolet in the car park. A blue-and-white joined them at two a.m. The couple were taking their work so seriously they did not hear it until its door was slammed. A panic whispered call on the intercom called a halt to Rakov's work. The couple were moved on. Rakov stopped further digging until the fresh couple arrived.

By three thirty-five a.m. the hole was a cube of roughly six feet. The intercom crackled into life again.

'Police approaching,' said a female voice.

The men ceased work. The girl in the car left the radio on transmit.

'Ain't you guys got homes to go to?'

'I'm sorry, officer. Are we doing something wrong?'

'Don't ask me, buddy. What's the lady got to say?'

'He's my boyfriend.'

'Do you have some ID?'

'Yes . . . ' There was a silence. Ultimately the police voice spoke again.

'It's an offence to behave in an obscene manner in a public place . . . '

'But nobody can see inside this . . . '

'I can and I did. What I saw was obscene by legal definition . . . '

'Officer. I can't afford to have a scandal . . . '

'You gotta wife too?'

'It's not that . . . '

'Shut up and listen. Make yourselves decent and report to the precinct in five minutes. We'll let the sergeant decide.'

Rakov waited until he heard a door slam before speaking.

'Gene, this is Harry. Is anybody else on standby to take your place?'

'No. But I can make a call as soon as we get away from the precinct. Or should we make a run for it?'

Rakov was quick to kill that idea. 'Act normally for God's sake. Did they show any sign of interest in us?'

'I don't think so.'

Rakov waited an hour. A new voice spoke; same codename.

'Hello, Harry. This is Gene. Do you read me?'

'Loud and clear,' said the major.

'There's nobody in sight. You can carry on now.'

By first light the team leader pronounced himself satisfied with the depth and size of the chamber and he was ready to start using the probe.

'How much noise will it make?' Rakov wanted to know.

'If the soil is swampy and there aren't too many rocks, it shouldn't be heard more than a few feet away. It's more a whine than a grinding noise. It's only a few inches in diameter and it just pushes its way through the ground.'

'How will it find the capsule?'

The team leader hesitated.

'We don't have too much to go on, major. We're using a type of echo sounder that will send back a signal when it homes in on ferrous metal. The time capsules seem to be made of copper, chrome and silver . . . '

'Which are non-ferrous and will give you no reading?' said Rakov.

'Right,' replied the engineer. 'But they do have an outer steel casing which should give us what we need. We already have a compass bearing on the granite monument, so we know roughly the direction.'

'The problem is the depth?'

'Right.'

'How about the power?' asked Rakov.

'The original electrical supply is still here. It was sealed off at the meter. No problem.'

'Get on with it.'

The whirring noise sounded too loud. Rakov halted it.

'Gene, this is Harry . . . ' he spoke into his radio.

'Go ahead, Harry.'

'We're going to be making a noise. Get out and walk about. Tell me if you hear anything.'

Rakov looked at the team leader and nodded. He switched on the probe. It was an odd sight. The small metal device had vanes which ejected in a flick-knife action to give it purchase, and the nose began a corkscrew movement boring its way into the earth, trailing its power line behind it. After a few minutes the metal tube completely disappeared and the only sign of its presence was the narrow power cable slowly being sucked into the earth.

'Hello, Harry. This is Gene . . . '

'Come in, Gene.'

'We can hear something a few feet from the wall where you are. Anybody who knew the area might want to investigate.'

'Thank you, Gene. Keep watch.'

The team leader looked up from his instrument panel.

'As we get deeper the noise level will reduce outside. Get him to walk round again in a couple of hours.'

At five minutes past noon on 17th October the team leader announced that he was locked on to a capsule.

'Which one?'

The leader shook his head.

'No way of knowing at this stage.'

'That means using the noisy stuff now?' asked Rakov.

The man nodded. Rakov looked at his watch.

'You'll have to wait two hours. Get some sleep.' He put one man on watch. He and the others climbed into sleeping bags.

The helicopter was Rakov's idea. A librarian from Upper New York State, posing as a Harvard historian, made a four-hour aerial survey of Flushing Meadow Park for educational purposes. The formalities were observed; police were notified and air traffic control OK'd it. It had the merit of not only drowning the noise of the drilling, it also made passers-by look up, which stopped them thinking about what was going on beneath their feet.

An unexpected problem was finding enough dogs to accompany the daytime look-outs. Few Russians kept them. They eventually managed to find three to accompany walking sentinels. The helicopter made off south at six p.m. Rakov ordered a rest period.

After thirty minutes Rakov spoke on the radio.

'Gene, this is Harry. We're starting now. Report anything you hear.'

'Harry, this is Gene. Understood.'

The mandrill was a two-foot diameter corkscrew with a tapering body, the operator steering it from the rear. The first part of the casing of the mandrill was threaded to give bite and drive. The remainder was smooth to polish the walls of the bored hole. The corkscrew plunged into the soil scooping up dirt and spewing it out the back. The hole was just big enough to take a man's body.

The first four hours were productive and without incident. The team leader was operating the mandrill, and loading the soil on to a sled which was hauled back to the enlarged manhole. From there it was shovelled into a wheelbarrow and piled along the corridor. The probe reported that the capsule was forty-seven feet below the monument, some one hundred and twenty-one feet distant, and on a known bearing. The soil was damp but not soggy.

Golitsyn was the next man to go down. Forty feet excavated, eighty to go! Rakov was pleased with progress. At this rate they would be out in under three days.

At the precinct, Officer Pierce, a Brit from Belize, who had settled in New York ten years previously, reported interference on his car radio. Nobody took any notice. He had a reputation as a perfectionist and pain-in-the-ass.

The mandrill went silent. Rakov talked to the look-out.

'Tell me what you see and hear, Gene.'

'There is a noise if I listen real hard. I can also feel it. But nobody seems to be aware of it.'

'We'll carry on. Out.' said Rakov.

The team leader gave the order over his telephone line with Golitsyn. Nothing happened. He spoke again. There was no response. The leader grabbed a face mask and air tank, dropped into the hole and scurried the length of the bore. Golitsyn was lying face down in water, no face mask. He tugged at Golitsyn's feet. No reaction. He couldn't reach his face. He hauled and heaved at the body, eventually getting him on to the sled. He tugged frantically at the line, scrambling backwards.

Mouth-to-mouth resuscitation brought Golitsyn back to life, but barely. He would be no use for further work. That would mean a greater load on the others. Durasov was next. The leader made him don the mask and switch on the compressed air before he left the hole. His first job was to report the performance of the pump. It was holding its own against the water. Another twenty feet had been dug when Gene called:

'Hold it! Problems!'

A police car was cruising slowly by and the driver seemed to be listening out. Officer Pierce was instantly alert when he picked up the faint voices of 'Gene' and 'Harry.' He stopped the car. The speaking ceased. He waited. It was not repeated. He got out. He saw a few cars in the park, a middle-aged woman ith a poodle, and two teenagers punting a football. He climbed back into his vehicle and adjusted the tuner on his radio. Nothing. He shrugged and drove off. Sunday was his day off and he was going to the ball game. He was an avid fan of the Jets.

The leader called Durasov back to the surface.

'We need to make a chamber.'

'What for?' Rakov wanted to know.

'It's too far to haul the soil, and we need somewhere as a staging post.'

'We're not climbing Mount Everest.'

'The principles are the same.'

'The longer we take, the greater the risk of discovery. We go on. No chamber!'

The team leader had no love of the KGB. He was a specialist engineer with an excellent work record and was highly regarded by the Party.

'I shall not continue. It would prejudice the mission.' He turned to Durasov. 'Pack up the equipment!'

Rakov couldn't afford another failure.

'All right, I agree, but if we're discovered it'll be on your head.'

The engineer nodded.

It took all night to make a hole roughly six-by-six-by-six in feet. The walls and sides were shored with timber. A look-out reported he could hear nothing when the chamber was being built. Rakov called off the car couples, and they worked through the night with no watchers.

By dawn on 18th October, they were ready to start the mandrill again. Another jogger reported vibrations under foot, but no perceptible noise.

A bird-watcher received permission to erect his makeshift hide of khaki plastic sheeting. The sergeant thought he was crazy. What birds could one observe in a city park hard by the highway? But it was harmless. The KGB ornithologist stayed in the bushes a hundred yards from the monument. He saw no reason to report the approach of Officer Pierce, who looked like any other Jet's fan in his blue jeans and walkman headset. The birdwatcher's radio was on transmit. Officer Pierce stopped a few feet from the Westinghouse granite slab. He cocked his head to one side. He tuned the dial on his radio. He lifted an earphone. He was puzzled. He heard through the speakers exactly what he heard without them. That was impossible. Then he noticed the sensation through his sneakers. (He took off the headset and listened). At this precise moment the bird watcher talked to Rakov.

'We have a visitor, Harry. Hold the drilling.'

Date: 18 October 1981
Washington, D.C.

They met at the Chagall bar. Lloyd was not impressed with his American counterpart. First impressions suggested a typical Ivy League hustler; brash, venal, with inherited arrogance oozing out of every Bostonian orifice, and the certainty that every problem could be solved with a bout of fisticuffs.

Tyson had a cold. He was confused and fed up. He loathed the British. They were stuck-up losers with no sense of humour and absolutely no appreciation of the finer things in life, like the profit motive.

'Is this really Chagall's work?' asked Richard Lloyd.

'Fake, but it catches the Russian and the Jewishness of his work,' replied Tyson.

'I'm impressed.' And he was.

'What d'ya wanna drink?'

'Gin-and-tonic?'

Lloyd knew it was unwise to pour ice-cold gin on to jet lag, but Tyson struck a nerve.

It was happy hour. Lloyd began to feel aggressive as he sipped the fourth gin. He boasted about Yugoslavia. Chuck didn't believe it. He retaliated by exaggerating his own importance in Alaska. Lloyd doubted that even Americans would have put such a person in the front line of their defences. Tempers began to boil, assisted by the alcohol. The manager of the bar watched the drinks going down, wondering if it would be necessary to ask them to leave, when Tyson got to his feet. Lloyd was just upright when Chuck threw a punch. It missed. They grappled, falling in a heap, collapsing the adjoining table, to the displeasure of the two blue-rinsed political wives enjoying their weekly character assassination.

It would ruin business for days. Tyson and Lloyd were deposited unceremoniously on to the street.

'What the hell did that prove?' asked a very angry Lloyd.

'It made me feel better.'

Lloyd's legs gave way. He slumped on the sidewalk, the continued effects of jet-lag, booze and a sore head getting their revenge. Tyson dragged him to his feet and flagged down a cab. The driver eyed them suspiciously, and reluctantly let them in. He closed and locked the glazed partition, and then used central locking on the rear doors.

'Don't give me no trouble or I head straight for the precinct!'

Tyson gave Ruth's address and concentrated on nursing his knuckles. Lloyd passed out.

Date: 18/19 October 1981
Flushing Meadow, N.Y.

Officer Pierce felt the vibrations underfoot. He put his hand down but felt nothing. He sat and still felt nothing. He donned the earphones. Nothing! He put them on and off. He heard the sounds of the park without them but not now with them on. He was baffled. He gave up. He was in his car, his hand on the ignition when the voice said, loud and clear: '*Vsyo nomalno. Devay, Harry, prodolzhay.*'

He whirled, searching for some clue to the voice. The park told him nothing.

Underground the mandrill was going full blast so was the water pump. They were forced to evacuate the tunnel when the rising tide threatened. Two hours elapsed before the leader deemed it safe to continue.

'We're there, Leader,' said Durasov.

'What can you make out?'

'Just a steel casing.'

'No marks?'

'No.'

'How long's it been there?'

'Can't tell.'

The leader spoke to Rakov.

'I'm going down.'

'It's two a.m. Monday morning. We've been here nearly three days. We've got to get it out before daylight.'

'Not a chance,' said the leader. 'Golitsyn. Make yourself useful. Work out how much compressed air we have left.'

Two and a half hours later the leader returned to the surface.

'We've found it. I drilled past the first one and then compared the age of the two casings. I'm pretty sure I know which is which.'

'How long to get it up?'

'Eight . . . maybe ten hours.'

'Minutes, you mean.'

'It weighs nearly a thousand pounds. It's sticking straight up. We have to make a chamber round it, to let it fall, hook a line to the eyepiece and drag it out.'

Rakov shook his head.

'Our luck can't hold.'

Golitsyn reported they had compressed air for two men for seven hours.

At eight o'clock that morning Officer Pierce handed in a written report.

'Vibrations!' said the duty sergeant. 'Ain't it occurred to you, peabrain, that the highway to La Guardia and Kennedy is right next door; not to mention the Els . . . '

'It's a different sort of vibration.'

'And have you never heard of CB radio! If the lieutenant reads this he'll send you to the nuthouse.'

'They know my reputation. I'm never wrong on something like this.'

'I remember a few false alarms that wasted thousands of man hours . . . '

'I caught three kidnappers when nobody else had a clue!'

'OK. I'll put it up.'

'When?'

'When I feel like it!'

The team leader appeared, grimy and exhausted. Rakov helped him out. 'Well?' The leader nodded. 'Good!' said Rakov. 'Start hauling away.'

The leader put out his hand. 'No.'

'What's wrong now?'

'It's too heavy.'

'What d'you mean?'

'We need block and tackle.'

It was nine-thirty a.m. on Monday 19th October. The ropes of the highly geared tackle inched the Westinghouse

Time Capsule through the sloping tunnel to the surface.

Officer Pierce heard and felt nothing, but he was curious about a line of subsidance that was not there on Sunday. He decided to see the lieutenant.

By ten thirty-eight the nose cone of the capsule emerged.

'Get the cap off!' commanded Rakov.

The team leader, totally exhausted, shook his head.

'Get the fucking cap off and that's an order.'

'Can't be done. Not here. We need to get it into a workshop with heavy equipment.'

'Use force. Anything to get it out and . . . '

'Risk damaging the contents?'

Rakov couldn't afford another mistake.

The team leader spoke to the birdwatcher. 'We need the truck, now!'

'Hold it, Harry,' was the intercom response. 'The policeman was here. He went away in a bit of a hurry. I think he found something.'

Rakov was livid with the engineer. 'I told you this would happen if we were down here too long.'

'I've done my job, Major, as fast as possible. It's your problem.'

Rakov grabbed the transmitter.

'Tell me when the truck's at the car park.'

The police lieutenant examined the area.

'What's so unusual about a dent in the grass!'

'It wasn't there yesterday!' said Pierce.

Then a section of earth subsided and the granite monument to the Westinghouse Time Capsules gently tilted.

'What did I tell you, lieutenant?' said Pierce smugly.

'Get the City Engineer here, on the double!'

The Dodge truck emerged from the wire-roofed building picking up speed as it crossed the grass.

'Hey there! Stop!' The lieutenant shouted. Officer Pierce

took aim and fired. The lieutenant knocked his hand just in time to prevent the premature demise of a five-year old and his mother.

Date: 19 October 1981
Georgetown, Washington, D.C.

Richard Lloyd wondered what had persuaded him to drink so much. He didn't need it, he certainly didn't feel in the mood for a binge. Thinking back on it he was surprised the comparatively few drinks he'd had – he had a very unhealthy tolerance for alcohol – could have affected him so much.

'Where are you?' Major Arthur Forbes asked down the telephone line.

'Washington, sir. As ordered.'

'Georgetown?' Chuck added.

'Where exactly?' pressed Forbes.

'I'm with Captain Tyson. At his family home in Georgetown.'

'Ah! . . . ' Lloyd wondered what that meant. 'You don't sound too good, Lloyd.'

Richard dealt with that smoothly. 'Bit of a headache, major. Jet lag. Didn't sleep too well.' It seemed to satisfy the major.

'What have you got to report?'

'I'm just checking in, sir. Captain Tyson and I will be sitting down to review the situation right away.'

'Don't sit on your arse all the time! And remember not to take the word liaison too literally,' said Arthur Forbes. Lloyd looked across at Tyson hoping he hadn't heard the last sentence, knowing he had to play games with him. 'And by the bye,' added the major, 'we've had our first report from the man in white.' Lloyd didn't know what he was talking about. 'No names, but your friend from Guildford' – Ah! Butterworth – 'He's in good health and enjoying the climate.' So he'd got in and out clean at least once. Would he be able to do it repeatedly?

'Has he had any more luck than me?' asked Lloyd innocently.

'Can't answer that. You don't have the security clearance for that information,' said Forbes pompously. Oh! yes, thought Richard. 'Keep in touch,' said the major and broke the connection.

Chuck handed Richard a tall glass of tomato-coloured liquid. 'Can't stand the stuff,' was Lloyd's reaction.

'This is special,' said Tyson. 'Cook makes it. Own recipe. Just the thing for your . . . headache. Down it in one.'

Lloyd eyed it suspiciously, took a breath, and launched his mouth at the liquid. He was three-quarters of the way down the glass when he realized it was fifty per cent vodka. He choked. Tyson watched him coughing and spluttering.

'You'll feel better now.'

'Don't ever do that to me again,' said Richard.

'You got any ideas where we begin?' asked Tyson.

'You're on the ground. This is where Tesla did his thing.'

Tyson wasn't about to give his ideas away.

'What's it worth?'

'What's what worth?'

'Information.'

'You mean money? You want me to pay you . . . '

'Trade-off!' said Chuck.

'I don't understand.'

'I've got something you want: what've you got I want?'

'Are these your orders?'

'Initiative. That's my orders. What's yours?'

'Liaison, which means working together! I'll share information with you, but I'm buggered if I'll horse trade.'

'What've you got?'

'Yugoslavia, for starters!'

'I told you about Alaska. Evens.'

'I'd already been briefed on the radar, Riga and the weather. You told me nothing. You owe me.'

'OK! . . . The secret's in the question of age. Tesla's friends, workmates were all his generation. I checked out his closest people and their known relatives. It was a hell of a job, but I've got a few possibles.'

'Give me your favourite.'

It went against the grain but he gave it.

'Ever heard of Kolman Czito?'

'And his son Julius? Who made the Trinity!'

'OK smartass. Julius had a daughter.'

'Did he now!'

'She's about forty-five . . . '

'That would make her seven when Tesla died. Not much of a lead!'

'That's not the point, Dick. Her old man didn't die 'til 1962. He must have talked about Tesla to her. Genius. All that.'

'That's not bad,' said Lloyd. 'How do we find out where she is now?'

'She's married to a top sergeant in the air force in Atlanta, Georgia. I'm not just a loud mouth. Under this brash exterior there's an intellectual genius just waiting to break out.'

12

Date: 19 October 1981
Atlanta, Georgia

Lloyd was not feeling well. The previous night's alcohol had not cleared the system when they boarded the Delta Boeing 727 for Atlanta. Clear air turbulence was now passing unpleasant messages to his stomach.

'I'm not sure we should be going to Atlanta,' said Lloyd.

'Why not?'

'I saw them make lightning and thunder, in Yugoslavia . . . '

'Oh yeah!'

'There were transformers and bloody great coils all over the place . . . '

'You told me. Last night.'

'Did I tell you about Tesla and Colorado Springs?'

'How he put the electric company out of business?'

'Yes!'

'We should be going there. That must be a lead of some sort.'

'Stop griping. A live one in Atlanta's better than an eighty-year-old power cut.'

Lloyd was glad when the 727 finally hit the ground and the air pockets stopped bruising his stomach.

Tyson used a payphone to call the office and let Heidi know where they were. She bawled him out for not using the Capistrano routine. She added: 'The ordure just hit the wind machine!'

'What?'

She told him about the theft of one of the Westinghouse time capsules. All Chuck could remember was doing a project on them at school. 'So what!' was Chuck's comment.

'The boffins reckoned it must have contained one of the three whatsits.'

'That's pretty way out!'

'They got everybody out of bed at Westinghouse, Pittsburgh, and that's the way it looks right now. I gotta go.'

Chuck called Georgetown to tell Ruth. She was away. There was no answer from the general.

'Any news?' Richard enquired.

'Nope,' said Tyson.

'Then why are you looking so . . . harassed?'

'I need thinking time.'

'Not that old barter routine!'

Tyson reckoned that if the Soviets had the first piece of the Trinity there wasn't a lot of point in holding back on the Brits. He told him.

'How will they get it out of the country?' Richard wanted to know. 'Diplomatic bag?'

Tyson shook his head. 'With something that important we'll X-ray everything and to hell with protocol. The KGB'll work that one out.'

'You can't monitor all the people who leave!'

'That's not as tough as it sounds. All hand luggage is X-rayed. We'll do the same for the hold.'

'How about the Mexican border?'

'Possible.'

'A private yacht could rendezvous with a Soviet submarine . . .'

'This is a job for blanket coverage by CIA and FBI and Customs and Immigration, but we could still lose out.'

'Has this information been given to our people?'

Tyson shrugged.

'I guess they'll be a bit busy for liaison . . . '

'I'll call the embassy. Let them . . . '

'Let them get on with it, man! We've got work to do!'

They took a cab to the First National Bank.

'What's this place in aid of?' asked Lloyd.

'Shakin' any tail. Walk! And keep your eyes open.'

It was a futile exercise. Downtown was crowded with people. A dozen KGB could have been following them. Tyson led the way into the black phallic symbol that is the hallmark of rebuilt Atlanta, the Peachtree Plaza Hotel. He rented a Hertz Skylark.

Tyson drove, using the Cobb Parkway exit to Dobbins Air Force Base. They found the street and number. The woman was remarkable for the clear, slate blue of her eyes.

'Mrs Brown?' enquired Chuck.

'Yes . . .'

'I called you yesterday, from Washington . . . Chuck Tyson, Central Intelligence Agency. This is Richard Lloyd from British Military Intelligence. May we come in?'

She hesitated, then stood aside.

'Is anything wrong?' asked Lloyd.

She started at the English accent.

'I already had a woman from CIA this morning . . .'

Tyson dealt with that smoothly.

'We've got so many people working on this thing we're tripping over each other.'

Her eyes had dark rings, her complexion was pallid. She was full of pent-up anxiety. Tyson seemed not to notice.

'We're here because of your father's connection with Nikola Tesla, and your grandfather's. We'd like you to tell us about it.' But Mrs Brown was still on the other subject.

'She had an accent, but it wasn't British. More like French or something like that.'

Tyson looked at Lloyd. KGB?

'Do you have identification?' she asked.

Tyson hadn't thought of that one. But he went smoothly into improvised patter.

'You should know better than that, Mrs Brown. CIA's

undercover. We don't carry cards in case . . . well you know . . . in case we get into a problem with the other side . . . '

'D'you have anything to tell me?'

It was a strange question.

'Excuse me?' said Chuck.

'Do you have a message for me?'

Lloyd felt they would get nowhere with Mrs Brown. He doubted if she was *compos mentis*.

'I'll give you the number of the CIA office in Washington. They'll vouch for me.'

'You gonna pay for the call?'

'Sure!' replied Tyson. 'Call collect.'

Mrs Brown dialled the operator. 'My name is Mrs Brown. I want to call a number in Washington. A government office, collect . . . ' She gave the number and waited. 'Tell them I have a Mr Chuck Tyson who says he's one of their agents and that they'll pay for the call . . . Thank you operator . . . Would you stay on the line please . . . ' She gave them an uncompromising look. 'They never heard of you. You're phonies!'

Tyson reached for the phone. 'Let me talk to the goddamn number . . . '

Mrs Brown continued evenly. 'I want you to leave my house right now or I get the operator to call the police.'

'Jesus, Mrs Brown,' said Tyson. 'D'you think I'd give you the number if I wasn't the genuine article . . . '

'Right now!'

She meant it.

Lloyd took Tyson's arm. 'There's no more for us here, Chuck. Our apologies, Mrs Brown. It's our fault . . . '

'Our fault, shit!'

'Shut up, Tyson,' said Lloyd mildly. 'We'll be back with official identification; if you want it, a police escort. We apologize for the inconvenience.'

He pushed Tyson firmly through the door.

'Stupid bitch! And you grovelled . . . I practically had

her. If only you'd kept your fucking English accent out of it . . .'

'She'd have called the fuzz . . .'

'Never!'

'I was watching while you were talking. We'd have been picked up. It would've taken a week to talk ourselves out of that mess. I don't know about you, but I can do without that sort of hassle.'

Tyson realized the trouble he'd have been in, not only with Rogers, for blowing his cover, but with the general. He didn't fancy facing that man after he'd screwed up.

'I need sleep.'

They checked into the Marriott Hotel at the junction of I-75 and the Perimeter 285.

Tyson awoke to a hammering on his door. The luminous clock fixed to the bedside table read 7.12 a.m.

'Go away!'

'Open up!' said Richard Lloyd, banging on the door again. 'We've got to get moving.'

Tyson staggered to the door.

'I've been on to the embassy,' said Richard. 'I think you call it pay dirt. Forbes has a contact in the Russian Embassy. He listened in on a phone call, a Southern accent; spoke about a ship leaving; the need to get the thing on board by morning.'

'That's all?' enquired Tyson.

'What do you want? Miracles?'

'It could be anywhere . . . nothing to do with the Trinity . . .'

'Right, but at this time . . . with the urgency . . . something had to be on board in a hurry, AND it's a ship. That's the easiest way to smuggle anything out of the country. How can we find out what Russian ships are . . . ?'

'That's not too difficult.' Tyson picked up the phone.

Ten minutes later he had three names and three ports.

'Take your pick. Long Beach, California; New York, Pier thirty-three; Savannah, Georgia.'

'Don't let's jump to conclusions. The Southern accent may mean nothing,' cautioned Lloyd.

'Long Beach is three thousand miles from where they pinched it,' said Chuck.

'By plane, nothing.'

'Still got to make a connection. Five hours in the air . . .'

'New York's the closest.'

'Are all these ships Russian?' asked Lloyd.

'One's East German.'

'Which?'

'Long Beach, California. I don't think they'd risk New York. The place'll be crawling with Feds and us. I don't rate Long Beach. It's five hours on a plane before they start.'

'And the German Democratic Republic is not always a favourite son of Mother Russia,' Richard added.

'Has Forbes told CIA about this?'

Lloyd wondered if Forbes would have decided to keep the information to himself. He played safe: 'Bound to have done!'

'So what do we do?' asked Chuck.

'Your boss told you to use your initiative. Mine told me the same. Let's do it?' said Lloyd wondering what.

Date: 20 October 1981
Washington, D.C.

Ruth was tired. She'd had a couple of days in Malibu to think through the complications in her life, professional and private. The result was sleepless nights and no solutions. She'd roused her pilot at 3 a.m. They'd hit thunderstorms and down draughts. She'd been airsick.

Jack Lubbock was at the gate to meet her, agitated. 'Where the hell have you been? Everything's been happening and it's all bad.'

That's when she saw Frederick, wide smile, running towards her.

Even Ruth's voice was tired as she said, gently: 'Get lost Jack. Just for me.'

'The Russians have beaten us to it. Pentagon thinks it's a joke. Stallybrass has made the Man put some beef into the CIA and FBI effort . . . '

He turned to follow her. She let her husband hug her. He kissed her deeply. Frederick saw Lubbock. He disengaged.

'How come I have to find out your movements from your secretary while generals have appointments?'

'I couldn't reach her either, Fred. Annie told me too.'

'What are you two up to?'

Ruth spoke directly to Lubbock, with meaning: 'I don't want to talk about your magazine now, Jack. I need a little time with my husband.'

'Magazine!'

She'd forgotten to tell him of her lie.

'Don't tell me you've come up with some other crackpot scheme . . . ' Ruth continued.

'Magazine? Crackpot? What're you talking about?'

'Don't call us! We'll call you!' said Ruth, and turned her back on the general.

Frederick raised the electric partition in the Rolls Royce Phantom Five. The chauffeur stared straight ahead.

'I think you'd better tell me about it, Ruth. And by the way, where've you been? I don't like my wife's secretary treating me like a syndication salesman.'

'I went to the cottage at Malibu. I thought you'd have guessed.'

'I rang. All day Tuesday.' She was in San Francisco.

'I walked the beach. I needed to think.'

'About Jack Lubbock?'

Ruth didn't know what he was getting at.

'What about Jack?'

'You're having an affair with him, aren't you?'

'Me and that gnarled old soldier! D'you really think . . . ?'

'I doubt if it's Stallybrass!'

She'd forgotten what jealousy could be like in a young love. 'There's nobody else.'

'D'you expect me to believe that? When every five minutes I see you closeted with the man, secret assignations?'

'Yes, and because I say so, and I'm your wife, a fact you've only recently seemed to notice.'

He acknowledged the truth of that. 'So what did you need to think about on the Malibu beaches?'

'You.'

'Oh! Did you reach any conclusions?'

'Not that I'll discuss in the back seat of a car.'

Frederick took her overnight Gucci case.

'We can talk in the bedroom . . . '

'I know where that'll lead. Let's go into the den.'

It was at the garden level, oak-panelled, with brown hide furniture, not unlike a London gentleman's club.

'Before your . . . change of behaviour last week,' Ruth began 'I was wondering what to do about us.'

'What d'you mean? We were getting along fine.'

'Just listen, Frederick, please. First there was the little matter of children.'

'We agreed on that, right from the . . . '

'You made the rule. I always wanted kids.'

'But you agreed . . . '

'I thought I could change your mind . . . '

'If that's the only stumbling block . . . '

'Shut up, darling,' she said sweetly; 'please! Before . . . last week, I'd almost made up my mind to get a divorce.'

'Divorce! It's out of the question!'

Ruth had to smile.

'Out of the question or not, I was thinking of doing it. Things were that bad. Then you told me about your Damascus! And that I'd never loved you! That hurt! Whatever you may think, I was in love with you. I would never have married you otherwise. It took two years for your . . . coldness or whatever it was, to kill that love. It took me another three to get to the point of divorce. And you asked me what I had to think about.'

Frederick collapsed into an armchair.

'What a fool I've been! Not to see. Not to give myself the chance to fall in love with you earlier. You talk about my lack of emotion. I've never been able to show it. I thought happiness was about getting on with people . . . enjoying work . . . being a success. I didn't know about falling in love. I wasn't prepared! Don't you understand?'

'I understand, my darling. But I don't know if it makes any difference. I don't know whether my feelings for you . . . the ones I had . . . when we married, are capable of being . . . raked up again.'

'Just give me a chance. I'll make it up to you. We'll go away. Bermuda? Europe? China? Say the word! Let me show you what I can be like.'

'Freddie . . . ' – he'd become a Freddie – 'We can't go away. Not now. What would the President say? First day in the important new appointment and it's vacation time!'

'Damn! Damn! Damn! I'll give it up, tell the Man it was a mistake . . . '

'Freddie! Don't go on . . . '

It was a small, helpless voice that said: 'But what am I going to do? I can't lose you now. I just can't.'

'You'll have to give me time . . . and not crowd me. You shut me out for so long I've got used to being alone . . . '

'Is there somebody else?'

'I've told you . . . '

'What about Lubbock? Stallybrass, and the others that come calling?'

'What about them?'

'If they're not here for . . . personal reasons, what's it all about?'

'You've got to give me room . . . and time. I may have no

right to ask it, but you've got to trust me. I'll do my best. I'll try to make it work again. Really I will. But as of now . . . it's all too sudden . . . it's a sea change you're expecting of my emotions. I don't know if they . . . if I can take it. If you push me, smother me, I'll run.'

'Oh my God! What have I done!'

Date: 20 October 1981
Savannah, Georgia

They emerged from the thirty-five minute flight by Eastern's DC9 into eighty degrees of Savannah fahrenheit. An Air Force jet screamed into the sky from the landing strip it shared with civilian carriers. Advertisements for Hilton Head beach and golf vied with guided tours of the balustraded mansions of nineteenth century Savannah.

There was a reassuring air of normality about the suntanned, wholesome-looking girl who took Tyson's credit card. 'You gen'l'm'n staying long in S'vannah?'

Lloyd answered in his most polished English.

'Probably not more than a couple of days, actually.'

'Gee! You must be from England. I can tell from the accent. It makes my legs go . . . Say something else in English.'

Lloyd laughed. 'When we've finished our business here, I'll treat you to a whole evening of my various skills, and see if you still have an appetite for the *mores* of the Anglo-Saxon.'

She stopped folding the car documents long enough to stare at Lloyd in frank admiration. 'Gee, that's just beautiful!' Her face froze into drilled formality. 'Y'all have a nice day now.'

It was white, over twenty feet long; Lloyd stared. 'You want to be inconspicuous!'

'Everything else was booked. You heard the girl.'

'But this is a . . . '

'Lincoln Continental, fully computerized, and on special

offer at thirty-nine ninety-five a day, unlimited mileage. That's a hell-of-a-deal.'

'Deals again!'

'It's got a lotta poke, man!'

'Where to?' asked Lloyd.

'This was your idea . . . '

'Let's head for the river.'

The cobbled quay was crowded with tourists gawping at a flea market of gold-dipped sand dollars and Christmas toys. The elegant buildings, where cotton slaves had been traded, had been restored and freshly painted, but now housed vendors of the arts and crafts of the Uncle Tom south. No ship was in sight. An old negro, sweltering in a heavy black suit, answered their question. 'You need the Ocean Terminal. Foller the river upstream! Fifth busiest port in the East!' he said proudly.

'What're you gonna do when we find this boat?'

'It's your country and you're CIA . . . ' said Lloyd.

'I supplied the first clue, Sarah Brown . . . '

'And screwed it up!'

'Come on, Lloyd. Stop bitching!'

'We need more information,' said Richard. 'When it's supposed to sail. That sort of thing . . . '

Tyson interrupted. 'We need to know if it exists!'

There was no mistaking the cyrillic script.

'We've got 'em,' whispered Tyson excitedly.

'Oh?' replied Lloyd.

'They can't get away.'

'Really!' said Lloyd.

'They can't go upstream, that's inland. They have to go thataway. It's fifteen miles to the open sea, and then territorial waters for three miles after that . . . '

'How does that help?'

'Time. If we screw up, call Rogers. He'll crank up the navy. They'll stop her. It's downhill from here on in,' said a grinning Tyson.

He asked a man wearing dirty jeans shorts: 'Can you tell me the name of that ship?'

'The Alex Bruno or something like that. Russian. God-damn commie junk!' He spat his disapproval on the grass.

'Thanks,' said Tyson.

'What now?' asked Lloyd.

Tyson scratched his head. 'I'll see if I can find out if any-body out of the ordinary has been aboard in the last few hours. Go bring the car a bit closer and call up your embassy for an up-date.'

Lloyd cautioned: 'Keep your eyes on that boat!'

'I know.'

Lloyd put ten quarters in the coin box. A familiar voice said: 'Give me your number. Don't, repeat DO NOT, give area code.'

'283 2900.'

'Wait there,' said Major Arthur Forbes.

Two people wanted to use the phone. Lloyd ignored them.

'Yes . . . ' said Richard.

'You know who this is?'

'Unless you're the world's best mimic.'

'Tell me what the cabaret act was . . . how it began.'

'What cabaret act?'

'When we first met.'

'This is ridiculous. I know who you are, and you . . . '

'Give me the answer or I terminate the conversation.'

Lloyd fumed at the pedantic major. He tried to remember. It was just before Greta arrived. He swallowed and told Forbes what he wanted to hear.

'Is there any news?' he said.

'Somebody left 16th Street early. He's KGB. We're pretty certain it's a Major Rakov. He had a shoulder bag with him, and he boarded a Delta flight at Washington National Airport at 7 a.m. for Atlanta, where he'd have to change for Savannah. He should arrive at 10.30 a.m.'

Lloyd looked at his watch.

'He'll be landing about now. Give me a description.'

'Forty, short, dark hair. Medium build. Ideal agent material, nondescript, easy to miss. No distinguishing features. But watch out! If he's in charge, it's because he's good. Two bodies have been washed up in New York. Could be his doing. What's happened your end?'

'We've found a Russian boat called the Aleksie Bruno . . .'

'I'll try and check it out.' Said the major.

'Tyson is watching it and asking questions.'

'I don't want you to get too close to Tyson.'

'Why not?' asked Richard.

Forbes hesitated. 'Natural caution . . . but it's more than that. If you get your hands on what we're looking for don't give it to Tyson.'

'We're working together! I've told him everything! How can I. . . ?'

'Get away from Savannah and him, and then call me.'

Lloyd was fed up. 'One good reason!'

'It's an order, captain.' And he broke the connection.

Lloyd parked beside an old warehouse. Tyson was with a veteran of the Second World War. They parted.

'What's goin' down, Dick?'

Lloyd told him.

'Plan of action?'

'You take the stern gangplank. I'll cover amidships. Whoever spots him first charges him down, grabs his bag and runs.'

'Sounds good,' said Chuck.

Lloyd counted twenty slow minutes on his Omega watch.

A white Adam cab pulled up at the entrance gate. A short dark man paid the fare. No shoulder bag! Then he reached into the back seat. Lloyd and Tyson saw the light leather shoulder bag.

An excited Tyson sauntered over to Lloyd.

'That's Rakov! Has to be! Description fits. Shoulder bag.'

Lloyd didn't trust the situation. It was too easy. Too pat. 'What's got into you. He's walking straight into our lap.'

'That's what's bothering me.'

'Fucking British caution. Forget it. Start walking, like we were tourists. I'll put my fist in his face, you grab the bag.'

'Anything you say,' said Lloyd.

It didn't go according to plan. He must have a sixth sense, thought Lloyd. They were seventy-five yards and closing when Rakov stopped. Lloyd and Tyson did likewise; a reflex action that gave the game away. Rakov ran. Lloyd and Tyson took off in pursuit.

They were heading east along Bay Street, the cobbles threatening broken ankles. Rakov turned away from the river, making for the town centre. Lloyd wondered if it was deliberate or panic. But dangerous KGB majors didn't panic. So what was his purpose? Lloyd kept running. Tyson was breathing heavily. Rakov was doing well, for an older man, thought Lloyd; but I can outlast him. As the chase lasted five, then ten minutes, he began to wonder. He was getting the pain of his first wind. He ran through it. Tyson couldn't keep up. Rakov kept on going, swerving in and out of pedestrians, across moving traffic, but still using busy streets. He turned a corner about a hundred yards ahead of them. When Lloyd reached the same point, he'd disappeared. He could have entered a dozen shops. Tyson arrived, panting. 'Jesus. Have you lost him?'

Lloyd caught a glimpse of a running figure in the warehouse area. He gave chase. Tyson followed, grunting. The KGB man disappeared into undergrowth. Lloyd raced after him. He climbed through the hulk of a crumbling corrugated-iron shed. Two shots spat at him. He dropped. Lloyd glanced behind him for Tyson. The rest of Savannah was going about its business as usual.

Lloyd scrambled to his feet and continued the chase. On

the other side of the building was the car park of the Visitor's Center and no sign of the Russian. Several hundred tourists were milling about coaches and parked cars.

The only other cover was the Old Railroad Station. Lloyd raced across the tarmacadam, halted and peered round the edge of the wall. No movement. He stepped inside. It had been lovingly restored, resplendent with Georgia Central Locomotive. There was a strange silence in the emptiness of the building. Grass grew between what was left of the old tracks. Lloyd imagined he could hear the cries of the wounded and dying Americans, French and British in 1779; one of the bitterest battles of the War of Independence. Of the KGB major there was no sign. He ran through the building to the throng of gaudily dressed vacationers.

Tyson joined him. 'We'd better go down either side of the crowd. Shout if you spot him.'

Rakov was not a tall man. The only thing that would single him out was the distinctive shoulder bag. Lloyd and Tyson scanned each figure and face, every bag. Richard sensed a movement in the middle of the crowd. He followed the line of it and took up position where he would appear. Rakov emerged fifty yards away. Lloyd put his fingers to his mouth and let out a harsh whistle. Tyson heard it, but couldn't see Lloyd or Rakov. Lloyd lost seconds whistling again. Rakov leapt up the steps to the street, and dashed through hooting traffic. Lloyd, and eventually Tyson, followed. Rakov steadied his arm against the wall of the Salvage Sales Company. He took careful aim. Lloyd went down. The first shot missed. Tyson, fifty yards behind, didn't hear the gunfire. The second went through his jacket, grazing his ribs. Rakov ran. Lloyd followed.

Another bullet chipped the wall. Lloyd ducked. He turned the corner of Telfair Square. Rakov was a hundred and fifty yards ahead. Richard followed. Chuck staggered after him, holding his side.

Lloyd wondered when the older man's strength would give out. Richard kept running but his breathing became laboured. Tyson was in worse trouble, and losing blood. Lloyd sensed Rakov slowing down. It was confirmed when he stopped to let a horse-drawn carriage pass. Richard felt a surge of adrenalin. In the next ten seconds, he gained ten feet; in the next twenty a further ten. They were pounding the sidewalks of elegant oak-treed squares lined with the multi-coloured façades of restored Victorian and Federal homes. Lloyd was st[illegible] gaining. Rakov jumped a contractor's ladder. His heel caught. He fell. Lloyd was triumphant. As Lloyd launched himself at the KGB man, he realized, too late, why Forbes had labelled him dangerous. Even as the Russian fell he was drawing his gun. As he hit the pavement he twisted and fired. The bullet took Lloyd in the left shoulder, the impact stunning. Lloyd felt for the leather bag. He grabbed the strap. To his surprise, Rakov let go. Then Lloyd knew why. He was on his feet, taking aim at Lloyd's head.

He shut his eyes. Instead of oblivion, there was a click. Rakov was out of bullets. Richard opened his eyes. Chuck appeared, shouting. Rakov looked from Lloyd to Tyson, to the bag. He had lost! He ran.

'Shall I go after him?' Tyson stuttered.

Lloyd had equal difficulty speaking. 'Don't bother. We've got what we came for.' He clutched the bag. 'Be a good chap. I think I'm in need of a medic.'

'Sure . . . sure. Don't move.' Chuck inspected his ribs. Satisfied, he said, 'D'you want to give me the bag?'

Lloyd smiled. 'Nobody's taking this from me after all the trouble. Get me a doctor, Chuck.' He closed his eyes. Tyson hesitated. Richard's eyes opened the moment Tyson's footsteps receded. He stuffed a grubby handkerchief on his shoulder, and made off at a lop-sided trot in the opposite direction. He entered the Department Store on Broughton Street. Propped in a corner of the mens' room, he dialled Forbes.

'Just listen,' Lloyd began. 'I'm in the toilets on the ground floor of Kress Department Store. I have the object. My friend is not with me. I am sick. Get somebody in here fast.'

'You need a code name!' Forbes was ever correct.

'Get help here fast before I flush the Trinity down the bog!'

Lloyd limped to the end cubicle and locked himself in. He hung the bag on the inside of the door, and eased off his jacket. The pain was waning as the shoulder began to go numb. Not a good sign. His fingers explored. There was no exit wound. Not a comforting thought. Blood was pumping out. He was no doctor but something told him that couldn't go on long. He pressed a yard of toilet tissue into the wound. He wondered how long he would have to wait.

He didn't know how much time elapsed. He wasn't even aware that he had passed out. He regained consciousness to the sound of a whispered:

'Lloyd . . . Lloyd . . . Are you there?'

He thought he must be dreaming because the voice was female. The call was repeated. This time he was sure.

'In here,' he croaked.

'Open the door!'

This time the female voice was unmistakable. It belonged to a woman in her late fifties. She was too large to be wearing Bermuda shorts.

'What a mess!' she said. 'Don't move. Stay still while I put something on that shoulder.'

Deftly, belying her awkward shape, she ripped away his shirt and bound the aching shoulder. She mopped up the worst of the blood.

'Who are you?' he enquired.

'Can you stand?'

He tried and failed. She swabbed his arm and plunged in the hypodermic.

The main door opened and two men entered. The taller one was saying, ' . . . and I told Shaun that if he ever placed an order without checking with me again, I'd cut off his balls, and where . . . ' when he caught sight of the Bermuda shorts.

The woman spoke. 'I'm a doctor. I'm giving my patient an injection. Either get on with your pee or leave us alone.'

There was a haughty shake of the head. 'I don't know about you, darling,' he said to his companion, 'but I'm bursting.' He stepped up into the stall. His friend left.

'Can you stand now?' she asked.

Richard felt a hundred per cent better, which wasn't saying much. He stood, and the world stood still, which was an improvement.

'Lean on me!' Lloyd grabbed the leather bag. 'Collect your luggage in the morning, young man . . . '

'Not on your fucking life!'

She shrugged. 'Whatever happened to charm and elegance! I remember the time that was a private word.'

13

Date: 20 October 1981
Savannah, Ga/Washington, D.C.

When Tyson returned the only sign that he hadn't dreamed it was the blood on the sidewalk. He searched the area. No trace of the bag either.

He called the Washington number from the Downtowner Motor Inn on Oglethorpe Avenue. He gave his codename and asked to be called back. He waited for thirty minutes. Nothing happened. He called again. His message had been passed on. After three hours, he broke the rules and called them direct. Rogers answered the phone breezily.

'This is Capistrano,' said Tyson cautiously.

'Hi, Chuck,' answered Rogers. 'What's doin'?'

'Didn't you get my message?'

'There's been a panic on. We can't respond to every phone call on the double.'

'Can I speak? On this line?'

'Sure. Why not?'

'When I tried to get somebody to vouch for me on this number, they said they'd never heard of me!'

'Full marks Heidi! Is that it, Chuck?'

'I'm in Savannah.'

'What're you doing in the south, boy?'

'I came here with the Brit . . . '

'Hey fella,' said Rogers, 'Who OK'd your transport, air ticket . . . '

'I used my credit card . . . '

'What was that you said about security, Chuck?' said Rogers sarcastically.

Tyson pressed on. 'I phoned in a report. From Atlanta.'

'I haven't had time to read anything.'

Tyson was calm. 'OK. Skip that. I take it you know about the KGB man who left their embassy for Savannah.' There was silence.

'Pete? Are you there?'

'Where d'you get this, Chuck?'

'The Brit.'

'Tell me.'

'Their embassy reckoned the KGB man had the piece from the Time Capsule, and was trying to get it out of the country on a cargo boat carrying grain to Kiev.'

'We can't discuss this on an open line.'

'I couldn't get a fucking answer . . . '

'OK! OK! Tell me the rest.' Rogers pressed a buzzer for Heidi to patch into the call. He activated the telephone tape recorder.

'We got the guy; the KGB agent.'

'Exactly how d'you mean, you got him?'

'We got there ahead of him. We were waiting for him. He had it with him. There was a bit of a fight. He pulled a gun. We got the piece.'

'You got the thing that was stolen from the Time Capsule?'

'Sure.'

'It's with you right now, in Savannah? . . . Forget I said that . . . I'll call you back.'

'Don't go. I haven't got it now.'

Rogers was beside himself with the suspense and the way Tyson was dragging out the story. 'Don't tell me where it is. This is an open line . . . '

'I don't know where it is. The Brit has it.'

'You let the limey walk away with it!'

'He was hurt, bad. I went to get help.'

Heidi came into the room. Rogers waved her away. She

put her hand over his mouthpiece. 'The director's on the line. He wants your hide!'

Rogers spoke quickly to Tyson. 'D'you know where it is? Yes or no?'

'That's why I've been calling you every ten minutes for the last three hours!'

'Give Heidi a number where I can call you back.'

The Director of the Central Intelligence Agency was a former four-star general, but there any similarity with Jack Lubbock ended. He was the closest the US Army ever gets to an academic. Brilliant at Yale in classics, top of his year at West Point, the only doubt about his eventually wearing the maximum gold leaf on his cap was that he was a below average performer on the sports field, but his qualities in tactics, strategy, logistics and leadership carried him all the way. When his retirement coincided with the vacancy at CIA, confirmation by Congress was a formality. He was held in awe by his staff, not because he was intimidating – as at least one of his renowned predecessors had been – but because of his ability to cut through distracting excuses and obfuscating detail and home in on the salient point. On this occasion he was quiet, and Pete Rogers was full of awe.

'I've had a telephone call from an English major who tells me he has a part of the Trinity and that it was given him by one of your officers. Is this correct?'

'I was going to call you about that, sir . . . '

'When? Tomorrow? After your vacation?' Sarcasm was only used by the director when he was really upset. 'What is the reason for giving it low priority?'

'There's been a communications foul-up. I've just this minute had the report myself.'

'Don't your people keep in touch on a regular basis?'

'Yes, sir. As I said, communications . . . '

'I want to know several things immediately. How did your man come across this? Where did he get his intelligence? Why wasn't it transmitted to my office? How come a British liaison officer was with him in the field? And finally, why did he give it to Captain Lloyd?'

So the director even knew the Brit's name. He was taking an interest. 'Right away, sir.'

'I'm taking a hard line on this one, Rogers, in case it's symptomatic of a general malaise in the service. American machines are the best in the world, but as individual operators we lag some way behind other countries particularly the British.'

'I'll give this top priority, sir . . . '

'The real urgency has been taken out of the situation on this Trinity piece. The Brits have it and I think we can rely on them to look after it!' The irony was not lost on Rogers. 'Now tell me about your man, Captain Tyson. Did he get on the track of this thing because he's an exceptional officer or was it luck?'

'I'll be in a better position to answer that when I have all the facts, general.'

'See to it, Rogers. And by the way, I don't like formality; sir is quite good enough.' There was no trace of humour in the remark.

Heidi walked in, eyebrows raised. 'Shouldn't we hold that boat? Just in case the Brits have screwed up?'

'You were listening on the other phone,' said Rogers dryly. 'D'you feel like telling the director to make sure he doesn't make a balls of his job!'

Heidi was not impressed with that argument. 'In this business one foul-up is seldom the only one!'

'Not me, baby! Get me Tyson, on the double!'

Date: 20/21 October 1981
30° 30′N 78° 30′W

Nobody was interested in Alexei Telinger as he boarded the ship carrying the kitbag. The captain chose the hiding place; a sheared-off disused pipe liberally smeared with grease, indistinguishable from other pipework in the engine room.

The red and black tug nudged the Aleksei Bruno away from Ocean Terminal One, and put into the middle of the river. Slowly – oh! so slowly! moaned Telinger – it took the grain-laden Soviet ship downstream. After two slow hours, the tug cut adrift. The American pilot was with them for another hour-and-a-half and still they hadn't reached international waters.

With no more than a mile to safety, the look-out shouted 'US coastguard approaching!'

The captain issued his orders. 'Get below, colonel. To the men's mess. You're crew, off-duty. Drink beer. Any questions, let others answer. Dirty your face. Smear some grease on those hands.'

The coastguard ordered the ship to heave-to. Men in steel helmets and flak jackets manned the four-and-a-half inch guns.

The first officer asked to see the ship's clearance from Savannah. The skipper glowered. His normal reaction. The coastguard lieutenant asked to see over the ship.

'Why?' asked the captain.

'Routine.'

'Our papers are in order. You have no right . . . '

'I could order you back to port for a full search. Take hours.'

Was this routine or inspired by what Telinger had brought on board? The skipper smiled. 'I'll personally show you round.'

'Not necessary,' said the first officer.

It took thirty minutes. Telinger was on his fourth beer when he heard the loud hailer on the patrol boat.

'The skipper wants to see you, lieutenant.' A few minutes later came the news: 'You're free to make way now, captain.'

Half-an-hour later, the pilot boat drew alongside. At last, international waters!

They made one more stop, for a private powerboat, with a white-faced Rakov aboard.

'Show me,' he said. Telinger wiped away the grease and took out the plastic-wrapped part.

'You undo it,' said Rakov. 'My hand is not too good.'

Rakov gazed at it in undisguised relief. It was the right one, the piece he had dug up from Flushing Meadow Park, the one Professor Vilkov had certified with the words:

'If there is such a thing as the Tesla Trinity, this stands a good chance of being part of it.'

'Is that a yes or a no?' Rakov had demanded.

'I'm a scientist, major, not a seer. All I can tell you is that the bauble you brought me from the Westinghouse home could not have any scientific secret hidden in it; this might. Until I have conducted experiments, together with the other two pieces, or however many more there may turn out to be, I can't answer you.' Rakov had had to be satisfied with that.

Vilkov had wanted to put it in his case in the hold of the aircraft back to Moscow. Rakov vetoed it.

'Then use the Diplomatic Bag,' said the professor.

'No,' said Rakov, and told him why.

'You know I make regular reports to the Kremlin,' said the professor. Rakov nodded. 'I shall tell them you rejected both my suggestions.'

Threats, thought Rakov. Why do we always have to use threats?

Telinger re-wrapped 'Father' in its plastic bag.

'Back here?' asked the major.

'Why bother?' Rakov nodded. 'We're in international waters!' said Telinger.

'When they find out we've still got it, they'll come looking for us. International conventions won't stop them boarding us.'

'No American could do that. Their laws are strict . . .'

'You've been brainwashed, colonel. If this was an American ship I'd sink it rather than let them keep this.'

'But you're Russian, and KGB. Americans couldn't . . . wouldn't do such a thing!' Telinger was so confident.

'We don't have a monopoly on ruthlessness. I could name a dozen US officers who would think international trumpeting a small price to pay for getting their hands on this.'

Rakov's eyes closed as another bout of pain struck. He slithered unconscious to the deck.

They carried him to the captain's cabin, and laid him on the bunk. Rakov insisted all he needed was rest, but when Telinger touched his hand he stifled a scream.

The seamen didn't trust the medical orderly. He didn't wash and was seldom sober. There were those who doubted he'd been on the course. It looked like a classic case of *blat*, influence, possibly a bribe to draw the extra roubles. His hands were dirty. He caused so much pain clumsily removing the glove that Telinger shoved him aside. 'And wash your hands!' The orderly grunted.

The hand was discoloured. There was pus at the sight of the wound. It smelled.

'I need to see the captain,' said Telinger. 'Don't you touch that hand until I get back!'

'This ish my job . . .'

Telinger hailed a seaman. 'Give this drunk a shower and sober him up.'

'Come along, comrade. You heard the officer.'

Telinger told the captain Rakov probably had gangrene and could lose his hand.

'Not my problem,' he replied laconically.

'Rakov needs a doctor, urgently,' insisted Telinger.

'So does half the Motherland, Comrade Colonel.'

'He's working directly for the Kremlin. If he dies it'll be your responsibility.'

The captain was not intimidated. 'I have orders about the major. Disobedience would mean more trouble than you can give me.'

'Did those orders tell you to kill him?' asked Telinger.

'They tell me to put him aboard a certain vessel. I shall do that.'

'And if the major is dead by that time?' asked Telinger.

The captain shrugged. He was delighted he had such explicit orders. He had a good life. The sea was his passion, his intimate, his perfect adversary. Whatever the weather, he was in his element. In foreign ports he enjoyed the camaraderie of other seamen, and the women, provided they were clean, and some even if they weren't. The bane of his life was the political officer, who never drank, never womanized, and always criticized. He demanded justification for every move the captain made, and threatened to put it in his daily report. His hatred of Chekists knew no bounds, and now he had the perfect opportunity to see the end of at least one of them, while being immune from criticism himself. If the bastard didn't die of his injuries, he'd not survive the transfer.

'I shall radio for instructions.' Telinger turned to leave the bridge.

'No, colonel. My orders also say radio silence – emergencies not excepted.'

'Show me!'

'Certainly, comrade.'

There was no room for argument. That was fine for the captain, but not for a KGB colonel, nominally Rakov's senior officer and therefore responsible for him.

'Send for the political officer.'

It made no difference. Having stood his ground against a Kremlin colonel, the captain took delight in telling the P.O. what to do with his 'direct order.'

Telinger decided to ask Rakov's help.

'Quite right, captain,' said Yuri, trying to muster a smile.

'Nothing must stop the rendezvous and my transfer.'

'But you could die!' said Telinger.

'I may lose a little limb, Comrade Colonel, but I don't feel like dying just at the moment. This is what we'll do, with your kind permission, of course, captain. This is, after all your ship . . . ' The sarcasm was not lost on the captain. 'You'll bring me some good Scotch whisky . . . I take it you have some . . . ' The skipper nodded. 'I'll take a little of that, while the comrade colonel reads your medical handbook.'

The captain nodded. Telinger wasn't happy.

The next hour was full of pain and whisky; whisky and pain; and pain and pain; and more pain. Telinger was no doctor. He was too careful and too slow.

At last it was finished. Telinger's clothes were stained with blood, pus and whisky. Rakov, who had consumed one-and-a-half bottles of Dimple Haig, was singing; bawdy peasant stanzas. He had no ear for music. Seamen smiled as they passed the cabin. The wind got up, and the long lurching swell was joined by short choppy waves with wispy white tops that made the ten thousand ton tub prance and buck. Telinger stayed with Rakov until the motion got to him. He left to vomit. When he returned Yuri had succumbed to the motion and gushed the contents of his stomach over the bedclothes and floor. Telinger shouted for help and made for the side again himself. The medic swabbed the floor, and stripped the bed and Rakov's clothes, clouting the hand and shoulder. Rakov stopped singing. He had a fierce headache and was struggling not to vomit.

'Get out,' he said.

'I'm quick, major. If I'd dealt with your injuries, it might've pained you a little, but it would have been over in five minutes.'

'And full of the grease and germs on your hands,' was Rakov's comment.

'Possibly. But I'd have held it under whisky for a while. Kill any germ that will.' He laughed and left the naked KGB major in the wet stinking cabin.

Telinger appeared with a change of clothes, and a fresh blanket. Rakov dressed himself in hard cotton overalls, and thick sweater. The temperature outside had dropped below freezing. The chill factor subtracted another ten degrees. The engine noise changed.

'What's that?' asked Rakov.

'The rendezvous. Are you ready?'

'God Almighty! In this sea?' He was suddenly very sober.

'And with that hand!' added Telinger. 'You'll never make it.' Not to mention the shoulder. The door was whipped back on its hinges by gusting wind. They reached the upper deck with Telinger holding on to Rakov's good arm with one hand and the storm line with the other. He nearly lost his grasp several times, and Rakov was forced to use his damaged hand to grab the rail. Visibility was down to two hundred metres. There was no sign of another ship. The captain was standing, legs akimbo, swaying to the erratic motion of the deck under his feet, uncannily anticipating every wayward movement, loving every minute.

'Are we there?' asked Telinger.

'More or less,' said the captain. 'In muck like this it's never easy to be exact.'

'Gospodi!' said Rakov.

The captain was amused. 'Nothing like a bit of weather to make good Party men invoke the Deity.'

'How will they find us?' Telinger wanted to know.

'The noise of our engines,' said the captain. 'And luck and persistence. Sooner or later we'll bump into one another. He raised his binoculars to a point about a quarter of a mile off the port bow. 'I think we have company,' he said. 'Whether it's ours or theirs remains to be seen.'

Rakov could see nothing, then he spotted a turbulence in the water as the black hull of a submarine broke the surface. The conning tower was quickly filled with figures. An Aldis lamp chattered its coded message. The captain gave the recognition signal.

'So far so good,' he ruminated. 'Now how are we going to get you across?'

Rakov was scared. He didn't like water, but he could swim. His hand was unusable, and his shoulder not much better. He was weak from the trauma, and being sick and drunk. The sea looked as if it would swallow any mortal thing so stupid as to enter its grasp.

The captain's attention was on the Aldis lamp. 'They want us to lower a boat.'

'What about a Breeches buoy?' Telinger did know something about the sea.

'The line would snap.' The captain picked up his internal telephone. 'Prepare the launch. We'll put it over the side with the major on board.'

'Get the . . . thing from the engine room.' Rakov gave the order to his superior officer.

The captain spoke casually.

'We'll try not to crush you going down. The launch has a strong engine. It'll handle this sea, you'll need to hang on with . . . both hands, and I mean both. Getting up that slippery hull will be difficult. They'll throw you a harness on a line. Jump in the sea and they'll drag you aboard.'

'I go now,' said Rakov without hesitation. The captain nodded.

Telinger returned with the Trinity.

'Tie it round my waist,' said Yuri, 'under the sweater.' Telinger did so.

The telephone buzzed. The captain listened briefly. 'It's all set,' he said flatly. A sailor appeared at the door dressed in oilskins.

'I'm Stepan,' he said.

'Shouldn't I be wearing some of those?' asked Rakov.

'Too much drag in the water.'

The wind would have hauled Yuri over the side if he'd

not hung on with both hands. If he'd been carrying 'Father' it would have been lost; him too. He ignored the pain and strode into the wind, following the yellow figure.

His first reaction to the launch was that it was too small to last ten seconds in the whirlpool below. It was resting on the deck, ropes at each end securing it to the davits. Stepan got in first and held out a hand to Rakov. He let go the rail and jumped. The sailor clasped him in a huge embrace that stopped Yuri being catapulted straight out again, but re-opened the shoulder wound.

'Sit down,' Stepan yelled. 'And hold on!' He waved his hand. The davits lifted them off the deck. They swung perilously between the steel arms as the small boat was buffeted by the gale. The pain in Yuri's hand worsened. The thing he feared most was passing out.

The sea came up to meet the hull of the launch. The ship heeled over. The davits dropped their charge. The thud should have ripped the bottom out of the boat, thought Rakov. He didn't have time for any further thought. He was struggling to stay in the boat as it bucked, and wheeled in the short savage waves. The engine dug deep into the water, and Rakov held the sides hard, stifling the pain. When he could bear it no longer he screamed at the top of his lungs, the sounds whipped away by the wind.

They were flung off-course a dozen times on their way to the submarine. Finally a line was thrown. It fell short. It was thrown again. It fell wide. The third shot had to be abandoned because the launch was about to be dashed to pieces against the black hull. Stepan revved the engine and sped away, describing a short circle back to his old position. The harness was thrown again. Rakov caught it and dragged the harness through the 'boiling' water. It was easy to see how to put it on, and secure the clasps. It was not easy to see how to do this with one unusable hand, and without being pitched into the sea. Stepan beckoned for Rakov to give him the harness. Rakov took off his lifebelt. The wind took it away; he didn't give it a second glance. He caught the harness with his bad hand, holding his position with the other. He got it past his bad hand and over that shoulder. Now came the tricky bit; using his good arm to get the harness over his head, and hanging on with the injured hand. He thought he would die from the pain. The seaman gave the leather strap a heave at the critical moment and tightened the strap.

He didn't know if it was the submariner pulling on the rope or the sea taking the launch away, but the effect was the same; Rakov was plucked violently from his seat and into the water . . . On the way over the side, his sweater was ripped against a metal gunwale, and the string tying 'Father' to his waist snapped. Two submariners pulled furiously to get Rakov aboard. The precious bag disappeared and then popped up again as the air held it momentarily afloat. At that second the line went slack and Rakov undid the fastener. In a flash he was free and swimming towards the bag, ignoring the searing pain from his shoulder. The launch was almost alongside the cargo ship when Stepan saw what happened. He revved his engine and turned the tiller hard over.

Rakov kicked off his shoes and swum strongly for the plastic. A wave gushed over him, filling his mouth with water, submerging him. When he surfaced again he was headed in the opposite direction. There was no sign of the bag. The helmsman of the launch was yelling and pointing. Rakov couldn't hear above the noise of the storm but he could see the direction. He spotted the bag, sinking, the air being expelled as it was buffeted by waves. Rakov's head was engulfed again with the sea. This time he had his mouth shut and he swam on. The submarine was now out of sight. The pain in his hand had at last gone. It was numb. The rest of his body was rapidly joining it. He lost sight of the bag. The air had been exhausted. It was on its way to the bottom.

Rakov thought it was the fin of a shark that touched his leg; it was shiny and clinging. Almost too late he realized it was the plastic bag. He dived, saw it and grabbed. He caught the bag, but its precious contents slipped through his grasp. With a superhuman effort he kicked deeper and held it. His relief was short-lived. He was drowning. He kicked with his feet but it was a paltry effort. It stopped his descent but didn't lift him. He kicked again, and again, and again. He wouldn't give up his grip on the Trinity, so he couldn't use his arms. His lungs choked with water, screaming for air. He was losing consciousness. Something tugged at his collar. He didn't care. Whatever it was, let go. Yuri Rakov relaxed. He remembered reading somewhere that drowning was not a bad death.

Date: 21 October 1981
Savannah, Ga.

Richard Lloyd was woken by a shocking steam hoot. Loss of orientation! A moment's panic. When reason identified the sound, he concluded he must be on board ship. When the room stopped moving he realized he was wrong.

An early sun was seeping through folds in the curtains. He was in a woman's bedroom, and the woman was sitting in a chair beside the bed, still wearing the Bermuda shorts. He took stock of his surroundings. There were frills everywhere; on the curtain pelmet, on the counterpane, lace on the edges of the pillows. The carpet was a soft powder blue. The dressing table was trimmed with blue and white scalloped lace edging. The fourposter bed had elaborate drapes in the same colours. His shoulder hurt, but the throbbing had gone.

'Feeling better?'

'Thank you, yes,' he said. 'Did you do all this? Take out the bullet?'

'What bullet? If I'd seen a bullet I'd have had to report it. Your shoulder was injured by a hit-and-run driver.'

'Really? Do you have my little leather bag?'

'Personally no, but it's in good hands.' Lloyd didn't like that.

'Whose?'

'Arthur Forbes.'

'Where is he?'

'He's gone to Atlanta, to somebody rather bright, he said.'

'I never even saw it.'

'I had a look. Didn't mean a thing!'

'Who are you?' asked Lloyd.

'Forbes said you had no need to know that.'

'You work for British Intelligence?'

She burst into musical laughter. 'Good God, no. I'm far too busy for games.'

'Then how come . . . ?'

'My husband was once a British Consul on the East Coast. I'm . . . Anglophile. Arthur couldn't call in the local constabulary apparently, so he asked me if I'd like to . . . help out.'

'It's very generous of you and your husband . . . '

'Don't bring George into this. He'd have apoplexy.'

'But . . . '

'He's on a golfing binge in Spain. How about something to eat? Bacon and eggs suit you?'

'Sounds like manna.'

Richard felt self-congratulation was in order. He'd taken on the KGB best and come out on top. Luck had played a part, but persistence was the key, and he had to admit it – a natural aptitude for the work. Pompous sod, he thought! Nothing else he'd done in his short life had given him quite the same excitement. Not quite true! His times with Marta were the best, but that was in a different compartment. He recalled the chase with Rakov – it was . . . exhilarating. Good word! What about that fleeting second when he looked into the rising gun? When Rakov stood over him and squeezed the trigger? He would save that up for future nightmares. But for now, on this new morning, it was good to be alive. As for Marta, even her face, which had dominated his thoughts for so long, was soft at the edges.

He felt good for a full five minutes more until Arthur Forbes entered the room. Lloyd waited for the congratulations. Forbes' voice was non-commital.

'How are you?'

'Fine, thanks to Margery here.'

'Yes . . . '

'Well, major. Don't just stand there. Do we have the secret weapon? Do I go to the top of the class?'

'No.' Forbes had a grim expression on his face. 'Neither do I.'

'What happened? You didn't lose it? Rakov didn't . . . '

Forbes shook his head. 'Nothing like that. He fooled you.'

Lloyd said. 'Impossible. I was there. I got the bullet in the shoulder. The bastard would've killed me if he hadn't run out of shells . . . '

Forbes wasn't impressed. 'I don't doubt it. Did Tyson tell you there were two thefts; one from the Westinghouse home, and the other from the Time Capsule?'

Lloyd nodded.

'Rakov had the one they took from the house. Decoy duck. You were set up.'

'Oh my God!' Lloyd was shattered. 'I got all this for . . .' and then he remembered his own sense of unease, when the chase began. 'Something wasn't right when I first saw him coming towards us. I thought, what's he doing getting out of the cab so far from the ship. But then he ran, the chase was on, and I got shot. But you must have stopped the boat.'

'It took me several hours to get here, collect the widget and have it checked out by a tame boffin in Atlanta. It's long gone.'

'Why not blow it out of the water?' asked Lloyd hopefully.

'They'll have had a rendezvous with a submarine by now.'

Lloyd still had questions.

'If Rakov was a decoy, are we sure the thing went aboard that boat?'

'There was a second man on the plane. We assumed he was Rakov's minder. Just after your little excitement, a man answering his description boarded the ship carrying a kitbag.'

'Oh! Hell!'

'Keeping it to ourselves has upset people.'

'Why didn't they stop it anyway? Tyson must have pushed the panic button when he lost me,' said Lloyd.

Forbes became even more lugubrious. 'My fault. I told them we had it, that they could relax. We're so much better than the Yanks at the subtle stuff.' His voice was heavy with irony.

'So it's down to me. I fouled it up.'

Forbes was fair.

'I don't blame you for being taken in by Rakov. The brigadier may not be so generous.'

Forbes stood up. 'I must be going.'

Lloyd stopped him. 'Tell me why I had to get it away from Tyson.'

Forbes gave a grim smile. 'It was a . . . hunch, actually . . . ' Lloyd couldn't believe it. Forbes nodded unhappily. 'We had a whisper about a private group involving Mrs Coverdale. Don't want amateurs playing our games, do we?'

'That's bitched it for me with Tyson and the CIA.'

Forbes was not helpful. 'I know, old chap. Bloody bad show.'

Lloyd's anger began to boil. 'Forbes! I was damned nearly killed and all in aid of a cock-up!'

Forbes became his steely cynical self. 'Spend a few days in bed. Catch a plane home. You can put your complaint in writing to the brigadier.'

'Give up now? No chance!' said Lloyd quietly.

'Anything you say,' said a tired major. 'It's been a day for bad news. Butterworth and Nicky managed to get themselves captured!'

'What! How?'

'Tell you all about it when you're better.'

Tyson arrived two hours later, with orders not to let the 'cockney son-of-a-bitch' out of his sight.

'I thought we were working this patch together,' he said.

Lloyd had had time to work out strategy. 'You're a fine one to complain. Leaving a helpless comrade . . . '

'To call the ambulance!'

'The Russian came after me again.' Lloyd told the lie with feeling.

'I don't believe it. He was finished.'

'He must've reckoned he was a match for a man with one arm.'

'You're a lying asshole.'

'Believe what you like.'

'How did you get away?'

'I made for the crowds, and managed to give him the slip.'

'Run the risk of walking into Savannah PD? Never.'

'He wants the Trinity as badly as we do.'

'True.' Chuck began pacing the room. Lloyd wondered what play the hustler would use next. 'I've been re-examining my attitude. I guess you're right. Trade-off doesn't make a lotta sense. I go along with you, share-and-share alike.'

Lloyd knew nothing had changed, but to humour Tyson he said, 'I'd like to share some really bad news with you, my friend.' And he told him how they'd been fooled.

14

Date: 25 October 1981
Georgetown, D.C./Atlanta, Ga.

The President sent Frederick to NORAD at Colorado Springs; an exercise in familiarisation and public relations for the new Defence Advisor.

Ruth called Lubbock. He told her to send for Tyson. Chuck told them everything. The general wanted to call a meeting of the group. Ruth told him she'd be out of town. Lubbock sulked.

She didn't know why she'd kept the purpose of her visit a secret from Lubbock. As she sipped a Perrier water and gazed down on the lush forests of Georgia, she wondered, again, about the phrase Sarah Brown had used: 'Do you have anything to tell me?' According to Chuck, it was a rambling non sequitur from a woman on the verge of a nervous breakdown. But Ruth was betting he was wrong. It was another of Ruth's hunches that made her want to see Mrs Brown for herself. And where had she heard the name Sarah?

She used General Rentacar, off the airport, and drove to the Brown home.

'You had an unfortunate experience. Tyson and Lloyd should've carried identification.'

A hint of fear came into the dark-rimmed eyes.

'Do you know who I am?'

'Sure! I saw you'all married in Beverly Hills. On the television.'

'You know who my husband is?'

'Frederick Coverdale.' It was said tonelessly, without significance.

'Don't you know what his job is?'

'Should I?'

'If you've been watching television lately, yes.'

'Excuse me, but I didn't think much of him. I know he's rich and all that, but he wasn't good enough for you. Cold fish.'

Ruth wondered what Mrs Brown would say if she knew what a change there had been in her husband.

'The President has just announced . . . '

'Don't tell me! I did see it. Somethin' funny. We ain't never had one before. Defence adviser?'

'You've got it.'

'I'm not bothered who comes. I only went on about ID because they didn't give me the message.'

'Yes . . . '

'So you'll be the one.'

'That's why I'm here, Mrs Brown. That's why the President personally asked me to come and see you. He wants you to know that the person you're talking to is genuine. He chose somebody you would recognize, so you'd have no hesitation talking to me.' She uttered the lie with what she hoped was understated sincerity.

'I don't have a problem with that. Just give me the message.'

Ruth called up further reserves of sincerity. 'Shall I tell you what the President said to me, only yesterday when he entrusted me with this delicate mission?'

'Nothin' delicate about it. Just give me the message.'

Ruth ploughed on. 'He said we know she's Sarah Czito, grand-daughter of Kolman, daughter of Julius, both of whom worked with Professor Nikola Tesla. We know they were both at her grandfather's funeral. We know the professor visited her after that . . . ' She was now gambling that her imagination would supply some fact to unlock Sarah's knowledge, ' . . . but for some reason best known to himself, the professor didn't give the message to any government agency. The President doesn't have a message to give you, Sarah.' She was almost nodding her agreement until the last sentence, when she blinked. It was as though a filter dropped over her eyes. Ruth had blown it. Now she would never divulge whatever secret she held. Ruth struggled to remember the O'Neill biography. She was sure there was no mention of Sarah Brown, or Sarah anybody else. But there was a Sarah. Who was it? 'You did meet Professor Tesla, didn't you?'

'If you don't have the message, I can't help you.' She obviously wanted to be shot of the responsibility for whatever it was. Did it account for the dark rims to her eyes?

'You met him when you were . . . how old? Seven? Eight? . . . No, that's unlikely . . . You were . . . what eleven years old when Tesla died?' Sarah nodded. At last a positive response. 'How old were you when you met him. What's the harm in telling me that?'

Sarah didn't answer immediately. Eventually she murmured: 'Five.'

What would Nikola Tesla have said to a five-year-old? Impossible to guess! Ruth needed more clues.

'When did you first meet him?'

Again the stubborn silence. Again, ultimately, Sarah gave the answer.

'At grandaddy's funeral.'

Did that help? Not a lot. What was the connection between Tesla, the Czito family and funerals? None. But wait. There was something. What was it? Didn't Tesla ask Julius Czito to bury a pigeon for him? Yes that must be it. What had he called the pigeon? Sarah. Ah! Was that the solution? If so, what about the pigeon? What do pigeons do? They carry messages? Was that it? Ruth felt ridiculous as she said:

'I have a message from a pigeon called Sarah. Is that what you want me to say?'

Jackpot! The relief flooded into Sarah's face.

'Oh thank God! Thank God!' she said. 'I've been so worried and anxious, ever since the first men came. When they didn't say it, I was shocked. Shocked, Mrs Coverdale. When the second man came, and then a woman, and then your two young men and none of them said it, I was so upset.'

'Have you kept this secret all these years? Even from your husband?'

'There y'have it. Maybe I should, maybe I shouldn't. I've bin happily married twenty-four years. I wondered. Should I tell him? When we first got wed. I sorta postponed it, you might say, and then time passed. When you've kept a secret from your dear one as long as twenty-four years, it's a bit difficult to come out with it all of a sudden.'

The secret was a dam. Now it burst and the taciturn housewife couldn't stop the words gushing out. 'It was at granddaddy's funeral, Queens, New York. I said something to the professor – I don't rightly call to mind what it was – I was a terrible talker in those days – and he said to me, "Is your name really Sarah?" I said, "sure is." And he said, "I have a pigeon visits me in my hotel. I call her Sarah. She's the love of my life." Just like that he said it: "The love of my life." Sounds strange saying it now. A grown man and all that, but at the time . . . I was no more than five . . . it was . . . it was just too beautiful. I have a little cry when I think about it. Gracious me! Here's you been standing all this time and I haven't even offered you a cup o' coffee. Where are your manners, Sarah Brown!'

Ruth smiled. 'I'm fine thank you. I'm just so interested in your story, I don't want you to break off for a minute.' Ruth wondered where Sarah had picked up her southern accent; it was so pronounced she was catching it herself.

It was a single family detached house, on two floors, built about ten years; comfortable and sparkling. The den had the look of teenager untidiness.

'Don't mind the clutter. You can't have children without

havin' a mess; so long as its clean dirt there's nothin' wrong with it. You sit over there, and I'm gonna get you a cup o' coffee, and a brownie I baked special this very mornin'.'

There was no point in trying to hurry Sarah, not after forty years of secrecy.

The coffee was good. The brownie reminded Ruth of her own childhood.

'Where was I?' continued Sarah. 'I remember. Calling on me! Call on me, I ask you? A grown man and a professor calling on a child of five! Who'd believe that? Well he did. My daddy, he was so pleased. He thought the world of the professor. He said granddaddy would have been so proud; him taking an interest in his lil' gran'chile. He asked my daddy if he couldn't give me a present; somethin' to remember him by, he said, when he was no longer here. Daddy said that was more than OK by him, thinkin' it would be just a little keepsake or somethin'. Instead, he comes by with a great van, and two men carry it into the house. It would barely fit into my room.' She saw the look of curiosity on Ruth's face. 'It was a wendy house!'

What an anticlimax! She'd posed as a government agent, taken the President's authority in vain – if Frederick found out, he'd never forgive – for a child's toy. 'How very kind of him!' she said.

'He made it himself, with his own hands. And this is what he said to me – and I've remembered every word of it – "One day somebody will come to you with a message from me. They'll say 'I know a pigeon called Sarah.'" Now you didn't say exactly that, and he did tell me to be careful . . . but given who y'are . . . I'm gonna show it y'all.'

They climbed the stairs. The wendy house was the centrepiece of the marital bedroom. It was grotesque. It occupied a third of the floor area. Sunlight flooded the room, giving it the effect of a bizarre palace.

'You ain't seen nothin',' said Sarah. 'Watch this.' She pressed a concealed button and the front walls and roof of the doll's house sprang apart, revealing a perfect living room in miniature.

Ruth made no attempt to conceal her disappointment.

'You mustn't stand in the light,' said Sarah, as though Ruth was committing sacrilege. She stood aside. A shaft of sunlight crept over her shoulder and hit the central feature of the living room, the fireplace, which seemed to come alight. It was an illusion, but something was acting as a refractor, a prism, giving off shafts of different coloured light. 'That's it!' said Sarah triumphantly.

Very pretty, thought Ruth.

'That's what you've come for!' added Sarah. She bent down and touched another release mechanism, revealing the brilliant surface of the heart of the 'fire.' It was made of a translucent material and there were lines running through it. Ruth knew she was looking at the second piece of the Trinity.

Date: 25 October 1981
Cien Fuegos, Cuba

Stepan, the helmsman of the tender, had strapped on the line from the submarine and dived overboard. At the second attempt he'd grabbed Rakov and dragged him to the surface. Even semi-conscious the KGB major had an unbreakable grip on his prize. The two men were hauled aboard the submarine.

It was an interesting journey for the captain of the nuclear submarine. Any Russian port was three weeks' sailing time away. The nearest haven was Cuba. The Americans knew this. They would not know what type of vessel was carrying the Trinity piece. They were bound to monitor every vessel into Cuba. Any unusual activity would pinpoint them and the captain didn't know what risks they might run to prevent the Trinity getting to Russia. If he went faster than normal cruising speed, the submarine's 'footprint' would stand out on the sensors. That meant three-and-a-half days to the south side of Cuba. He wanted to enter Cien Fuegos by night, but there was a morass of islands and a six-and-a-half mile coral shoal to be negotiated. Strong tidal streams and a sharp bend made navigating the narrow entrance to the harbour hazardous.

It was two-thirty-seven p.m. on a bright sunny afternoon that the captain ordered the ballast tanks blown and the black prow broke through the water. The captain manned the conning tower as they glided past the round stone-built lighthouse of Punta de los Colorados with the square flat-roofed houses alongside, to the anchorage at Ensenada de Marsillan.

General Yakushenko did not appreciate being rowed across, or climbing the slimy plates. Professor Vilkov enjoyed his companion's discomfiture.

'Where is he?' 'Y' demanded of the officer of the watch.

'In his cabin, Comrade General. I'll show you the way.'

Rakov looked bad; his skin grey, his cheeks sunken. His eyes showed signs of fever.

'Well?' said the general. 'Are you going to lie there all day?'

Rakov was silly enough to think that after such success the general might relax the malevolent mask. He should have known better.

Everything still hurt; his shoulder, hand, lungs; only vodka seemed to help, and the ship's surgeon had rationed it. Complete rest for two weeks and he might recover the use of his shoulder and avoid the loss of a hand. He was lucky to be alive.

The general looked at the object on the table. No reaction! The professor took his eyes off Rakov's face and switched to the object of all the fuss. He didn't touch it, he just looked. Then he slowly walked round the table. It was several minutes before he spoke. 'I wonder what it is!' he said.

Date: 25 October 1981
Washington, D.C.

Heidi was fed up. She was not alone. She, and a hundred other agents had racked their brains for days on original approaches to the Tesla connections. She called some on the telephone to make appointments. Those who did not complain about being harassed were, if anything, worse; they saw her call as an opportunity to rake over old reminiscences. And yet, among those tales could be the clue that would lead to the very thing she was looking for. She just had to listen and listen and listen. The most difficult part was keeping her concentration. The fact that she taped every interview didn't help, because she still had to recognize a lead when it appeared, and fire questions to make sure every part of memory had been tapped. Heaven help those who had to interpret the tapes, find a lead out of the hours of inconsequential chat about what granny said George had said Manny had said Tesla had said.

It looked like a scene from a bad 'B' movie. They were seated at a large round table, the men in their shirtsleeves, pretending to play poker. It was Marvin Bennett's idea because he did play cards every Saturday night. Eustace had entered into the spirit of the occasion with a green eye shade. Jerry Brand had on a black satin mini-dress, and red bandana round her head. Marjorie Swanson was not amused.

'Where is it?' Wilshire wanted to know.

Ruth was emphatic. 'I'm not telling anybody. All you need to know is it's safe.'

'And if you get hit by a truck?' Bennett wanted to know.

'They'll know it was the Mafia, looking at you lot,' said Swanson cryptically.

'What do we do with it?' Ruth wanted to know.

Bennett had no doubt. 'We get the best damned lab in

the United States to work on it, and beat the Russian sons of bitches and the CIA . . .'

'Impractical,' said Wilshire. 'Security for one. Any lab will take it straight to government.'

'What's your solution?' asked Eustace Vanderpage quietly.

'Take it to the White House.'

Jerry Brand exploded. 'After we've been to all this fucking trouble?'

'We don't have the facilities to make use of it.' Wilshire again.

'Buy 'em. We've got enough between us to buy a dozen labs,' said Marvin Bennett.

'What do you think?' Henry Hale asked General Jack Lubbock.

'I think we've got to get it to the President. Our terms of reference, our very existence as a group, is to help our country, not to go into competition with it. Arthur's right. The boys who've done the basic research have got to have this baby, and fast,' he replied.

'Take a vote on it?' asked Senator Stallybrass.

Ruth intervened. 'I hope we're unanimous on this,' she said looking at Marvin Bennett. He hesitated and then nodded.

'How?' said Ruth.

'Who?' added Jerry Brand. 'Who takes it? Ruth?'

Stallybrass was quick with the answer. 'That'll blow her cover. Frederick'll have to resign. Any heroes?'

Swanson's contribution was 'How about a yellow cab.'

Jerry Brand was not amused. 'This is serious, Marge.'

'Couldn't be safer than in a yellow cab? Who'd suspect. And we can make it anonymous.'

Bill Reiman said, 'They'd probably blow it up as a terrorist bomb! I move Arthur takes it; acting as a lawyer. I'll retain him if he's sniffy about the ethics; I'll even pay him a dollar to make it legal. His client wishes to remain anonymous, and has told him he is one of a number of people who are putting their services at the disposal of the national interest, and this is the living proof! How about that?'

Date: 26 October 1981
Akademgorodok USSR/London, England

Professor Vilkov didn't believe in the Tesla Shield; it broke too many laws. But he was giving it his best effort. If he made it work it would demonstrate his single-minded devotion to Rodina. If he failed, every reputable scientist would say it was inevitable. The telephone rang.

'I have nothing for you, Major General Yakushenko,' said Vilkov. 'It's far too early. And we're working with one-and-a-half hands tied behind the back without at least one more part of the model.'

'Would you like me to quote you to Comrade Brezhnev when I see him this afternoon?'

That was bad news. 'The Academy of Sciences at Akademgorodok is working twenty-four hour shifts. No avenue of research is being overlooked. More resources are being devoted to it than any western nation could afford. We shall be first with the answer – as soon as the KGB has supplied all the material.'

Yakushenko was riled. 'KGB secured that piece; under the noses of the Americans. That's a KGB success. It hasn't been matched by corresponding diligence by your department,' and terminated the call.

Vilkov called for his assistant: 'Not enough effort is going into Tesla research . . . '

Lyubov gulped. 'We can't take any more people off the nuclear side. The military are already complaining . . . '

'I can't help that. I am being pressed *from the very top* – you understand who I mean?' Lyubov did. 'Damn the military! I want another team to start from scratch. What's Anastas doing?'

Lyubov consulted a chart on the wall. 'He's booked for a spell at CERN, Geneva, next month. He's completing the getting up of an experiment – something to do with new particles, Vector bosons.'

'Is this a joke?'

The young man looked hurt. 'No, Comrade Professor. It says so here. It's a matter of prestige. If we solve it before the Americans it'll cause an international sensation.'

'What are you thinking of, Lyubov? Letting them work on projects of no practical value, when we're on the brink of controlling the planet!'

'Yes, Comrade Professor.'

'What do you mean, "yes"' said Vilkov icily. 'He must stop that work. Get him on to Tesla.'

'And what do we say to Geneva?'

'Talk to me about it nearer the time.'

'But the trip's planned, arrangements made, accommodation booked. Equipment's been ordered to arrive on certain dates. Do I cancel all these things?'

'Not now, Lyubov!'

Date: 27 October 1981
Havana, Cuba/Atlanta, Ga./Washington D.C.

No sooner had Rakov settled into his bed at the embassy in Havana for at least a week's 'rest' ordered by his doctor, than the general demanded his immediate attendance. Yuri climbed painfully to his feet. He staggered. A tumblerful of vodka put that right.

Rakov was the only agent who knew it all.

'Y' ordered him back to the US. He protested. He'd been exposed, identified. He'd be arrested for the killings in New York, executed!

'Are you frightened, Comrade Major?' was his superior's sneering comment.

The truth was, yes, but not for his own safety. 'If they take me, where does that leave the search for the Trinity?'

'I've got to have more!' said Vilkov. 'One part on its own is useless.'

'What about Telinger? He's handled it. He speaks the language. He wasn't compromised.'

Major General Yakushenko's voice was loaded with contempt. 'Sybarite, lotus eater!'

The speed set Rakov's nerves on fire. Previously there'd always been time to plan, to prepare the mind for the task ahead. This expedition was conceived in horrible haste. Within forty-eight hours of arrival, he was on the nine-thirty a.m. Cubana Airlines flight to Mexico City. It was an hour-and-twenty minutes late taking off and he only just made the Eastern Airlines connection to Atlanta, Georgia. He was travelling on a forged British passport, and supposedly continuing a long vacation taking in Amelia Island, Florida, where an apartment had been rented in his new name. It would all check out, so they said. Rakov was not fooled. Given time, KGB operations could be executed well; the one thing they were bad at, was improvisation, and speed. It usually ended in disaster.

Rakov had taken simple precautions. His hair was now light brown, shorter, and the parting on the other side. He had one inch lifts in his shoes and he dressed differently, blue blazer with brass buttons, grey flannel trousers and pseudo club tie. Archetypal cricket club member on holiday.

The immigration officer was friendly. 'How long are you going to be with us, Mr Lesser?' he asked. Rakov held up two fingers of his good right hand; the other was planted firmly in his pocket. 'Two weeks. Gonna take in Orlando while you're here?' It's a great day for adults as well as kids.' Rakov didn't know what he was talking about. He nodded. 'Give Walt my best, and whatever you do, don't miss the magic submarine. I tell you, it's so realistic my wife got claustrophobia!' Rakov didn't wish to be reminded of the sea. 'I'll mark it for three months, Mr Lesser. Have a nice vacation.' Rakov nodded. He handed in his stamped customs declaration and rode the escalator to the main concourse. He cancelled his Washington flight and checked into the Marriott Airport hotel. He was asleep as soon as he climbed between the sheets.

He woke at three a.m. He felt worse than before he went to bed. His left hand was throbbing again, his shoulder stiff. He inspected the plaster; there was no sign of blood.

He arrived at Washington National Airport at eight-twenty nine; on time at the 'gate.' He took the coach service to the city centre, and used a payphone to call his contact at the embassy.

'What happened to you? You were supposed to be in at seven-twenty last night! I've been waiting by this phone all night!'

'Bad luck,' said Rakov, in no mood to put up with the tantrums of subordinates.

'What have you got set up for me?'

'I shall have to make a report . . . '

'Make anything you like, but tell me what my orders are.'

'I am going to give you a number. You are to write it down . . . ' The pedantry irritated Yuri. 'It's a telephone number. Do you know what that means?' Rakov had the code in his head.

'I know what it means.'

'486 7869. Call that number in exactly five minutes.' Rakov dialled the transposed number from another payphone. He thought he recognized the voice of a senior KGB officer.

'Do you have another number for me?'

Rakov was at a loss. Then he remembered and gave the last three digits of his army number. 'Good. No arrangements have been made.'

'Why not?'

'It'll be safer if you choose, at random. Check into a motel. We've activated a sleeper. He's not at the top, but he has access to the right information. You must not – repeat must not – make any attempt to identify him.'

'Why not?'

'Usual reason.' So they were assuming he would be caught and given a truth drug! Reassuring!

'Call me at eleven twenty-five a.m. with the number of your motel. He'll call you.'

'How will I know him?'

'He'll ask if you have any Dunlop Maxplys . . . '

'Maxplys?' asked Rakov.

'Tennis rackets . . . You'll say you have to check and call him back. He'll give you a time and a number in the usual code. Meet him as soon as he can manage it.'

'What's my regular contact?'

'This number, ten a.m. and four p.m. daily.'

'And in emergency?'

'Go via Viktor.'

Rakov was surprised. 'But he's in . . . '

'I know where he is.'

Ruth put it in a box, wrapped it in gold and silver striped paper, and stuck a blue bow on top. It looked like any anniversary present from Neiman Marcus.

She needed a story to cover her visit to Atlanta, in case Frederick became inquisitive. She picked up the telephone to call Ed Jamieson. Her husband walked into the room. She wasn't expecting him until the weekend. She put down the phone. He gave her an enveloping hug and a long kiss.

'God! I missed you!'

'Me, too,' said Ruth, automatically.

'Does that mean you've finally made up your mind . . . ?'

'No, Frederick, just that I haven't had too much time . . . '

'What've you been doing? I thought my being away would give you the ideal opportunity . . . '

'Lots of things . . . '

'I called. Jennings said you'd gone to Atlanta.'

'Yes,' said Ruth, improvising. 'I went to look at a site for an office building.'

'I thought Jamieson did that for you.'

'Fulton County Commissioners can be tough on zoning changes and we have to buy now, unconditionally. I had to size it up. It's a lot of bucks.'

Frederick pointed at the box. 'Is this for me? Present on my appointment?'

Ruth answered too quickly. 'No . . . '

His eyebrows rose. 'What is it?'

Her mind went blank. 'It's . . . it's a surprise.' She was tired; edgy because of what lay ahead when Wilshire took the box to the President, and emotionally exhausted wondering what to do about her husband and how to keep him from finding out about her Tesla efforts. Success in that area seemed to have created even more problems.

'You know I don't like surprises,' said Frederick. 'I'll open it now.' He picked it up.

'No . . . Not here.'

'Why not here?'

Ruth desperately searched for a reason. 'It's not the right time or place.'

Frederick was now thoroughly suspicious. 'I think you'd better explain what's going on.'

She couldn't tell him the truth. Not yet. It would ruin everything, assuming she wanted everything not to be ruined, about which she hadn't had time to make up her mind. What could she say? She improvised.

'I want you to open it in the bedroom.'

'Why?'

'You took me by surprise when you made love so differently . . . '

'I told you why,' he said softly, silkily. She hesitated, but then knew she had to go through with it, knowing what his reaction would be.

'I thought you'd like a surprise from me.'

'I don't understand. There's only one thing I want and that's to win back your love.'

'This may help.'

He shook his head.

'I love surprises . . . invention . . . your new technique. I thought it would be nice if I made a contribution. My surprise for you, my darling is something unusual. Very expensive and extremely arousing. Unfortunately I have the curse so it would not be the best time to try it out, but tomorrow . . . '

'Have you been to a sex shop? Have you bought a so-called marital aid?' He shuddered, as she had anticipated.

She nodded, smiling, she hoped seductively, feeling wretched.

'I thought yours was supposed to be the sensitive sex: men the coarse breed. You don't seem to comprehend what I feel for you. You have my whole being, my soul, assuming I've got one. I'd give up life itself for you.' He said it quietly, but the emotion behind the words was intense. 'And you think it's . . . lust!' He turned his back, and left the room, closing the door softly.

Ruth had never admired him more. It went a long way to resolving her doubts about staying married to him. She felt wretched and frightened.

Date: 27 October 1981
Washington, D.C.

The arrangements for the meeting broke every rule. Rakov was to go to the appointed place and wait, indefinitely. He wouldn't see his contact, only hear a voice. There was no proper recognition code, just a reference to something said in the last phone conversation. The venue was even worse; better for a mugging than a meet; a downtown multi-storey car park, at ten p.m. He was to stand in the corner nearest space 5130. He should not move or leave until his contact appeared and had, in turn, left.

Rakov didn't like anything about this trip. The hairs on his neck were prickling, suggesting he was under observation. If so it was a professional because Yuri Rakov couldn't spot him.

He took elaborate precautions. By the time he reached the car park he was reasonably sure he was alone. He parked the red Honda Accord at eight thirty p.m.

Cars and people came and went. Nobody noticed Rakov. By nine fifty-five p.m. fewer than a dozen cars were left. Nothing happened for another fifteen minutes.

Rakov heard nothing until the voice spoke – in a whisper. 'How is your motel?'

How could anybody have got so close without Rakov hearing? I must be ill!

'It's OK' he said, 'but I have trouble remembering the phone number: 567 8981.'

The whisper continued, urgently: 'There's a private organization at work, looking for the same thing we are. There are top people involved, and big money. You must find out about it.'

Rakov asked 'What can they hope to achieve?'

'Government's slow, bound by rules. Private groups ignore legal restraints.'

'Give me names.'

'Start with General Lubbock.'

'What d'you want me to do about them?'

'Take them out of the game. Wait an hour before leaving.'

That was not good enough. He had to know how far the CIA had got, what leads there were to follow up. 'I need to know quite a few things. I'll make it as short as I can, but I can't operate without something to go on . . . ' There was no answer. 'Are you there?' No answer. 'Say something. I need answers.' He'd gone. Damn. And again he'd heard nothing. How could that be? How could a man walk so quietly? Was is it a man? Of course. It was always a man. He tried to recapture the intonation of the whisper. Inconclusive. What was the smell? Perfume? Yes! But faint. What brand? James Bond would have known, or was it after-shave, or soap?

Why was he concerned? After the warning about identification? Rakov was an old hand. Nothing beats information. The more you know the better prepared. It had saved his life.

What should he do about the private group; led by a general? It was another difference between their two countries. How could any system survive if the state allowed private groups to operate. That was why police needed power, and why everybody had to have a passport. You could strangle such things at birth. He couldn't take this as a serious threat. Even with a general involved. He would tell his contact at the embassy. Let him get on with it.

He waited until seven a.m. when the flow of cars began, and then drove out. The attendant who took his money didn't look up from the sports pages.

The British government's passion for public expenditure cuts ruled out Richard staying at hotels, so the assistant press officer was persuaded to give him a bed some miles out of town. Lloyd was congratulating himself on his prowess on the wrong side of the road in the rented blue Pontiac compact when the accident happened. It was early morning – far too early by Richard's standards – the beginning of the rush hour. The traffic was moving at a steady twenty miles per hour. Lloyd couldn't say what drew his attention to the red Honda Accord travelling in the opposite lane, Japanese cars were commonplace in the States. His eye flicked across the windscreen, and registered the face above the wheel. From that point the accident became inevitable.

Richard's first reaction was disbelief. The Honda's window was open, and was no more than fifteen feet from the Pontiac. A small crowd waiting for the 'DONT WALK' sign to change obscured his view momentarily, but his head followed the car. The Russian became aware that somebody was staring at him and glanced across the central reservation. His reaction at first mimicked Richard's, disbelief; it was quickly followed by recognition and – Lloyd could see it in the eyes – the brain's automatic reflex to imminent danger: fight or flight. That was when the car Richard was following braked, and the Pontiac tried to climb up its exhaust pipe. Two cars further up the line were involved in the shunt. Lloyd grappled clumsily with his seat belt, intent only on getting out the car and seeing the Honda's registration number. He was too late. Rakov had chosen flight and was weaving in and out of traffic. Richard sighed and turned to deal with three irate drivers. On this occasion his English accent didn't help.

When he finally got to the office, the others were sceptical.

'You're not even conscious at that hour, Dick,' said Chuck Tyson, remembering the night he'd spent at Georgetown.

'I tell you it was him,' Richard insisted. 'He couldn't have been more than ten, fifteen feet away!'

'How can you be sure?' Rogers wanted to know.

'Have you ever lain on a street in Savannah and had a guy stand over you with a gun in his hand pressing the trigger?'

'Point taken,' said Heidi.

'And he recognized me. I saw the fear!'

'It doesn't make sense,' said Rogers. 'After all that hassle with you surely he'd have left the country.'

'Don't ask me how or why but that guy's here, in Washington.'

'I'll get the mug shots; make sure.'

'You feeling OK?' Chuck asked.

'I'm not hallucinating!' said Lloyd crisply.

'You lost a lot of blood. Medical shock's no joke . . . '

Heidi brought in a thick book of photographs. Lloyd and Tyson recognized the same picture immediately.

'That's him!' said Richard. 'Younger and thinner in the face, and the hair's parted on the other side now, and much lighter in colour. Chuck?'

'That's him all right.'

Heidi quoted the details:

'"Number 45 – Rakov, Yuri. KGB Major." He's served two periods in the States. Seventy to seventy-two he was at the trade delegation in New York, his real job monitoring the conduct of Russian staff. Seventy-four to seventy-six he was third secretary at the embassy, a straight espionage assignment, contact with agents that sort of thing. That's when this photo was taken. No record after that.'

'What do we do about him?' asked Lloyd.

'I can check with immigration,' said Heidi.

'Jokesville!' said Tyson. 'He'd never risk using his own name.'

'Nonetheless, I'll check with the records,' said Heidi, making a pencilled note.

'Why not call in the FBI?' asked Lloyd. 'He's wanted for God knows how many crimes in Savannah. We're witnesses to those.'

'The prime object of our operation,' said Tyson, 'is to get our hands on the next two pieces of the Trinity. He's still here, despite the risk. So somebody thinks he's got a good chance of finding them. If we lock him up they'll only send in another agent who we won't know. Our best bet is to find him and watch him. If he strikes pay dirt, we nab him and the Trinity as well.'

'We didn't exactly shine the last time we tried conclusions with Mr Rakov,' said Richard Lloyd ruefully.

'This time,' said Heidi with a certain smugness, 'we shall have the full resources of the agency mobilized!'

'Would you excuse us just a minute, Heidi?'
'Sure.' She took the book and left.
Lloyd wondered what ploy was coming next.
'I've had time to do some thinking; while you were recuperating. I'm still mad at you for walking off with the bag, even though it was useless, but you did a pretty good job in Savannah. Americans don't like coming second, and although I got a little graze from the bullet, you got to him first, you took the full impact of that shot, and if he hadn't run out of ammo you'd be dead. Mainly because I couldn't take the pace. There's another thing we're not very good at: saying sorry, but I'm sayin' it, Richard.'
'You don't have to . . . '
'Let me finish . . . I ain't too proud of the way I've been treating this thing . . . trying to turn it into something for the money . . . I just wanted you to know I'm gonna do something about getting fit and you won't hear me talking about trade-off again.'
Was this a new Chuck Tyson? The sincerity sounded good. Lloyd wouldn't make any hasty judgements.
'Thank you, Chuck. I'm sure we'll get along fine.'

Yuri Rakov drove hurriedly to his motel and checked out. He wiped every surface clean of prints, paid his bill in cash, and drove to the nearest pay phone. It was five minutes before ten a.m. He waited and then dialled the number. 'This is Dunlop. Do you have an order for me?'
'Give me your number.' Yuri used the code. He was called back in eight minutes.
'Yes. Maxplys. What do you want?'
Yuri told him about Lubbock's group and what the mole wanted done about it.
'I'll pass it on to Centre,' the contact said.
'And I've been spotted; by the Englishman.'
'Careless! Centre will not be pleased.'
'It was bad luck! Do you have a safe house for me?'

'You know your orders. Choose other accommodation at random.'

'Not now I've been seen. They'll check every motel!'

'I have no authority to make any change in your orders.' And he cut off the connection.

Yuri decided to call Viktor in New York.

The CIA agent dialled her office from the motel lobby. 'I've found him. He checked out this morning about nine thirty. What do you want me to do? . . . OK.'

She gave the desk clerk a visiting card and told him to call if Rakov showed up again. Waste of breath!

15

Date: 27 October 1981
Washington, D.C.

Heidi's first surprise was the security guard on the door of the manuscript room at the Library of Congress. He was built like a football player but spoke in a whisper, like a 'queen' from Polk Street, San Francisco. 'You need to register – sign on at the desk. They'll ask you for ID. Then you'll have reading rights for two years.'

My God! thought Heidi, am I going to be chasing Tesla clues for ever? The clean-cut librarian in the paisley sweater gave her six reels of microfilm and directed her to the Minolta Video machines. She mastered the forward and reverse actions, and how to turn the picture through ninety degrees.

She looked around the room at the fifteen or so other occupants of desks and consoles. Who were they? Academics doing research for a thesis? Was one of them, like her, trying to find a literary clue to a war-stopping weapon? Was one of them moonlighting for Leonid Brezhnev? The most unlikely candidate was an overweight matron in a purple pant suit. She didn't look like an academic, which meant she was probably the KGB agent! Heidi smiled at her paranoia.

For the next two hours she read the inconsequential correspondence passing between R. U. Johnson, assistant editor of *Century* magazine and the great man, mainly complaints from Mrs Johnson that Tesla failed to come to dinner yet again. Then Johnson was fired and Tesla had to send him money. If there was any truth to the story that Nikola was having it away with Mrs Johnson there was no sign of it in these exchanges. There was also no sign of any lead to the Trinity.

Next came reels of letters to and from Tesla's secretary George Scherff; interesting but nothing that could be described as a clue. She had high hopes of the correspondence with George Westinghouse junior, but was again disappointed. She didn't bother with the Samuel Clemens letters. Of what consequence could the thoughts of the great Mark Twain be in the search for the Tesla Shield? That was the end. Nothing! She decided to flip through the Mark Twain.

She almost missed it. She could understand why others had passed it by. Scientists would have regarded it as fanciful rubbish; non-technical people would have taken it at the value of the postman who had scribbled on the envelope. 'Not delivered. Addressee dead!' The only reason Heidi read it was that she was bored with details of polyphase alternating current, steam turbines and thermo-magnetic motors. Tesla had written to his friend:

> 'Dear Mr Clemens,
>
> I am sending this letter through the mail as the bellboy at this hotel came back this morning with a remarkable tale of your demise, which I know cannot be true as you visited me in my room two nights ago.'

She looked at the date; 3rd January 1943. Tesla died on the 7th. Was he hallucinating? Could anything he wrote at such a time be of any value? She continued reading.

> 'I wanted to send you money, my friend, because I heard you had financial difficulties. I can understand your situation having been in similar circumstances myself on a number of occasions when, without the timely help of good friends such as Mr J. P. Morgan, and Mr G. Westinghouse junior, my work would have suffered irreparable harm. Indeed when I first landed on these shores I might well have starved to

death but for the help of those who subsequently became my friends.

I say this to you, my friend: please call upon me at your convenience. It seems I shall be confined to my bed for a few days yet. I should be pleased to see you, and to give you such practical assistance with your difficulties as lies within my power.

I have a small gift for you. It has no value. I have never been a person to set store by worldly possessions, but you have been so kind to me on many occasions, I should like you to have something by which to remember an old friend. It is a piece of needlework executed by my mother. It depicts the church in the village of Smiljan where I was born, and where I spent some of the happiest days of my life and where I first became aware of the great beauty and power of nature.

The church is much in my thoughts as my days draw to a close. I hope I have fulfilled some of the purposes for which my Maker, if he exists – as to which my doubts will soon be indisputably resolved – put me here. That I have not achieved all of which I was capable was inevitable; I am only human, and by definition fallible. I have tried to leave a legacy that will improve the lot of my fellow man. Some are patented, although I set precious little store by such bureaucratic procedures, some are not. Some are still in my head and I will take them with me. There are a million discoveries still to be made by others. I wish them well. I hope my work will help them with their endeavours. I have left a few clues, intentionally or otherwise which I hope they will find of use, and I have not forgotten the church of my childhood.

Yours sincerely,
Nikola Tesla.'

It was the very last sentence that caught Heidi's attention. It didn't follow from what he'd said before. It was a new thought. What did it mean? On the surface it was a reference to his mother's needlepoint, but was it? He used the phrase 'the church of my childhood.' Heidi dismissed the idea as far-fetched. She continued reading.

After another forty-five minutes she gave up. Her mind kept returning to the letter. Finally she asked the custodian if she might make a photostat.

The woman in the purple pants waited until Heidi had left. She placed her books on the central counter and glanced at the cartons of film. Her eyes widened as she recognized the Tesla name. She spoke to the paisley wearer.

'May I look through this Tesla-Clemens film? I must have missed it the other day.'

The President's schedule was full for the day. Wilshire had no special status to give him access to the White House. He made it known that he would talk to no one but the Man, and that national security was involved. He was eventually put through. 'Mr President, this is Arthur Wilshire. I need to see you as a matter of greatest urgency . . . '

'What's it about?' The Man was terse.

'It's too sensitive to discuss through an open line. I need to see you personally.'

'Hasn't my secretary told you I have a full calendar in fact for a week ahead?'

'Indeed she has, Mr President. I'm afraid what I've got can't wait, and I am not at liberty to see anybody else.'

'You're not at liberty!'

'I am a lawyer. Those I represent . . . '

'Who? Who are they, Mr Wilshire?'

'I'm instructed not to disclose names.'

'I won't deal anonymously with anybody!'

'Mr President. I think you know my reputation on the Hill. I won't waste your time. If you trust my judgement – and many in the GOP think highly of it – I think you should see me. I need fifteen minutes, maybe less.'

'Noon!' said the President.

The blue-uniformed White House guard told Wilshire to open the package. 'Only in the presence of the President!'

'Then you don't get past me, sir.' He pressed a button. The alarm sounded. Wilshire was surrounded, weapons were drawn. Wilshire would not permit the box to be opened. His ID and appointment were confirmed. A detector was produced and the package was pronounced free from explosive devices. At five minutes past twelve, Wilshire was ushered into the Oval Office. An aide was standing by the President's side.

'What have you got there?' said the President pointing to the box.

'May I approach this my own way, Mr President. My job isn't easy.'

'What's it about?'

'Survival,' said Wilshire mildly.

'Huh! What area of activity are we talking about here? Army? Navy? Missiles? What?'

'I suppose the general heading would be our country's defence,' answered Wilshire. The President pressed his intercom button.

'I want Mr Coverdale in here fast. If he's not in the building, find him.' He disconnected. 'Start talking.'

'I represent a number of clients who are people of influence . . . who work for their country in ways that are not always obvious . . . '

'If you mean they make heavy donations, say so.'

'That's not what I meant, Mr President.' The intercom buzzed.

'Yes?'

The secretary's voice was calm and efficient. 'Mr Coverdale's on his way up.'

'Send him right in.' And he nodded at Wilshire to continue.

'My clients do various things, control different companies carrying out all manner of research, some of it for government agencies – and I'm not here to talk about that aspect, I merely mention it to give you some idea of the scope of the people I represent – and a lot of it in private speculative fields of engineering, high-tech, electronics; you know the sort of thing?'

The President nodded.

'It was during such activities, that they stumbled across certain material which they now believe may have a security application for United States defence.'

'Why the secrecy? The anonymity? Why didn't the company call up the Pentagon and tell 'em about it?'

Before Wilshire could answer, there was a tap on the door and Coverdale entered. His step faltered as he saw the gold and silver wrapping and blue bow. He blanched.

'You OK, Fred?' asked the President.

Coverdale recovered his composure with difficulty. He couldn't take his eyes off the box. If it did contain some arcane sexual aid, what was it doing in the Oval Office of the President of the United States!

'I'm sorry, Mr President, would you mind repeating that. I lost my footing on the rug.'

'Arthur Wilshire represents a bunch of guys who've stumbled across something they think's mighty important to defence. Carry on Mr Wilshire. Tell us why your anonymous clients didn't take it to the Pentagon.'

'What's in that box is something government agencies have spent millions trying to find. The Soviets have devoted even more resources to it. My clients know the significance of this . . . thing. They know they can trust the President of their country, but with something this hot, they don't know who else can be trusted.'

Wilshire had everybody's attention now. The President spoke. 'What is it?'

'We . . . that is my clients, believe it to be a part of a

model made by one Nikola Tesla, known colloquially as the Tesla Trinity.'

Coverdale was fast with his question. 'Has a scientific test been run on it? It's easy to be fooled!' The question was a reflex; what Coverdale was really thinking was how did Ruth get hold of it? What was her connection with these people? Was it a group working outside legal frameworks? And what did that do to his position?

'It's been in my clients' possession less than twenty-four hours, but its provenance is beyond question. It was given personally to my clients' contact by Tesla himself, together with a message that emphasized its secrecy and importance.'

Frederick had dragged his mind away from thoughts of his wife's behaviour and was now concentrating on the implications of the job in hand. 'How old is this contact? Tesla was eighty-six when he died in 1943!'

'Middle-aged,' answered Wilshire.

Coverdale was dismissive. 'Then I don't think we can take this too seriously, Mr President. Tesla would never have entrusted the secret to a child!'

Wilshire was equally dismissive. 'He left one piece buried in Flushing Meadow Park!'

'Where did you get that information, Mr Wilshire? That's a serious breach of security,' said the Man.

'I'm sorry, sir. Lawyer's confidentiality.'

'I'm not so sure about that.' He turned to his aide. 'Get lawyers to check it out.'

'Yes, Mr President.' The young man made a note.

'Let's take a look at your treasure, Mr Wilshire.'

The Defense Advisor intervened. 'Don't you think it would be better if I got a scientific team to do that?'

'No, I don't Fred. I want to see it for myself.'

The President disliked Arthur Wilshire. Since Watergate, lawyers had had too much say in what the President could and could not do. Here, at last, was a lawyer out on a limb and he would take a shot at chopping it off.

Arthur removed the silver bow and scotch tape. He unfolded the paper. The box showed that it had once held a year's supply of PX soap.

The President was disappointed. 'I expected something impressive, spectacular even. This is just a . . . an ornament. Which way up's it supposed to go?' he asked. The President tried it on all its sides. 'It doesn't seem to make a deal of difference. What are these lines running through the middle of it?'

'That's what it's all about, Mr President, or so I'm informed.'

'Shall I take it now, Mr President?'

'No, Fred. As Wilshire says, we've spent a few bucks trying to find this damned thing. I won't have it smashed when you fall over your feet again. Get General Beely over here with an armoured car, and some marines to look after this . . . whatever it is.'

The woman left the Library of Congress and made a phone call. She hailed a cruiser yellow cab and gave him an address in Sewards Square in the south-east side of the city. She arranged her briefcase neatly on her lap, its handle firmly grasped in her right hand.

Rakov made his call at four p.m.

'You're to meet the sleeper again. Urgent. Same time and place. Tonight.'

Rogers, Lloyd, Tyson and Heidi were grouped round Pete's desk staring at the photostat of Tesla's letter.

'I don't know,' said Rogers. 'I just don't know whether it's a hidden message or the meanderings of a dying mind.'

'Have we got any better leads?' asked Lloyd. Rogers gave him a withering look. 'So why not go for this?'

'How?' asked Tyson. 'Where do we start?'

'The letter talks about the happiest days of his life,' speculated Lloyd. 'We know he had tremendous affection for his mother – how proud he was to tell everybody she could tie three knots in an eyelash with her bare fingers – mother . . . mother . . . "church of my childhood" – that must mean Smiljan.'

'So what!' said Heidi.

'His father was a parish priest. He was in charge of the church at Smiljan where he grew up, where his mother was . . . ' It sounded feeble even as he said it. The telephone rang. Heidi answered it with a simple 'Hello.'

'Who is that?' said the voice.

'493 1217,' said Heidi barely concealing the boredom in her manner. It was the wrong number, but the code identified her for the right caller.

'I suggest you pay a little more attention to security, in future,' said the CIA director. 'Use the scrambler and put me on to Pete.' Heidi gulped and handed him the instrument.

'It's the director. For you.' Heidi punched the scrambler switch.

'Yes sir . . . '

'Anything to report?'

'No, sir. We have a lead of sorts, but we can't seem to make any sense of it.'

'What sort of a lead?'

'Probably the last letter Tesla wrote to somebody who'd already been dead twenty-five years.'

'It doesn't sound promising.'

'We'll give it a bit more effort until something more . . . promising comes along.'

'It has.' The director waited as if for applause.

'Really, sir?' said Rogers encouragingly.

'That fat legal lobby cat Arthur Wilshire walked into the White House this morning with one third of our target.'

'A part of the Trinity?'

'Indeed. Now where did he get it? That's what the President wants to know. What I want to know is how a lawyer sitting behind a desk can find something my worldwide network can't!'

'You want me to bug a lawyer? Arthur Wilshire! He'd spot it in a New York minute. It'd be another Watergate.'

'The Man wants to know where he got it. So do I. That means we've got to find out who his clients are . . . '

'Sir . . . we can't do things like that. It's against the law.'

'I want a team set up with cameras. I want photographs of everybody going into his building.'

'What do I do about this letter?'

'The Wilshire business takes precedence over everything. Its a direct order from the President. Let somebody else work on the goddamn letter.' The line went dead.

'We've got work to do,' said Rogers. 'Heidi, get on to photographics. I want a twenty-four hour shift set up. Then get hold of the real estate division. I want plans of all buildings near Wilshire's office in the 700 block.'

'What about the letter?' Tyson wanted to know.

'I guess that had better be your baby.'

'We'll go for it!'

'How?' asked Lloyd.

'Use the outer office, you two,' said Rogers.

'Give me the letter,' said Chuck as they settled in the other office. '"I have not forgotten the church." If that's any sort of a lead, it means he put the final piece of the Trinity in the church at Smiljan.'

'That letter's forty years old. He made the model, say twenty years before that. If you're right, if he put it there, he did so fifty or seventy years ago. What makes you think it's still there?'

'Churches keep things they're given; sometimes for hundreds of years,' said Tyson.

'We've got to make the assumption. And remember, it's an open library. The opposition could have this letter.'

'Ask Heidi.'

Rogers didn't like the interruption.

'Was there anybody else in the library who could have seen what you took?' asked Lloyd.

'Only one person stood out, in a purple pant suit! And yes . . . I glanced back through the glass doors on my way out. She was standing at the desk.'

'If she was the stake-out, would she have been able to get a copy of the letter?'

'Easily, I'm afraid,' Heidi admitted.

'We have a race on our hands,' said Tyson.

'If, if, if!' said Lloyd.

16

Date: 27 October 1981
Washington D.C., Points East

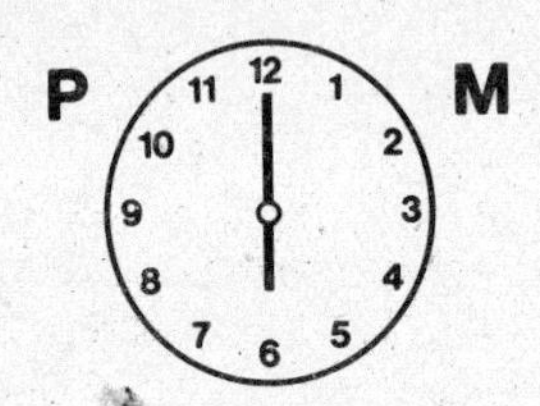

'There's a ten o'clock flight from New York to Zagreb tonight,' said Tyson to Lloyd. 'JFK – Pan Am.' Lloyd looked at his watch. Tyson spoke into the telephone again. 'Is there a connecting flight that'll get us to JFK in time? . . . OK. Thanks.' He replaced the receiver. 'We need to leave in the next fifteen minutes. The Washington/New York shuttle will not technically give us enough time, but without luggage and any luck . . . '

Lloyd was not happy. 'We can't both take a chance on missing the flight. They may be ahead of us for all we know.'

Tyson was irritated. 'There's no alternative. Yugoslav Airlines doesn't have anything tonight.'

'There must be another way of getting to that bloody country.' Tyson handed him the telephone.

'I've only been hanging on the end of this thing for an hour. You try your luck, buster!'

'What about a government plane?'

'What sort of government? Air Force? It would take a week to get permission to land. Then the answer would be no.'

'Ruth has a Lear jet. What's its range?' asked Lloyd.

The idea interested Tyson. 'It would have to refuel somewhere. I'd have to talk her into it.'

'It would cost a bomb in fuel.'

'What's money! We'll both go that-a-way.'

'No,' said Lloyd. 'Anything can happen with long distance plane rides. I'll take my chances with Pan Am. You go in style.'

'How do we get the model out of Yugoslavia?' asked Tyson.

'Busk it.'

'What does that mean?'

'You'll have the private jet somewhere handy – Zagreb looks the nearest,' said Lloyd looking at the map of Yugoslavia on the desk.

'How do I get it through customs?'

'I see what you mean . . . I could lay on a boat – private yacht, cruising the Adriatic, calling at . . . say Zadar.'

Tyson stood up, decisive. 'Let's do it. You set up the boat. Get Forbes to call me at Ruth's. Call me when you get to New York.'

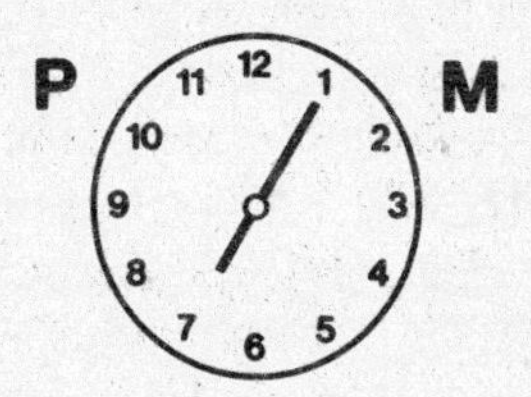

They met in a busy, darkened bar in one of the tree-lined streets of Georgetown. The young executives and secretaries of professional Washington were beginning the weekend with a liquid happy hour. Rakov's contact kept looking about him nervously. Rakov blew out the candle.

'Does that make you feel safer, comrade?'

'You don't seem to realize. The CIA are everywhere. Nobody is safe.'

'What do you want with me?' said Rakov calmly.

'You're to go to Smiljan.'

'Where's that?'

'Yugoslavia.'

'Why?'

The embassy man told him.

'Why me? They know what the damn thing looks like. Why not send somebody closer?'

'The general says it must be you.'

'How do I get there?'

'That's being worked out. But you have to meet the sleeper first.'

'Has everybody gone mad!'

'I don't set the priorities.'

'I know nothing about Yugoslavia. I don't even speak the language.'

The contact ignored that. 'I have a new passport for you. You're a woman.'

'Absolutely not!'

'Not my idea. Orders.'

'To pull that off you need to walk like a woman, talk like one. I'm not made that way . . .'

The contact was not impressed. 'I'm just the messenger.'

'It's the surest way of blowing my cover.'

Ruth rapped out the orders. The Lear would be diverted from Los Angeles, much to the disgust of Ed Jamieson who was on his way home in it at the time. It would land in Washington at one-thirty a.m. It would take time to file a flight plan, get refuelled and the pre-flight checks done, and they'd need a fresh crew.

Frederick walked in. 'I need to see you, Ruth.' His mood was ominous. Ruth guessed why. 'Chuck, I need a little time with my wife. It could take quite a while. Do you have plans to go out for the evening?'

Ruth put a hand over the mouthpiece of the telephone and spoke to Frederick. 'Not now, darling. This is important.' Frederick was not amused. He took the phone and replaced it in its cradle.

'This can't wait.' He said it mildly.

'I'd better . . . ' said Tyson.

'Don't leave yet, Chuck. We haven't finished making your arrangements.' She was also cool, but there was a dangerous edge to her tone. Frederick continued.

'Leave us!' he said.

'I don't like being ordered about, Frederick; especially when I'm making important arrangements.'

'What arrangements and how do they concern this officer?'

'Chuck needs to get to Yugoslavia in a hurry. He can't use Air Force planes for various reasons. I've offered him the use of my Lear.'

'I can't allow that.'

'It has nothing to do with you, Frederick. It's my plane and my decision.'

'I am the President's special adviser, and I'm telling you not to do it.'

Tyson spoke, nervously. 'I need to use the bathroom.' He left the room.

'Why did you tell me lies about that box?' The change of subject came as no surprise.

'What box?'

'The one with the gold wrapping that was going to get me all excited. Arthur Wilshire presented it to the President this afternoon in my presence, on behalf of certain anonymous clients, one of whom is you. Who are the rest? Jack Lubbock? Arthur Wilshire himself? Who else?'

'I don't know what you're talking about?' Ruth said it defiantly. A straight denial, relying on the coincidence of two similarly wrapped boxes seemed the best bet. Why hadn't she thought to change the paper!

'Bring me the box. We'll open it together. In the bedroom, if you like.'

Why hadn't she thought to buy a damned dildo and wrap it like the box? 'I can't do that.'

'Surprise. Surprise.'

'I was . . . upset by your reaction. I took it back.'

'You can do better than that, Ruth. Where is your . . . originality now?' She said nothing. 'And now I find you getting further into business of state. Private airplanes, no less. What will it be next? Gun-running?'

'I'm not ashamed of what I'm doing. I'm proud of it. Nothing you say will stop me.'

'OK. I'll call the President, give him your name, and those of the others and my resignation.' He stretched out his hand for the telephone.

Ruth was panic-stricken. 'Don't! For God's sake, Frederick.' He didn't pick up the instrument. 'I need time to . . . surely we can work something out.'

Frederick was cool. 'What do you suggest?'

'Do you have to tell him?'

'Of course I do. My job isn't only Russians and spies and terrorists; it's anybody who threatens the United States.'

'We're no threat. We're helping.'

'Don't be naïve.'

'I'm serious. We all are. That's the very reason for . . . '

'You can't make that sort of judgement. You can't usurp the functions of government because you feel patriotic.'

'It's not like that!'

'It's exactly like that.'

Ruth thought for a moment. 'What do you want me to do?'

'My duty is clear. Report and resign. I realize there couldn't be a worse time for a national scandal. It would undermine the authority of the President.' Ruth began to breathe more easily. He had a plan and that must mean hope. 'Your activities will cease at once. You'll tell your friends they're blown and the group disbanded.' Ruth's mind was beginning to think she could give him any promise he wanted and still carry on, until he continued: 'You will convene a meeting of all members of your group here tonight. I will talk to them.' It could not have been worse, thought Ruth in despair.

'I need time to think about this, Frederick.'

'Five minutes. Then I call the Man.'

'What about Chuck? That's genuine business for the CIA. He absolutely has to get to Yugoslavia.'

'Why?'

'They've got a lead on the third piece of the Trinity. He hasn't told me what it is, but he needs to get to Yugoslavia fast. The other side already has the same information and may beat him to it.'

'Ruth, I don't seem to have got through to you. You can't play international war games. You're a private citizen. You're not even a politician or in the administration. You have no standing, no business even knowing what's going on. Tyson has no right coming to you. That's a breach of security for which he will be disciplined.'

'For God's sake, Frederick, can't you throw away the rule book just for once – when your country's survival is at stake!'

Frederick's anger was frightening. 'Rule book! Is that what you think it is. What do you know of what is going on on the international front? What do you know of the exchanges between the President and Brezhnev, between ambassadors; what do you think the Pentagon's up to?

NATO countries? Do you think they're sitting on their asses waiting for the results of your puny efforts. Good God, woman, your bungling interference could start the Third World War!'

Ruth was crushed. She had no answer. There was silence in the room for several minutes. 'All right, Frederick. I'll call them . . . I can't promise they'll come . . . '

'You realize, of course, it's the end of us.' He said it so softly she almost missed it.

'This has nothing to do with us personally, Freddie. It doesn't affect what I feel for you.'

His face was devoid of expression, hard, impersonal, as she had known it most of their married life.

'You really don't understand me, either the before or after my . . . foolish exhibition. Trust! That's what I'm all about! That's what I could always depend on, from you. This isn't just lack of trust, it's deceit. It puts at risk all I've ever wanted out of my professional life. I'd no idea I could be so wrong about anybody.' And she had to take it because every word was true. She couldn't hold back the tears. He looked at her without pity.

Tyson knocked and entered.

Ruth turned to look out of the window. She cleared her throat. 'Chuck . . . you'll have to do as Frederick says.'

'I'm sure my director'll clear it if you give him a call.'

Frederick would have none of that.

'When your director gets the facts he'll clamp you in irons, young man.' That silenced him. 'You will report back to your office and do whatever it is you have to do through the usual channels.'

The flight was closed. The agent at the ticket desk said there was no hope of Lloyd boarding the flight. He ran at full tilt to the gate, waving his ticket. The huge door of the Boeing 747 dropped and was clamped from the other side. The agent shook his head. 'Please,' said Lloyd, out of breath. 'It's life or death. It really is.' The agent looked through the priest's hole, holding up one finger. The purser rang the captain of the plane. Lloyd held his breath. Sixty seconds passed. The door began to rise again. It was 2205 hours.

Date: 28 October 1981
Washington, D.C.

Rakov was back in the shadowed corner of the car park. It was one a.m. He kept trying to detect his contact's arrival, but his concentration span expired.

The whisper began. 'They have the second part of the Trinity.' Rakov gasped. He had no suspicion they were even close.

'Are you sure?' he said.

'It is confirmed!' The whisperer was not pleased to have its word doubted. 'They have a lead to a place called Smiljan in Yugoslavia . . . '

'I know about that,' replied Rakov. 'I'm leaving to chase it down myself. Is there anything else?'

There was no answer. The whisper had left as silently as he/she had come.

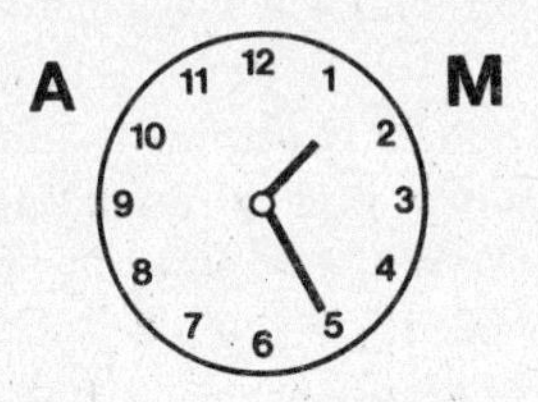

Richard Lloyd had tried to sleep on the plane, but his mind was preoccupied with the permutations of what lay ahead. Forbes had responded immediately. 'Leave it to me, old boy. Give me a ring from Zagreb. I'll let you know the form.'

'What about code?'

'Stuff it,' Forbes had said. 'No time to be elaborate. I'll tell you in a roundabout language. Use a public phone.'

At last he began to doze when the captain's voice came through, quietly, soothingly over the public address system in the darkened cabin.

'I sure hate to wake you folks up back there, but we do have a little bitty problem up here. Nothing serious, but we're getting a malfunction on one of our fuel gauges, and rather than run any risks we're going to put down at Prestwick, Scotland, just to check it out. We won't keep you there any longer than we have to. Have a good night's sleep, now.'

Tyson had thought about the scene with Frederick. He could understand his point-of-view. He was the President's special adviser. Ruth had blown her cover and he'd put a stop to her activities. OK but he still had his job to do. He was at Washington National Airport betting that Ruth hadn't cancelled the Learjet.

He was on the strip when the short ladder dropped to the ground. Out stepped Ed Jamieson. 'What's going on?' he demanded.

'Government business, Mr Jamieson. This aircraft has been commandeered for service use . . . '

'Commandeered! Who started the war?'

'I'm not at liberty to discuss that.'

'Let me get at a telephone. Ruth Coverdale had better be informed of this!' He strode away. Tyson held his arm.

'These are Mrs Coverdale's instructions, and I don't think she'll be thrilled at being woken up at two a.m. to confirm them. What do you think?' Jamieson contemplated his future and decided it was more important than a row about a missed schedule.

'Where's the bar?' he asked.

Tyson was on tenterhooks for two hours, while the formalities were completed, expecting any moment that the phone would ring, and orders come stopping the flight. None did. At three thirty-five Eastern Daylight Time, he was airborne.

It was nine-thirty a.m. Greenwich Mean Time. Lloyd called Forbes in Washington, where Eastern Daylight Time made it four-thirty a.m. Yes he had arranged for a private yacht to steam at full throttle from Rimini to Zadar. The owner, chairman of a multi-national aerospace company based in London, would be only too happy to put his private passion at the disposal of HM Government for five thousand dollars a day. That was fine provided Lloyd ever got anywhere near Zadar, Smiljan or Zagreb. The airline gave the usual commentary every thirty minutes. meanwhile how about having another breakfast with the compliments of Pan Am? He tried to get there by other means but connections were difficult and the odds favoured the Pan Am flight getting him to Zagreb fastest.

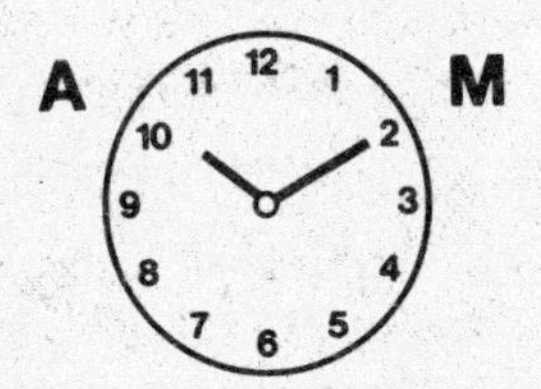

Rakov shaved twice, cursing his dark beard. He splashed on cologne and then realized nuns probably didn't use after-shave. He struggled with the whimple which wouldn't sit right on his hair. He pulled the brown habit over his head and lastly the black veil. He felt stifled and ridiculous. An unmistakably male face glared back at him in the mirror. Or was it? The shoes were two sizes too small. The Air France agent curtsied! 'Have a nice flight, sister.' As the beautiful metal 'bird' soared into the American sky, Rakov sighed in relief to be free of the clutches of that New World's justice. It was ten-ten a.m. Eastern Daylight Time. Rakov's relief turned sour when he considered that his country's enemies had a start of many hours on him, and that the chances of his recovering whatever was at Smiljan church were almost nil.

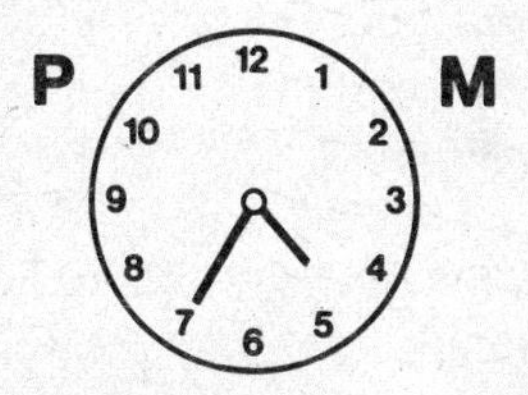

Tyson woke refreshed. He had not realized what difference a full-length bed made to a transatlantic flight. He looked out of the window and saw nothing but cloud. He walked through to the cockpit.

'How did you sleep?' asked the captain.

'Great. Great. How are we doing?'

'Fine. Right on schedule. We're due over Zagreb at seven thirty-seven local time.'

'Shall we beat the Pan Am flight? It left JFK at twenty-two hundred.'

'Not in a million years. They'd be there five, six hours ahead of us.' Chuck snapped his fingers, irritated to be beaten by Lloyd. 'Want me to check?'

'Why not.'

'Hello Zagreb. This is Learjet Alpha X-ray. Can you tell me if the Pan Am flight from New York has landed yet?'

'This is Zagreb . . . hold one minute please . . . No. It diverted to Prestwick with engine trouble. No E.T.A. as yet.'

Tyson heard it and rejoiced. The pilot continued the conversation. 'Do you have clearance for our landing yet, Zagreb?'

'Is there a problem?' asked Tyson.

'Don't worry, we often get this. These Iron Curtain countries are not used to the private plane set. It takes them a while to go through the red tape. It'll be OK. You're a rich tourist and they want dollars!'

'Hello Learjet Alpha X-ray . . . this is Zagreb. Negative on clearance for landing.'

The pilot came back quickly. 'Zagreb, this is Alpha X-ray. Repeat that please. Did you say negative?'

'Negative Alpha X-ray.'

'Do you mind telling me why, Zagreb, I've flown five thousand miles from the United States . . . '

'We cannot give you clearance to land. No request for permission was received before your take-off time, according to our records, and so we cannot give permission to land now.'

'Zagreb . . . this is very inconvenient. Please check your records again. I personally telephoned before take-off from Washington DC. I was assured it would be in order . . . '

'Stand by, Alpha X-ray . . . I will check again.'

'What is going on?' Tyson wanted to know.

The pilot looked uncomfortable. 'The guy I spoke to said he was sure it'd be OK . . . You were in one hell of a hurry to get off. I took his word for it.'

The speaker crackled into life again. 'Alpha X-ray . . . This is Zagreb . . . We have a problem. Too much air traffic and not enough senior staff on duty. I cannot get you a clearance. Sorry Alpha X-ray. Good luck, and out.'

The Pan Am 747 took off at six p.m. Flying time: two hours thirty-two minutes to Zagreb.

The great thing about flying Concorde is not its comfort; it is rather cramped; nor its food which, apart from the caviar and cold lobster appetizers, and the Dom Perignon, is prepared in heated trays because of space restrictions; it is the smoothness with which every request is treated, the remarkable way difficulties melt in the path of the highest paying passenger in the air. So it was that Rakov was met personally at the gate at Charles de Gaulle and escorted to the departure lounge for Lublijana, Yugoslavia. The nun mimed her thanks; Carmelites, Rakov remembered, were largely a silent order. He did not immediately check in, but sought out a toilet. Just in time he remembered to go through the door marked 'Dames.' He closed the cubicle door and quickly changed. When silence finally indicated he was alone he emerged from the cubicle in shirt, sweater and pants. At the door, he encountered an ample matron, shepherding two young daughters. 'Pardon, Madame,' said Rakov in his most charming manner, 'Je vous m'excuse. C'est terrible . . . terrible . . . ' Madame smiled at an innocent mistake.

Tyson landed at Venice at seven p.m. He spent ten minutes listening as the pilot tried to get clearance to land at Zagreb, and then rented a car. At seven-thirty p.m. he was in the driving seat of a Fiat 132, distance to Yugoslav border at Sezana 164 kilometres; and then another 237; say 250 miles.

Rakov made a phone call as he waited for embarkation. He was angry that he was kept in Washington to hear a message the sleeper could have phoned in.

He felt the nudge as the aircraft was pushed from the departure gate. It was seven-forty-seven p.m. The stewardess announced that their flying time to Ljubljana, Yugoslavia, would be one hour fifty minutes.

Tyson had a frustrating time getting out of Marco Polo Airport and on the freeway to Trieste. Construction work was causing traffic chaos. As soon as he hit the autostrada he put his foot to the floor of the new Fiat. At roughly one hundred miles per hour he should get to the border in the hour; nine p.m.; and beat that damned Brit, and the goddamn Soviets.

The Pan Am flight's arrival was announced on the visual display unit at Zagreb: 'landed at 2132 hours – 9.32 p.m.' There had been no time to arrange a forged passport, so Lloyd was using his own. He prayed that at nine-thirty p.m. on a Friday night the immigration boys would have other thoughts on their minds than high security checks. His luck held. He was issued his tourist pass for thirty days along with the three hundred travel-weary Americans from his jumbo jet. By nine-forty-five p.m. he had completed the formalities for renting and was sitting behind the wheel of a Skoda.

Rakov had not wanted the 250 kilometre drive from Ljubljana to Smiljan; hence his phone call. A hard landing put him finally on the ground at Ljubljana at nine-thirty p.m. He did not attempt to use his KGB status. He told the immigration officer he was on vacation. The customs inspector was interested in the nun's habit in his overnight case. Rakov had debated ditching it in Paris, but feared the consequences of its discovery. He explained that they were needed for a play being produced, in Moscow where such things were hard to find. It brought the intended smile from the Yugoslav, who let him through at nine-forty-six p.m.

He was met by a harassed KGB lieutenant. 'You didn't give us much time, major.'

'Don't give me excuses. What arrangements have you made?' The lieutenant was good-looking with full lips. Another time and place, thought Rakov.

'A private plane will take you to Zadar. A rented car will be waiting.' Rakov smiled. The lieutenant was agreeably surprised. He lowered his eyes. He guided Yuri to the tarmac, where a Cessna stood waiting, the name Aviogenex painted on the side. 'Are you coming with me?'

'Unfortunately major, I have to go back to Zagreb. I got you as many maps of the area around Gospic as I could find. As you didn't tell me your exact destination, I could do no more.'

'Get me into the air,' said Rakov.

Tyson waited in line at the border at Sezena. He was upset. He had done the journey in record time, but for the last thirty minutes he had been waiting for the single border guard to inspect each vehicle, and then for the clerk to issue the tourist pass. It was not until nine-fifty p.m. that he was free and on his way to Gospic, over two hundred kilometres away.

Lloyd found the first forty-four kilometres from Zagreb to Karlovac easy and fast. They took twenty minutes. The next leg was through a so-called tourist road, picturesque, but single lane and winding. He passed through the small town of Rakovica – noting the coincidence of name wryly – at ten-fifty-eight p.m. Eighty-six kilometres to go; another hour?

Rakov's Cessna landed late. The tower at Zadar made the private plane circle while international traffic took precedence. It was ten-fifty-nine p.m. before Rakov was at the car rental agency desk. It was closed.

Tyson was pleased with himself. He was making good time and the Fiat drove well; not to be compared with his Camaro back home, but it gave him no trouble. He was taking a corner rather fast in the ancient city of Rijeka when it happened. True he was moving quicker than the speed limit, actually about twice the permitted velocity, but he wouldn't be beaten a second time by Lloyd. The truck entered from his right, without warning, applied its brakes far too late, and hammered into the side of the Fiat, carrying it across the road and into a shop window, where it came to rest. Tyson examined himself and was surprised to find that apart from a few bruises he was unharmed. His watch told him it was eleven-o-five p.m. He grabbed the door handle; it would not move. He smelled leaking gasoline. The truck driver was singing.

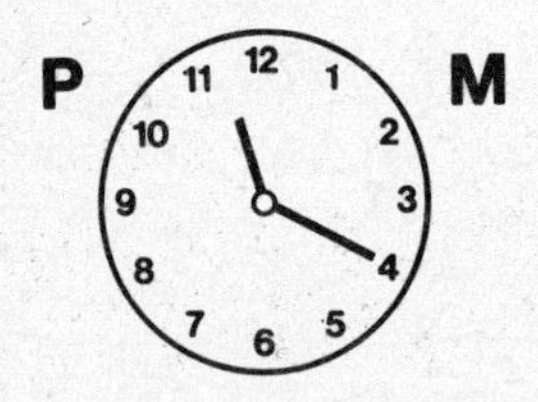

Yuri Rakov cleared Zadar airport at eleven-twenty p.m. He headed north to Karlobag, 90 kilometres away. The E27 was the coast road, normally crowded with holiday traffic.

Lloyd was having difficulty keeping awake. The windows of the car were open. He was travelling at speed, but the overnight flight and the frustrating delay at Prestwick were finally catching up with him. As he passed into the National Park at Dreznik-Grad, he put his foot down hard. He realized he must have dozed off for a second or two when he saw the signpost for Udbina; he had missed the road to

Gospic. He braked and tore his map open. It looked quicker to go on to Udbina and turn off, getting back to Gospic via Medak. He raced the engine and the tyres protested as he angrily let in the clutch. It was eleven-forty-three p.m. when the tyre blew.

There was another crash of glass as a friendly motorist used an axe to smash the rear window of the Fiat. Tyson clambered out. A police car arrived. Its two occupants wandered over. One of them got out a notebook. Neither of them spoke English. The truck driver stopped singing.

Date: 29 October 1981
Smiljan, Yugoslavia

There was a nearly-new moon. The light it cast was minimal. Lloyd was looking for a church steeple, having given up hope of finding a signpost to Smiljan. He approached the lee of a wooded hill and saw two buildings on his right. He stopped. One was a house, the other a ruin. He decided to investigate. He was definitely in the right place on the map for Smiljan but what had happened to the church? It was the ruin; there could be no doubt. It was on the spot. There was the dry-stone-built tower with its long narrow windows, and then the squat square shape beneath. It had once been the Serbian orthodox church where Tesla's father was pastor, but it was no longer a place of worship. The walls were crumbling; moss and other vegetation grew through the stonework. Now what? Was it all a self-induced hoax? Was the letter to Mark Twain a reference to something entirely different? It would seem so. Even if it wasn't, even if Tesla had presented the third part of the Trinity to this church, what had happened to it? Where would he even begin to look?

A light breeze fanned his face and a door knocked against its architrave. Lloyd turned his attention to the house. What was it? It was in darkness and didn't seem to be inhabited yet it was in good repair. Lloyd examined the flapping door; the wood was splintered round the lock. He listened but heard nothing. He struck a match. Inside it was neat and beautifully laid out. Was it somebody's home? No. That was not right. He realized it must be Tesla's old home restored as a museum. Had the Trinity piece been housed here? Possibly. What was the explanation of the broken lock? Could Rakov or one of his men have beaten Lloyd to it? Possibly. He struck another match. On a table were artefacts from the church. There was something wrong with the symmetry. There was a gap in the middle of the display. He struck another match. There was a scratch mark and a faint outline of dust.

It was then that he heard the low rumble of an engine; somebody trying to start a car in motion. He ran. The engine caught, was revved, and crashed into gear before Richard got back to his Skoda. It started at the third turn of the key. He ground it into gear and let in the clutch, leaving a spray of gravel in his wake. He could see the headlights ahead of him. The other car had a start of less than a mile. Lloyd would close the gap. Having got so far, he would not let a Russian win the second round of their encounter. The road was narrow and winding. He drove into every corner, crashing from bank to bank, using brakes only as a last resort. They were nearing a main road. Suddenly the lights of the leading car were doused. Lloyd was not troubled; he had the spot precisely calculated. He killed his own engine and coasted the last few feet. He left the door open. He located the other car and approached quickly but silently. He flung open the door. The interior light disclosed a young man and woman in each other's arms. The girl screamed.

Yuri Rakov also saw the sign announcing the town of Rakovica. He took it as a good omen as he looked down at the remarkable thing beside him.

It would have cost a fortune to have made today, he reflected, even if there were anybody alive with the necessary skills. He did not think it was made of gold, it looked and handled more like brass, the surface of which was worked with many figures. It stood on almost human feet, each pair pointing outwards. Its base was scalloped, with a figure wrought into each shield. Then there was a band of brass with rectangular shapes of zinc let into them. Four roughly circular columns with elaborate filigree branches and leaves rose from the base to meet a replica of the rectangular base of brass and zinc. Nestling inside in a cradle of brass formed to take each point of contact was the familiar translucent quartz that he had taken from Savannah to Cuba. There was no doubt: this was 'Ghost,' the third part of the Tesla Trinity.

BOOK III
Fusion

'History is just the portrayal
of crimes and misfortunes.'

Voltaire,
(*L'Ingenue*, Chap. X)

CERN is the European Centre for Nuclear Research; its laboratory spans the Franco-Swiss border with 110 hectares in Switzerland and 450 hectares in France. It is located at Meyrin, a small village a few miles south of Geneva and within sight of the Jura mountains; the Rhone wends its peaceful way to Lac Léman passing CERN from east to west, north of the complex.

There are twelve member states of CERN – Austria, Belgium, Denmark, West Germany, France, Greece, Italy, the Netherlands, Norway, Sweden, Switzerland and the United Kingdom. The USSR, USA and China use the facility by invitation.

About 1,500 scientists have unrestricted access to the four hundred thousand million electron volts of energy which the most powerful of the CERN accelerators generates in its high energy physics experiments to seek out the structure of matter. Its most recent finding is confirmation of the existence of subatomic particles called Wand Z, which helps the theory linking electromagnetism and the weak nuclear force. This has led to the belief that space may have not three dimensions but as many as ten. Einstein's theory that gravity is an expression of a curvature of three-dimensional space and time, has been expanded by Kaluza who pointed out that if space had only four dimensions it would be possible to describe electromagnetism geometrically as warps in the fourth dimension.

Ten dimensions is a concept almost impossible for the mind to grasp, but such is the extraordinary range of thinking and experimentation of the scientific community at

CERN. It is one of the finest examples of co-operation across political and national boundaries to improve man's knowledge of his universe.

Nikola Tesla would have been in his element at CERN. He would have rejoiced in the knowledge that a principal unit of modern physics is named after him – a Tesla. He would also have known that access to CERN's accelerator would have enabled him to demonstrate the validity of the theory behind the Tesla Trinity.

17

Thursday 29th October 1981
Washington, D.C.

At 8 a.m. Frederick was in his temporary office behind the White House. Papers with government insignia littered the desktop. He tried to concentrate but his mind kept wandering to his personal problem. He had never had to cope with such strong feelings. Never had emotion entered into competition with his duty, not even when his mother had been at her most demanding. Even then he had known exactly what the priorities were; personal affairs took second place to work.

It wasn't a question of willpower – he had enough of that for ten men – it was the confusion in his mind he couldn't handle. He knew what he should do. The course of action was clear. He should see the President, tell him everything and let him decide whether to sack Frederick and arrest Ruth and the others. But another part of his mind told him that the Man had appointed him to take responsibility, not hand it back at the first sign of a problem; that if he could not deal with an irresponsible wife and her intermeddling friends, he wasn't fit to be the office cleaner, let alone National Defense Advisor. This was reinforced by the conclusion that his own departure so soon after appointment would cause a crisis of confidence in the nation's ability to defend itself. And then he heard his mother's voice telling him these were excuses to protect the female. She'd warned him, repeatedly, about the effect of a certain type of woman. 'I warn you about Ruth Granby,' she had said. 'She's too rich and independent. She's not to be trusted. Marry her and sooner-or-later she'll bring you down!' He knew it was her normal possessiveness, made worse by advancing senility, and yet a small voice persisted that there was a truth in it, and that Ruth herself had proved it by her actions.

Perhaps his confusion was a simple matter of his still being in love with her. He could contemplate that without an attack of emotional jitters. It could be so, but he could leave that out of the equation without difficulty; that was where willpower came in. He would simply dismiss it as a factor worthy of consideration. If only he could resolve the other parts of the problem. It didn't occur to him that the reason for his confusion was the conflict of emotion and duty.

He decided to be the strong man and take the full responsibility for action upon himself; that was what the President would want, in fact insist on. They would separate – even the thought caused a churning pain – yes, separate, quietly. He would take an apartment adjoining the White House. If anybody bothered to enquire why, the story would be immediacy, security, long hours; everybody would understand. 'Divorce her,' said his mother's voice.

'For God's sake shut up!' he replied, and realized he'd said it aloud. The sooner he got out of this house and away from whatever was destroying his thought processes the better. If that was true – and it was – why did he delay in sending for Ruth and telling her his decision. He looked out of the window. Some leaves had still to fall.

He looked at the clock, and realized, with a shock that he must have been staring into space, his mind a total blank for nearly twenty minutes, a thing he had never done before. He jammed his finger at his secretary's button on the intercom: 'I'm going for a walk!' he said defiantly.

'Shall I tell security?' She was a new girl, a physics major from Yale who knew the administrative handbook from

cover-to-cover. Already she was beginning to irritate him.
'No!'
'I have to tell them anyway, sir. It's my job,' she added with polite indifference.

Palo Alto, Ca.

Christopher Hackett watched with concern as two muscled twenty-five-year-olds manhandled the package.

'Lift the goddamn thing, don't shove it. That's seventy five thousand dollars worth of sensitive equipment. Don't treat it like a . . . '

The two men in the back of the truck swore, and then set about moving the machine more carefully on to the forklift. Two white-coated technicians steadied it as the motor took the crate down to ground level.

'She delivered!' said Hackett. 'You've gotta give the lady credit. She came through!'

Hackett's assistant was Julia Black, a graduate of Berkeley of three years' standing; cool, competent, neat and professional, with a healthy percentage of cynicism in her make-up to counter-balance her boss's ideological commitment. 'And she will no doubt expect her pound of scientific flesh.'

'Yes . . . '

'You made the deal!'

'I know. But that thing she brought me won't work; it can't work!'

'Tough!' was Julia's comment.

'How can I justify taking men off important work to prove what I already know?'

'By contemplating that without that lady and her ancient oscillator you would never have owned this lovely toy.'

Hackett looked at her without malice. 'You're fired,' he said dolefully.

'Not again!' she sighed. 'I'm going into town.' She left him walking round the wooden casing, licking his lips.

He prised the nails out and lifted off the wooden struts. Eventually the gleaming metalwork was free of its timber shroud, and four men eased it from its pallet.

From a cupboard in the corner of the laboratory, buried under a pile of magazines Hackett pulled out the Tesla memento. 'Gene . . . ' He called across to a young man with his eye glued to a microscope, who reluctantly looked up. 'Catch!' And Hackett tossed over the oscillator that had cost Ruth Coverdale a quarter-of-a-million dollars. 'See if you can make that work!'

'What the hell is it?'

'Find out!' And Hackett went back to his new bauble.

Georgetown, D.C.

Ruth didn't see Frederick for the rest of Wednesday. She didn't know where he slept. The only contact was a note given her by Jennings.

> 'I want your group at the house at ten a.m. sharp, tomorrow. No excuses.'

She was waiting for him at 9.45. Five minutes later she heard his key in the front door lock. 'Frederick,' she began. 'We have to talk. Certain things have to be discussed. I can't go into this meeting or whatever you want to call it, just like that.'

He answered her as though she were an importuning Representative for a democratic state. 'I've told you my position. You've introduced a fundamental breach of trust into our relationship. That can't be undone. The consequences are inevitable.'

'What consequences?'

He didn't know why he hesitated. He had it quite straight in his mind ten minutes ago. 'I . . . you . . . I can't trust you again. I . . . can't take you into my confidence, so I can't go on living in this house wondering whether I've locked every drawer which might contain confidential papers . . . '

'So it's divorce, is it?'

'Of course not. That's unthinkable. We shall live separate lives. We shall come together for official functions. You will remain my wife.'

'No, Frederick. If I'm not to be trusted it's your duty to get rid of me.' Two could play at this sort of game.

'I have no intention of divorcing you or giving you grounds to divorce me. But that's beside the point. Your duty to your country comes first . . . '

'Frederick, sometimes you're a joke!'

His anger flared. 'If you'd spend two minutes thinking what damage your adventures could cause your country you'd go down on your knees and beg forgiveness! The least you can do now is behave with dignity and allow me to try and minimize the damage.'

Jennings knocked and entered. 'General Lubbock is here, sir, with Senator Stallybrass and Mr Reiman.'

'Show them in,' said Coverdale. Jennings nodded his head and withdrew. 'Where are the rest?'

'Bennett's racing his America's Cup challenger in Australia. Arthur Wilshire said anybody who turned up might just as well sign a confession.'

'I had something like that in mind,' said Frederick.

Jennings opened the door to admit the three men, plus Marjorie Swanson and Jerry Brand. Lubbock had his jaw stuck out. Stallybrass was concerned. Reiman was calculating the odds. Jerry was looking forward to the excitement, and Marjorie Swanson wanted a fight. She began:

'What gives you the right to tell me how to show my love for my country?'

'You should be handing out medals,' said Jerry. 'But for us – or rather your brilliant wife – the Commies would probably have the whole Tesla shooting match by now.'

Thursday 29th October 1981

'Good point,' said Lubbock.

Frederick kept his temper with difficulty. 'You people don't seem to realize how much trouble you're in.'

Lubbock continued: 'If the Russians get this weapon before we do, the American people will have more trouble . . .'

'You're an illegal organization, interfering in matters of state, putting the defence of this country at risk,' Coverdale continued. The telephone jangled. Frederick glowered at it. 'I told them no calls . . . ' Ruth picked it up, and listened.

'It's the White House.' She handed the instrument to her husband.

'Coverdale . . . Yes . . . Yes, Mr President . . . You mean right this minute. I am in the middle of a tricky situation. . . Yes, Mr President. Right away.' He pressed another button on the telephone. 'I want my car. Now!' He banged down the telephone. 'I won't repeat this. You're going to break up your little gang and sign a written guarantee about future conduct. . .'

'Or what? You call in the FBI?' Stallybrass asked. 'Your own wife is involved. Your new job would be blown right out of the water.'

Frederick looked at him with cold eyes. 'I don't advise you to try me.' He opened the door.

'Just one moment, Coverdale,' said Jack Lubbock. Frederick hesitated. 'Purely from a military point of view, the President couldn't afford such a diversion at the present time. Ask him.'

'I'll give you twenty four hours . . . ' said Frederick.

Washington, D.C.

The top Pentagon 'brass' were already assembled in the Oval Office when Frederick was shown in. The President lost no time in introductions. 'We believe the Soviets may have another piece of the Trinity.'

Thursday 29th October 1981

'How? When?' asked Frederick.

The President told him about the Tesla letter to Mark Twain, and the race to Smiljan.

'Why didn't the agent take the original?' asked a four-star general. 'We'd have had it to ourselves!'

'She didn't know what she had,' explained the CIA director. 'It was a hunch; inspired guesswork.'

'How did the Soviets get on to it?' asked Frederick.

'KGB had a woman in the library, waiting for just such a thing to happen.'

'What do our scientists say about the one piece we have got?' asked the four-star general.

'They're working on it,' said the President. 'Not very hopefully.'

'What do they say about the fact the Russians are two-to-one up on us?'

The Man was not his usual urbane self as he answered. 'I won't kid you, gentlemen. This is about as serious as it gets. The assessment of the National Scientific and Technology Committee is that we must assume they now have the necessary level of expertise to put a shield round their territory which we could not penetrate.'

'When?' That was a chorus of voices. Others added 'How soon?' 'How long have we got?'

'Hold it!' commanded the President. 'It's an assumption, not fact.'

'Good as,' said the first general again.

'I won't have that. We have one of the three pieces of the puzzle and it's distinctly possible that what stopped them going for it when they had the blow-out at Riga, and when they couldn't repeat that weather stunt, is still gonna stop 'em.'

Frederick was on the President's side. 'We can't make doomsday assumptions this early in the game, gentlemen. I agree with the President. What we need now are cool heads.' Frederick pressed home his point. 'They won't be able to do anything in a hurry. These things – whatever they are – will have to be built, tested. That could take years.'

'That may be true,' said the President, 'but only maybe. For all we know it may be a fairly simple device to make. If that's so, we may have no time at all. I won't take the best option on that any more than I'll go with the worst case scenario. These are still assumptions at this stage. Does anybody have any concrete proposals?'

'Can't we stop the Soviets getting it out of Yugoslavia?' asked the Navy's man.

'If we knew where it was we might. We do have a map . . .' An aide spread it out on an adjoining table. They all rose to pore over it. The aide pointed to a red ring. 'That's Smiljan. They could hole up anywhere along that coast until a boat comes to pick 'em up. They could head for any one of a number of airports; Zadar is the closest, or Zagreb, Ljubijana, Sarajevo, Pecs; or there's the Hungarian or Rumanian border.'

'The Russians are not on the best of terms with the Yugoslavs. Couldn't we use that to put pressure . . . ?' asked the four-star general.

Frederick was unequivocal. 'They won't make trouble with Moscow. Since Tito's death they have their hands full trying to keep the eight republics and regions together.'

'Fly it, drive it; post it even,' said the director. 'Who'll ever know.'

'Gentlemen,' said the President. 'That's enough chat. I want your recommendations in writing a.s.a.p!'

Mid-Atlantic

Lloyd made contact with Tyson through the US embassy in Belgrade. They met at the airport and boarded a 747 for New York.

Forbes had been uncomplimentary. 'I can accept the

Yank's foul-up, but we're supposed to know how to do these things.' Lloyd's protestations that he had no control over mechanical failure of aircraft bore no fruit. 'Excuses! You're there to make things happen, not have them happen all over you. Get back to Washington on the next plane.'

Tyson's director was equally scathing. 'You don't even have the excuse that they drive on the wrong side of the road. Were you drunk?' he'd asked.

'No, the other guy was,' had been Chuck's reply.

'Why the hell couldn't you keep out of his way!' There didn't seem a lot of point in answering that one. 'Come back, and bring that Limey with you, at least he got to the right place!'

Georgetown, D.C.

After Frederick Coverdale's departure for the White House, Ruth's group discussed the problem and got nowhere. It was stand-off; each side had everything to lose by carrying out its threat. They thought they held the trump card because it would force Frederick to resign. The senator didn't buy that.

'Coverdale's just the sort of guy you can't rely on to do the honourable thing, and that's probably why the President picked him.'

Ruth nodded.

'If we were right to set up in the first place,' said Marjorie Swanson, 'what's so different now that Frederick knows?'

'He could put us all in the hoosegow,' said senator Stallybrass, 'and at my age that doesn't have too many attractions.'

'We knew the risks!' said Jerry Brand.

'I say we carry on,' said Ruth.

'What will you tell your husband?' asked the senator.

'That I'm a dutiful wife, and I've persuaded you all to be

good boys and girls and do as teacher says.'

'And you would ask us to go along with that?' persisted the senator.

'Sure. Why not?'

'OK by me,' said Swanson. Jerry Brand nodded her agreement. Reiman spoke to Stallybrass.

'What's buggin' you, senator?'

'Something about hiding behind skirts . . . '

The women laughed.

'That's a sexist remark . . . ' began Jerry Brand.

'I'm serious,' said the senator.

'I don't like it either,' said Lubbock grumpily. 'I don't need a woman . . . '

'You fools!' Ruth was angry. 'This isn't a virility contest. I'm the best person to put the lid on Frederick, and that's exactly what I'm going to do. If any of the rest of you want out, that's also OK by me!'

Karlovac, Yugoslavia

Major Yuri Rakov was given a rendezvous in Karlovac at six a.m., a long wait. He had found a secluded spot where the car lay concealed most of the night. He did not sleep.

He was surprised to see Aleksei Telinger stroll up to his vehicle at six-fifteen a.m., fifteen minutes late, as Rakov complained.

'Good morning, hero,' said Telinger.

'You're late. I nearly wasn't here. Then you'd have been in trouble.'

'I know your orders. You were told to wait; no matter how long. Where is it?'

'In the trunk. Did they send just you? No back-up? No guards? No guns?'

'Let's get it!'

'Where are you taking it?'

'You don't need to know that.'

Thursday 29th October 1981

Rakov exploded. 'I'm in charge of this operation . . . '

Telinger interrupted equally fiercely. 'The Americans got the third piece; from somebody we'd already seen. That's a major bungle and we're answerable for it.' Rakov paled.

He got out of the car and unlocked the trunk. Telinger looked at the elaborately carved columns and the Trinity piece nestling within it. If he was impressed, he didn't show it. 'You don't mean you've carried it around openly like this?'

'I don't travel with wrapping paper.'

'Put it in there,' said Telinger, pointing at the leather bag.

'What do I do with this?' said Rakov, showing Telinger the nun's clothing.

'Your problem,' said Rakov's superior. He turned and waved. A black Mercedes 450 drew alongside, its driver and two other occupants were part of the heavy mob. Telinger drew the zip across the top of the bag.

'What do I do now?' asked Rakov.

'Drive to Budapest; the embassy. They'll have your orders.' He didn't say goodbye. Rakov watched the powerful machine draw smoothly away. He drove to Karlovac motel and slept.

Friday 30th October 1981
Washington, D.C.

Rogers was fed up with trying to put names to the many faces visiting Arthur Wilshire's office, and then trying to work out who was going to see him, and who was consulting one of his numerous partners.

'It's hopeless,' said Rogers to Heidi. 'Half the Congress uses these offices. How am I supposed to spot the bad guys?'

'Tell him,' said Heidi.

Friday 30th October 1981

'I've tried. The director seems to think that a job with the Company means you must be able to work miracles. Has there been no sighting of Lubbock at Wilshire's place?'

'Not once. Not even a phone call.'

'I thought we had a positive make on one call,' mused Rogers.

'It was too short to get a voice print, and innocuous.'

'What about the tail on Lubbock?'

'Plenty of names of people he sees. Ex-officers in all three services, politicians, Pentagon personnel, Ruth Coverdale . . . '

'I would have thought that was suspicious for starters,' said Pete.

Heidi shrugged. 'Ruth's father and the general were buddies. Family friend. And in view of her husband's position I can't see her as a candidate for skullduggery.'

'I wonder . . . ' mused Rogers.

Heidi's interest in that subject was at an end. 'How much longer are you going to keep those jet-lagged captains in the outer office?'

Pete was still wondering about Ruth Coverdale. She didn't fit the pattern of old pals of a retired army man. The age gap was too great, and he didn't think there were any interests in common. 'What have we got on the lady?'

Heidi was surprised. 'Are you going to investigate the National Defense Advisor's wife? Don't you like eating?'

Pete had the feeling Ruth was the odd one out, and he needed to satisfy his bug of curiosity, if nothing else. 'We must have her on file. Dig it out, and send in the young men.'

'The director won't like it one little bit.'

'So nobody's going to tell him, are they?' said Rogers with feeling. 'Now bring in Lloyd and Tyson.'

Pete wasted no time on pleasantries. 'This is the second screw-up. You guys are making a habit of it.' Both began to protest. 'If I thought you two were merely unlucky, I'd get you shifted pronto. I can do without accident-prones. The director bawled me out at six a.m. today. He also told me Colonel Aleksei Telinger was seen entering the Soviet Embassy in Belgrade just after ten, yesterday morning.'

'Any sign of Rakov?' asked Tyson.

'Any reason we believe he was the one who took the bauble from the Tesla museum?'

'Just feel,' said Lloyd. 'It doesn't sound too logical, I know, but . . . I got the feeling it was Savannah all over again.'

'OK,' said Rogers. 'Let's assume it was Rakov. Where does that get us?'

Lloyd tried to make his sleepy brain function. 'Assuming Telinger went with Rakov to Savannah, and took "Father" aboard the ship, it's a fair bet they'd put him out in the field with Rakov to get the third piece of the Trinity . . . '

'So?' said Tyson, not convinced.

'Telinger has what we want and he's in his embassy in Belgrade.'

'You want to bust in there and get it?' Tyson was incredulous.

'You got a better idea?' asked Lloyd.

'How do we know it's still there?'

Rogers put up his hands to stop further argument. 'I think we can rely on the director to have taken whatever action's possible on that score.'

'I'm not satisfied,' said Lloyd. The three others looked at him in amused surprise. 'I'm going to talk to Forbes.'

Washington, D.C.

The President looked grim when Frederick Coverdale walked in. 'The Brits had an SAS team en route to Yugoslavia to snatch Telinger and whatever he was carrying. The Prime Minister vetoed it. Right, but a pity. Have you found out when the next Soviet pouch leaves Belgrade?'

'One left yesterday; a special at noon,' answered Coverdale.

'We had no warning? Nobody on to it?'

'The director tried, but his sources are unreliable, and it was Sunday. We must assume they've got it out and have now put the two parts of the Trinity together, Mr President.'

'We have our own people working inside Russia,' said the President hopefully.

'All they've told us so far is that there's the tightest security ever on something!'

'This is bad . . . ' said the President.

'The Chief Scientific Advisor's waiting, would you like me to sit in?'

'Send him right in.'

He was a tall, scholarly man, thin with stooped shoulders. His eyes gleamed a cool intelligence. Rex Hirshfield was a New Englander from Boston, an American aristocrat to whom everything, including academic excellence came easily.

'The bottom line, Mr President, is that we're getting nowhere fast,' he said laconically. 'I have all the men who can usefully be employed on it, working round their joint and several clocks. It is not made any easier by the fact that they are good scientists being asked to work on something they don't believe in . . . '

'Doesn't patriotism count for anything?' asked the President.

'They're practical men; in a scientific sense. Unless you can show them there is technical feasibility to what they're doing, they're bound to be sceptical. I don't think it's affecting their effort, but it must affect enthusiasm . . . '

'Where, exactly, do you stand, professor?' asked the President dryly.

Friday 30th October 1981

'I try to do my job as well as I can. I use a mixture of national threat, and scientific competition with the Ruskies . . . "Don't let them get there first, boys . . . "; that sort of thing. I think I know how to get the best out of them.'

'Will their best be good enough?' the leader of the American nation wanted to know.

Hirshfield shrugged. 'Who knows! I do have one contribution to make to the debate.'

The President showed some fire. 'What we've got here is a losing war with Russia, which they can't lose. Haven't you grasped that yet!'

'I'm sorry if I give that impression. My father always told me I'd need to show a little more enthusiasm to get anywhere in the American hustler race. I've given it one hundred per cent, Mr President. Tesla is not really my field. But if, as they say, what he was working on was an entirely new physics, then there are no experts, as yet . . .'

'Get to the point, professor,' urged the President who did not like academics.

'Yes, sir . . . As I see it there are two possibilities . . . no three. I don't think we'll be able to crack it with the one piece we've got. We'll bust the proverbial gut, but my best guess is we won't get there. Second, given their state of the art, the Reds may be able to put the act together with just two pieces of the puzzle; but in my book it's a big maybe.'

Frederick entered the conversation. 'What are you suggesting? That neither of us will get the secret?'

'That could be, but that's not what I'm thinking. I think they'll need outside help.'

'Where from?' demanded the President.

'What does new physics suggest to you, Mr President?'

'Not a damn thing,' he replied with asperity.

'Where is the most fundamental physics research being done?'

'I don't like guessing games, professor.'

Friday 30th October 1981

'This is far out stuff. We've got no precedents. All we can do is think laterally; think the unthinkable. If there was a conventional solution we'd both have been there a long time ago. I want to share my thinking with you; that's why I asked to see Coverdale. I wanted an outsider's view on my ideas.'

Frederick answered the earlier question. 'You're talking about particle physics?' The Bostonian nodded. 'The high energy accelerator?' Again he nodded. 'But why should they need to go outside? They have one of their own.'

'Not enough output.'

'Accelerator, you say?' said the President. 'Don't we have one of those things? I saw it in one of the budgets. Costs a damned fortune. You think they'll ask to use ours?' He was rather pleased with his joke.

'No, Mr President. There's one in Geneva with a four thousand million electron volt capacity.'

Frederick shook his head. 'This makes no sense. What they do at CERN is examine matter, anti-matter, the smallest things in the universe; pure physics. The main argument against the money spent there is that it has no practical application . . . '

'Except to improve man's understanding of the place he inhabits,' added the professor. 'I know all that. But one of the experiments there is designed to catch forces, elements, that are firstly invisible – that's no big deal – but that pass straight through the earth, leaving no trace. Neutrinos, they're called. What Tesla described – insofar as he described it at all – was the opposite of neutrinos; a new physics which enables an element or force, which is invisible – to act as a solid or destructive force to anything approaching it. Now I may be crazy, but my hunch is they may not be able to understand the new principles of this weapon or screen, even with the third part of the Trinity – remember Tesla himself wasn't able to carry out any experiments; even for him it was still all theory – they may still need the sort of facilities only CERN at Geneva presents.'

The President and Frederick were silent. At last the occupant of the White House spoke. 'Where does that get us?'

Frederick added, 'I don't buy it. They've got their own accelerator. It's too far-fetched, and it's only . . . '

'Speculation.' The professor completed the sentence. 'I know that. But I thought you would want to know my thinking, however useless it may turn out to be.'

The British Embassy, Washington D.C.

Lloyd viewed the imposing Lutyens creation that was the residence of Her Majesty's ambassador with a sense of pride. Some might call it over-blown, but for Richard it spelled out the grand manor, the Hunt balls and gracious living of the Old Country. Outmoded maybe; out-of-touch with the pop tempo of the times, but solid, dependable and full of tradition. But it was not his destination. He was bound for the glass and concrete rotunda that was the home of chancery; the offices. It too was evocative, but of Hercules Road not Kensington Gardens.

Arthur Forbes strode ahead of him along the straight corridor, through prison-grey painted doorways, and ultimately into a nondescript office. This building must, at one time have been considered elegant or, at least avant-garde, but now was just another example of a design that time had passed by. Of the dense tapestry of autumn colour that was the immaculately tended embassy garden there was not a glimpse.

Forbes was depressed and not only by his surroundings. 'There's nothing to stop the Russians turning two pieces of the Trinity into the Tesla Shield.'

'We can't just sit on our hands,' Lloyd protested.

The major told him that British and American scientists

were pulling out every stop; intelligence services of all NATO countries were putting every available man into the search for clues; the electronic bugs on satellites, in aircraft, at sea and on land were all programmed with the urgency of the task. 'All I'm saying is that there's little the likes of you and I can do to influence the course of events.'

'Why not bomb Akademgorodok?' Richard asked, seriously.

'I suppose it's a possibility. I doubt if anybody would sanction it.'

'Because it would start the Third World War?'

Forbes said the main objection would be that it was far from certain 'Father' and 'Ghost' were there. He admitted it was the most likely place for the research to be continued, but they had had no luck in positively identifying where either piece had gone, and embarking on a mass bombing, even of conventional explosives, could not be justified simply on the balance of probabilities.

Lloyd changed the subject. 'What news of Butterworth and Nikki in Yugoslavia?'

'Not good. We tried to warn Nikki's wife but she'd already disappeared, whether into police hands or hiding we don't know. We believe they're giving Nikki a hard time . . .'

'Physically, you mean?' Lloyd was very upset.

Forbes said they could not be sure. The information that came out of jails was unreliable. It was nearly all rumour; one prisoner heard somebody screaming, coming from the general direction of Nikki's cell. The embassy had been able to take a formal interest in Butterworth and the word was that he hadn't been harmed, was being questioned at length, and kept incommunicado from other prisoners.

'Can't something be done?'

'All we can do, we're doing. It's one of the risks.'

Forbes told him that there were signs that the Trebinje

project had been stopped. The embassy staff had picked up gossip on the scientific circuit that they were stalled without the use of controlled nuclear explosions. That debate had now gone to the Yugoslav Politburo where the best guess was that building a nuclear plant would be killed for lack of funds, or Russian reaction, or Anglo/American trade repercussions.

Lloyd felt an acute sense of anticlimax. 'There must be something we can do. Surely the Prime Minister won't just sit back and do nothing? Not that lady!'

Moscow, U.S.S.R.

General Yakushenko and Professor Vilkov were at Vnukovo Airport when Telinger stepped off the plane. All three stood by the cargo doors as the diplomatically-sealed wooden case was unloaded. The general couldn't wait. He grabbed the crowbar from the baggage handler, ripped away the struts, and tore out paper shavings. 'Well?' he said impatiently to the professor. 'Is that it?'

Vilkov would not be hurried. He lifted it, and inspected it from every angle. He replaced it and turned to the general. 'I think we have it.'

'Good, good. Excellent.'

'I shall not know for certain until we get it to the laboratory and compare it with the other piece, but shall we say it looks promising.'

Salisbury Plain, England

The Prime Minister sat with the brigadier as they watched a display of anti-tank gunnery at Bulford army camp. The Defence Secretary was on her other side. Even though the guns were nearly a mile away the sound as they were fired was strangely muted, a thud, rather than an explosion, and the puff of smoke reluctantly left the barrel after each round a moment before the noise reached them.

Friday 30th October 1981

'What are you recommending, brigadier?' asked the Prime Minister.

'A commando raid on Akademgorodok to take or destroy . . . '

'On Russian territory?'

'Tell me what else we can do, Prime Minister and I'll willingly . . . '

'It would be suicide,' added the Defence Secretary.

'Indeed,' said the brigadier.

'Is it feasible?' Her question surprised the brigadier. After her outright abort order on any bombing, he thought she would shy away from any physical interaction.

'We don't know for sure. Akademgorodok is remote and we don't have accurate plans or maps. We're OK on streets and general layout of the town, but we don't know what security they have, how many defenders or how they're armed. We need a few satellite pictures – high resolution stuff. Can you twist an American arm or two?'

'I don't think that'll be a problem, provided they've got one going over the right spot; arranging a detour might be more difficult.'

'Are you giving me the go-ahead?'

'Yes,' replied the Prime Minister of Great Britain without hesitation. 'Will Captain Lloyd be with them?'

The Defence Secretary coughed. 'Are you sure this is wise, Prime Minister?'

'I'm authorizing a feasibility study, and combat training in readiness for an actual assault on the target. I'm not setting H-hour or even D-day yet.' She turned to the field officer with a smile. 'I expect you'll be wanting to get on, brigadier. Then I can enjoy the rest of the manoeuvres.'

He gave the smartest salute since his passing-out parade at Sandhurst.

Friday 30th October 1981
Budapest, Hungary

Rakov was treated warily when he arrived at the embassy. 'We rather expected you earlier, Comrade Major . . . ' said a hesitant third secretary.

'Did you!' was Rakov's reply. 'Where are my orders?'

'If the major will come with me . . . '

He was shown into a plainly furnished small office. A few minutes later the third secretary returned with sealed envelopes.

'We received this signal at ten o'clock this morning, and this one . . . ' there was another envelope, ' . . . half-an-hour ago.' Rakov took them and turned his back on the man.

The message was a fine example of brevity and clarity:

'Proceed at once to Moscow Centre – by air.'

The second message was almost as good:

'Ignore message No. Y/10/27/1. Proceed at once to Akademgorodok for authentication procedures. Fly.' The second signal, ominously was signed with the single letter 'Y.'

'Can I do anything more for the Comrade Major?' Rakov had forgotten the bureaucrat was still there. What did 'authentication procedures' mean? That Vilkov hadn't seen it, or had seen it and was expressing doubts, or had thought it was the real thing and was now having reservations? Or was the general up to his usual tricks of striking terror?

'Yes,' replied Yuri. 'Tell me where I can get a decent meal, and if I've got time to eat it before catching the next plane to Novosibirsk.'

18

Monday 9th November 1981
Cambridge, Mass.

There was a period of uneasy calm, reminiscent of the false start to the Second World War; a no-mans-land in time and activity. At all levels there was tension, as inactivity fed imagination with forebodings and suggested one impossible solution after another. On the scientific scene there was sustained if sceptical application. Increasing political pressure for an answer hindered rather than aided this effort.

But the tourist in Boston walked the Freedom Trail, past the statue of that earlier experimenter with lightning, Benjamin Franklin, little realizing that the fight was still being fought, on the laboratory benches of the Massachusetts Institute of Technology.

Hereford, England

Richard Lloyd sweated and groaned through more fitness training with the Special Air Service, preparing for the assault on Akademgorodok.

Akademgorodok, U.S.S.R.

Major-General Yakushenko had no patience. He believed it a synonym for idleness. He didn't believe time had any therapeutic value. It was a span during which maximum pressure had to be exerted on everybody to ensure that an even tolerably acceptable work norm was achieved. The centralized, over-bureaucratic system aided and abetted the wasting of time. If he had a free rein he would shoot a few people every day *pour encourager les autres*. Stalin was a great man, a dire loss to the motherland. The pusillanimous bunch who had taken his place were lily-livered status quo compromisers. These thoughts were culminating in a satisfactory lather when the architect of his present frame of mind entered his office.

'Have you solved it?' demanded Yakushenko.

'We are making headway, but it's slow. We shall need more time,' Vilkov answered uneasily.

'You've had a week already.'

'We don't have all the pieces of the Trinity. If we had – if your department had been more zealous in its function . . .'

'That's just an excuse for your own incompetence. Stalin would have shot Rakov for letting the imperialists get the third part of the Trinity. You, too, in all probability!'

'You are in charge, Comrade General. You would have been the first to face the firing squad,' said Vilkov calmly. Yakushenko scowled. The professor continued: 'We need access to the CERN accelerator at Geneva.'

'Why not use our own?'

'It's not up to the job.'

'What do you expect me to do about it?'

'We have an invitation to carry out certain particle physics experiments there next week. I propose to send in a different team, who will carry out our work instead.'

'Won't they suspect something?'

'Yes.'

'Then how will you deal with that?'

Vilkov was patient. 'It's a non-military set-up; pure science. They won't be looking for trouble. They are normally interested in what we do, but only on an academic level. We shall find a plausible cover story for the work we're doing . . . it won't fool anybody but by the time they realize what we are really doing we'll be away.'

'What exactly is the nature of the work you need to do?'

'In technical language?' asked the professor with a glint

in his eye, knowing the general's inability to grasp scientific material.

'Now is not the time for jokes, professor.'

'There's the problem of focus. If you aim a beam of energy it's difficult to prevent diffusion as it gets further from the power source.'

'I thought you needed the broadest diffusion to give the effect of the screen or wall,' said the general.

'Precisely! The two parts of the Trinity tend to confirm that we are dealing with a new form of physics. New dimensions at the interface of time and space. We need access to a very powerful nuclear accelerator. CERN has it.'

'After all this effort and risk, you still can't give me the answer without . . . '

Vilkov interrupted. 'Tesla never made it work. He wanted two million dollars and three months . . . '

'That was eighty years ago! Scientific knowledge has made huge advances since then. Surely any competent scientist, given what you have, could . . . '

'We began this research with unanimity of all our scientists that the Tesla theory was nonsense.'

'What about Riga and the weather?'

'They were the first breakthroughs, but they weren't conclusive. We couldn't even prove they were related to Tesla's work. We thought so but it was all still experimental guesswork. We think . . . I repeat, think, that CERN may help us. That's all I can say. There are no guarantees.'

Palo Alto, Ca.

In San Francisco there was no enthusiasm for the Tesla box. It stood in a corner, and Hackett was gazing at it, mesmerized. 'The trouble is I don't care. I'm just going through motions.'

'She won't think she's had much value for her money . . .' said Julia Black.

'Don't remind me! As you say, she did deliver, and so far

I haven't, and that bugs me. I'm going to do my sleep trick.'

'Come again?'

'I shall read all the notes and papers on the subject just before I go to bed.'

'What's that supposed to do?' Julia Black wanted to know.

'Based on sound scientific, or rather medical theory; that the subconscious has greater resources than the conscious mind. It has every experience stored in its memory. Plug in the problem consciously, just before sleep, wake up to the answer!' The failure bothered Hackett. He stared at the old metal box, as if willing it to give up its secret.

Julia was not impressed. 'Freud called them the unconscious, and the intelligent minds.'

'You should try it yourself, sometime,' said her boss.

'If you promise to keep yourself out of my dreams I might just do that.' She took a lipstick from her bag, and twisted the bottom so that the carmine Revlon greasepole emerged erect from its gold sheath. She applied it to her mouth, and then passed her tongue over both lips. The effect was provocative.

'What did you say?' asked Hackett, absent-mindedly. Julia looked at him, and sighed.

Georgetown, D.C.

General Jack Lubbock was pacing Ruth's drawing room in Georgetown. 'I can't stand the inactivity. Why haven't we taken out Akademgorodok with conventional bombs? We don't need to go nuclear. What are we doing to guard the one piece of the Trinity we have got? Jesus! When is there gonna be some goddamn action!'

'Frederick's right about one thing; we've got scientists, and army and Pentagon and NASA and heaven knows who else working on this thing. What can we add now?' said Ruth.

'Where's that nephew of yours?'

'He's been officially warned off by his director. I won't have his career put further at risk.'

Lubbock did not agree with that sentiment, but kept the thought to himself.

Maryland, U.S.A.

The National Security Agency's monitors and computers were working overtime on the problem. Their listening and photographic facilities, in space and on the ground everywhere from Alaska to the Russo/Chinese border, were programmed to monitor every significant military and political move across the world's chessboard, and sound an alert if any action or combination of activities threatened the security of the United States. Computers printed out any item relating to certain key words, like Tesla, Trinity, defensive screen, death beam, and a hundred other words which the computer itself suggested might mean a happening related to the shield. They did not pick up an apparently innocuous telephone conversation, at low administrative level indicating that certain Soviet citizens would, and a number of others would not, be making use of facilities at *La Centre Européenne pour la Recherche Nucléaire*, because nobody had told the computers that CERN was a key word.

Wednesday 11th November 1981
Lexington, Mass.

Chuck Tyson had surveyed MIT by road along Memorial Drive, from the Charles River, on foot, and even by helicopter. He had not liked what he saw. Some buildings were old, grand and magnificent, sitting cheek-by-jowl with tall concrete slabs and modern brick mid-rises. All were densely packed together and an easy mark for a hit team. He discussed the problem with Rogers, who talked to Hirshfield.

Wednesday 11th November 1981

At night, they moved the entire operation to the Lincoln Laboratory at Lexington. This is located within the secure perimeter of Hanscombe Air Force Base, where missile defence penetration systems and satellite communications are designed and tested.

Tyson was reasonably satisfied with the standard of alertness of the airmen on guard duty, but he organized mock attacks by CIA teams, which increased vigilance and frightened the academics poring over their intricate and sensitive instruments.

A few days of that was enough to get security to the level he wanted. He then planted electronic bugs in every room they were using. For the last four days he had been boringly wending his way through the tapes. So it came about that he heard about CERN, when Hirshfield repeated his worries to other scientists.

'Why don't I go check it out?' Tyson asked Rogers.

Rogers put his feet back on to the tutor's desk in the office they had commandeered for the duration of the project. 'You wouldn't know a nuclear accelerator from your asshole,' he replied without interest.

Chuck Tyson was close to mental boil-over point. He'd always had success in his life. Naturally ambitious, he'd strived for first place in everything from schoolroom to playing field. When boredom threatened he turned entrepreneur, not for the money but for the excitement, the risk and, above all, for the thrill of success. Savannah and the trip to Smiljan were his first important solo roles, and on each he'd failed; and try as he would, he couldn't find anybody to blame. He was now itching to get back into the action to prove he was still as good as he'd always been.

'I want to go to Switzerland.'

'Got a line on a few watches?'

'Nobody's checked out CERN. I want to do it. I feel useless here. I can't sit on my ass all day waiting . . . '

Wednesday 11th November 1981

All lethargy left Rogers, who sat suddenly upright. 'What did you say?'

'I'm bored sitting on my . . .'

'Before that!'

'Nobody's checked out CERN . . .'

'Are you sure about that?' The significance struck Tyson at that moment.

'Jesus! You don't think . . .'

'I don't know. But if we need CERN the chances are the Russians may.'

Three telephone calls later they learned of the imminent arrival of a new clutch of Soviet scientists at CERN. It took Rogers' mind off the CIA file on Ruth Coverdale which he had shoved in a drawer when Tyson strode into his office.

Washington/London

The President spoke to the Prime Minister.

'The Swiss government say they have no power to intervene. CERN is an international outfit run by you, and eleven other European nations.'

'I have spoken to our ambassador there,' she replied. 'He has told the Swiss what the Soviets might be up to and suggested the Federal Government took an even-handed stand . . .'

'What does that mean?' The President wished he understood more of what she said.

'The laboratory is owned and operated by its members, of which the USSR is not one . . .'

'Neither are we!'

'Precisely,' said the Prime Minister. 'So the Swiss have just announced that they will not welcome to their country, non-members of CERN – until further notice. Rather neat, don't you think, Mr President.'

As he said to Coverdale later: 'I used to think this British understatement was a pain in the ass, butt it has its uses.'

Wednesday 11th November 1981
Palo Alto, Ca.
Christopher Hackett did not have a dream, he had a nightmare. Thousands of his monitoring machines were stretched out in rows either side of Long Island Sound and as far as his eyes could see. He began by trying to count up how much it would cost him to buy these thousands of seventy-five thousand dollar machines. The cheque, when it appeared for him to sign, was as long as Manhattan Island. As he picked up the pen – as tall as the Empire State building – an earthquake tremor rumbled and the machines began a dance. Fissures appeared in a jigsaw across Manhattan Island. All the machines were gobbled up. The aquiline face of Nikola Tesla appeared, surrounded by a full-bottomed judge's wig. He began his summing-up. Hackett leaned forward, trying to hear what he was saying, but the closer he got the fainter the thin voice became. Tesla's image began to fade. The sound of the alarm woke him. It was five a.m. He had set it an hour ahead of his usual time. He fell out of bed, tired, with a dry mouth. He brushed his teeth and drank some water; it tasted foul. He staggered into the laboratory, and wondered how he could induce his imagination to work when his body was in such bad shape. He sat at his high stool and looked at Tesla's box. He gazed at the dials, each of which was working with smooth precision. He looked at the numbers of the sequences already used. Lacking inspiration, he opted for perspiration and decided to go through every one of the routines again, checking each step along the way, hoping for a miracle.

He was asleep hunched over the bench when Julia Black blew into his ear. 'You're a fine advertisement for Freud! I suggest you go back to bed.'

He looked balefully at the machine. It stared back at him, plodding its programmed way through the range of tests and producing zero results.

Friday, 13th November 1981
Moscow, USSR

'You're asking us to cause the most serious international incident since the start of the Great Patriotic War!' said a Politburo member.

Rakov knew drastic action would have to be taken to make the Trinity work. Every Russian was taught from childhood, that its enemies surrounded Rodina. Only constant vigilance, powerful defence forces and unabated effort in new weaponry and technology, would prevent the Motherland's invasion and subjugation. He had thought Yakushenko would go to Moscow, see his superiors and a decision would be taken. What he had not anticipated was to be wheeled personally before the Politburo and told to justify his plan. But here he was and they were listening. It was interesting that Yuri Rakov might go down in history as the man who started the Third World War.

'Comrade Borisnov, since we have been denied access to the only facilities that will perfect our defence, we must use other tactics.'

'That, at least is logical,' said another member.

'What do you think NATO will do when we invade Switzerland?'

'And France!' added another voice. 'The accelerator also runs under their territory.'

'If they know it's us and why we are there, they may respond with force.'

'Are you suggesting we declare war?' asked Borisnov mildly.

Rakov was hasty with his reply. 'No, Comrade Minister. I am proposing a hostage situation; at least a pretend terrorist raid.'

'In what cause?' asked another sceptical member.

'Armenian Freedom Fighters International.'

'Where will you get them from?'

'They will be KGB, pretending to be terrorists. They will

take existing scientists hostage, and demand the release of all political prisoners held in Turkey.'

'It won't fool anybody!' said Borisnov.

'I agree, comrade, although we do have some Armenians in the Cheka who will make it look genuine. But we will not be dealing with our normal enemies, only the Swiss. They have a tradition of neutrality . . . '

'They're in the Western camp!' said the sceptic.

'We only need a short time. The Swiss will do nothing precipitate. The psychology of a hostage situation is that the attackers want a swift acceptance of their demands; the authorities prevaricate to let time break their nerve. We shall make urgent demands, they will give us the time we need.'

'The Americans will tell them to destroy you,' said Borisnov. Rakov felt the whole committee was against him.

'The Swiss are stubborn. They won't take orders from the Yanks. None of the hostages will be Americans. They'll be Dutch, Belgians, Spanish and Swiss! Mostly Swiss. They won't risk those lives just because Reagan says so.'

That produced an interested silence. Borisov addressed Vilkov. 'How much time will you need?'

Vilkov had tried hard not to be impressed by the Politburo, but he was sweating. The laconic man who dealt so easily with 'Y' lost control of his lower lip. He stuttered 'We . . . we . . . don't know, Comrade Borisnov. Days . . . maybe a week. It is impossible to be precise.'

'Could you fail?'

'Nothing is certain in these experiments,' replied the professor.

'What are the chances?' Borisov wanted to know.

Vilkov didn't want to answer that. 'The best I can do is to give the odds as two-to-one against us finding the solution.'

Yakushenko couldn't keep quiet at that. 'With great respect to comrade members, that is not the only consideration. We must ask ourselves what the odds are of the Americans getting this weapon if we don't gain access to CERN.' Borisov gave the hint of a smile, well aware of the tension between the major general and the professor.

'What are those odds, Comrade Professor?'

'We are ahead of them and we have two pieces of the Tesla Trinity. They have one.'

Borisov returned to Rakov. 'Why choose an Armenian group?' he asked.

'To confuse the issue. A number of genuine terrorists are Russians, from Soviet Armenia. There are KGB with Armenian backgrounds and accents. We have a full dossier, we can make it sound convincing.'

'You make it sound easy, Comrade Major,' said the sceptic.

Rakov shook his head. 'We will plan carefully but things always go wrong. People will die; theirs and ours, but I think we can buy enough time for the professor to do his work.'

Saturday 14th November 1981
Palo Alto, Ca.

Hackett was a modern man. He thought most relationships were likely to be transient, and so had avoided marriage. He had lived with two women at various stages in his life, the most recent, an ambitious journalist, had taken off for a lucrative television job in New York and he did not know when he would see her again.

Hackett tended not to distinguish between male and female at work; they were either good or bad, and that was all that mattered. He had not realized, until he found himself suggesting a meal after a late Saturday session in the laboratory, that he found Julia Black's company so – he tried to find the right word – comfortable; that would do for the moment.

Saturday 14th November 1981

She suggested the Fish Market. All he could remember of the restaurant was that it didn't serve liquor, only beer and wine, and he needed a martini, or at least an old-fashioned. They didn't take bookings and there was a thirty minute line. He began to think the whole idea was lousy. They went anyway.

It was crowded and noisy, neither of which Hackett needed after a long hot day in the laboratory. But two large glasses of Wente Brothers Chablis took the edge off his irritation and he began to enjoy himself and his companion. The white fish was gleaming and succulent, topped with a creamy hollandaise. Julia chose a vintage Franzia, from a small winery near Modesto in Northern California, which was nectar.

As he drove his favourite Blazer pick-up back through the Saturday night traffic Julia snuggled up to him. As he turned off the Oregon Expressway to Page Mill, he felt a stirring in his loins. Julia put her hand inside his shirt and traced the pattern of his ribs with a feathery touch. In the shadowy light cast by the dashboard she noticed a swelling in his pants. She sighed speculatively. 'H'mmmmm . . . ' Hackett shuffled in his seat.

'Don't do that,' she said quietly. 'You'll disturb it, and it was doing so nicely on its own. Now I shall have to help it.'

He turned into Adestradero Road. Her right hand gently explored the growing bulge. The bench seat of the Blazer was a distinct advantage over the buckets of supposedly sexy models like the Porsche. It was a warm night.

Men were always difficult, she thought, as she glanced at the well-cut jeans, with their battered brown belt. The shirt didn't matter, that would soon give way to careful undoing of buttons or ripping apart, as the mood took them. Where and how would she begin?

Hackett was alcoholically mellow. He didn't speculate on what lay in store for him in the next few minutes. He thought, idly, and without too much commitment one way or the other, that it looked like a slow-building, sensual climax to an agreeable evening, and that was fine by him. He was wrong.

Julia tugged to free the belt from its clasp. She unfed the strap through its loops. The volume of the bulge increased by a satisfactory ten per cent, her technical mind told her. So far so good. The top button of the pants was stiff – not the only thing, she thought. It yielded to increased pressure. Her hand crept inside to ensure that when she undid the zip, no tender flesh was caught. The swelling member was encased – just – in tight Hom bikini briefs. She drew down the zip. It proved unsatisfactory. The zip was too short, the pants themselves too tight. She could not free the jeans or the bikini briefs, and all the time the organ was increasing its volume and making a thoroughly untidy jumble of everything. She leant across him, putting her right arm round his back, and grasped the back of the jeans. She did the same thing with her left hand. 'Lift your buttocks,' she commanded quietly.

He didn't think buttocks the most romantic word to use, but keeping both hands on the wheel, and concentrating through a vinous haze on maintaining course and speed, he braced his left heel and right foot against the floor and lifted his haunches a couple of inches. She slipped his clothes down, and his member sprang free, shuddering a second or two before attaining its full erection. He put out his right hand and touched her leg. She replaced his hand on the wheel. 'There'll be plenty of time for that later,' she said. 'You concentrate on getting us home.' She bent low. Her tongue traced the outline of his pubic hair. Fingers massages his testicles. His member responded with an attempt to beat its previous best volume performance. The Blazer weaved across the centre white line. He hastily corrected its path. Must have been that second bottle, he thought.

Saturday 14th November 1981

He began to suspect that things might go wrong when he felt her lips close on the very tip of his penis. He had blinked a couple of times earlier on in the exercise, but this time he had positively to close them, and hold on. She removed her lips from the tender area to say: 'Is something wrong?' She was responding to his tenseness.

He knew the idea was to play the game with maximum cool. 'Something on the road,' he said. She nodded, and returned her lips to their former place, only this time rather lower down, taking more of his inches into the warm moist cloister of her mouth. Her right hand continued to stroke and knead his tautening sac, as her tongue played its tune up and down the length of his organ. Even at that stage he thought he would be able to stay in control.

He was prepared for the climax. He had his eyes wide open, a passer-by might have said staring wide. His hands gripped the wheel tight. What he had not bargained for, or even realized, was that her left hand had crept round his right buttock and was now centred on the cleft. She continued the oral stimulation and massage and sensed the moment when he would fulfil the promise she had been exacting from his person. At that moment her left index finger entered his unsuspecting anal canal.

Surprise combined with ecstasy to clamp shut his eyes and shoot both feet straight to the floor, rigid, as the sensation engulfed his senses.

At this point the road curved through the pastoral scene. Hackett's favourite truck, without its master's sure touch, ignored the bend and rode the brief grass shoulder before launching itself into space. The journey through the cool California air matched the time span of Christopher's climax; the distance travelled was no more than a hundred and fifty feet; quite enough to have ended, rather prematurely, two promising careers, but fate did not have that in store for Julia and Christopher. Instead it provided an agricultural holding, the gemstone of which was a magnificent greenhouse, burgeoning with a new strain of huge and ripe orange pumpkins. The forward momentum of the Blazer slowed when the wheels lost their traction; its weight dragged the underside of the engine housing into a confrontation with the gable end of the main timber frame of the greenhouse. The panes of special glass thoughtfully provided a second crash barrier, and finally the Blazer settled with a satisfactory thud, its four wheels, and chassis nestling into a bed of squashed pumpkins.

Julia Black found the event rather pleasing. She normally had trouble with orgasm. She thought altogether too much attention was paid to it, both in the media and by her friends, until, that was, today. She could not say what was the determining factor. Maybe it was the launch into the cool mountain air, at the *moment critique*, combining with the racing screech of the engine that brought about her first multiple orgasm.

There was a stillness and a quiet as they opened their eyes. There was also a lack of movement which required explanation. And then they saw the shattered glass, great green leaves and heard what sounded like a hundred farts, as the pumpkins exploded under the weight of the Blazer. As the last pumpkin died a stillness descended on the low Altos hills, followed by a rumbling noise.

'Did you feel it?' asked Hackett.

'Feel it!' replied Julia, delicately wiping nucleic acid from the corners of her mouth, 'I practically swallowed it!'

'Not that!' said Hackett, 'that!' Julia sensed the tremor.

'Wait 'till I tell the girls Hemingway was right. The earth does move!'

'It's the San Andreas Fault and it's going to be a biggie,' said Christopher. 'We'd better get back.'

They picked their way through the broken glass and suppurating fruit, and reached the road. Hackett ran the last hundred yards. Julia wondered where he got the energy.

He crashed the door open and rushed to his instruments, which registered an escalating score on the Richter Scale.

'This *is* going to be something else!' he said excitedly as Julia entered the room. But she was not looking at him or the instruments.

'What's happening to the box?' she asked.

'What box?' he said, still gazing in rapt attention at his instruments.

'The Tesla thing,' said Julia. 'It's jumping about all over the place.'

It was screwed to a central steel stanchion which was the main vertical support of the roof, reaching down into the foundations. 'Don't bother me with that now. Look at these readings. We could be in for another disaster!'

The truth dawned on Julia Black. 'Chris,' she yelled. 'You left the experiment running!'

Chris was only interested in what his precious instruments were telling him. He looked round, irritated at the interruption, prepared to dismiss her claim when he saw what was happening to the box. He then realized that there was something very unusual about this earthquake: they were on top of its epicentre.

19

Monday 16th November 1981
Moscow, U.S.S.R.

After two days sitting in an office at Moscow Centre waiting for news, Rakov was called to Yakushenko. 'You realize what happened was unprecedented. A mere major being accorded an audience of the Politburo?'

'Indeed, Comrade General.'

'This time your mistakes will not be treated as kindly as I have dealt with you. Your blunder in America, in letting the third piece of the Trinity slip through your fingers . . .'

'I did recover the other two, Comrade General!' With this much backing from the Politburo, Yuri did not feel so intimidated.

'You failed your country, Rakov, and for that the punishment is usually severe. You've been given a rare privilege by your motherland, an opportunity to redeem yourself.'

The injustice of it made Rakov protest. 'But general . . .'

'Silence!' What was the point in arguing? He'd got what he wanted.

'I want detailed plans by tomorrow; a list of arms, transport, men, and their various skills. I will decide how much can be granted.' They both knew that every aspect of the plan would be vetted at the top.

'Certainly, Comrade General.'

It took him a day to find out what was available and where. It was frustrating work. The Russian civil servant is not at his best on the telephone; he likes everything in triplicate, and he will then sift it for ambiguities, possible misinterpretations or incorrect addition or subtraction. If he finds any of these, the request will go back whence it came.

Monday 16th November 1981

He had to put his general on the line frequently to get any action at all, sometimes even information.

Rakov sought out Vilkov.

'How many men will you need?'

'Twenty,' answered the professor.

'Impossible,' said Rakov calmly. 'You must do it with less.'

'Tell me why,' he replied.

'Logistics. I am taking forty men to hold CERN. It is probably insufficient by a wide margin, but I have to think how they will be fed.'

'There is a canteen there; several in fact. They will have enough for all of us.'

'I can't take that risk. Certainty is what we must have. What will you say if I tell you we must surrender after three days because we have no food or water left?'

'What's a few days without food!'

'I have to get them into Switzerland. The more there are the more difficult. Visas have to be obtained, or faked, passports, photos; the administration is a nightmare. Special servicemen will have to be smuggled in.'

'Fifteen. The absolute minimum,' said the professor.

'I need full names and addresses, today.' The professor called his office on the telephone.

'What about "Father" and "Son"? The two parts of the Trinity. How are we going to get them through?'

'My God! Why do you need to take them?'

'They are what this is all about, or had you forgotten.'

'The risk is too great, Comrade Professor. Suppose they fall into enemy hands!'

'Their safety is your problem, Yuri Rakov. The sooner you get me to CERN with the two parts of the model, the sooner my responsibility will begin and yours end.'

If only that were true thought Rakov, but with forty men

guarding a tunnel seven kilometres long, he began to think the task impossible.

Georgetown, D.C.

Ruth hadn't seen Frederick for over two weeks. He'd slept away from the house, and she'd not even had a phone call. She'd tried to lead a normal life, paying more than her usual attention to her businesses, irritating her managers with requests for up-dating reports on progress when none were necessary.

Ruth knew it was the lull before the storm, and that she was, at present powerless to make anything happen, as she'd told Jim Lubbock. She was half listening to 'Good-morning, America' and news of another tremor in California registering 4.1 on the Richter scale, when Frederick walked into her bedroom.

Ruth's first reaction was that he had his old familiar, formal face back on again. He soon confirmed it.

'I thought I'd allow a decent interval to elapse before making contact again. I've thought things over and decided that there's no need to be uncivilized about it.'

Ruth's answer was quiet and calm: 'You pompous bastard!'

Anger lit up her husband's eyes. Ruth was surprised, and rather pleased; she'd try it again. Frederick was annoyed he'd allowed his anger to show. He'd been so sure he'd kept away long enough to break his crazy addiction for the woman. Sixteen days should have been enough.

'I don't think calling each other names will help, and in case you've forgotten, I am . . . ' He didn't finish the sentence. He was going to say 'the innocent party,' but it was not the note he wished to sound. What he wanted to say was: 'Please forgive me for being a pompous bastard, and how the hell can we get back to where we were two weeks ago, but the other side of his brain told him it would be a denial of principle.

'. . . the wronged party?' Ruth completed the sentence for him, sardonically.

Frederick hadn't heard her. 'What did you say?'

Ruth changed the subject, not suspecting the battle going on in her husband's head. 'To what part of your duty do I owe this visit?'

'I'm going to MIT tomorrow. It's official. Wives are supposed to go along. I told you about it last month.'

'And you actually want me there? After you've used words like betrayed?' Ruth's look was, she hoped, scornful.

He managed to get out the line he'd prepared: 'It would look bad if I went alone.' His look was cool, official. What he felt was that her company was the most important thing in his life at that moment, and for God's sake say yes.

The telephone rang. She picked up the handset. The long distance bleep preceded the voice of Christopher Hackett.

'Speaking,' said Ruth.

'We've cracked it,' he said. Ruth's excitement was immediate. She was back in the game! In spite of Frederick! Hackett continued: 'But it's not what you thought it was . . . '

'I'm sorry. I've got somebody with me. I didn't get that last bit.'

'It's nothing to do with the Tesla Shield.' Having struggled to keep her excitement from Frederick, she now tried to keep disappointment from her voice.

'Oh! Do you wish to discuss it with me, or . . . '

'Did you hear the news tonight?'

'Give me your number. I'll call you back.'

'They said it was another little rumble from the San Andreas, but it wasn't. Your old box did that.' He gave her the number. She didn't write it down. She was too busy trying to work out what, if anything, it meant in the plan of things. She replaced the receiver.

'Well, will you come?' asked Frederick, still formal, still hiding his churning feelings so well Ruth let her anger show.

'No! Damn and blast you. No! And get out of my house!'

Akademgorodok, U.S.S.R.

Rakov went to Academy of Sciences HQ to tell Vilkov of the final plans.

'You will be flown to Ljubljana, Yugoslavia, where you and your team will pick up a coach that'll take you across the border into Italy. At Palmanova you'll change to an Italian coach . . .'

'Why all this chopping and changing?'

'The Italian border is the easiest way into the West for us, particularly from Yugoslavia. An Italian coachload of tourists will attract less attention than a Russian.'

'Will you be with us?'

'My face is known. I will go . . . I'm afraid I can't tell you how I'll get there.'

'Am I permitted to know how "Father" and "Son" will be travelling?'

'Not really, but I can tell you that one will be with me, and the other will be under heavily armed guard, all the way.'

'I thought you said getting across the border was impossible with armed men,' said the professor. He wasn't really interested and didn't want or need to know but inconsistencies bothered him.

'I said difficult, not impossible. I have found a way, tortuous and dangerous, but the safest I can devise.'

Tuesday 17th November 1981
Lexington, Mass.

The Air Force DC9 made a smooth landing at the Hanscombe base. A guard of honour welcomed Frederick Coverdale. The President's Special Advisor walked briskly across the tarmac to be greeted by the Chancellor of MIT.

Officially the occasion of Frederick's visit was to be shown round Lincoln Laboratory and its satellite program. Assistants, tutors, graduates and technicians were introduced. At last, he was alone with Hirshfield, who came quickly to the point.

'We are making some progress; not enough.'

'What are your conclusions, so far?' asked Coverdale.

Hirshfield got out of his big leather seat and paced the room. He gazed out of the window marvelling at the richness and beauty of autumn colours. 'I'm not prepared to say too much at the moment. With only one part of the puzzle, all we can do is make guesses.'

'You don't have to defend the research process to me, professor. I know it takes time. The great thing is to get it right.'

'I'm not saying we ever will. I am still a sceptic about the whole idea. But what we are working on – what the one piece of this so-called Trinity seems to point at – is extra low-frequency. It's not a line of research I would have taken, but the Trinity thing points that way, and it was the Russian explanation for Riga.'

'Suppose the Soviet Government put out that story as a blind?'

'Exactly. It's too neat. Is there any possibility that the Trinity piece we have is a fake?' asked the professor.

'Every chance,' answered Coverdale. 'I'm not so starry-eyed as some of my colleagues. I think your scepticism is healthy. I would encourage you to work on the theory that Tesla may even have misled himself.'

Tuesday 17th November 1981

'I thought you were committed to making this work,' said Hirshfield, with surprise.

'I'm not a fool, Hirshfield,' said Coverdale earnestly. 'Nor am I, frankly, carried away on the same wave of enthusiasm which has hit the President and some of his other advisers. I'm not prepared to see a whole bunch of our national resources, at a time of economic recession, poured down a hole with no bottom to it. I want to see you people do steady basic research, putting one sound block on another, until we know what we've got; if we've got anything.'

Hirshfield was amazed. 'It's the first sane comment I've heard since the damned thing started, but aren't you just a little worried the Ruskies will get there first?'

'Of course, but getting the science of it wrong through haste is the worst option.'

'I do want one thing. I need to get into the CERN facility in Geneva with some of my people.'

'I'm afraid that won't be possible. The Swiss Government has denied access to the Russians and ourselves.'

'Surely you can find a way round that. I know the Swiss are supposed to be neutral, but . . . '

'Why do you need it?' interrupted Coverdale.

'There's no apparent connection between weapons and particle physics, and most scientists dismiss any idea of a military application, but Tesla talked of a new physics. If that wasn't all hogwash, we have to open our minds to new thinking.'

'OK but why CERN?'

'There are certain elements about this Trinity model that suggest the use of an accelerator. The Trinity isn't the weapon, or the shield or whatever it is. It is – for want of a scientific word – a formula, an elaborate clue to the principles on which the screen is based. Tesla himself said it would take him three months to perfect it. We can speed that up, but we have to get on the same wavelength, if you'll forgive the pun. Our own accelerators are not quite man enough for the job. CERN is unique.'

'Do you need to take the Trinity piece with you?'

'We're trying to complete it – make the Trinity complete. It's a hopeless task; there are so many permutations. That's one of the reasons we need CERN.'

'I can't permit our part of the Trinity to leave the United States. What would happen if the Russians got their hands on it. Here, we can guard it. Overseas, who knows!'

'We have made copies,' said Hirshfield.

'Copy! Original! What's the difference if the Soviets get their hands on it . . .'

'If we can't take it with us there's no point in going!'

'Some risks are acceptable and some aren't. And if you do get to use CERN when the Russians have been denied it, would you care to speculate on their reaction?'

'The diplomats can keep the lid on that,' said the professor confidently.

'It's out of the question.' Frederick was firm.

'I am surprised, Mr Coverdale. I expected you to take a different line . . .'

'Defending the Union has two aspects: offensive intelligence to establish Soviet state of the art and intentions; and keeping the nation's secrets safe from its enemies. On both scores taking this country's most prized secret on a hazardous journey to Europe on a scientific fishing expedition is out of the question.'

Palo Alto, Ca.

Ruth had regretted her hasty anger as soon as Frederick had slammed the bedroom door. She would quite have liked to go on her first official trip with him, but his behaviour riled her into losing her temper. At least he, too, had lost some of his cool. Was he becoming more human?

Tuesday 17th November 1981
Duty and principle were such a large part of his make-up, she doubted that any emotion could make a dent in it.

On impulse, and to put as much distance between herself and her husband as possible, she took the Lear jet to San Francisco.

'But it's in pieces,' she said to Christopher Hackett.

'Soon put it together again,' he replied. Julia Black smiled. Ruth noticed.

'How soon?'

'Couple o' days?'

'Oh . . . ' said Ruth, disappointed, but not knowing why.

'I'll try and make it by tomorrow night.'

A few hours in her Malibu cottage would help sort out her thoughts. Julia Black was quietly sizing up the rich young benefactress.

'How did you do it?' asked Ruth.

'Unremitting and dedicated research round-the-clock et cetera . . . '

Julia stifled a laugh.

'At these prices I want the truth,' was Ruth's caustic comment.

'OK. We tried everything and couldn't make it work. So I devised a little automatic testing device which was programmed to put the box through all the wavelengths, with all the permutations of settings possible on the box. We'd already done something similar by hand, and got nowhere. We turned it off at night and when there was nobody here . . . ' Ruth nodded. 'Two days ago we went out and forgot to switch it off. When we got back it had hit the right note; ergo! An earthquake!'

'Was that what parked you on top of the greenhouse?'

'Ah . . . well . . . ' Hackett began; Julia gave him a clenched fist salute. 'Not exactly, that is. Yeah. That's just about what happened.'

Julia joined in the conversation. 'I was there. The earth

moved us right off the road. It was some experience I can tell you.'

Saturday 21st November 1981
Odessa, U.S.S.R.

The trucks ground their noisy way through the tree-lined streets of Odessa not disturbing the sleeping occupants of its wooden houses. At the docks they converged and stopped. Small arms, supplies and men arrived at the assembly point. A gentle lapping swell rocked the equipment as it was stored in the cargo hold of a flying boat whose first destination was to be the Tyrrhenian Sea.

Lexington, Mass.

Tyson put a tape on the deck. 'Wait 'til you hear this!' Rogers' face was impassive as he heard the argument between Hirshfield and Coverdale. 'What did I tell you!' said Chuck.

'Who authorized you to bug the professor? Not to mention the President's Special Advisor?'

'You put me in charge of security. I didn't specially put a tap on Hirshfield – there's one in all the rooms.'

'You tired of earning a living?'

'You heard him. What's your opinion of the son-of-a-bitch?'

'I don't necessarily agree with him, but if that's the way he sees his job . . . '

'Give the tape to the director!'

'Why should I do that?'

'Coverdale's sabotaging our defence!'

'Cool off, Tyson.'

'He's frustrating Hirshfield's efforts to get the Tesla shield for America. Whaddya call that!'

'You don't get to be the special adviser unless you're a damn sight brighter than most; us, for instance. I value my job; the money, the pension and Uncle Sam – in that order, and I'm not about to tell anybody I've put a bug on the President's number one.'

'Christ, Pete. What's the matter with you!'

'The professor pushed; his privilege. Permission denied. That's the adviser's privilege. If Hirshfield wants CERN bad enough, he can figure out a way round Uncle Frederick. I'm not paid to mess with those guys.'

'In that case I'll . . . ' stormed Tyson.

'Tyson . . . ' interrupted Rogers, 'you're out-of-line putting in the bug, and out-of-line in everything else you've said tonight.'

'I've gotta do something about this!' Tyson stuck out his jaw.

'What's happened to you, Chuck?' asked Rogers, sardonically. 'Where's the bucks in this? What happened to the great entrepreneur?' Chuck glared at him. 'And I thought you always looked out for numero uno!' Tyson was confused. The jibe hit home. For once he had no ready quip. 'They're big boys out there,' Rogers pursued his advantage. 'They can look after themselves, and Uncle Sam. Don't mess with it. You'll only collect bruises.'

Sunday 22nd November 1981
Como, Italy

Rakov and Telinger had no trouble getting from Yugoslavia to Italy, the colonel in his Brooks Brothers sports jacket, Calvin Klein shirt and narrow tie, even looked like a tourist. Rakov's Russian-made two-piece suggested an unemployed undertaker.

Yuri had given some thought to the vehicle they would use. It had to be sturdy enough for the journey and yet ordinary to Italian eyes, unremarkable. Of the KGB-owned cars available, there were: a Lambourghini, which was too ostentatious, although Telinger favoured it on the double-bluff theory as well as a personal preference; plenty of

Volkswagens, but Rakov wanted an Italian car; an Alfa, big enough for comfort, only two years old, dark blue. The engineers took a whole day cutting out a segment of the chassis, and making sure 'Father' would fit inside without weakening the structure.

They turned right in Milan and headed for Como and parked in the square. Rakov got under the car, wiped the masking grease from the hinged lid of the chassis aperture and took out 'Father,' which Telinger carried in a photographic shoulder bag. By the time they reached the outskirts of Chiasso, his shoulder was aching.

Rakov was none too happy about the arrangements for the next stage of their journey. His encounter with so-called professionals in New York left little respect for their expertise or discretion. The guide they now awaited was supposed to be different; a leader among smugglers of everything from Chinese H to 'black' lira. This well-established border activity had acquired the status of a cottage industry. Neither government made much effort to stamp it out.

'Let me have the bag,' he said. Telinger willingly handed it over.

'I'm not fit to meet anybody. I need a wash . . .'

'Shut up, Aleksei!'

Telinger followed Rakov into the white-painted bar. Three of the tables were occupied by knowing old men. Conversation stopped. Rakov was not impressed with the public choice of meeting place.

He ordered beer, brandy for Telinger. They sat in silence. The locals stared at them.

She was about thirty, but could be more, thought Rakov, lean and fit, but the skin on the fair face did not have the lines or stretching of a person exposed to the elements. She strode across with her hand held out. 'You must be the one who phoned.'

Rakov nodded. She turned to the other occupants of the

bar. 'They want to see the Alps on foot. "What do you want to smuggle across?" I ask. "Nothing" they say. "Then why come to me?" I demand. They say "You were recommended by a man in Milan . . . " I ask you, who knows of little me in Milan?' The men roared with laughter.

'Why are you doing it, Rita?' asked one of the younger men. She rubbed her fingers together in the international gesture for money.

'"I don't care," I said. "The price for being guide is the same, smuggling or no smuggling." Show me your money, my friend,' she said to Rakov. He pulled out his wallet and carefully counted notes.

'Here, give it to me,' she demanded, taking the leather pouch. 'Ask anybody round here. I can always be trusted with money.' And they all laughed again as she counted out two hundred thousand lira and returned the wallet to Rakov. 'For half-a-day of my time, my friend. Any longer and it will cost you another hundred thousand. Are you ready?'

The two men nodded. 'Andiamo!'

They were soon off the road and beginning the long climb. After half-an-hour she stopped.

'You might just as well have taken out an advertisement in the newspaper,' said Rakov accusingly. She smiled.

'You don't understand my people. They would have known as soon as we met that I was on a job. They will think it is smuggling; heroin, or black money, and they will keep quiet about it; one must play the game correctly.' She looked ahead, then at the sky. 'You need a rest; just ten minutes, no more. I'll slow the pace because it gets steeper. We need to be over the top and down the other side before darkness.'

Lexington, Mass.

'Is Mrs Coverdale there?', Tyson asked down the telephone.

'Not at the moment, sir. Do you wish to speak to Mr Coverdale?'

'Where can I reach her?'

The Welsh butler was pedantically correct. 'I do not have a number for her. You could try Los Angeles . . . '

'Thank you, Jennings, and . . . don't bother to tell Mr Coverdale about my call.'

'Very well, sir.'

He looked at his watch – eight p.m.; that meant five o'clock, L.A. time. He called.

The answerphone reminded him it was Sunday and gave him an emergency number. Mike Jamieson answered. 'I don't have a number,' he said. 'If she checks in do you want her to call you?'

'That's OK' said Tyson. 'I'll catch up with her tomorrow.' He thought: that's another day lost!

Chiasso, Swiss/Italian border

The climb was terrible. Even Rakov, who thought he was fit, had difficulty keeping up with their lithe guide. She made no more jokes and only spoke to urge them to climb faster or curse them for idleness. Telinger was in a poor state. He shoes were more suited to a *thé dansant* than mountaineering, his hands were a mass of lacerations where he had grabbed at rock outcrops to prevent a fall. His face was covered in perspiration, and a deathly white.

'We'll have to stop,' said Rakov to the guide. 'He'll die!'

She gave Telinger one contemptuous look, and nodded. 'Five minutes; even that may cost us our lives if this mist gets any thicker!' Telinger got out a cigarette. She took it from him and threw it away. 'Don't make your breathing even more difficult!' Telinger closed his eyes and was instantly asleep. Rakov massaged his calf and thigh muscles. She handed him two white lozenges. 'Glucose. Eat them.' She woke Telinger, who groaned with the pain in his legs and hips. He ate mechanically, tasting nothing but bile.

Sunday 22nd November 1981

After exactly five minutes, she made them set off again. It took another twenty minutes to reach the top. 'From here it is downhill.' If it was meant to encourage them, it did, but only momentarily. Telinger made the mistake of relaxing, when they set off downhill, not realizing that he would need to impose almost as big a strain on other muscles to control the steep descent. He fell at the third step, heading fast for the edge and a two-thousand foot drop. Rakov dived for his legs and just managed a rugby grip around the ankles. The guide was not amused. As Telinger and Rakov lay on the ground, she knelt and felt the legs and ankles of the weaker man. She stood up. 'Nothing is broken,' she said. 'Let's go.'

'For God's sake,' gasped Telinger. 'Can't you see I'm hurt!'

She had no sympathy. 'If we don't get below two-thousand feet before the mist closes in, we shall have to spend the night on the mountain, and in those clothes you'll die.'

Rakov helped Telinger to his feet. The going was faster, but every step on now blistered feet was painful for both men. The air became more moist, and visibility lessened.

'We must hurry,' she said. 'It's not far now. Just a couple of hundred feet and we shall be safe.'

She teased them into extra speed by lies, pretending that rest lay round the next corner, the next outcrop of rock. Telinger fell twice more. Rakov collapsed when his ankle turned on a stone. Both men retreated within themselves, conscious only of the need to put one step in front of the other; nothing else mattered. Only gradually did Rakov become aware that they were no longer descending, and the path was broader and more even. He looked up and saw, through the gathering dusk, a flicker of artificial light.

'Are we there?' he croaked.

'What you can see is your destination; Mendrisio Railway Station,' she replied.

Sunday 22nd November 1981

Telinger mumbled: 'We can't go there looking like this.'

'All my customers look the same!'

Monday 23rd November 1981
Washington, D.C.

Chuck was not sure there was anything Ruth could do about Frederick's attitude to Hirshfield. General Lubbock was out of the mainstream of influence. Experience told him that anything he did would get him into trouble. His motto had always been 'never volunteer' unless there was a clear advantage to be gained. So why was he even bothering? What Pete said was right. Hirshfield could take care of himself. He'd already made an enemy of one of the nation's top men; why do it again! He tried to tell himself it was a simple matter of competition with the Brit, the need to prove himself. But he suspected there was a deeper motive; he didn't know what to call it; he didn't want to call it anything. Was it conscience? Patriotism? God! What awful words! He phoned for an interview with the CIA Director. He said it was urgent.

The director was an old-fashioned man; a stickler for discipline with a detestation for any employee who went over a superior's head. He listened with a blank face and cold eyes. Chuck offered him the tape. He pointed to the desk. 'I had a phone call about you,' he said, 'telling me you're unreliable, not suited to intelligence.'

'I can explain that . . . '

The director ignored the interruption. 'I asked for chapter and verse. I was told I should be satisfied with the fact that the authority for the statement was in a high place. I pressed. Eventually Mr Coverdale appeared from the woodwork. I don't like interference in CIA internal affairs without supporting evidence, of which I was given none. I said I would take no action. I was wrong.'

'Sir! May I explain?'

'You are unreliable. You bug the President's adviser

without authority, and then refuse to pursue it through channels. You're a disgrace. Dismissed.'

'Sir. I'm entitled to put my side of the story.'

'Put it on tape, captain! You're dismissed.'

Palo Alto, Ca.

Ruth gazed at her new box. It was not as pretty or polished as the one she had taken from Cheyenne College; the metal casing was grey, unpainted, and there were scoring marks where the riveting machine had slipped. It was bigger than Tesla's original – it fitted into a large suitcase – and was heavy.

'For maximum effect it should be buried six feet deep in rock,' said Hackett. Ruth was only half listening, wondering what she was doing here. 'You need to apply exactly crossed electric and magnetic fields, held in precise ratio, and so for that purpose the current has to be held constant to better than one part in ten thousand. The frequency at which the fields oscillate is of crucial importance and has to be tied to a value consistent with the fields' strengths as well as with their ratio. Even small deviations in any of these variables will prevent function. Under no circumstances are the settings on the instrument itself to be touched.'

'You don't expect me to remember that!' said Ruth.

'There are written instructions.'

Hackett demanded to know what she wanted it for. The truth was that she didn't know. She paid a quarter of a million dollars for what she thought was a breakthrough that would give Uncle Sam the Tesla Shield. That she could have wasted such a sum on a box that was nothing to do with her purpose shocked her deeply. She could never admit it to Lubbock. The fact that it could apparently spark off an earthquake was so irrelevant she could hardly take it in.

'D'you realize what you've got here?'

'Not really.'

'The capacity to make earthquakes!'

'I suppose that's what I paid my money for.' She didn't care. She had two preoccupying thoughts in her life, her husband and the Tesla Trinity and this thing didn't fit into either scenario.

'It's not as simple as that.'

'You want more money? There's a word for that sort of thing!'

'What's with you? Money, money, money! This box is of immense scientific interest. It could help us understand earthquakes, maybe even prevent them.'

'Don't ask me to give it to some damned university. I just paid a fortune to get it away from one of those.'

'I'll have to write about it; for publication.'

'Not on my time and money.' She didn't know why she said it.

'People have to know about it.'

'Absolutely not!'

'Why?'

'I paid through the nose for what you've done. You guaranteed me discretion and that nobody would be told. I'm holding you to that.'

'You told me it was part of the Tesla Shield.'

'You knew you were getting into Tesla!'

Hackett spoke urgently. 'Every scientist has laughed at the story of Tesla making an earthquake in New York, because they know it's impossible. This proves he actually did it!'

'So what!' said Ruth.

Hackett lost his temper. 'The fucking thing works and that changes everything!'

'Not for me,' said Ruth. 'And not our agreement.'

'I'll publish anyway.'

'And I'll use a battery of lawyers to put you out of business. By the time they've finished you'll be unemployable.'

He knew that was no idle threat. 'You realize it's dangerous.' He said it quietly, almost an aside.

'What do you mean?'

'Think what an enemy could do with the ability to make earthquakes.'

'I suppose it could have some potential,' said Ruth, 'but it's got to be near something like the San Andreas fault to make it work.'

'I didn't say that.'

'You're sitting on top of the most volatile shifting continental plate in the world. That's what you set off, it wouldn't work just anywhere.'

'There's no San Andreas fault in Lower Manhattan!'

Ruth's interest stirred. 'Do you mean just anywhere?'

'I think so.' Ruth still couldn't see any relevance to her plans. 'So you see why I must publish.'

'Out of the question.' A commercial reaction. Never give anything away.

'This is probably one of the greatest scientific discoveries of all time! I don't think our defence chiefs would like it handed on a plate to Brezhnev, and I imagine your husband will have more than a passing interest.'

'Put it in the car,' said Ruth, 'and you're coming with me.'

'Where to?'

'You'll see.'

'I'm busy!'

Ruth gave him a hard look. 'You're the one who thinks this thing is so goddamn important. We're going to put it somewhere safe.'

Five minutes later, the limousine was taking them back into San Francisco. The box was in a battered suitcase tied round with rope, on the floor between them. Ruth took no chances. She told the driver to leave them at the airport.

Monday 23rd November 1981

When he was out of sight, she hailed a taxi and they headed for Downtown.

The vice president of the bank promised complete discretion and two keys for the box in the vault where the suitcase was deposited.

'Who else knows about this?' asked Ruth.

'Just Julia. Julia Black, my assistant.'

'Can you guarantee her silence?'

'I think so.'

'You'd better be right!'

20

Monday 23rd November 1981
Off Syracuse, Italy

The flying boat left the Yugoslav coast at two thousand feet and descended to two hundred feet above the waves of the Adriatic to keep under NATO radar. It was a dark night with low cloud base. US satellites would have difficulty identifying it, as it landed twenty miles east of Syracuse. Quickly and silently men and equipment were transferred to a cargo ship flying the Liberian flag.

Twelve hours later the ship docked. It was a brilliant sunny day, and the bay was beautiful. The port area was not a thing of beauty; cranes, coal wagons, shunting railway stock mingled with assorted mounds of tarpaulin-clad imports and exports. The sleek Italian in expensive grey mohair, arrived in a nondescript Fiat. His driver adjusted his sunglasses, and carefully scrutinized the area. The passenger alighted and shook hands with several officials, who greeted him with a deference that suggested money and power. He boarded the ship and was escorted to the captain's cabin. He chose cognac which he sipped in tiny measures. He listened to the request, weighing the strength of the silent KGB officer.

'Several of my sailors have not seen the city before,' said the captain. 'They would like to go ashore, but their papers, regretfully are not fully in order. They will cause no embarrassment to you or to your beautiful city; in fact they will stay no longer than to drive through and on elsewhere . . .'

Monday 23rd November 1981

'So they will not be spending their wages with my people?'

'They . . . I will be happy to compensate the traders for their lost business . . . '

'Ah, so. And they will be travelling on to . . . ?'

'Another destination. Another country.' The man was interested in that information.

'May I, perhaps, be of assistance in that respect also?'.

'It is not necessary, my friend, but thank you for your offer,' replied the captain. 'And certain goods were unfortunately omitted from the ship's manifest. A clerical error at port of embarkation, you understand . . . '

Grey suit put his finger to his mouth. 'That is more difficult. Different people are involved. When would you wish to unload this . . . cargo?'

'As soon as possible, and then we will be gone.'

The man paused again, deep in thought. He gazed at the captain and his 'adviser.' 'I will require your assurance . . . we have been doing business together for some years . . . I would hate to see that terminate in any sort of unpleasantness . . . '

'Naturally . . . ' assured the captain.

'I would require certainty that the goods are not . . . shall I say in competition with the products of . . . my friends,' said the man with a smile in which there was not even the hint of warmth.

'Certainty is . . . ' began the captain. The KGB officer whispered into his ear. He listened and nodded. 'My adviser will personally add the sum of ten million lira to the amount already agreed.'

Grey Suit was surprised and did not hesitate to show it. 'That sum is sufficiently large to raise doubts about the . . . venture as a whole . . . '

Again the KGB man whispered. The captain nodded

again. This time the KGB officer spoke. 'You have one minute to say yes or no, or we take the business to other . . . friends.' He said it without menace. It was a plain statement of fact.

Grey Suit did not hesitate. 'I accept your assurance. If I . . . and my friends are mistaken in doing so, you appreciate there will have to be a reckoning.' That too was said without menace. If the captain was not playing straight, Grey Suit would arrange for problems, not only there but at other ports; his continued good health would also be in doubt.

Washington/London

'We have a problem, Ma'am,' said the President into the telephone. 'The United States is not a member of CERN. In denying the Russians access, you've also kept my people out.'

'I realize that,' said the Prime Minister evenly.

'We now need it.'

'Can't it wait? Surely, stopping the Soviets perfecting this weapon is more important than pure science at this stage.'

'We need it for the same reason the Russians do. We're evidently working on the same lines.'

'As you say, Mr President, we have a problem. Can I call you back?' asked the Iron Lady.

Two hours later she did so.

'Our ambassador has had a word with his opposite number in Basle. What we have is an . . . arrangement. The Swiss do not normally enquire the nationality of the technicians working on our team there. They will not do so now.'

The President wondered if this was a plan to ensure that the Brits were in on whatever Hirshfield discovered. He couldn't help admiring the 'footwork.' 'I think that will prove satisfactory. Thanks, Mrs Prime Minister.'

Monday 23rd November 1981

Lexington, Mass.

Rogers signed a recommendation to his director that further surveillance of Arthur Wilshire's office be terminated. Tyson entered the room with a familiar question. 'Has he acted yet? On the tape?'

'The President says Hirshfield gets to go to the land of the cuckoo clock,' said Rogers, sealing the envelope. 'You've drawn a new job; get this "Son" to Geneva, Switzerland, via London, England. Any ideas?' Rogers didn't seem concerned about what Chuck had done.

'Pan Am?' said Tyson, only half seriously.

'Has its merits, but on the whole I think not.'

'Military job? Air Force One?' asked Tyson.

'I think we might go supersonic. I'll call and find out what we've got.'

'What about a decoy?'

'What are you talking about?' asked Rogers testily.

'You know how much the Reds would love to get their hands on this baby. I'd hate to see somebody nick it en route. Tell whoever needs to know the decoy story; the real route we keep cosy – just you and me . . . '

' . . . And the director . . . '

'You and me, Pete. You and me I can trust. Anybody else then his secretary knows and the press department gets a briefing in case anything goes wrong, and you might as well tell Carl Bernstein.'

'I'll go along with that,' said Rogers. 'Make up a fake parcel; same size and weight. I'll get the director to lay on a special flight with an Air Force U-2 or whatever. Then get yourself a new identity and get booked on tomorrow's Concorde to London. I'll alert somebody to meet you.'

St Rhemy, Switzerland

Each scientist from Akademgorodok was assigned a new KGB 'wife' for the occasion. Some were annoyed, others embarrassed, but the majority reaction was a mixture of interest and lust. They were disappointed; each woman made it plain that duty came first, second and last, and any thought of marital rights would be answered by a headache, for the husbands.

The crossing into Yugoslavia, and then Italy passed without incident. They changed coaches and ate at Palmanova. The autostrada took them past Milan to Novara, and the long climb through the Alps to the Swiss border. Vilkov told them to act like any bunch of Russians on holiday. 'I hope we don't have to look that unhappy,' quipped one of the older men. He was quickly shut up by the KGB leader, a fearsome woman with her mousy hair crunched into a bun at the back of her head; she was Vilkov's 'wife' for the journey. He had tried unsuccessfully, to swap her for one of the prettier ones. She had not taken it well.

The Swiss border guard was hunched over a paperback in his kiosk. He took no notice of the coach. The Italian driver – a good Party member – kept the engine running, hoping to be waved on, but knowing that he dare not move without a signal. It didn't come. Eventually, the guard closed the book with a slight smile, and then looked up to see what he had on his hands. He glanced down the length of the vehicle and its full passenger load. The driver thought they would be let through. He was wrong.

'Passports!' the Swiss border guard demanded. The driver presented the forgeries.

The coach passengers watched an angry silent scene in the guard house. Vilkov became increasingly nervous. Eventually, the driver returned, a thunderous look on his face. 'These capitalist manure eaters have the effrontery to suggest that Switzerland can beat Italy at football . . . ' Blaring horns of traffic persuaded the angry fan to get on with his job. The coach entered Switzerland.

Tuesday, 24th November 1981
Hereford, England

Lloyd was bored. He had spent two weeks getting fit, and had lost twenty pounds in weight. He'd studied plans of Akademgorodok until he could recite every measurement in his sleep. He repeatedly asked when they would be given the signal to go. He was told to be patient. He was drinking beer in the mess when Major Forbes sauntered in; in regimental blazer and grey slacks, with a tie that looked as if he normally used it to keep up his trousers.

'You have news. We can go?' asked Lloyd, his hopes rising.

'No,' said Forbes. 'Just a social visit; buy you a drink; find out how you are; if the shoulder's healed.'

'Bugger!' said Richard Lloyd.

'How is it? The shoulder?' Forbes repeated.

'Lot of fuss about nothing according to the quacks here,' replied Lloyd. 'Did you say you were buying?' Forbes nodded. 'Make mine scotch; a double, as you've come empty-handed.'

'I didn't say that,' said the major enigmatically, and he ordered two large whiskies. 'I've come to tell you that, in my opinion, permission will never be given for your little exercise.'

'Oh Christ!' said Richard. 'After all that effort. It makes you want to . . . '

'We do have some other ideas for you,' said Forbes, and told him about CERN.

'Where do we fit into that scenario?'

'When the Kremlin finds out we're going full blast on the accelerator they've been denied access to, they may not be thrilled.'

'Tough tit.'

'The intelligence assessment is that they might try something physical,' said Arthur Forbes mildly. He began the arduous task of cleaning and then filling his pipe from a weather-beaten leather pouch.

'They wouldn't dare!'

'Probably. But as Lloyd's personal invasion of Russia had been called off, I thought you'd like to work up a defence strategy for CERN – just in case.'

'Waste of time,' said Lloyd.

Forbes blew through his pipe stem, spraying dottle over Richard's shoes. 'Sorry about that. Filthy things, pipes.' He started filling it.

'They'll just bomb it,' said Lloyd. 'Much cleaner.'

'It's buried under God-knows-how-many-feet of concrete. It's nuclear-proof, so they say.' While Lloyd digested that fact, Arthur Forbes completed the smoking ritual by setting a match to the inverted bulb of the old Dunhill. Then he righted it and pushed down the red hot tobacco with a blackened thumb.

'Your mouth must be on fire!' said Lloyd.

'Quite right,' replied Forbes. 'Got a good glow, this one. Father gave it to me for my twenty-first.'

'Do I have any choice?' asked Lloyd.

'Not really. I've got plans and such-like, in the car. You'll need to make a model of the accelerator and the terrain. Here's something to be going on with,' and he drew a torn aerial map of CERN from his pocket, showing the route of the accelerator, its proximity to the Alps and Lac Léman.

As soon as Lloyd saw it his mind engaged the problem, and he began applying the lessons of Akademgorodok in reverse.

Lake Maggiore, Italy

Communists in Italy comprise more than one ideology, from those locally oriented, like the comrades who run the local government of Bologna more efficiently than any other city, to extremists who would promote a Khmer-

Rouge type slaughter to purge the country of its middle class millions. Somewhere in between are the elements that support the USSR, right or wrong. They include the rich and famous and even some of their scions. One such edged his father's elegant motor cruiser close inshore near Laveno. Vito was twenty-three with pointed Valentino features marred by a complexion pitted by a childhood ailment.

He had gone through various phases in his short life, seeking ever more from a life in which his father's wealth ensured he was denied nothing. It gave him only transitory satisfaction. He soon tired of the *dolce vita*; dropping out and drugs had their moments; a stint when he bent his mind to academia lasted but a few months. And then he fell in love with communism; it was a form of chastisement, a rebirth, expiation for the too many good things his family ostentatiously enjoyed.

His friend, Angelina was not into dialectical materialism; some comrades might even have described her as a hedonist, not that she would have known the meaning of the word; she was too busy practising the art to waste precious pleasure hours on books and learning. She was short, blonde and the gods had been generous with her mammary equipment.

Vito awaited the arrival of the KGB men with impatient excitement; it was his first assignment of any significance. He imagined his father's rage if he were caught; it would undoubtedly be bad for business, it would cost him a few hundred million; his mother would have to cancel a few dinner parties. He smiled at the thoughts.

There were two trucks, and six men. The others had dropped off at various points to cross the border individually. It took half-an-hour to load the boat and store the wooden cases below decks, a back-breaking procedure interrupted several times by passing vehicles; one, a police van, stopped. Vito thought his heartbeat would burst his chest, but even police officers need a pee and a cigarette.

The Italian/Swiss border divides Lake Maggiore about seven miles south of Locarno, without any demarcation. Two patrol boats, one Swiss, one Italian, guard the interest of each nation. It is not a demanding exercise, and they know all the boats on the lake. Rakov had chosen this route because he was not prepared to risk a customs inspection at a land border crossing. The only worry with this method was a spot check by a patrol boat, unlikely unless something suspicious attracted its attention. Hence Vito's invitation to Angelina; a reassurance of normality.

The engines throbbed into life. Vito cast off bow and stern, and the million-dollar craft drew smoothly away from the shore and into the middle of the deep lake. He could see no sign of movement through his binoculars. He eased the throttles forward. The sharp leading edge of the bow rose as it cut its way into the still water.

They had been travelling for about an hour when Vito became aware of another craft keeping station with them and about half-a-mile on their starboard side. He guessed it to be a patrol boat; but whose? The Italians were less enthusiastic about the job than their Swiss counterparts.

'Take off your T-shirt,' said Vito.

'I'm cold,' said Angelina.

'This'll warm you up,' replied Vito.

'That's different,' she said, and peeled off the thin cotton top.

Vito turned on the radio, the thundering beat of reggae cut through the night air. 'Wanna dance, beloved?' he said.

'Who's going to drive the boat?'

'I am.'

'So how do we dance?'

'Not me; you. I want you dancing on deck where I can see that . . . wiggle from your hair to your hips,' he said enticingly.

Tuesday 24th November 1981

'Like this?' she said, indicating her naked torso. 'What if they come up from downstairs?' He had tried to teach her more nautical language, but it had not been successful.

'I'll put their eyes out,' he said evenly.

'Would you?' she said eagerly. 'For me?'

'Nothing less,' he replied.

'Turn up the sound,' she giggled, and climbed on to the deck.

There was about a square metre of space, and only the overspill light from the wheelhouse; it was enough. 'Go baby!' said Vito as he increased the volume.

The patrol boat reacted to the music. Its spotlight swept the yacht from stern to bow, and returned to the gyrating figure on the deck.

'Keep going, baby!' urged Vito.

'But they'll see me!' she protested, but Angelina enjoyed the limelight.

The lake police kept station with them, the light concentrated on the blonde dancer. As she got used to the idea, her dancing became more raunchy.

'Now come inside,' Vito said, as the voice of the announcer told them the time was one a.m.

The spotlight followed. Vito cupped one breast and kissed her. He heard laughter on the patrol boat. Its light was killed and it turned away.

They reached the north-west shore between Brissago and Ascona in two-and-a-half hours, and without further incident. The unloading was smooth and quick. Soon the Russian soldiers and their supplies were road-bound again, well inside Switzerland and headed for Geneva.

Meyrin, Switzerland

It was cold, but spacious, and conveniently near CERN and Cointrin Airport. A polite KGB lieutenant thought it would be ideal. All manner of problems were presented by the landlord. Lawyers had to be consulted, references taken up, documents had to be signed. The Russian, speaking immaculate French, and giving no clue to his nationality, produced his wallet, which was nicely bulging, and mentioned it could be a cash transaction, and that he would not be wanting receipts. The 'black economy' was an international language and the Swiss were as avidly in its favour as the Moscovite chauffeur who used his state-owned Volga to 'moonlight' as an unofficial taxi-cab.

'Are you asleep?' Telinger asked.

It had been an exhausting two days. They had arrived just after midday and gone straight to the warehouse. Telinger had wanted to check into the Hôtel des Bergues and 'recover from his unaccustomed exertions.' Yuri had soon disabused him and set him to work on the telephone, checking arrangements for the scientists and their 'wives' at hotels and boarding houses. They had taken a taxi to within half-a-mile of CERN and reconnoitred on foot. They did not cross the border into France. Cattle grazed on fields above the seven kilometres of nuclear tunnel that spanned the two countries.

'I wonder how our scientific friends are getting on,' asked Telinger.

'What do you mean?' asked Rakov.

'I wouldn't care to share a bed with some of their new "wives."' Rakov laughed. 'Hand picked, most of them, by me personally.'

'You're a sadist,' said the colonel.

'I chose them for their records in combat and on the ranges,' said Rakov. 'Although there was one who looked promising.'

'Male or female?' asked Telinger, thinking of Anton.

'Female, of course,' said Rakov calmly. 'Let's go back.'

'Have you a cigarette?' asked the colonel. Yuri threw his packet. The match flared, casting a flickering shadow through the windows of the bare office. It momentarily illuminated the inside of the big void that was the main part of the warehouse, with its metal corrugated roof, and the 'hangar' doors at the far end, ample enough to permit trucks to load and unload out of sight.

'How do you feel?' asked Telinger. It was not a question Rakov welcomed. He didn't examine his feelings. It added to tension. He preferred to occupy his mind with the practical details.

'OK' Yuri replied and lit a cigarette.

'What do *you* think'll happen?' asked Telinger.

'The Swiss police are a hard lot. They'll isolate us or try to; siege tactics, I imagine,' replied Rakov.

'When the scientists have done their stuff, and we've radioed the results, how do we get out?' asked the colonel.

'We shall demand transport to Cointrin, and an aircraft to take us to Libya.'

'Taking the hostages with us?'

'Of course.'

'Balls,' said Telinger quietly. Rakov said nothing. 'We have no chance of getting out of there; you know that. We'll either be dead or in a Swiss jail for the next twenty years.'

'You think too much,' said Rakov. 'I'm going to sleep.'

21

Tuesday 24th November 1981
Washington, D.C.

Ruth found Chuck's note in the second drawer of her jewellery box.

> 'I'm on my way to Geneva via England. Things are hotting up. It looks as if we might be a bit nearer a solution once our guys get going on the CERN accelerator. I'll try to call you from there.'

Ruth decided to tell Frederick about the box. Her openness would demonstrate that she had abandoned clandestine activity. She rang his office. He was out. She left a message. No response. She did that several times with no result. So, he'd decided not to talk to her! Damn him!

Heathrow, England

Lloyd was pulled out of yet another session on strategy to defend CERN when he and his team were sent to Heathrow to escort Chuck and his 'luggage' to Hereford.

The army helicopter with its five man team, arrived as the delta-winged Concorde landed, its needle nose drooping as its rear wheels screeched on the concrete. It halted at the end of the runway near the SAS group.

'Catch!' said Chuck.

Lloyd fielded it. 'If this is what I think it is, you certainly like living dangerously.'

'Hi!' said Tyson. 'What's happening?'

Wednesday, 25th November 1981
Meyrin, Switzerland

Rakov trained the 'soldiers' all morning, and then brought in the scientists for a briefing. 'Once inside that place, there's no coming out because we've forgotten something. It must be perfect the first time.'

Pinned to the wall were enlarged photographs and drawings of CERN. Each soldier's area was marked, and so were the buildings the scientists were to occupy. Sleeping, cooking and eating sections were marked. The most vulnerable points would be given the strongest weaponry, the shoulder-mounted anti-aircraft missile launchers. 'You'll spend the night here,' said Rakov. 'Departure six a.m.'

The men and women began to disperse. Vilkov spoke to Rakov.

'Are you happy in your work, major?'

Rakov smiled. 'Everybody's worried about my welfare. It's touching.'

'Do you have any particular concerns about tomorrow? If so I would like to know.'

'No, comrade professor. I'm reasonably certain we can hold the situation for three days, after that . . . who knows.'

'And I can't guarantee that will be long enough.'

'I know.' What the professor did not know was that neither he nor any member of his team was to be allowed to fall into the hands of the enemy alive.

Georgetown, D.C.

For two days Ruth had tried to contact her husband. She had now given up and was trying to write him a letter. She was tearing up the fourth attempt to put her point across succinctly, but with urgency, and without committing what ought to be a state secret to prying eyes, when Jennings entered with a message: 'Would it be convenient if the Master called at four o'clock?'

Surely nobody used such archaic language, even in Wales, today, thought Ruth. 'Yes, Jennings.'

Perhaps she should have been more conciliatory in her greeting: 'I've been trying to reach you for two days. Is the White House so inefficient it can't carry messages?'

'I received a note of your calls. Did it not occur to you that I might not wish to see you?'

'Then what the hell are you doing here!'

Frederick was past introspection into his emotions; he was furious. 'I'm here for an explanation.'

Ruth sighed, exasperated. 'What's got up your pompous nose this time?'

The insult made him even more angry. 'I warned you of the consequences of meddling in affairs of state, but I find that you and your nephew are playing for even higher stakes; going to the President, no less.'

'I don't know what you're talking about. We've done absolutely nothing since I last saw you.'

'Then how did you get to know Professor Hirshfield wanted to go to Geneva, and that I'd vetoed it?'

'Who's Professor Hirshfield?'

Frederick snorted his derision at the denial. 'I'm trying my damndest to keep the nation from getting into a war situation. I stopped Hirshfield going to CERN and taking the Trinity out of the country because that's what's in the national interest. Your nephew told some cock-and-bull story that the CIA director swallowed and the President's just bawled me out for being ultra cautious. You and your co-conspirators are obviously. . .'

'I know nothing of any of this.'

'Why lie? I know! I've checked back through sources. It was Tyson who blew the whistle on me.'

'If Chuck did such a thing, he didn't tell me. I've never heard of Hirshfield, and all I know about CERN is what I read in old *Economist* magazines at the dentist.'

Wednesday 25th November 1981

One part of Frederick wanted to believe her, but logic said she had to be lying.

His reaction had been to tell the President about Lubbock and the rest, but the countermanding of his orders on Hirshfield had put that into a different light. A complaint now would look like sour grapes; it would diminish him in the Man's eyes, and worse, he probably wouldn't be believed. 'My respect for you has reached a new ebb.' He turned on his heel.

'Don't go, Freddie . . . ' To her surprise, what she intended as a demand, turned into a plea on which her voice cracked, making it sound emotional. It stopped her husband, but he didn't face her. 'I've just come back from California. Something happened there that I have to tell you about.' He slowly turned, his face a mask. 'I went originally to Colorado Springs to . . . ' And then she realized what his response would be. He would take it as evidence that she was still working on Tesla in defiance of him, and he would almost certainly think she had just been lying. She clamped her mouth shut.

'Yes?' he said, impersonally, as though admonishing a careless secretary. 'What was so important that you had to leave seven messages for me at the White House? Colorado Springs! That sounds like Tesla.'

She could think of no words that didn't sound deceitful and devious and make her out to be the worst of liars. She turned away from him. Tears threatened to break out, but whether for impotent rage or emotion about him she couldn't tell. If only he'd unbend just a fraction, she'd be able to tell him. She needed so little from him.

'Is it?' This time it was more demanding.

'Damn you, Frederick,' she said in quiet frustration. 'I can't talk to you when you're like this. You'd better go back to . . . wherever.'

Thursday, 26th November 1981
Cambridge, Mass.

The time was two a.m. Rex Hirshfield was in bed, his mind pre-occupied with coming events. There had been no time to go out to dinner. He did have a quiet time with his wife over Scotch whisky at midnight. It was not much of a farewell party. Their relationship was sound, a companionable marriage of similar temperaments and intellectual interests. There was not much overt demonstration of affection, but an underlying current that ran smooth and strong; neither liked being parted from the other. This time it was different, because he could not tell her how long he would be away, and he didn't want to frighten her with words like danger.

He let his breathing become shallow, feigning sleep, but her hand sought his. They made sensible use of the next half-an-hour. Then she slept. He wondered what the next few days would hold.

Washington, D.C.

There was entertainment at the White House, a glittering occasion. The men showed off their women. The President proudly projected the First Lady to centre stage. Encore followed encore, and it was after midnight when Frank Sinatra sang 'My Way.' He would have sung for another hour if she had not decided enough was enough.

The party broke up, and the guests departed. Sinatra took the band for a drink; the President joined them. She went to bed murmuring 'He'll regret it.'

Hereford, England: 6 a.m.

Lloyd got out of bed, slipped into a track suit and went to wake Tyson. Jet lag had attacked; Richard decided to leave him. He and the other four members of his team ran for five miles through the dew-strewn countryside of Herefordshire as the sun did its best to warm up the day.

Thursday 26th November 1981

London: 6 a.m.

In London the British Prime Minister was at her desk, at work on the morning's mail. She had a heavy schedule ahead of her. By ten a.m. she would have disposed of a crop of civil servants. At ten-thirty there was a cabinet meeting. At noon she would visit Northern Ireland; a surprise, she hoped, for all but a handful of people charged with ensuring the IRA did not get to the airstrip before her. The job absorbed and fulfilled her. Each day was filled with action, information and demands to which her character responded with enthusiasm. Had the Prime Minister known what challenges would be presented to her before darkness fell, she might not have been so eager for her day to unfold.

Geneva: 7.10 a.m.

KGB 'soldiers' were aboard the trucks, with their arms and supplies. The hangar doors swung open, the engines coughed into life, and they moved out.

Vilkov and his colleagues waited nervously in groups. Telinger spoke to them. 'Don't worry, comrades. The *Cheka* will secure the place for you, and then you can get on with the job of solving Tesla's little conundrum.'

'What happens if Comrade Rakov and the others can't get in? If it goes wrong?' There was always one pessimist.

'Then you'll go home none the wiser,' replied Telinger. 'But that won't happen. CERN is a civil installation. It is not guarded . . . '

'They are mad,' said the talkative one. 'At home it would be surrounded by wire and guards and towers. Don't these people know what their enemies might do to such a valuable . . . '

'Careful, comrade,' interrupted Telinger. 'We are that enemy!'

It broke the tension; there was laughter.

Thursday 26th November 1981

Lac Léman pinpoints Geneva with its famous Water Spout. The grandeur and essential Swissness of the four and five storey buildings surrounding the tree-lined deep blue water are dwarfed by the snow-cloaked Alps. Geneva is a unique combination of tradition – the first recorded mention of the town is by Julius Caesar in his 'Commentaries' in 58 BC – and modernity; the 'luxus' international hotels and world organizations, health, meteorology, telecommunications and intellectual property; not forgetting the longest-running international show in town – the Disarmament Conference. Meyrin, where CERN is located, is typical European suburbia, cleaner than France, smelling fresher than Spain and as neat as Holland, a mixture of residential, commercial and industrial buildings. On this fine crisp November morning, the Swiss were leaving their homes for offices and factories unaware of the globally-significant events about to engulf their old city.

Just past Les Pommeries the first truck turned left into Route Paul and stopped at Building 55, the CERN reception office. Rakov sat in the passenger seat, and pressed the button which flashed a dull red light twice in the rear of the vehicle. Two KGB men flipped back the canvas flap and dropped over the tailgate. In sports jackets and slacks they strolled to reception, one studying an open folder. It was normal, disarming. 'I need to lay these out on a table,' said the first. The uniformed attendant nodded, and they went inside. There was one other occupant, drinking coffee from a battered mug held in both hands. The two Swiss looked, uncomprehending, at the gun which appeared in the hand of the first KGB 'soldier.' The second man produced a revolver.

'We would like you to come with us and get into the back of the truck. You will come to no harm.' It was said politely, but there was no choice. They looked at each other and the guns; they shrugged. The second Chekist stayed behind.

Thursday 26th November 1981

The first task was to isolate key people; the two directors-general, the five members of the directorate, the executive chairman, board members and secretary, the research board chairman, and chairmen and secretaries of experiments committees, the leaders of theoretical and experimental physics and data handling divisions, and the leaders of common services divisions. KGB herded them into the experimental hall.

Two offered resistance. One was pistol-whipped. The other, CERN's most dedicated chauvinist, did not like the idea of being 'captured' by a woman. He arrived at the hall white-faced, crouching to contain the pain in his bruised testicles.

Rakov addressed them: 'Ladies and gentlemen, you are hostages. We are representatives of the Independent Republic of Armenia. Our people are in slavery, denied our birthright, denied basic human rights. We have certain basic demands. We shall hold you here until those demands are granted. As long as you behave, you'll be treated well. Anybody who makes trouble will be shot.'

The executive board chairman was not afraid. 'And what if your demands are not met?'

'We're not asking for anything unreasonable. When they see that we're serious, they'll give in.'

'What about our families?'

'They'll hear soon enough.' Telinger gave the signal for the Russian scientists to join them from the warehouse. Rakov continued. 'Work will carry on as normal but with certain changes.'

'I can't permit that,' said the director-general. 'This equipment is highly sensitive; it has cost millions to build, years to perfect . . . '

'We will not harm your accelerator,' replied Rakov.

'Then what do you want it for?'

'We too have our scientists. They have great respect for the work that is done here. There are certain experiments they would like to carry out that have not been possible in our homeland.'

'I still can't permit it,' said the man whose responsibility was the world's most famous physics laboratory.

'Would you please step forward,' Rakov said politely to the executive board secretary, a self-effacing man in his forties. He moved closer to Rakov, hesitantly. 'Please face the director-general.' The man did so.

Rakov drew his own pistol and put it to the secretary's head. 'We wish for no unpleasantness, but unless you give your full co-operation, I shall shoot this man, and after him another, and another.'

KGB 'soldiers' round the room shuffled their feet and raised the muzzles of their weapons. The head of research stuck out his jaw and tried to outstare Rakov. In a few seconds his nerve broke. He looked helplessly at the other directors-general; they gazed back. 'What do you want?' he said to Rakov.

'You will not regret your decision.' Rakov replaced his hand-gun in its shoulder holster. 'Our team will arrive shortly. You will instruct staff that an emergency experiment is to be carried out in place of existing work.'

The necessary orders were given. KGB took up position in key areas. Cars brought the scientists. They stopped at reception. It looked calm and normal; no passer-by would have an inkling that Europe's foremost physics laboratory was occupied by an alien armed force.

The scientists took their allotted work-stations smoothly and quickly. Vilkov and his senior men went to the main control room. Speed was now critical. The experiments had been planned in exact detail in Akademgorodok. Rakov intended that news of the occupation be delayed as long as possible.

Russian scientists avoided contact with CERN-based colleagues who would know them personally, but Rakov was under no illusion that sooner or later it would happen.

Everything went according to plan for the first few hours. The scientific team set up their first experiment. Night shift workers were allowed to go home. New staff coming to work, were, where possible, allowed to carry on normally. A big proportion of the work-force; engineers, maintenance people, administrators, didn't know and didn't need to know what experiments were being conducted. If certain people behaved strangely, few remarked on it; it was a fact of any corporate existence, and the Swiss are respecters of authority. Staff who saw too much made supervised telephone calls; guns encouraged convincing lies. By two p.m. the first experiment was ready to go. Vilkov accidentally blew their cover. There was a problem with one of the intersecting storage rings. Each consists of two interlaced circles, three hundred metres in diameter, crossing at no less than eight places. Bursts of accelerated protons are sent to the rings from the proton synchrotron until there are two circulating beams, each containing several hundred million protons. These beams circulate for several days without loss of protons provided the magnetic fields which guide them are perfect and the tubes in which they travel are kept at a very high vacuum. The problem was the vacuum, there was a leak. Several attempts were made to cure it electronically, but without success. Eventually the strain began to tell on Vilkov and he went personally to the area with the problem. He was recognized by the experimental physics facilities leader.

'What are you doing here, Professor Vilkov?' he asked.

The Russian was nonplussed. He realized his mistake immediately, but his brain would not adjust to the new danger.

'Professor. . . Are you all right?'

Vilkov recovered enough to mutter 'Kidnapped. They kidnapped me.' It was an incredible statement.

'Where? How? We were told all Russians had been banned entry into the country.'

'It's a long story. I'll tell you when it's all over.'

'I don't believe you, Vilkov. You are part of them. This is no more an Armenian takeover. . .'

'Shut up, Mencken,' roared the professor, 'or somebody will shut you up.'

But the West German scientist doing his stint at CERN, and only three months from going home after a five year appointment, was too shocked. 'The Swiss Government forbade you use of the accelerator. What are you doing here? Is this a Soviet operation? Yes, of course it is . . .'

Two KGB officers revealed their weapons. One of them spoke into his personal radio.

Vilkov said calmly: 'I suggest you remember what you were told outside, and take a look at the armoury. We don't want anybody to get hurt, do we?'

The West German maintained his defiance for a moment longer. Then he shrugged, and looked at Vilkov with disgust. 'So you are all Stalins under the skin!' Vilkov said nothing. It was true of many citizens of the Motherland.

Rakov entered. Vilkov told him what had happened. Rakov nodded. He spoke to the KGB guards. 'Nobody is to leave this area, except the professor, without my personal order. Is that clear?'

'And if they try? Do I use this?' asked an armed Chekist. He was looking forward to the opportunity, Rakov thought, sourly.

'If you have to, and can justify it to me afterwards.'

Washington: 9.55 a.m.

Rex Hirshfield and his team assembled in the Concorde lounge of British Airways at Washington International Airport. There was a holiday air about the trip. Although supersonic travel was scientifically 'old hat' for all of them, for those who had not experienced it before it was either a schoolboy thrill or it exacerbated their claustrophobic fear of flying. They talked about the flight and the delights of Europe awaiting them, the antiquity of buildings and places that made the United States look like a kindergarten country. Few of them enthused about the experiments, despite morale-boosting speeches by Hirshfield.

The flight was called.

Hereford, England: 4 p.m.

Richard took Chuck for a run, two miles; a warm-up, but Tyson was puffing like a fifty-year-old at the end of it. They had a meal, Richard showed his friend round the barracks. The SAS took him through the assault course. Lloyd's fears were confirmed. His friend was unfit for any strenuous action.

'Don't you keep fit in the US Army?' asked Lloyd of his freely perspiring friend.

'I used to work out in the gym every day in Alaska. Washington's all chairborne exercise and frozen daquiris.'

'We'll have to do something about that!'

As they towelled off after a shower Lloyd said, 'SAS work in teams of four. Each is a complete unit, self-sufficient in everything from combat and logistics to medical aid. I've been grafted on the side of one of those teams, which they don't care for too much. Now they're going to have to take you on board as well. You are not as welcome as buds in May so keep your head down.'

'Aye, aye, sir,' said Tyson throwing up an exaggerated salute. Lloyd was not amused.

'I mean it, Chuck. This will be no picnic.'

22

Thursday 26th November 1981
CERN: 5.30 p.m.

It was inevitable the news would leak out. Rakov didn't know who was responsible, and it didn't matter. The first sign was a phone call from the local police, rather naïvely wanting to know if everything was all right at CERN. 'We've had a report that there are men with guns out there. Is this true?'

'Everything's under control,' said Rakov evenly.

'We will send out some men. Don't worry.'

'I wouldn't do that,' said Rakov.

'We must do it. We can't have people with guns . . . '

'Put me through to your senior officer please,' replied Rakov.

'Who is speaking?'

'I am a representative of the Independent Armenian Republic. My name is not important.'

'Hold the line.' In less than a minute another voice came on the line.

'To whom am I speaking?' he said.

'Who are you?' replied Rakov.

'I am the senior police officer. Who are you?'

'I speak for the Armenian Republic. Our human rights have been denied us by the Turkish Government. The rest of the world will not help us. We have to take our own steps. We have a number of the world's leading scientists under protective custody . . . '

'What do you mean? "Protective custody?" Protected from whom?'

Thursday 26th November 1981

'We have certain demands that must be met if these people are to be released unharmed. I wish to speak to a member of the Swiss Federal Government.'

'That is not easy . . . I cannot guarantee . . . '

'I know what your tactics are in these situations. You will cut off communications and other supplies. If that should happen; if the telephone is cut off or the electricity – even the power to the accelerator – we will kill hostages. The same will happen if any attempt is made to attack CERN. We have armed guards all round the buildings and in the tunnel itself. We'll shoot any intruder. This is no bluff. We are prepared to die for our country.' The thing that carried conviction was the matter-of-fact tone of Rakov's voice, free from the hysteria of the fanatic.

'I need to know more . . . ' Rakov terminated the connection. It was five-thirty p.m. in Geneva, four-thirty p.m. in London and eleven-thirty a.m. in Washington.

London: 4.50 p.m.

The wire services had the news on teletype, radio stations carried the bare outline.

Atlanta, Ga: 11.55 a.m.

Channel Six News was the first on the air with the story in America.

Moscow: 8 p.m.

Yakushenko watched the chattering facts come through on the teletype. He picked up the telephone and called the Kremlin. 'They have declared themselves. They've had almost nine hours on their own. Their first experiment should be complete.'

'Let me know how they get on.'

'They will only use their radio when they have the answer we're waiting for.'

Thursday 26th November 1981

'Suppose Washington decides on an air strike?'

'We have a modified TU-126 Moss transport with airborne detection radar on stand-by.'

'They'll force it down!'

'Not if they over-fly neutral Austria. It'll take station at 30,000 feet over Geneva and be able to see several hundred miles up-track of any attacking force and vector in our own planes.'

'What have you got for interception?'

'Two groups of MiG 25s in high level holding patterns over Pilsen, with flight refuelling provided.'

'H'm,' said the Politburo member as he replaced his instrument.

Geneva: 6.00 p.m.

The Swiss hostage squad was on its way to Meyrin and the local army commander put his best troops on stand-by.

Paris: 6.45 p.m.

The French Government was the first to the telephone.

'This must be a joint operation,' said the Foreign Minister from Paris.

'Difficult,' said his Swiss counterpart. 'As far as I know they have not occupied any French territory.'

'They have men in the accelerator tunnel!'

'The hostages are on Swiss soil!' exclaimed the Basle diplomat.

'How did they get so many men and arms into Switzerland?'

'I don't have that information yet. You may send a representative to Geneva, but we remain in charge!'

'Head of Chancery at our embassy will make himself available initially as liaison. We're prepared to airlift a hostage team from Paris with senior gendarme and deuzième bureau officers to take charge and give advice.'

'I will seek instructions,' said the Swiss.

Thursday 26th November 1981

'We have linguists on the way who will listen to their voices and tell us what nationality they are,' said the Frenchman.

'They have already identified themselves.'

'But where, exactly, are they from? We need that information,' said the voice from Paris, 'and another thing, can we agree no precipitate action without further consultation?'

'We will not initiate action, but I reserve the right to respond to violence, if there is any,' said the Swiss.

'I suppose I'll have to agree that, but French lives must not be put at risk. Some of our most eminent physicists are there!' The Foreign Minister took a firm line on that.

'We'll do our best. But there can be no guarantees.'

Washington: 12.45 p.m.

Pete Rogers heard the news on his car radio. He pulled into a gas station and called his director.

'It's Rakov!' said Rogers.

'How do you know?'

'It has to be him!'

'Hunch, you mean?'

'Why would Armenians or any other terrorist outfit choose a place requiring so much manpower? Only somebody with an army could mount this. It has to be the Reds.'

'I'll think about it. This is no easy ride.'

'Please call the President, sir. I think it's that urgent.'

'I don't have enough facts yet. Get me those and I'll act.'

'I don't have access to what's going on over there, sir.'

'Where's Tyson?'

'Still in England I assume.'

'Can't he get there?'

'He's working on defending the place.'

'Maybe they'd better start thinking about how to attack it!'

'You want me to tell him?'

'I'll get on to the President.'

'What do I tell Tyson?'

'This thing's complicated. The Brits will want to get in on the act. It's on Swiss soil so their government will raise all sorts of hell. State'll take a week to understand it . . . Call Tyson. Tell him what's going on and to be ready for anything.'

London: 5.45 p.m.

The brigadier called the Defence Minister. 'I think you should alert the Foreign Office, and the Prime Minister.'

'How well do your chaps know CERN?' was the minister's reply.

'They've not had much time.'

'Could we tell the Swiss we have an SAS detachment, ready to try an Iranian Embassy-type storming of the place?'

'I'll get them working on it right away.'

CERN: 6.45 p.m.

Rakov placed video cameras to monitor the approaches. He watched troops take up positions surrounding the main buildings. The Swiss would send in a team, armed, well-trained, probably quite ruthless. He was not bothered. They wouldn't let them loose for days yet.

In the main control room Vilkov gave the order: 'Run it!' Nothing appeared to happen, but the accelerator screens told him what he wanted to know. 'Not bad, gentlemen, but we have a long way to go. Let's set up for Number Two.'

'Shouldn't we think about rest, Comrade Vilkov?' asked Ashensky, a brilliant physicist with a vodka problem.

'We've made a good start. Tomorrow should see it finished.' Vilkov walked Ashensky round the room, a firm, painful grasp on his elbow. 'I don't care what you think of these experiments, you're going to do them, and we're going to work on them until we are successful. Do you understand, Andrei Ashensky?'

He was sullen. 'I don't work my best . . . nobody does when they're physically exhausted. I need something for my nerves.'

Vilkov took a silver hip flask from his pocket. 'One swallow! That's all.'

'Yes, Comrade Vilkov,' he murmured. He smelled it, nodded. 'I envy you your connections.' He took a long pull, Rakov prised it from his lips.

Vilkov told Yuri he needed the use of the computer room.

'Can't you program from here?' asked the major.

'Yes, but the printer is in the computer room.'

Rakov beckoned one of the KGB guards. 'Go with the professor. Stay with him.'

The telephone rang. A new voice spoke in English. 'This is the Chef de la Police de Sûreté – the Chief of Police for Geneva . . .'

Rakov made his first mistake. 'I understand what that means. What do you want?'

'I am giving you the chance to surrender peacefully. If you put down your weapons, you will not be harmed.'

'I've told you I will negotiate only with a member of the Swiss Federal Government.'

'Tell me your name.'

'It's not important.'

'How can we communicate if I don't know who you are?'

'This is not police business. It is political. I must speak to a politician who can negotiate the legitimate demands of my people.'

'You're putting innocent lives at risk. Set them free and we'll talk.'

Rakov simulated anger. 'The Turkish Government

massacred hundreds of thousands of women, children and old men. They have enslaved a nation. You expect me to listen to appeals for innocent people. Our cause is people, a whole people living in abject conditions, tortured, starved, homeless, dying by the thousand. Bring me a member of your government or I'll give you one of your innocents – dead.'

The police chief replied calmly. 'Please leave this telephone line open for our negotiations. Is that agreed?'

'Agreed,' said Rakov sharply.

'I'll see what I can do. I make no promises.'

Geneva: 6.50 p.m.

The policeman turned to his linguistics expert. 'What do you think?'

'He's good. He sounds convincing, but I'm not sure.'

'But is he Armenian?'

'No, but he may represent them.'

The police chief reproved him. 'Let me interpret the evidence, just give me the facts. What is his nationality?'

'I can't be sure. He speaks English with an accent; a bit phoney, but fast and fluent. He has lived in an English-speaking country, probably America, but I don't think he's a Yank.'

'Is he Russian?'

'Why do you ask?' enquired the linguist.

'Is he?' insisted the policeman.

'It's a possibility, but not the only one.'

'What else could he be?'

'I prefer not to commit myself until I have thoroughly analysed the tape.'

'You must be quick. Lives depend on it.'

'I'll take it to my laboratory.'

The whine of the police siren sped the expert on his way. Further delay would help Rakov.

Thursday 26th November 1981

Washington: 1 p.m.

Frederick Coverdale was present when the Secretary of State saw the French-born Swiss Ambassador, a well-dressed diplomat, looking vaguely like Louis Jurdan, with elegant manners, and a brisk style.

'How can my government help the people of the United States?' said Eduard Dupois.

The Secretary of State was a 'hawk.' 'We need to know if the terrorists at CERN are genuine or if they're the Soviets putting on an act.'

'The signs are that they are genuine,' replied the ambassador.

'What signs?'

'Their demands are in line with those made by other Armenian groups.'

'Is he Russian? You've got experts who can tell you these things.'

'They're not sure.'

'Get other experts. Have one of ours. Play the tape over the satellite.'

'This is a Swiss problem. While we welcome help from the United States Government, until it is proved there is some American interest at stake . . . '

'Don't you realize what's going on. If they're Russians, they could be writing the end of our way of life in that accelerator. And the much-vaunted neutrality of Switzerland will be about as much use as . . . '

Coverdale interrupted smoothly: 'We do have a legitimate concern for reasons we cannot make fully clear to your government at this stage. But the Secretary does not overestimate the seriousness. However the President appreciates that your government cannot invite US help until you are on sure ground politically.'

'There's a lot to be done. We have to ascertain the reaction of the Turkish Government. We have to liaise with the

French. There are many Swiss lives at risk. We are also host to eminent scientists from other European countries. We have responsibility for their safety. We must consult with them.'

'Fred: we've got to tell this guy what this is about!'

'Not without the President's clearance, and he feels he can't make disclosures to other governments without the agreement of Congress.'

'I don't believe it. I don't believe any of it. What's got into you, Fred. You're supposed to be the President's right hand on this sort of thing. You know what's at issue. Survival! And you throw technicalities at me!'

'I know the score, Mr Secretary, but we have responsibilities to other countries on whom we may have to rely if the situation gets worse. We can't prejudice the future by premature action now,' Coverdale insisted.

The Secretary tried a new tack with the ambassador; in calmer tones. 'OK. You win. But will you, as a matter of courtesy between friendly nations, do just one thing for us. It cannot possibly cause an international incident. You can do it on your own authority. You need consult nobody.'

'We always try to be good neighbours. What is your pleasure?' the Swiss diplomat asked.

'Turn off the power.' He said it calmly as if ordering a coffee.

The ambassador considered the request reasonable, but pointed out the snag. 'They say they'll kill hostages if we do that,' replied Philippe.

'Bluff!' said the Secretary.

'We won't call it at this stage.'

'Why not?'

'Suppose they carry out the threat and the victim is Belgian or Chinese?' the Swiss said coolly.

'Have you got Chinese holed up there too?'

'We don't know who they've captured, Mr Secretary.

Until we know who and what we're dealing with, my government will tread cautiously.'

'We can't stand still for that,' said the Secretary.

Frederick intervened smoothly. 'What the Secretary means is that we shall have to ask the Swiss government to review the situation as a matter of urgency, and keep it under review.'

'That accelerator has got to be stopped. If you don't do it, I sure as hell . . . '

The National Advisor 'killed' that. 'Threats can lead to diplomatic relations being broken off. That's in nobody's interest.'

Eduarde Dupois stood. He was terminating the meeting, a breach of protocol, and the first sign of his anger. 'I will convey the precise nature of the American response, to my government,' he said coldly. 'I assure you there will be no misunderstanding.'

London: 6.30 p.m.

The British Foreign Secretary told the Prime Minister, in his charming and elegant voice that one of their own language experts had heard the tape. In his opinion the spokesman was Russian. 'I rang the Russian Ambassador and asked if it was true.'

'When in doubt, do the obvious,' said the Prime Minister. 'Quite right, Foreign Secretary.'

'He professed himself outraged on behalf of the Socialist Republic. They deplored the action of terrorists.'

'Which told you nothing,' said the PM.

'Not quite. His response was not spontaneous, as it would have been if he'd been caught unawares by the suggestion. It was as if he had expected the accusation and was ready with his answer.'

The Defence Secretary intervened. 'But isn't that always so with the Soviets. They're so defensive.'

Thursday 26th November 1981

The Foreign Secretary defeated that argument with blithe, legalistic logic. 'That's not the point. The significance is that there was definitely not an innocent response. If there had been, we might have been able to rule out Russian involvement. As it is, we know it is still an option. My advice, Prime Minister, is that we try to persuade the Swiss to turn off the power . . . '

'But they'll start killing; maybe somebody of world eminence!' said the Defence Minister.

'The power station is fifty kilometres away, and the supply is carried overhead. They could plead a storm, plane crashing in it, any plausible excuse to make it more difficult for the terrorists to carry out the threat.'

'And if they still do so?' asked the Defence boss.

'If they are genuine terrorists, they can have no technical need of the accelerator. Only if they are Russians, trying to crack the Tesla Trinity do they need it. Either way, it's worth the risk.'

CERN: 7.55 p.m.

Night fell at Meyrin; floodlights covered the CERN buildings. One effect was that Rakov could not see what was happening behind the lights. Three hours passed without word from the Swiss. Vilkov analysed the results of the first experiment. His team were puzzled by what the computers told them. They mounted another test.

'How much more time do you need?' Rakov asked. Vilkov was bad-tempered.

'How do I know! We've barely started yet.'

'Give me some idea. I can't carry on a negotiation not knowing how much time I'm bargaining for.' Vilkov stopped working on his calculation and sat back, concentrating. He said nothing for several minutes. Rakov didn't interrupt his thoughts.

At last Vilkov spoke. 'The only scientific answer I can

give you now, is that I don't know. After we complete the next two experiments, and provided they give us the information we want, I would guess two, maybe three days. That's the best I can do and in reality it's little more than guesswork.'

Rakov was not happy. 'Can you tell yet if you'll be able to solve the Tesla problem?'

'We wouldn't be here if we didn't think so, but that's only the first stage. Next we have to find out if it'll work in practice.'

'You mean you'll never know until you try it out? Against incoming missiles?'

'We can do better than that. We need the accelerator to discover the new physics that Tesla talked about. The three-part model Tesla made does two things: it describes a new way of looking at the scientific problem. The accelerator will help us understand the way in which matter reacts in his new physics. If we can understand that – and the model basically is a description of that new thinking – then Tesla will have told us his secret. We should then know how to build the screen.'

'And you still need the accelerator for that stage?' asked Rakov.

'Quite possibly.'

'So we can't get out after the first stage?'

'CERN also has the most extensive computer system in the world,' said the professor. 'Once the accelerator tells us what we want to know we can program the computer and it should complete our knowledge.'

'There are computers everywhere. Why not send the accelerator information to Moscow and let them get on with it?'

'We're still way behind in computer technology,' said Vilkov, 'thanks to Stalin. Our equipment couldn't do the job.'

'So we have to stay until we finish both stages?' Vilkov nodded. 'Tell me,' added Rakov, 'when you've put it all together, and we've sent back the information on the high speed transmitter, what then?'

'The scientists at Akademgorodok take over. They'll have no trouble making the Tesla Shield.'

Heathrow, London

The Concorde carrying Professor Hirshfield and his team landed at 2137 hours local time. They were taken to the American embassy in Grosvenor Square where they spent the night.

Geneva: Midnight

The Swiss Minister of Justice did not look his usual neat urbane self. He had removed his jacket and loosened his tie. The Geneva chief of police kept his coat on and tie tightly knotted. Now was not the time to let standards lapse.

'How much have you been able to pick up?' asked the minister.

'The long-range microphones give us the occasional words here and there, but not much of any value so far.'

'In what language?'

'It's a mixture, I'm afraid, minister. The trouble is that there are several hundred regular staff there. What we're picking up is mainly their conversation, some of it in French, German, Dutch, Swiss/German . . . '

'Anything in Russian?'

'We think so.'

'But you cannot be sure?' pressed the minister.

'No.'

'How about cameras?'

'We can't get near enough to fix them into the walls.'

'Have you tried?'

'Not yet, minister.'

'Then how do you know?'

'There are many buildings. Which one should we try?'

'If they are Russians they must be using the main control room.'

'They have guards on that.'

The minister was frustrated. 'Surely you can get a camera in somewhere to tell us who we are dealing with.'

'I'm working on it. Meanwhile I'm waiting for a check on the number plate of the truck they used. The cars were rented locally by various people. We are doing the legwork on that but it could be days before we come up with any useful lead. They don't use credit cards. Cash is not traceable. And I'm afraid we don't know how they got into the country. If they are Armenian or Russian they probably used Italy, and either walked across a border, or used one of the lakes. They could even have flown in under our military radar screens.'

'But the equipment! They didn't walk that in!'

'No. But that's not difficult. We can't check every truck. Thousands cross the border every day.'

The telephone rang. The minister listened and then handed the instrument to the police chief.

'Yes . . . ' He listened for several minutes. 'Ask the Italian police if they will continue with their enquiries. It's urgent.' He replaced the receiver thoughtfully, and spoke to the minister. 'One truck has a Bologna registration. The number is false.'

'Another dead end,' said the minister disgustedly.

'Not entirely. Bologna give us a direction.'

'By sea? The Adriatic from Yugoslavia?'

'Possibly . . . '

'So?'

'False passports? Hundreds could walk through any airport or border crossing. Only if they acted suspiciously or didn't have a visa when they should have, would they be stopped. The equipment is another matter. We ought to be able to get a trace on that.'

'How? How?' said the minister impatiently.

'I've been on to immigration and customs control.' The policeman pointed at Bologna on the wall map. 'That suggests a communist connection. If I were trying to get arms into Switzerland I'd get them first to Italy.'

'Land or sea?'

'There are ports in the south where they could practically unload a whole ship without questions being asked. The Mafia would have to be taken care of, but that's only a question of price.'

'Can you check that out?' asked the minister.

The policeman did not answer directly. 'May I ask what the government's position is on this?'

'We are still waiting for information before we decide how to act. If it is an Armenian terrorist group, we shall isolate them, spin out all deadlines, and try to wear them down.' The policeman nodded. 'We'll keep the Turkish Government informed and co-operate with them unless they ask for something we don't approve of. The usual thing . . . ' The telephone rang; for the minister. After a while he put down the instrument grimly. 'The British want us to cut the electricity and take the consequences. So do the Americans!'

Friday 27th November 1981
CERN: 4 a.m.

Professor Vilkov was beginning to show signs of the strain. His face had a washed-out look, and his shoulders were drooping; his temper was short. The others were not in much better shape. 'Are we ready?' asked Vilkov. Heads nodded agreement. 'Let's go!'

The scientists looked anxiously as the voltage surge every

eleven seconds hit the accelerator and caused the bombardment of millions of particles against one another on collision courses. After fifteen minutes, Vilkov expressed himself satisfied and the accelerator was closed down. Now began a period of waiting while photographs of the collisions were made available, and the computer analysed the results and the photographs.

'Gentlemen. I suggest we all get two hours' sleep.'

Rakov told Telinger to find a bed. He was tempted to get some fresh air but knew he could be identified within minutes from an infra-red photograph. He found a corner of an unoccupied office and went through a strenuous exercise programme. In a lather of sweat, but feeling better, he flopped down on a mattress in the main control room and told the guards to wake him as soon as it was light.

Hereford: 5.20 a.m.

The brigadier arrived. There was physical activity everywhere. Richard Lloyd and Tyson, in denims, with packs and carbines, were completing a fast jog. Tyson looked terrible.

'I need to see you two right away,' said the senior officer. He was unshaven. He knuckled his eyes. 'It's taken all night to get the Swiss to agree to take you chaps on board as advisers.'

'Just the two of us?' asked Lloyd.

'Let me finish,' said the brigadier testily. 'You and your team. The hassle was over your team-mates and weapons.'

'So is there any point in going, sir?' asked Lloyd again.

'For Christ's sake listen, Lloyd. That's what the all-night chat was about. They realize this may turn out to be something rather different from the usual terrorist game-plan, so you can take your weapons and equipment. It will all be logged and checked on arrival at Cointrin Airport, by Swiss army officers, every round of ammunition! You will act under the command of the Geneva police chief. However, buried in your gear will be a special transmitter which will give you direct communication with me via satellite. You will be under apparent local command but if I give you the order over that transmitter, you will say goodbye to their orders.'

'And if it all gets screwed up you'll deny everything?' asked Lloyd innocently.

'Naturally,' said the brigadier.

Tyson joined the conversation. 'Time's getting away from us, sir. Every minute takes the Soviets closer to busting the Tesla thing wide open.'

'I know that,' said the exhausted brigadier. 'The Swiss won't make a move until they are certain it's not a bunch of terrorists.'

'Bloody hell!' was Lloyd's comment.

'There are a few hundred Swiss there. They do have a problem. We see it differently, because we perceive the greater threat.'

'When does the US cavalry get in on the act?' asked Tyson.

'It doesn't. Your President is happy to leave the local situation to us,' said the senior officer blandly.

'Six men? To take on dozens of armed KGB? And that's it?' asked Lloyd incredulously.

'I don't believe it!' said Tyson.

'Those are your orders,' said the brigadier in a tired voice.

Lloyd's comment was crisp. 'You're expecting us to act on our own initiative. We could easily cock it all up if we don't know the full picture.'

The brigadier thought for a moment. 'You may be right at that. OK. Here's the situation. American and British bombers have been scrambled, and are ready to take out the CERN facility.'

Friday 27th November 1981

'Christ!' said Tyson.

'The accelerator tunnel's underground and supposedly bomb proof,' said Lloyd.

'We know that,' replied the brigadier.

'Conventional bombs will just bounce off.'

'The main control room is above ground. We're going to knock out enough to ensure that the accelerator is out of action.'

'I'm sorry to press this but I've been looking at the plans. Anybody who wanted to hole up and not get winkled out could do it.'

'Precise calculations have been made, Lloyd. The bombers will carry what is necessary to do the job.'

'Will we get any warning if that is to happen?' asked Tyson. The atmosphere was tense. Lloyd wondered if they were being invited to a suicide party.

The brigadier was careful in his answer. 'This is a volunteer situation. Nobody will be ordered to take part.'

'How long?' asked Lloyd.

'The airborne attack force is maintaining position thirty minutes from target.'

'So we may have that long to get away.'

'Maybe,' said the brigadier.

23

Friday 27th November 1981
Washington: 12.20 a.m./Moscow: 8.20 a.m.

It was a nervous aide who rang to say the hot line from Moscow had been activated. The President was a man who liked his full ration of slumber. He grumpily splashed cold water on his face, demanded hot black coffee and went to the communications room. He hated the unnatural pauses while interpreters did their work.

The Soviet leader was terse. 'You have bombers in the air, preparing for an attack on a European target.' The President said nothing. On a notepad he wrote the word 'Coverdale' and signalled to his aide that he wanted him here now. The Russian continued. 'Can I take it your silence indicates that you accept my statement as fact?'

'You may not,' said the President.

'You deny it?'

'Have you completed what you wanted to say?'

'No.'

'When you've finished I may comment; not before I know what this is about.'

'We have always encouraged the Armenian people's aspirations to nationhood . . . '

'Come now, Mr Chairman, do you expect me to believe that your interest is altruistic?'

The communist leader was abrupt and angry. 'Part of Armenia is in the USSR. My government's record in promoting their language and culture is without parallel. No less than fifty churches flourish with well-attended services, and no interference from the state. We're very interested in what happens to Armenians. We deplore their plight, their lack of a properly-recognized homeland. The Turks massacred over one million of their number – one half of the world population of their race – in 1915!'

'Do you approve of terrorism?'

'Of course not, but we will not stand by while you kill Armenian nationals whose only objective is survival. Nor will we allow the West to drop bombs on CERN.'

'What makes you think we have any intention of doing so?'

'I've given orders that any military aircraft heading for Geneva are to be shot down. This is not bluff, Mr President. As you will know from past incidents, we don't hesitate to destroy planes which threaten our national interest.'

The President was shaken. 'I hear what you say, Mr Chairman. I'll consider it with my advisers and respond through this telephone as soon as possible. May I take it you will be available?'

'You may, Mr President.'

Grosvenor Square, London: 11.30 a.m.

Professor Hirshfield asked, for the third time, when they would be setting off to Geneva. He was told, again, that no decision had been made, and that every effort was being made to get permission.

Georgetown: 7.00 a.m.

General Jack Lubbock arrived at the Coverdale house for breakfast with Ruth. They ate at the long polished rosewood table in the dining room. When Jennings left the room the general spoke: 'It's all happening in Geneva; at the CERN laboratory.'

'So I hear,' replied Ruth wryly.

'It's Rakov and a KGB goon squad, of course.'

'So talk of Armenia is just a smoke screen?' enquired Ruth.

Friday 27th November 1981

'Damned clever,' said the general admiringly. 'It explains why they speak Russian and confuses the hell out of the Swiss.'

'What is the US of A doing about it?'

'If we're not careful, between diplomatic protocol with the Swiss, and the President afraid to take any action without Congressional approval – which could take weeks – I'm afraid we'll lose this mother to the Reds.'

'They've still got to build it,' said Ruth.

'Don't kid yourself, my dear. Once they've got the technical answer out of CERN, we're in a time vice, with no way of stopping the clock.'

'We could crack the Trinity too,' said Ruth.

Lubbock contemplated his finger nails. 'Stand-off! The best of all solutions. But if they get the answer and then blow up CERN, which is what I'd do if I were in their position, it's all over. They take out Kansas City or LA, our Minutemen bounce off their Tesla Shield, and we'll all start learning the Cyrillic alphabet.'

'I suppose our group was a pretty puny effort, even before Frederick got on to us,' mused Ruth sadly.

'If I could lay my hands on some sort of nuclear device, frankly I'd plant it on CERN right now and to hell with consequences.' Jack Lubbock was suddenly a grey old man, forced to be a spectator as terrible things happened to his beloved country.

'It's not all lost,' said Ruth. He looked up, not very interested, assuming, in his chauvinistic way that nothing of military significance could come out of the mouth of a woman. 'Do you remember the box of tricks Fritz Lowenstein gave to Cheyenne College?'

'What are you talking about?'

'It turned out to be the oscillator Tesla used to make an earthquake in Lower Manhattan.'

'Really!' Lubbock was not interested.

'It works,' said Ruth calmly.

'Congratulations,' said the general sarcastically.

'It can cause an earthquake.' She let that thought hang in the air.

'I don't think you quite appreciate the spot we're in, Ruth. Our civilization is about to go down the Russian tubes. We need to call a full meeting of the group. We need to put maximum pressure on the President for a nuclear attack on CERN.'

Ruth shook her head. 'It'd never work.' She handed him Hackett's instructions for operating the oscillator. 'Read that, Jack.'

He did so. 'Scientific mumbo jumbo!' he said. Ruth patiently explained what had happened to Lower Manhattan and more recently to Palo Alto when the machine was properly tuned. Lubbock was not impressed.

'You don't understand the nature of the problem we're dealing with here. We need to kill those bastards in the next few minutes, flatten them and the whole goddamn CERN place. That means bombs, rockets . . . whatever it takes. Our only chance is to make the President see it that way.'

'Russia won't stand still for us bombing CERN.'

'They won't know until it's too late.'

'Suppose they already know?'

'How could they?'

'They must be monitoring every move we make.'

'What's the alternative?'

She told him. His expression was impatient boredom when she began. It changed to indulgent attention while he waited for a suitable pause in her diatribe to demolish her ridiculous proposal in a few pithy sentences. It ended with him saying nothing and thinking hard.

Friday 27th November 1981

Moscow: 3.00 p.m.

The Politburo member phoned Yakushenko. 'We're not prepared to rely on one TU-126 to give warning of NATO response.'

'We need round-the-clock capability. Two standby aircraft!'

'The Chairman wants something on the ground. You are to organize forward tactical radar; an air control post with fighter controllers.'

'Where?'

'A remote hilltop in Switzerland covering approaches from the north and west. Use helicopters.'

'We could have a range problem, even with M1-6s.'

'I thought they could carry up to sixty-five passengers.'

'After the American fiasco in Iran I'd recommend at least two M1-6s plus two back up; and extra fuel carried on board.'

'See to it.'

CERN: 5.10 p.m.

It was tantalizing. Vilkov knew they were close. He'd been certain the second experiment would prove his theory. The results would be analysed through the computers. After one further test with the accelerator, they would have the secret. But it hadn't worked out like that. The computer results were satisfactory up to about the halfway stage, thereafter they were gibberish; there was no other word for it. Vilkov and his men stared at photographs of what the accelerator had done in its multi-billion volts collisions; and then at the calculations the computers had spewed out. There was an ominous silence.

'Did we make a mistake?' demanded Vilkov. Nobody responded to that. 'Have you checked right through the programming of the experiment, Andrevich?'

'Two, three times, absolutely correct.'

Friday 27th November 1981

'What about computer malfunction?'

'Rubbish in, rubbish out is more likely,' was the contribution of Ashensky.

'Did you put rubbish into the computer?' asked Vilkov with asperity.

'Not my job,' said Ashensky smugly.

The man who was responsible put up his hand. 'There is no possibility of that. I checked it myself twice, after my staff had already done so. And we have just checked it again.'

'So what do we do?' asked the professor.

Ashensky was the only one to volunteer a suggestion. 'Why don't we carry on with the third experiment we were going to do?' said Ashensky.

'Don't be stupid!' shouted Vilkov. 'How can we when we don't have the information?'

'That's conventional thinking, and from what we've discovered so far, nothing is conventional about this new physics of Tesla's.'

'You're not making sense,' said Andrevich.

'Have you been drinking, Ashensky?' demanded Vilkov.

His response was to be expansive rather than annoyed. 'If only, dear comrades . . . Do you remember the assumptions we made about Jupiter and Mars? When we got there we had to re-write many of the theories about our universe. This is similar. Normally, at this stage, we would go back to our respective laboratories, and start the whole process again. We'd come back to CERN in due course. But we don't have the time. What else can we do? I say let us do each of the experiments we had planned, leaving out the information we had assumed we would collect from earlier experiments, and see what happens.'

Vilkov was reluctant to take the suggestion seriously because he didn't trust any alcoholic, but the others liked the idea.

Friday 27th November 1981

'When you say it – just like that–' said Andrevich, 'it sounds stupid, impossible; hit-or-miss at best . . . '

'How do you fill in the blanks? The information we haven't got?' asked another.

'Make more assumptions,' said Ashensky blithely.

'Like what?' said Vilkov.

'Why don't we try for a consensus on what is the most likely, and the most unlikely result from number two, and program the accelerator on that basis, and see what we get.'

Rakov entered the room. 'How much more time do you need, Comrade Vilkov? I can't contain this situation much longer.'

Vilkov waved him away. 'Don't interrupt now. We're busy.'

Rakov was insistent. 'I have to know and know now!'

Vilkov's frustration burst through in rage at the interrupter. 'We don't know and I'm not in the guessing business. Fuck off, comrade!'

Washington: 11.10 a.m.

Coverdale was against it, so were his two principal civil servants. The State Department bureaucrats were appalled at the duplicity involved and for long-term diplomatic relations with Switzerland.

'We can't wait for confirmation,' said the Secretary of State. 'We've got to stop them using the accelerator. If it costs a few lives, we lose a few! The American position on a hostage situation is well-known. Our own diplomats take that risk.'

'They know what they're getting into. These people aren't even Americans!' said Coverdale.

'When will we know for certain if it is the Russians in there?'

The director of the CIA was sombre. 'You've got it, Mr President. We'll never be sure until we get them out. The

Politburo sure as hell won't announce it. None of the guys in there is going to show himself, and the Swiss won't let us fix a listening bug.'

The President stood up to indicate the meeting was over. 'I'm going to talk to the British Prime Minister.'

Frederick wondered what Ruth was doing.

Geneva: 5.20 p.m.

The Justice Minister looked at one of the several antique clocks in his police chief's room, and wondered where he got the money to indulge such an expensive hobby. He'd missed his lunch. He was an able politician, but at fifty-five, he didn't perform well on an empty stomach.

'What do you have?' he asked.

The police chief's tie was still in a neat knot, but the shirt was looked ragged. He told his minister that the truck belonged to a fully fledged communist cell of a pro-Soviet group. 'We've found the port where they landed the equipment, in the south, with Mafia help. We haven't been able to find out where it was loaded.'

'At sea?'

'Probably.'

'What chance is there of shooting a bug into one of the walls?' asked the minister.

'We don't know which buildings have guards, or which ones the terrorists are in. We've got some listening ears in the outer buildings but they've told us nothing.'

'The British and Americans want us to mount a supposed attack, as a cover to plant microphones. What do you think?'

'It's a good idea,' said the policeman. 'If you don't mind a few people getting shot.'

'In the attack, you mean?' said the minister.

'I think these people are ruthless. I think they'll kill,' said the chief of police.

Friday 27th November 1981

'Can you be sure?'

'I've been in a few of these situations. This man's a tougher proposition. He's cold, and I'd say ruthless.'

The minister thought he saw a potential breakthrough. 'Doesn't that tell you something about who they are? Who we're dealing with?'

'I don't doubt they're Russians.'

'Then what have we been wasting our time for? Missing my lunch?'

'You wanted evidence. My personal opinion, based on twenty-five years as a policeman, is not evidence. I could be wrong.'

The minister shook his head in exasperation. 'I need food. Will you join me?'

'No thank you, minister. I'll get a sandwich sent in. You're welcome to share it with me.'

The look on the minister's face told the police chief that he had just committed *lèse majesté*. He grinned for the first time in twenty-four hours.

23

Saturday 28th November 1981
Cointrin, Geneva: 3.30 p.m.

The Royal Air Force Hercules drifted down to a slow smooth landing at Cointrin. It was met by a posse of Swiss military vehicles. Lloyd and Tyson exchanged salutes with their counterparts. The SAS team drove a scout car and small truck down the ramp at the rear of the aircraft.

'Two vehicles?' said a surprised Swiss.

'There are six of us,' said Lloyd. 'You may inspect them if you wish.' The Swiss, surprisingly, waved his hand dismissively.

'We trust the English to keep their word on such matters.'

Lloyd was relieved. 'Lead on. We'll follow you.' He climbed aboard the scout car.

CERN: 3.40 p.m.

Professor Vilkov was doubtful. Under normal circumstances he would not have sanctioned the use of the accelerator for such an enterprise, but circumstances were far from normal, and time was running out. He was in the main control room and his colleagues were looking anxiously at him; all except Ashensky who was smiling sardonically, not bothered. Vilkov nodded. The seven kilometre length of the world's most sophisticated accelerator hummed as the surge of power was called up from the power station fifty kilometres away, which in turn automatically drew on the resources of power in the Swiss and French national grids.

Vilkov watched the instruments register each phase of

the accelerator's activity. It seemed to be working. At last the final surge of power arrived and discharged itself. Vilkov gave the order to switch off, and the slow process of analysing the results began. Had it been a waste of time? Would they have to admit defeat, and let Rakov try and negotiate their return to Mother Russia? The time was five-thirty p.m.

Cointrin, Geneva: 5.32 p.m.

The Swissair DC 9 from Paris touched down at Cointrin. A few minutes later General Jack Lubbock made his way from the plane, through a cursory immigration examination of his passport, and through the main doors into the arrival hall. He was met by another sixty-year-old General Jo Roskill. 'You look like death,' he said to Lubbock with a smile.

'And you look twenty years younger. If that's what retirement in this angel cake country does for you, I might just have a piece of it for myself.'

'They make you show a whole bundle of bucks before you can live here; or you could marry a rich widow-woman,' said Roskill.

'That's not totally impossible,' said Lubbock. 'What have you got for me, Jo?'

'Dinner at my house first, with Elizabeth. Then I thought we might have a few drinks and I'll show you the town.'

Irritation, close to anger flashed across Lubbock's tired face. 'I told you this fucking thing was urgent . . . ' and then saw the smile on his old friend's face and knew he'd been kidded.

'It's all set up. Not the best-looking industrial building you ever saw. In fact it's going to be knocked over pretty soon for redevelopment, but it's got three phase power, and I managed to get it connected, and a telephone.'

'I hope you didn't mind my getting you involved in this

thing,' said Jack Lubbock, with concern.

'Delighted to have something to do. Now tell me what it's all about.' Roskill was quite relaxed.

'You'd rather not know,' said Lubbock with finality.

'I thought it might be one of those.' But Roskill was smiling like a schoolboy. 'Private mission for the President?' he asked with a twinkle in his eye. 'Unofficial. I've done a few of those.'

'Not exactly,' said Lubbock as he sat in the passenger seat of his friend's Mercedes 450. 'Elizabeth, you said. I take it from this smart-looking piece of machinery that she is a rich widow-woman?'

'Right on, pal.'

'How did you manage it, you plug-ugly monster?'

'She loves uniforms.' And he changed the subject back to what he was most interested in. 'What do you mean? Not exactly?'

'Look, Jo. I'm very grateful for what you've done, but I would be doing you a serious mischief – not to mention your Elizabeth – if I allowed you to get in any further. So far all you've done is rent an old building for an old friend and you can't go to jail for that.'

'Are you planning a bullion heist?' asked Roskill.

'I wish it was that simple.'

'At least tell me, Jack. Let me make up my own mind,' said the other retired general. One look at his face was enough to tell Jack Lubbock that his old friend was longing for part of the action missing in the luxury of his idle life.

'It's dangerous and you may not approve. I shall have to ask you for a pretty solid promise not to breathe a word.'

'Since when did you and me need that sort of talk, Jack!' said Roskill, nettled.

'Since neither the President nor anybody else in the administration knows what we're about – at least I sincerely hope they don't.'

Saturday 28th November 1981

'Ah!' said Jo Roskill, and then he smiled. 'So somebody's at last got the guts to go out on a limb! I take it it is for the stars and stripes and not some private ruckus.'

'Right on, general,' said Lubbock.

'So tell me what I'm about to be court-martialled for, you old goat,' said General Joseph Roskill.

Grosvenor Square, London: 6.33 p.m.

'Why couldn't we have been aboard the Hercules that went to Geneva?' asked Professor Hirshfield.

The Head of Chancery was apologetic, yet again. 'You don't realize the hassle we had to get those guys in. As it is there's only one American among them.'

'Does the ambassador realize my mission was personally ordered by the President?'

'Yes, professor,' said the harassed official, 'but we've got all sorts of panic on at this time.'

'I want to see the ambassador!'

The civil servant shrugged. 'I'll see what I can do, sir.'

CERN: 7.35 p.m.

The United States and British Governments had a hard time convincing the Swiss that it should happen. It was hedged with conditions. No Swiss lives were to be put at risk. No Swiss troops or police could be used.

The action began with a telephone call to Rakov. 'This is the Chef de la Police de Sûreté . . . '

'What do you want?' asked Rakov.

'To whom am I speaking?'

'I am the representative of . . . '

'I know that. Your name please!'

Rakov was annoyed at the repeated demand for his name. 'You may call me Omega.'

'Is that your name; your real name?'

'Yes,' said Rakov in a shout.

Saturday 28th November 1981

'What is your nationality?'

'I am Armenian. That's all I'm going to tell you.'

'As you wish. I am telephoning to tell you that the Swiss Federal Government has agreed to appoint a minister to negotiate with you. He is with me now. He is the Minister for Justice, Monsieur Le Brun. I will put him on the line now . . .'

The minister cleared his throat, and touched his tie nervously as he took the telephone. 'This is Le Brun . . . Minister of Justice. What do you wish to say to me?'

'How do I know who you are?'

'Any Swiss will recognize my voice if you put them on the line.' Rakov had no wish to do that.

Lloyd, Tyson, and the SAS, dressed in jeans and sweat shirts were poised at strategic points behind the searchlights illuminating CERN. They carried sten guns, and a back pack filled with explosive devices.

'All right,' said Rakov. 'I'll accept who you are. Here are our conditions for freeing hostages. We require the release of all political prisoners by the Turkish Government; that a plane be put at their disposal; DC9 or larger, with full tanks. When they are in the air and out of Turkish airspace I wish to talk with their leader by radio. Then we want a similar plane made ready at . . .'

At that moment the searchlights went out. Lloyd, Tyson and their four SAS men charged into the CERN complex of buildings, shouting and letting off thunder flashes.

'What's that?' yelled Rakov. 'What double tricks are you playing?' He shouted to a KGB guard. 'Bring one of the hostages to me at once.' He continued speaking to the minister. 'Call those men off or I will kill hostages beginning now!'

The rehearsal for the incident had been minimal. The policeman told his minister to act normally – to panic!

The minister had no relish for the part. He was

frightened and his voice betrayed that fear. Perfect! 'I don't know what's happening. I can't see anything.' He shouted at the police chief. 'Find out and stop it this instant.'

'Immediately, minister,' the chief shouted back, not moving.

'Monsieur Omega! Monsieur Omega! This is not authorized action. I don't know who's responsible.'

Rakov put his hand over the instrument and spoke with calm but urgent authority to his second-in-command. 'It's too early for a full assault. I don't know what they're up to. Make sure your men shoot to kill.'

Outside, several KGB 'soldiers' had emerged and were looking for targets at which to shoot. They let off bursts of fire every time they saw the flash of an explosion. The SAS men seemed to be running aimlessly but there was a careful pattern and timetable, the objective to create a diversion while Lloyd and Tyson planted listening devices on the walls of the main control room, and the computer centre. Lloyd crept along the side of the first building keep careful watch. He glanced quickly round a corner and saw the outline of a figure with a machine carbine. He tried the next building.

Lloyd kept to grass or concrete on which his Adidas sports shoes made little sound. He rounded the last building in front of the computer set-up and saw three guards. One fired a burst just wide of him – a blind shot he decided. He waited, hoping at least one of them would move off in another direction. None of them did.

Chuck was at the wall of the control room. He gouged out a piece of mortar, and plugged in the tiny metal transmitter. He covered it with a rubberoid sealant, and then reached down to smear it with earth. He was nearly caught in the beam of the searchlights as they were turned on again exactly three minutes from the time the area was plunged into darkness.

Saturday 28th November 1981

A KGB guard entered the control room, jabbing his gun into the ribs of a terrified Belgian scientist of about forty, who was gibbering with fright.

'What's your name?' shouted Rakov.

'Gilbert . . . Maurice Gilbert. I am scientist for peaceful work. Only peaceful . . . ' He was shouting and crying at the same time.

'Did you hear that?' Rakov shouted into the telephone. 'Unless the attack stops this instant . . . '

'It is not an attack. Not by us. Not by the Swiss Government . . . '

'Stop it now or I kill this Belgian.'

The lights went on. The noise of explosions abruptly stopped. The silence was unnerving. Gradually the senses picked up the noise of traffic on the main roads.

'Who was responsible for that?' the minister demanded in a stern voice of his chief of police.

'It was hooligans . . . young people with firecrackers taking advantage,' he replied, loud enough for Rakov to hear.

'They must be caught and arrested. Bring them to me immediately!'

'Yes, minister.' The policeman leaned back in his chair.

Le Brun spoke again to Rakov. 'You heard my order to the chef de la police. It was nothing to do with us. Please don't act against that poor man.'

Rakov didn't know what to do. He was puzzled. He didn't believe it was hooligans. The main thing was that the attack had stopped.

'You have one hour to obtain the answer of the Turkish Government,' said Rakov.

'That is impossible.'

'Otherwise I shoot hostages.'

'You might just as well start shooting. There is no possibility of getting the Turkish Government even to meet in that time, let alone make a decision on your demand. We'll need at least twenty four hours.'

Rakov was elated. If he was to maintain the fiction that they were an Armenian Terrorist group, he had to keep the pressure of time on the authorities. 'I will give you twelve hours. Not a minute longer.' And he put down the telephone.

He turned to the senior KGB man present. 'I want a thorough search made of all buildings; inside and out. I want to know what that was all about.'

'Yes, Comrade Major,' he replied. Rakov looked across the room at Telinger whose features had begun to relax.

'Would you go with him, please, Comrade Colonel, and make sure that nobody shows themselves more than necessary.' Telinger nodded.

Lloyd shook his head. 'Sorry, Chuck. I was pinned down. Couldn't get anywhere near the building.'

'Not to worry,' said Tyson. 'At least we have one bug attached. And it helps even the score; you and me!'

They joined the minister and police chief in their official caravan. The police radio operator listened carefully to his headphones. He turned a couple of knobs, and then a smile crawled across his face, and he held up his thumb.

'Thank you,' said the minister, dismissing them.

'We've earned the right to hear what they say!' said Tyson.

'That's not permitted. It's our business now.'

Lloyd and Tyson looked suitably disappointed.

They rejoined the SAS team. The signals expert adjusted his dials, and finally pronounced himself satisfied: 'Clear as crystal,' he said, raising his thumb.

Over Pueblo Colorado: 11.35 a.m.

Ruth wondered what people without money did when confronted with the logistics problems which had just melted away when she pressed buttons. A phone call had her Lear-jet awaiting her when she arrived at Washington National Airport, fully fuelled and ready for take-off. Another call had chartered another jet at San Francisco. The most difficult part had been to persuade Christopher Hackett to get out of bed.

CERN: 9.55 p.m.

Telinger woke Vilkov. 'You're wanted in the control room.'

'Have we done it?' he said excitedly.

Telinger was not sure. 'I detect a certain air of quiet satisfaction!'

Vilkov swung his legs off the camp bed and rubbed his weary eyes. 'Let's find out.'

Even Ashensky had some enthusiasm. 'It seems we might be on the right track,' he said.

'Show me,' said Vilkov.

Ashensky handed over the computer summary sheets. Vilkov flipped quickly through them. 'Yes . . . I see . . . Yes . . . What about the photographs?' Andrevich laid them before his professor.

'What do you think?'

Vilkov studied them for several minutes. 'This is not conclusive. In fact it may not tell us anything,' he said.

'I don't agree,' replied Ashensky. 'There's a trend in the results of the last two experiments. We must continue along the same lines – increase the strength of the magnetic fields in the collision chamber still further, change the angle between the electric and magnetic fields to allow for relativistic effects, and continue to vary the rate and duration of the pulses. We'll soon see if the particles we produce have the two properties we're looking for, dispersal and the correct charge-to-mass ratio. If the experiment works, the output beam from the collision chamber will widen as it leaves, but its energy won't be dissipated.'

'What about mass?' asked Vilkov. Andrevich answered.

'I've done a few sample equations . . . if you'll look at the blackboard . . . ' Vilkov scanned the myriad of calculations.

'Let me make sure I understand the principles . . . Yes . . . ' He stood for a moment with furrowed creases on his forehead, then his face cleared. 'Yes. I see. That is good work, my friend; very creative, if I may say so.'

'Thank you, professor.'

'But it means we need one or two more experiments before we know for sure?' asked Vilkov.

'Only one, I hope,' said Ashensky.

'How long will it take you to set it up?'

'This one is not so simple. A few hours.'

'Right. Let's get on with it.'

CERN: 10.15 p.m.

The SAS signalman looked up from his set. He was the only Russian speaker in the team. 'They're Russians all right, and Rakov is there. I heard his name mentioned. They've got the result of number three, and it's all go. One more experiment and they've cracked the Tesla Trinity!'

Lloyd spoke urgently. 'Get me the brigadier, and be ready to send the tape in clear.'

The signaller made contact and handed Lloyd the headset. 'Their experiments are a success, sir. They're setting up for the last one now. They're close!'

'Stand-by. I'll contact Super Sunray and call you back.' Super Sunray was the Prime Minister.

'Don't you want to hear the tape in full?'

'Personally no. Send it while I'm on the other line,' said the brigadier. Lloyd looked at his watch; it was ten-twenty p.m.

Saturday 28th November 1981

Over Duluth, Wisconsin: 12.30 p.m.

Ruth Coverdale and Christopher Hackett landed within a few minutes of each other. Hackett lugged the heavy suitcase containing the oscillator aboard Ruth's Lear.

'What are you going to do with it?' he asked.

'That's no part of our deal,' she replied.

'If you're gonna try and start something seismic somewhere, I need to know; and that's professional, not personal.'

'Hackett, I've told you you can publish when I get my hands on this baby. Go ahead. That should satisfy you.'

'We both know how long it takes to get anything into print.'

'What do you think I'm going to do? Raise Manhattan again?' asked Ruth.

'The urgency tells me you're gonna make this baby do its tricks. Give me one good reason why I shouldn't call the fuzz.'

Ruth wondered what sort of lie would keep him quiet for the necessary length of time, whatever that might turn out to be.

'Suppose I sing God Bless America and talk about the land of the free.'

Hackett pondered that for a moment. 'For real?' She nodded. 'For really real?' She nodded again. 'You'd better tell me about it.' She shook her head. 'So it's down to me. You want me to trust you.' She nodded. 'I don't trust anybody with money, and you could buy most of the ones I've met.' Ruth still said nothing.

Christopher gave her a hard look, trying to read behind the eyes. All he saw was worried, serious determination. He made up his mind. 'Don't sing above a top B flat or you'll set it off in mid-air.'

Ruth called the flight attendant. 'Wake me half-an-hour out of Geneva.' She took a pill and was asleep by two p.m.

Saturday 28th November 1981
Central Zone Time, nine p.m. Geneva time.

Washington: 5.10 p.m.

The Secretary of State challenged the Swiss Ambassador. 'We know they're Russians, and KGB.'

'That doesn't solve the problem that they've taken Swiss hostages as well as others.'

'What response have you had from the Soviets?' asked Coverdale.

'They're not surprised some speak Russian. It's the native language of many Armenians.'

'Prevarication!' said the Secretary without hesitation.

'That may be,' said the Swiss, 'but saying so doesn't alter the fact that many innocent lives are at risk.'

'You've got to go in there, ambassador,' said the Secretary, 'with necessary force and get them out.'

'Why should we do that?'

'They're gonna get the secret of a weapon that'll wipe out freedom everywhere, even in Switzerland.'

'We've always maintained strict neutrality. We won't abandon years of successful policy to deal with a one-time emergency.'

'One time and for always!'

'We see this as a confrontation between the two superpowers. My government doesn't intend to take sides,' said Philippe urbanely.

'What are you going to do?' asked the Secretary, controlling his temper with difficulty.

Coverdale coughed. 'You must understand the high level of concern of the United States and governments of the other NATO nations,' said Coverdale.

'We have nothing to gain, and everything to lose by precipitate action,' said the ambassador. 'The loss of life will be considerable – and for what? Two competing nations fighting over yet another ultimate weapon! We've heard it all before, from mustard gas to the cobalt bomb, and you're still here. We're not impressed,' said the Swiss Ambassador.

'What will you do?' asked the Secretary stonily.

'Continue negotiations for the release of the hostages.'

'A charade!' exploded the Secretary of State. 'And if the Soviets get the weapon and blow the top off your mountains!'

'Years ago,' sighed Eduard Dupois, 'we came to the conclusion there was little we could do to stop the super-powers making war. We've provided nuclear shelters for most of our people. Each household keeps enough food there to survive a month. If you are right, our precautions will have proved timely.'

A little later, Frederick tried, yet again, to reach Ruth. Jennings thought she might have gone somewhere in the Learjet. Frederick called for her flight plan.

Meyrin: 11.37 p.m.

The brigadier's voice travelled clearly from London to the satellite and into Lloyd's earphones. 'You are no longer under Swiss command. Pack up quietly, and get away. Your orders are to cut off the power supply to CERN. You have the location of the cables. We would prefer it looked like an accident, but the most important thing is speed.'

'And afterwards?' Lloyd had asked.

'Stay loose. Evade capture, but remain in the vicinity of CERN. The fun will start when you knock out the accelerator.'

25

Saturday 28th November 1981
Washington: 6.45 p.m.

Frederick Coverdale phoned the National Airport and was told that the flight plan of Ruth's Lear jet took her to Denver, Colorado. It meant nothing to him. He called Lubbock; no answer. Stallybrass said he didn't know where either of them were, or if they were together.

Arthur Wilshire gave a lawyer's stonewalling reply: 'I can't think why you should imagine I have any knowledge of your wife's whereabouts.'

Frederick feared war would result from the CERN incident. He was desperate for Ruth to be somewhere safe.

He searched everywhere in the Georgetown home for a clue and eventually found the name Hackett and a California telephone number.

Julia Black answered: 'He went to Denver. Who's calling him?'

'I'm Frederick Coverdale, the National Defense Advisor. Get him to call me the minute he returns – no matter what hour!'

Sunday 29th November 1981
Les Voyrieres, Switzerland: 12.22 a.m.

The two helicopters left the safety of Czechoslovak air space and entered Austria at low level, flying at their maximum speed. Several times, during the nerve-racking journey of five hundred miles, they were challenged in English, the international language of the air, but feigned radio malfunction, and escaped without enemy aircraft forcing them down.

Sunday 29th November 1981

They flew through the narrow corridor between Lac Léman and the Alps and crossed the French border between Chavannes de Bogis and Chavannes des Bois. The last eleven kilometres, in French air space, was the most dangerous. If detected, NATO defence aircraft would have no hesitation in shooting down Russian military helicopters.

Five minutes after crossing the border they landed. The goon squad was deployed in defensive positions while the equipment was off-loaded and both ships refuelled from drums carried on board. Eight minutes later the helicopters were airborne again.

A French Mirage jet buzzed them but broke off as they crossed the Swiss border.

The Russian forward air control post was quickly camouflaged in white. The KGB border guards who made up the goon squad manned their AA missiles and waited, five thousand two hundred feet up the north-west slope of an Alp, and began shivering.

Near Les Baillets: 12.25 a.m.

It took Lloyd and Tyson fifty minutes to find the right spot. The land sloped gently upwards towards a range of snow-covered peaks. The granite looked stark and intimidating. On the lower slopes the harshness was softened by lush conifers topping a carpet of greens. Occasionally there was an outcrop of rock, just the tip visible as punctuation in the verdant growth. Planted firmly in this idyllic setting were the tall electricity pylons, ghostly sentinels in man's march of progress.

The SAS explosives expert reckoned that quite a small charge would dislodge a boulder weighing perhaps thirty tons, which, provided it took the predicted direction, would bring down the nearest pylon and cable with it. The signs of the detonation could be concealed from a casual examination.

Six men took cover. Lloyd nodded. The engineer's wrist

turned. There was a dull thump. At first they saw nothing. A faint wisp of smoke floated away. The boulder was still in place. They approached cautiously. Another ounce of plastic would have been enough.

'Try again?' asked Lloyd.

The engineer shook his head. 'Let's give it a nudge.' Six shoulders leaned into the granite. 'On a count of three!' said the bomber.

In eerie light the stone ambled into the air, hit rocks below once and then hurled itself at the base of the pylon. The metal stanchions shuddered, like a slumbering giant attacked by an irritating midget. But the essential balance of the structure had been disturbed by the impact and the steel struts began to buckle; the weight did the rest. The 'meccano' tower slowly, arthritically collapsed. The cable seemed in two minds but, eventually it gave up the struggle as millions of volts short-circuited in a spectacular shower of dissipating energy.

'I think we'd better clean up and get out of here, gentlemen,' said Lloyd.

Saturday 28th November 1981
Washington: 8.10 p.m./Palo Alto: 5.10 p.m.

Frederick picked up his private phone at the White House.

'My name is Hackett. I'm returning your call.'

It took some persuading, but by using the weight of his office Frederick made Hackett tell him everything. 'Where's she taken the damned thing?'

'She wouldn't tell me.'

'You'll be hearing from me,' was Coverdale's closing threat.

Several minutes later Denver Air Traffic Control told him the Learjet was bound for Geneva. Rage mingled with fear for her safety. He contemplated getting the air force involved. 'Where is it now?' he demanded.

Saturday 28th November 1981

'Assuming she maintained course and air speed, she would have left US air space at about 2.30 p.m. Mountain Zone Time.' Nearly four hours ago! 'She'll need to refuel in Northern Canada, probably Frobisher Bay. She's got a fair tail wind so my guess would be she's already taken off again and is somewhere over the Polar Cap.'

Sunday 29th November 1981
CERN: 1.36 a.m.

Experiment number four was in full spate when the lights went out, the video display units lost their ghostly green glow and the hum of the air-conditioning unit whispered to a halt.

'Get light somebody' shouted Vilkov.

A dim emergency system came on.

'What happened?' said Vilkov. There was no reply.

Rakov entered the room. 'Is this something to do with your experiment?'

'Most unlikely,' said Vilkov.

'Right,' said Rakov, turning to leave.

'What are you going to do?' asked Vilkov anxiously.

'As you so nicely put it when I asked about your business, fuck off, Comrade Professor.' And he said it with a calm that was more chilling than any exhibition of anger.

Rakov found Telinger in the computer centre. They went into a small office nearby, their conversation more akin to an off-shoot of a company board meeting, than the signing of a death warrant. 'We need to put the maximum pressure on,' said Rakov.

'A Frenchman! When his body hits the sidewalk the international stink will force them to restore the electricity.'

'I think he should be Swiss,' said Rakov.

'That will make them angry, maybe even stubborn.'

'It's not their fight. They will judge public opinion as

being against wasting Swiss lives for Armenia or Russia or America.' Rakov's argument was persuasive.

'OK. Who?' said Telinger.

'How about a Swiss director-general? They have two of them.'

'It doesn't leave us much in reserve if we go for a top dog at first. How about one of the clerks?' said Aleksei Telinger.

'Male or female?'

'Do we want to make them really mad, or just comply with our demands?'

'The latter,' said Rakov with emphasis.

'Definitely not female. The Swiss get upset when you interfere with their women.'

Rakov was looking at a list of senior personnel. 'This one looks promising; Gunthardt, executive board secretary. Swiss.'

'Brilliant!' said Telinger. 'Important, but not vital. An administrator, with whom not too many identify.'

The door opened, a female KGB guard said:

'It's the telephone, Comrade Major. The police chief,' she said. 'He sounds agitated.'

'And so he should. Tell him to wait; I'm busy. But first, see if Herr Gunthardt is on the premises. If he is, ask him if he could spare us a moment.'

She left them. Telinger was the first to break the silence. 'How are you going to do it?' he enquired.

'You hold his attention. I'll do the rest.' Rakov lifted his trouser leg and tested the steel of his knife.

The KGB guard knocked on the door. 'This is Herr Gunthardt.' Rakov advanced on him with his hand outstretched. It was a disarming gesture.

The Swiss/German took the Russian's hand. He was in his early forties, a spare man, with sallow complexion; a worrier, a good administrator.

Sunday 29th November 1981

'I'd like you to meet Colonel Telinger. He has a problem of logistics he would like to discuss with you,' said Rakov.

Telinger also held out his hand, and it too was shaken. 'We don't want to make this any more unpleasant than we have to for those of you who are forced to remain, and so we wondered if you would think it a good idea if we were to . . . ' Rakov moved behind the Swiss secretary. He took a quick firm grip on Gunthardt's hair and drew the sharp steel deeply across his throat. The man put both hands to his neck. He tried to scream. It came out as a strangled gurgle. Blood gushed, soaking his clothes as he sank to the floor.

'Did you have to do it that way?' asked Telinger.

'I have no quarrel with this man. It's the quickest and least painful death.'

The police chief was anxious. Rakov came on the line.

'Yes?'

'I wanted to tell you, Monsieur Omega, that we don't know what caused the power cut. It wasn't us or anybody on our authority. We are doing everything possible to restore the supply.'

'If you will look behind building number 129,' said Rakov dispassionately, 'you'll find the body of the first victim of your stupidity; Herr Gunthardt, Swiss secretary of the executive board. If power is not restored in half-an-hour, there will be two more bodies to join his.'

'Listen to me, Omega . . . '

Rakov replaced his receiver.

Saturday 28th November 1981
Georgetown: 9.40 p.m.

Frederick was spending the first night at home in a month. Sleep would not come, so he dozed on the leather chesterfield in the den, beside the telephone. All efforts to contact her in the air failed; atmospheric problems. He had left an urgent message that she should ring him on the Georgetown number as soon as she landed. He thought of having somebody from the embassy meet her but they had their hands full with the CERN crisis.

He couldn't believe Ruth seriously contemplated trying to use her 'earthquake-maker.' At any other time and place he would have dismissed the very idea as ludicrous. But fear had been with him since Denver had mentioned Geneva, fear that she would get in the way of the violence; terror that he would never see her again. He had to stop her, somehow. He dialled Geneva Air Traffic Control again. The Learjet was on schedule.

Sunday 29th November 1981
CERN: 2.45 a.m.

The police chief looked down at the body being loaded into the back of the ambulance. No siren wailed as it drew away. Time had no further meaning for the administrator with the sallow complexion.

'This is down to those SAS,' said the policeman. 'I want them found, and I want them arrested. They will answer for this.' He returned to the caravan. 'Do we know where the damage is?'

'Out in the country,' replied the radio operator, 'near Les Baillets. A pylon is down.'

'How long will it take?' asked the police chief.

'Can't say yet. They have to rig up a new tower.'

'Don't they have portable ones? Surely . . . '

'It's some way from a main road. There's no means of getting there quickly.'

'Call in helicopters.'

London: 3 a.m.

The Foreign Secretary's telephone rang. He got wearily out of bed, trying not to wake his wife. 'I'll make tea,' she said.

Sunday 29th November 1981

He went to his study.

'You have violated our agreement,' said the Swiss ambassador without preamble.

'That is a strong accusation between friendly powers. Unless you can substantiate it I shall have to ask for a formal apology.'

'I'm talking about men's lives. We admitted your team to our country on the understanding that they were to be under Swiss command. They've destroyed an electricity pylon, cutting off the power to CERN. The terrorists have executed one of our senior officials, a Swiss. I am instructed by my government to lodge a formal note of protest in the strongest terms, demanding an apology, the immediate withdrawal of your men, and compensation for the relatives of the victim.'

'I cannot, of course, comment, until I am in possession of all the facts. Meanwhile I hear what you say, and must immediately tender my government's regret that there has been loss of life in this tragic affair. I cannot accept any responsibility until you have presented the evidence for your allegation and a full investigation has been carried out. What exactly is the evidence?'

'Your men have disappeared. The power has been cut off. It must have been them.'

'I take it these are assumptions.' The Minister was at his most urbane.

'A pylon was destroyed. It must have been your men who did it. Who else could possibly have had either motive, means or knowledge of what it would mean?'

'I can think of quite a few. Turkish patriots opposed to the Armenians? What explosive was used?'

The ambassador went on the defensive. 'The substance has not yet been identified.'

'Was the pylon destroyed by explosion?' asked the Foreign Secretary.

Sunday 29th November 1981

'What does it matter what method was used?'

'Obviously when a power line goes down there can be a number of explanations. In this country the usual reason is high winds.'

'It was a calm clear night.'

'So it could not have been a natural phenomenon!'

'Of course not.'

'Forgive me, Mr Ambassador, but you do not sound entirely certain. Are you witholding information?'

'First reports indicate that a huge rock was the immediate cause of the pylon's destruction . . .'

'So we are dealing with natural causes.'

'Fifty tons of rock does not dislodge itself for no reason!' said the exasperated ambassador.

'Perhaps it was already unsafe? Come now. Aren't you reacting hastily before the facts are known. This will look different in the morning.'

'I'm instructed to hold your government responsible for the one death and for any subsequent deaths that result from your actions.'

Swiss airspace: 5.55 a.m.

As the Learjet began its descent to Cointrin, the airport for Geneva, the flight attendant brought Ruth a note:

> 'Please telephone your husband at Georgetown as soon as you land. Urgent.'

Ruth nodded. So he knew, but what did he know? Who had talked? It could only be Hackett. Frederick knew she had a box that might be able to start an earthquake. Would he believe it? Surely not; it smacked of science fiction. So why did he want to speak to her? Presumably to give her another lecture on loyalty and private citizens interfering in matters of State. She'd heard that one. She screwed up the note.

Sunday 29th November 1981

Grand Bois de Roulane: 6.10 a.m.

Lloyd and Tyson and two SAS men were asleep. The radio receiver was tuned in to the bug in the wall of the main control room. Another commando scanned the slopes below their hiding place through night glasses, the images intensified by infra-red, another Tesla discovery.

At six-ten a.m. he woke Lloyd. Tyson also stirred and opened his eyes. 'What's goin' on?' he asked blearily.

'Is the power back on?' asked Lloyd.

The radio operator shook his head. 'But they seem to have by-passed it,' he said.

'What do you mean?' Lloyd was now fully awake, so was Tyson.

'The man called Ashensky brought Vilkov back to the control room. It seems they've found a way to finish the tests using only the computers.'

'That won't help them without power,' said Lloyd breathing in relief.

The radio man persisted. ''Fraid not. They only need the direct power line for the big surges to run the accelerator. The computer set-up needs far less.'

'They still don't have electricity, man,' said Tyson.

'They have an emergency generator,' said the signaller.

'Which gives a low light. Not enough to run the most complex computer bank in Europe,' said Lloyd.

'They've rigged the generator so that with all other uses blanked off, they can squeeze enough out of it!'

'Are you sure about this?' said Tyson.

'That's what they're saying,' said the radio signaller.

'See if you can raise the brigadier,' said Lloyd.

It took a long five minutes. He told his superior the situation.

'How close are you to CERN?' asked the brigadier.

'About five miles.'

'Get back there and stand by to attack.'

Sunday 29th November 1981

Cointrin: 6.15 a.m.

Ruth walked through the green customs lobby with her heavy suitcase on a metal trolley. Lubbock was waiting for her.

'It's all set up and ready to go,' he said, taking the bag, and hefting it into the trunk of his friend's Mercedes.

'Where are we in relation to CERN?' asked Ruth as they set off through the busying streets.

'We can see it from the roof of our building; about half a mile.'

'And nobody suspects anything?' said Ruth.

'About us? Why should they?' Lubbock asked. 'They think all their troubles are up the street.'

Ruth nodded. 'What exactly do you have in mind?' asked Lubbock. 'I mean how are we going to find out if the situation is sufficiently desperate to warrant using this thing?'

'Did you get that radio?'

'That won't tell us anything.'

'Maybe, but it's an obvious source of information and we mustn't overlook it. Next, Stallybrass is going to keep close to the President; try to find out what orders he's giving, and what results are coming through.'

'How does he tell us?'

'I have to call him with our number here – I take it we have got a telephone . . . ?'

Lubbock nodded. 'What's our fall-back position?' he asked, knowing there wasn't one.

'I hoped I might have gotten something from Chuck before I left. I made arrangements for any call he made to be patched through to the Lear, but nothing,' said Ruth.

'He won't know how to reach you even if he does get the message.'

'I'll give Jennings our number here.'

Lubbock laughed.

'What's funny,' asked Ruth.

Sunday 29th November 1981

'Here we are at the worst crisis in the history of the world and the liberty of freedom-loving peoples is in the hands of a goddamn Welsh butler!'

Ruth did not respond to Lubbock's mood. She said, drily, 'Since you invoke His name, I would remind you that His Son was a carpenter.'

26

Sunday 29th November 1981
Georgetown: 12.25 a.m./Geneva: 7.25 a.m.

The telephone woke Frederick. He grabbed it: 'Ruth . . .'

'This is the White House, Mr Coverdale. The President would like you here right away sir.'

Frederick looked at his watch. Ruth should have just about landed. 'It's not very convenient. I'm expecting an urgent call.'

The White House aide was polite but firm. 'A car will be with you shortly. The President asked me to emphasize that this has the highest priority, and that even minutes count. He means immediately, sir.'

Damn and blast! He dialled Geneva again. The front door bell rang. Frederick waited for Geneva to answer. Jennings, in dressing gown and pyjamas, knocked and entered. The voice from Geneva told him his message had been passed to the Learjet which had landed at 6.15 a.m.

'The car from the White House is here, sir.'

Frederick gazed at the telephone, willing it to ring. 'I'm expecting an overseas call from my wife, Jennings, but I have to go to the President. Tell her to call me there, but in any event, get a number where I can reach her and call me with it yourself. It's urgent and it's official.'

'I understand, sir.'

Frederick fixed his butler with his most serious expression. 'Don't fail me on this, Jennings.'

Washington: 12.46 a.m.

The President spoke on the telephone to the Prime Minister.

Sunday 29th November 1981

'I'm giving the Air Force Commander orders to attack as soon as they have their target in sight,' said the President.

'Agreed,' she said.

'Pinpointing the computer centre.'

'Can we agree on procedure if our aircraft are attacked by enemy planes?' asked the Prime Minister.

'They defend themselves. My airborne commander has orders to use his own judgement.'

30,000 ft. over Geneva: 6.59 a.m.

The observer, in the TU 126 Moss Transport manning the radar, was 25, the only son of a prosperous Moscow prosecutor. His mathematics degree from his hometown university and father's unwavering support for the party, guaranteed him an enviable place on the ladder of military preferment. He noted the change in the pattern of activity of the enemy aircraft.

'They're breaking into two groups, control. The RAF Phantoms are heading due east, possible target Geneva, and hold it a moment . . . yes, they're going low level. That's reduced their ground-speed to something like eight hundred miles per hour. But don't rely on that. They have Mach 2.2 capability at higher altitudes. The other group is presumably the American F111s and F15s . . . yes . . . I confirm that they are headed north-east. Will continue to observe both groups.'

Bay of Biscay: 7.00 a.m.

The British commander was Air Commodore 'Digger' Smith, so named because he had spent three years on detachment with the Australian Air Force and had never lost the accent. He was too old at the game to be overexcited at the prospect of action, or at least he would not allow it to show in his voice. 'OK lads,' he twined laconically, 'this seems to be it. Target – attack.' The detailed plan had been worked out long before. Only if Digger and his squadron failed would the Yanks join the party.

Moscow: 9.00 a.m.

Major-General Yakushenko and the air force marshal watched as the enemy aircraft were moved on the plot board. A calm voice announced: 'We've lost enemy Phantoms from radar.'

'Last heading?' snapped the marshal.

There was a pause. The voice intoned: 'Six aircraft heading north-east, six aircraft due east . . . '

The marshal didn't wait to hear it. 'Must be Geneva! Where are our fighters?'

'Eighteen MiG25 Foxbats in holding patterns east and west of Pilsen,' came the calm reply.

'Order ten MiG's on to heading to intercept Phantoms; low level.'

Meyrin: 7.01 a.m.

While Lubbock and Roskill worked on Hackett's instructions for mounting the oscillator, Ruth called Stallybrass and brought him up-to-date. He had no news. The President had been too busy to even talk to him. There was a news blackout on everything. She called Jennings.

'No, ma'am, Captain Tyson has not called.'

'When he does, give him this number.'

'Mr Coverdale said to be sure to get you to call him at the White House.'

'Thank you, Jennings. I'll do that and . . . by the way . . . there's no need to give Mr Coverdale this number.'

'I understand, ma'am.'

CERN: 7.02 a.m.

Over six hours had elapsed since the killing of the Swiss hostage. The search for Lloyd and the SAS went on. There was silence from the terrorists. The police chief was uneasy. The Minister of Justice phoned. 'Low flying aircraft are heading this way; six in all.'

'Is that so unusual?' asked the policeman.

'Unidentified. No air traffic control clearance.'

'What do you make of it, minister?'

'Hold on a moment. Another message is coming through . . . ' The police chief waited. 'Another force – also unidentified and uncleared is heading in from East Germany.'

'So British or Americans are coming and so are the Russians. One presumably to attack and the other to try and stop it. What are your orders?'

But the minister was receiving another signal. 'Now we have a third group, from France this time. Tell the terrorist leader what's happening and to get all the people out.'

Rakov heard him in silence. 'I don't believe you. It's a ruse to get us out.'

The policeman was cool. 'Get them out of there or you'll all be killed.'

Rakov still did not believe him. 'Call off the aircraft or I will execute more hostages.'

The policeman still kept calm. 'That's stupid. I don't know who they are; they're approaching Swiss air space without permission. We assume one lot want to destroy you and the others are trying to stop them. Don't bother to kill any hostages. Leave them there and the air attack will do it for you.'

Rakov believed him. 'How long have we got?'

'Minutes.'

'How about the Russian planes?'

'How do you know they're Russian?' asked the policeman. Rakov didn't answer. 'Get out fast or you'll all be dead.'

Rakov had a better reason for wanting the hostages out

when the bombs fell; they would distract his men from their main task. He told Telinger: 'Get rid of them; everybody we don't need. Keep only the chairmen of boards, and the director-general.' Telinger left. Rakov returned to the computer centre where Vilkov was concentrating on information being printed at bewildering speed by the banks of chattering machines.

'How much longer, professor?' he asked quietly.

'Soon. Don't interrupt me,' he replied, not looking up. He checked another figure, and then spoke urgently to the woman beside him. 'Somebody programmed one wrong digit in that last run. Find it and correct it. It's somewhere in these numbers.'

Rakov debated whether to tell him they were about to be bombed, and decided there was no point. They would know soon enough. 'Is there any way this can be speeded up?' Vilkov gave him a withering look.

Geneva: 7.04 a.m.

Lloyd reckoned they could reach CERN by seven-thirty five a.m. with luck. The driver maintained a steady speed, taking no chances. He was the only one not checking weapons. Lloyd calculated that they had enough for about fifteen minutes' combat. After that it would be hand-to-hand. The watch on Lloyd's wrist showed seven-o-four a.m. when they hit their first traffic jam; Sunday church-goers.

Moscow: 9.05 a.m./Washington: 1.05 a.m.

'Don't insult my intelligence, Mr President,' said the Soviet leader. 'My information is accurate. US Air Force F111s and British Phantoms are heading towards Geneva, to attack the Armenian patriots.'

'Mr Chairman, I'm still awaiting information myself. I don't have all the facts, and until I do I can neither confirm nor deny what you say.'

'This attack couldn't be mounted without your direct command.' The President said nothing. The Russian continued. 'I've given orders that if your force approaches CERN, our aircraft will shoot them out of the sky.'

The President became angry. 'This is not your territory . . . '

'Nor yours!' interrupted the Russian.

'These terrorists are your men, KGB. And we both know why they're there!'

'Call off your attack and I will call off my fighters.'

'If American aircraft are attacked they will respond. Our technology is superior to yours, as you know.'

'I know there are a lot of theories, most of which have not been tested in battle conditions, Mr President. Are you going to call off the attack?'

Moscow: 9.07 a.m.

'How many aircraft have we in the air?' the marshal demanded.

'Ten MiGs on converging course with the Phantoms, eight holding over the Czechoslovakian border.'

'What's the Geneva ETA of the Phantoms?'

The controller consulted his computer read-out ' . . . Nine minutes.'

'And the F111s?'

'Nineteen minutes.' The marshal made up his mind quickly.

'Tell the remaining eight MiG 25s to head for Geneva and engage and destroy the Americans.'

'Yes, marshal.'

'Will they succeed?' asked Yakushenko.

'Who knows!' said the marshal. 'Actual combat's a bit different from training missions.'

Meyrin: 7.22 a.m.

The traffic cleared quite quickly. Lloyd and his team left

Cointrin Airport on their right as they took the Matgin road, bearing left at La Citadelle and then taking another right at Les Vernes. The road was narrow and pot-holed. They reached Les Arberes where they turned into the Swiss side of Bois Tollot. They parked out of sight of the road. Hugging the trees they set off at a smart trot through the fringe of the wood alongside the French border. They stopped within a few yards of the CERN perimeter, and watched as hundreds of men and women streamed from the CERN buildings. 'Sunray, this is Lionheart . . . ' said Lloyd into his radio. 'They've released the hostages. They're pouring out.'

The brigadier's response was matter-of-fact. 'Our bombers will arrive within minutes. Stay five hundred yards clear of the computer building. If the planes fail to destroy it, go in yourself and finish the job.'

'Understood,' said Lloyd. 'Wilco and out.'

French/Swiss Border: 7.26 a.m.

Digger Smith knew it was too good to last. He registered the heat-seeking missile when it was almost too late. His number two released a thermal decoy while Digger kicked the rudder for a fast turn. The missile took the bait. They were momentarily blinded by the explosion.

'Bandits! Bandits!' he yelled, breaking radio silence. He was too late to save one Phantom which exploded in a belch of flame and debris. Another lost a wing and began spiralling to the ground before the fighter cover located the Soviet planes and engaged them. Digger knew it was hopeless as soon as he realized they were outnumbered by the Foxbats. Two of the enemy were downed by British missiles, but a third explosion took out another of the F4s. The commodore called up the other attack force.

'Hank, this is Digger. It's your show now. We seem to have bought it. Good luck.' And he began to fly for his life.

Sunday 29th November 1981

He didn't stay on one course for more than three seconds. He weaved in and out of hills and mountains at times only twenty feet above the ground. He sensed one pursuer cartwheel as a wingtip caught a piece of mountain. He thought he might just make one pass over the target. He sighted Lac Léman. Two MiGs locked on to his tail. Digger steadied for his run-in. At eight hundred miles an hour he only needed a few more seconds. The Soviet pilots unleashed a missile apiece. Digger never felt a thing.

Over Lac Léman: 7.28 a.m.

Hank Schuster was 27, and a brilliant pilot. He was young to be a captain, and had been less than thrilled to be posted to England. Son of a Tennessee mountain farm hand who made his money out of gut-rotting moonshine liquor, Hank fell in love with the slow-moving agricultural people of Kent. None of this did him much good as he sped to his appointment with destiny over the Swiss Alps.

In the holding pattern over the Bay of Biscay he had wondered if he ever would see action. He had thought he would run low on fuel and he recalled long before there was any fighting. False alarms had happened so often before, he found it difficult to believe, even now, that this wasn't just another exercise which the 'brass' had decided to make extra-real. The thoughts passed through his head in less than a second because it was taking all his concentration to hug the contours of the French terrain only a few feet below him. He had no chance to look about him. He was concentrating one hundred per cent on his instruments and the church tower he thought it might be a good idea to avoid. When its tower bellowed into an eruption of masonry and glass and smoke, and he realized he had company, he yanked hard on the stick, just avoiding a collection of religious debris. His computer told him he was forty-one seconds from target when he spotted the second batch of killer

MiG 25s despatched by the Russian marshal.

He switched on his radar jamming device, and told his co-pilots coolly: 'Hey you guys, we've got company. Sarby and Wyatt stay on course for target. Let 'cover' deal with the interference. Take avoiding action but get to that . . . ' He could not complete the sentence because the tail section of his F111 was shot away by a Soviet missile and he found himself ejected and dropping like a brick to meet the earth only fifty feet below him. He saw one other USAF plane destroyed and two Foxbats.

Wyatt's jet screamed across Lac Léman at wave-top height with three Soviet fighters in pursuit firing everything they had at him, but miraculously missing as he dodged and weaved. He steadied momentarily, took aim and fired. Half a second later a Russian missile homed in on the heat of his engine, entered through the rear opening and exploded, cutting plane and pilot into a thousand pieces. Time: 7.31 a.m.

Meyrin: 7.31 a.m.

The oscillator was wired firmly to the main vertical girder which was bedded into the granite on which the foundations were built.

'What do we do now?' asked Roskill.

Before anybody could answer, the building was rocked by the deafening sonic booms of fighter aircraft cutting through the air only feet above the roof. The building heaved to the shock of two explosions as missiles struck CERN. A second later, the roof and walls were splattered with the detritus of Wyatt and his disintegrating aircraft.

They rushed to see what had happened. They were too far away to hear the screams of the injured and dying. A pall of black smoke was forming over the accelerator complex. It was impossible to tell which buildings had been hit.

Ruth said. 'The planes have gone. That was it?'

Sunday 29th November 1981

'They'll be back,' said Lubbock.

'Whose were they?' asked Roskill.

Lubbock had no doubt. 'The Man's got his balls back. That was a US Air Force plane that made the hit, and the pursuers were Soviet. The problem is how the hell do we find out if they did the job.'

Roskill pointed to an elaborate radio painted dull green standing in the corner of the room.

'If only we knew what frequency anybody is using, and who we are trying to tune in to,' said Ruth logically.

Roskill smiled. 'I know the regular channels used by NATO forces in West Germany.'

At first all they picked up was the anguished calls of commercial aircraft wanting to know who was shooting at whom, and being told that Cointrin was closed to all traffic and they should divert to Zurich.

The telephone rang. 'That'll be him!' said Ruth excitedly, picking up the receiver. 'Chuck, this is Ruth. What we need to . . .'

The voice that interrupted her was Frederick's, and there was no trace of pomposity. 'Ruth, it's me, Freddie. Don't hang up; please don't hang up.'

'Frederick, it's too late. I know what I'm doing . . . '

'I only have seconds to say this . . . I love you . . . I don't care what you've done . . . I don't care what happens to me, but please, please get away from that place . . . '

Ruth's voice softened. Lubbock and Roskill returned to the radio. 'If only you'd said that a week ago . . . I think I love you too, but we both have things to do . . . '

'In the name of God, my darling, don't . . . '

'Don't worry, Freddie. I'll be all right. I'll call you when it's all over.' Ruth gently replaced the instrument.

Roskill's radio found the local police frequency and urgent calls for ambulances. More faintly they heard what sounded like manoeuvres on Luneberg Heath. They so nearly missed it. Lubbock thought it was a commercial pilot. Roskill continued the slow pan of wavelengths. Ruth said: 'I think I recognize the voice. Can you go back?'

There was nothing but a hum. Then Richard Lloyd said clearly and distinctly: 'Damage only to surface buildings, Sunray. Nothing below ground as far as we can see, and the two hits were wide of the mark. When can we expect the next strike? That one was close.'

The brigadier's voice was fainter. 'That's it. We seem to have taken a pasting. It's now down to you. You have your orders. Good luck! And don't hang about!'

Ruth looked at Lubbock. 'You're the general.'

He said, rather pompously, 'We need a military appreciation of the situation.'

'Who's going to give us that?' asked Ruth sarcastically.

'I am!' said Lubbock waspishly. 'What do we know? One: the Russians still have control of CERN. Two: they are minutes from cracking the Tesla thing and sending the nitty gritty back to Moscow. Three: the air attack failed to destroy the target. Four: your friend Lloyd, possibly with Chuck, is out there somewhere trying to do something about it himself.'

Roskill added, 'The target's underground, presumably in the tunnel.' The others nodded in agreement at the assessment. 'How much damage will this thing do?' asked Roskill. Lubbock looked at Ruth.

'It did a fair bit of mayhem in California.'

'I don't like the odds against those guys on the ground. We'd better give them a hand,' said Lubbock lightly.

'There's thousands of people out there!' said Roskill.

'How can Chuck and Richard get through a steel door, into the tunnel, locate the right people, and blow them away in the time available?' asked Lubbock.

'It's not possible,' said Ruth.

'I agree,' said Lubbock. 'Throw the switch!' Roskill

gripped the black plastic handle which would make the connection with the three-phase electrical current.

Grosvenor Square, London: 6.35 a.m.

Hirshfield turned off his electric shaver, washed his face and returned to the bedroom to hear the announcer on BBC Radio Four say: 'here is a news flash . . . ' He turned up the volume. 'News is coming in of an air battle taking place over Geneva in Switzerland. American and Russian planes appear to be involved. No official announcement has been made and so far there are reports of some bomb damage, but no information about casualties. We'll bring you more as soon as we have it. And now back to . . . '

The professor didn't bother to listen any more. He knew there was now no prospect of him getting to the CERN accelerator.

27

Sunday 29th November 1981
CERN: 7.36 a.m.

Two explosions rocked the room and the machines on which Vilkov and his men were working. The generator seemed about to fail, but picked up again. Rakov was the first to recover. 'Damage, professor?'

Vilkov looked at what the various computers were doing. 'Can't tell. Give me a minute.' He glanced swiftly at the print-out. 'This is all garbled. We'll have to start again.'

'Start again!' exclaimed Rakov. 'Surely . . . '

'Just the last run,' re-assured Vilkov. Ashensky turned off the computers, spoke to the man beside him, who began hammering the keyboard, his fingers flying over the plastic digits at bewildering speed.

'How long?' said Rakov.

'Minutes,' said the professor.

Rakov nodded and took Telinger on one side. 'We don't know what else they have planned for us, but we shall have to assume some sort of ground attack.'

'The message has to be encoded before it's sent,' replied Telinger.

'Two minutes for the last computer run, say three minutes to encode the information, say ten seconds to send. We need our first line of defence outside the tunnel. Pack the remainder in here, in case they get through that steel door before we've done the business. And hurry.'

Telinger emerged to find CERN in chaos. There were fires and smoke everywhere. Men and women were screaming. A delirious man walked past him, with one arm missing, the exposed tissues pouring blood. With a shock,

Sunday 29th November 1981

Telinger realized he was Russian. He had trouble rounding up the KGB. They were dazed with the effect of the attack. He chose defensive positions for ten men and three women, made sure they had ammunition and returned to the tunnel.

Meyrin: 7.37 a.m.

'What's the matter with the goddamn thing?' asked Lubbock, raging at Tesla's oscillator.

'Losing your temper won't help, Jack,' said Ruth quietly. 'Hackett told me this might happen. It's a question of minute adjustment. Unless you hit exactly the right wavelength it won't work. You have to pick up the precise resonance of the earth. Obviously there's a tiny variation here compared to Northern California.'

'The rock composition and geological formations are quite different,' said Roskill.

'You see!' said Ruth.

'OK,' said Lubbock, still impatient. 'But what do we do about it?'

'Watch me,' said Ruth. On the front of the metal casing were four calibrated dials. Hackett's piece of paper showed the exact position for each dial. She checked. They were correct.

'Is it the same principle as Ella Fitzgerald breaking a glass with a certain pitch to her singing note?' asked Roskill.

'How the hell would I know?' said Lubbock.

Ruth made an adjustment to one dial. 'Throw it,' she said to Roskill. The oscillator began to whirl, the noise increased, but nothing vibrated with it. Ruth drew her hand across her throat. Roskill turned off the power.

CERN: 7.37 a.m.

Lloyd had given the others a time of seven-thirty-eight a.m. exactly as the start of the attack. He looked at his watch. It still lacked thirty seconds. He was alone, crouching behind building 28 at the junction of Routes Balmer and Einstein. He checked his automatic carbine. The ammunition clip was full, the safety catch off. He set it for three round bursts, the most effective. As he peered round the corner a single shot missed him by a foot. He wasted no further time. Picking up a large stone, he threw it. The other man reacted with a shot. Lloyd emerged, took quick aim and pressed the trigger. Three shots rang out. The spread was minimal. He had time to register the jerking movement of the man's upper body, assuring him he had a hit, before he ran the length of the building across Einstein and ducked behind building 253. He peered through the window. KGB men and women were loading their weapons. He smashed a window pane and lobbed in a grenade. He ran across Route Veksler and flung himself to the ground as the explosion occurred. Shooting from the other side of the complex told Lloyd Tyson and the four SAS had begun their attack.

CERN: 7.39 a.m.

The chef de la police was assailed on all sides for help, information, ambulances, hospital facilities. His men abandoned their cordon to help the wounded, put out fires and drag bodies from the wreckage.

'I can only tell you, minister,' said the chief, 'that two bombs or missiles exploded. They demolished buildings 300 to 303 and most of 255 to 350. The jet that launched the attack was shot down and the wreckage struck about a kilometre away.'

'What's the situation inside CERN?' asked the minister.

'The bug is not picking up anything from the main control room. They must be in the computer centre. We have no listening device there.'

'Could they have come out with the other hostages and be making their escape?'

'I doubt it. The last we heard they hadn't completed the experiment, let alone transmitted it to Moscow.' The noise of Lloyd's grenade in building 253 filtered through to him. 'I have to go, minister.' He handed the instrument to an assistant and ran out of the caravan.

Meyrin: 7.40 a.m.

For the fourth time Ruth made a minute adjustment to the dials, and nodded to Roskill. He pressed home the lever. The oscillator wound itself up. This time there was a distinct difference. At first they were puzzled. It was as though the machine had acquired a new tone, it seemed to sing. They were witnessing the accord of oscillator and its setting. The three-phase power provided the energy to transmit vibrations from the machine, through the girder as a conductor to the rock beneath them. Much as the granite on which Lower Manhattan stands was stimulated into reciprocal tremors, so the subterranean part of the Alpine massif was now rumbling as its resonance was invoked. Shock waves throbbed away from the man-made epicentre.

'OK' said Ruth. 'That proves it works. Turn it off while we listen to what's happening to Lloyd.'

Roskill pulled up the lever, disconnecting the power. It had no effect. The noise made by the oscillator increased. She waved her hand behind her. 'Don't wait for my signal, just turn it off.'

'I have,' shouted Roskill. Ruth whirled and saw the lever in the up position. The oscillator had been cut off from its power source, and yet the machine carried on with its own momentum, increasing the severity of the vibrations with every moment. The girder to which the machine was screwed was holding firm, but everything around it was shaking.

Sunday 29th November 1981

CERN: 7.41 a.m.

Rakov raised his head as a grenade exploded nearby. He asked for the third time: 'Well?' Vilkov studied the words and symbols. Andrevich and Ashensky looked over his shoulder.

'It can't be right,' said Andrevich. Vilkov nodded.

'We need another run on the accelerator,' said Ashensky.

'No chance,' was Rakov's firm assertion. 'What the hell's wrong?'

'We've got an answer we don't understand,' replied Vilkov. 'Check the program,' he ordered.

'I did,' said Ashensky, 'twice.'

'Check it again.' He pulled out sheets of paper and began searching through them.

Rakov heard the sound of sub-machine guns and automatic rifles. 'They're here! Think of something fast or we're beaten.'

'Why don't we send what we've got so far. Let the Moscow computers sort it out?' offered Andrevich. It was a sensible suggestion.

'We would have to send everything we've done up till now to enable them to make any sense of it.'

'But we'll be there. We can do it ourselves!' said Ashensky. There was no reply. Vilkov and Rakov looked at the ground. It dawned on the Russian that they might not get out of the place alive. Vilkov handed his hip flask to Ashensky. He took a long pull, and offered the flask to the others.

'Do something!' commanded Rakov. 'Do something!'

Ashensky looked up. 'There's nothing wrong with the program.' Vilkov made up his mind.

'Run it again.' The operator pressed the buttons. The discs began to rotate, the machine hummed.

Sunday 29th November 1981

At first they thought the vibration was coming from the banks of computers.

CERN: 7.42 a.m.

Lloyd and Tyson lay side-by-side looking at the red-painted steel door. Lloyd said, 'I'll cover you.'

Tyson extracted the pin from the grenade, stood, and bowled it over-arm. It struck the door, and landed in the lobby made by the dug out earth. It exploded with a clanking bang. The two men looked up. There were some scratches on the door, but it held fast.

'That was a waste of time,' said Lloyd.

'What do we do now?' asked Tyson.

'Call up Reg. He should have the anti-tank gun.'

'If he's survived.' Tyson spoke into his personal radio. 'Reg – this is Chuck. Can you get over to us? We're at map reference F-3.'

A breathless voice responded. 'I'm a bit pinned down at the . . .' The sound of machine gun fire crackled over the radio at the e same time as they heard it live from two streets away. They listened. They heard the thud of a grenade, and then the chatter of three short bursts of automatic fire. The laconic voice of Reginald Arkwright came through to them. 'Now what was it you wanted of me, my Yankee friend?'

'We need your long tube . . . '

'Hang about!' he said.

A sudden violent tremor threw Lloyd and Tyson a foot into the air. 'What the blazes was that?' said Lloyd.

Tyson, who had been in Malibu in 1976 when an earthquake registered over 6 on the Richter Scale said: 'Feels like an earthquake.'

'They don't have them in Switzerland.' The tremors continued, making him a liar.

Sunday 29th November 1981

They ducked as gunfire erupted all round them. Arkwright ran and leapt to their position, knocking the wind out of Tyson as he landed square on his back. 'Good-morning, gentlemen,' he said. 'Now what seems to be the problem?' Lloyd poked his head up long enough to let off three bursts of fire in the direction of the bullets which had chased Arkwright. There was one scream. Lloyd nodded in satisfaction.

Tyson pointed at the steel door. Arkwright unclipped a metal tube and turned his back-pack to Tyson saying, 'Get out the ammo. A couple should do it.' Arkwright loaded, aimed and fired. They hugged the ground as another hail of fire descended on them. Lloyd surfaced and let fly more bursts of fire. A grunt preceded the sound of a body falling. They looked at the door. There was a hole in it, but it was still on its hinges.

Arkwright nodded at Tyson, who handed him another shell. Another hail of fire, this time two machine guns, instead of three, Lloyd noted. Arkwright fired. Another hole appeared but still not big enough for a man to get through.

'I'll have to use the sticky stuffy,' said Arkwright. 'Cover me on a count of three.' He took a ball of grey plastic explosive from his pack and said quietly, 'One, two, three!' He waited a second while Lloyd and Tyson commenced firing, then ran, crouched low.

The concrete was spattered by bullets striking his wake. He reached the door, and lay flat for a second. He broke the grey ball into four, and moulded one into each of the two lower corners of the red door. As he stood to place the other two, his body arched as machine gun fire raked his lower back.

'I think I'm going to need some help,' he stuttered.

Lloyd's personal radio chattered into life as another SAS made contact. 'Where are you, Richard?'

'Tell him,' said Lloyd to Tyson. 'I'm going in to finish that door.'

'F-3,' said Tyson. 'And we need somebody to get some baddies off our backs.'

'Coming,' said the singsong Welsh lilt of guardsman Tiny Evans.

Tyson began firing as Lloyd ran to join Arkwright. A hail of fire followed him. Tyson's cover was just enough to spoil the KGB aim.

Arkwright looked bad. He grinned at Lloyd. 'Detonators!' he said, opening his hand, exposing four metal 'cigarettes.' Lloyd moulded the plastic to the shape of the two top corners of the door.

'Banzai!' yelled Evans, announcing his imminent arrival.

Tyson stood to give covering fire. Lloyd loosed off three bursts.

'Made it,' said Evans. Lloyd shouted back.

'I'll wave.' He did so.

Tyson and Evans opened fire. Lloyd fixed one explosive, jammed in the detonator, and dropped to the ground. He waved again and they repeated the trick. The fire of the Russians was more ragged. Tyson counted a total of three guns firing at them.

'How about you and me getting out of here?' said Lloyd. The gaping hole in Arkwright's stomach made it a somewhat bizarre invitation.

'I'm rather comfortable here, sir. Why don't you . . . ' and his head lolled to one side, the open eyes, now seeing nothing. 'God bless,' said Lloyd quietly. He yelled to Tyson. 'I'm coming back . . . '

The two men gave covering fire. Lloyd hit the ground beside them, winded. In less than a minute the plastic exploded. When Lloyd peered at his handiwork the door had disappeared, so had most of Arkwright's body.

Another earth tremor shook the ground and debris

began falling on the concrete roads in which long cracks and eruptions appeared. Tyson fired a burst. There was no answering fire. Lloyd leapt to his feet and ran for the door, followed by Tyson and Evans. One machine gun opened up. A bullet felled Evans with a wound in the ankle. Lloyd felt part of his left ear disappear. He tossed a grenade through the open doorway, paused for the explosion, and rushed in with Tyson at his heels.

Moscow: 9.45 a.m.

The marshal sat grim-faced waiting for news. Yakushenko said to nobody in particular: 'Why don't they tell us what's going on?'

'They never do,' said the marshal dryly. 'Since generals stopped going into battle at the head of their troops, they have had to rely on imperfect communications to tell them what is happening, usually when it's too late to do anything about it.'

'Why has there been no transmission?'

'A dozen reasons,' replied the marshal. 'One of them could be the radio silence you ordered.'

Meyrin: 7.46 a.m.

'Where's the goddamn hammer?' shouted Lubbock.

'In the car,' replied Roskill.

'Get it for Christ's sake.'

The building was shaking violently. As Ruth looked up at the roof she could see that it would shake loose from the walls at any moment and come crashing down on them. She was shaking with fright. Roskill made a dash for the door, returning a few moments later with the hammer. As he came through the door, part of the wall collapsed, burying him.

Ruth and Lubbock scrabbled at the rubble to get him out.

'I'm OK' gasped Roskill – a palpable lie. 'Get the hammer and stop that thing. We must have destroyed half of Geneva.'

Lubbock used his hands like a shovel, bruising and tearing his flesh. He found the wooden handle, and jerked it out, scattering debris over Roskill. The roof buckled and caved in. The hammer was pinned under the general's body which was being crushed by the steel girder.

London: 6.47 a.m./Washington: 1.47 a.m.

'Do you have any news?' enquired the Prime Minister.

'Warsaw Pact countries have gone to full alert, ready for war.'

'NATO must respond,' said the English woman indignantly. 'We didn't start this.'

'There's a satellite report coming in now,' said the President. 'Two CERN buildings have been taken out; the wrong ones. There are no holes in the ground so presumably the experimental work is continuing. What report from the SAS team?'

'Nothing since they began their attack. There are only six of them. I imagine they have their hands full.'

CERN: 7.47 a.m.

Vilkov, Ashensky and Andrevich were crouched over the printer as it jerked out its staccato messages. It seemed interminable to Rakov, who was listening to the SAS assault with mounting apprehension.

'For God's sake,' cried Rakov, 'don't you know yet?'

The scientists didn't hear him; they were concentrating on the flow of words and symbols, trying to interpret the meaning, desperately hoping that a miracle would unfold and tell them Tesla's secret. Ashensky thought he saw the answer emerging. 'That's it! That's it! I can see it . . . ' only to be disappointed when the next bunch of numbers made no sense. And all the while the ground was lurching and heaving under their feet; segments of plaster were shearing off the ceiling and showering them and their machines with dust and grit and lumps of masonry. The printer chattered on its chosen programmed course, so far ignoring the havoc around it.

It was a race between the violence of the earthquake, and the speed of the machine to interpret man's calculations. The computer at the end of the line tilted as the ground beneath it subsided. It fell on its side in a shower of sparks. The printer hesitated, and then decided to ignore its stricken mate.

The surviving KGB tensed, their weapons aimed at the gaping hole where the steel door used to be.

The printer stopped. At first Vilkov thought it had been knocked out. When he looked at the figures, he revised his opinion. 'I think this is it!' Ashensky and Andrevich were puzzled. The figures told them nothing more than before. They weren't identical to those they had earlier rejected, but the variations were minimal.

'How can you say that, Comrade Professor?' asked Ashensky.

Vilkov was almost pensive as he answered. 'We are looking for something that corresponds with what we know, and yet Tesla told us it was a new form of physics, as new as black holes could have been to him. This is the solution. This is it.'

'But I don't understand,' said Andrevich, 'with or without a drink. And you, professor, don't understand it either.'

'Not completely,' said Vilkov, 'but I understand enough to be certain this is the only answer we're going to get.'

'What do we do with it?' asked Ashensky.

'Transmit,' said Vilkov.

'All of it?' exclaimed Andrevich.

Sunday 29th November 1981

'The last page first!'

Rakov was bothered by the silence at the steel door. He was sure the attack had not been beaten off, and that the last push would take his enemies through the door and into their inner chamber. 'For Christ's sake stop arguing and send! They'll be on us any second.'

'Encode it,' said Vilkov decisively. The computer operator hit the keys with speed and precision. 'We need two minutes,' he said to Rakov, who merely grunted. He was tempted to leave the inner room and join the defending force in the main part of the tunnel. Instinct told him to stay with the high speed transmitter until the secret was safe with the Motherland.

The shock waves of a grenade in the tunnel knocked them to the ground. The computer operator was the first to recover. He checked that the encoding machine was still working, and continued flicking his fingers across the keyboard.

Rakov's first line of defence was immobilized by Lloyd's grenade. The KGB defenders furthest from the open hole that had been the steel door, survived. Four machine guns were trained on the hole. They opened fire as soon as Lloyd and Tyson's bodies were launched through the air. They narrowly escaped the bullets and lay, pinned to the ground. Evans, slowed by the injury to his ankle, was not so lucky. Bullets from two machine guns found their mark, and stitched a pattern across his chest and stomach practically severing his body in two. It was not immediate oblivion. His brain had time to register extreme pain. His piercing scream stunned even the KGB defenders.

Lloyd and Tyson lay full length on the floor of the tunnel, unable to move. Tyson, just below their arc of fire, began crawling, embracing the ground, to the opening he had just come through. Lloyd stayed put. Tyson got through. If Lloyd was to stand any chance of getting in, there had to be covering fire or a diversion, preferably both. He had two grenades left. He put them carefully on the ground at his feet. He eased Evans' carbine from his fingers. With a gun in each hand he edged his way to the entrance. He hefted each carbine into an upward elevation and pressed the trigger repeatedly. Bullets ricocheted off the roof in a lethal random hail. He heard sounds that could have meant hits. When the returning fire ceased, he took the pin from one grenade and hurled it far to his left, and then did the same in the other direction.

As the second grenade exploded Lloyd leapt at the door of the inner room, crashing it open. Tyson followed in Lloyd's wake, landing on the ground and rolling over, his carbine clutched to his chest.

Meyrin: 7.48 a.m.

Tears and sweat drenched Ruth. The pain in her arms from the unaccustomed strain on little-used muscles was almost unbearable. Jack Lubbock's shoulder was at an odd angle, and the weight of the girder had crushed his chest. She could see no sign of breathing. Somehow she had to move the huge metal. She heaved once again. The girder slid from his shoulder to his knees which gave out a nasty crunching noise. At the same time Lubbock's chest heaved and a long drawn sigh came from his lips. 'I'm sorry, Jack . . . I'm sorry . . . ' and she wiped away more tears. She now had to move Jack to get the hammer. She wondered if she had the strength or courage to inflict yet more pain on the mutilated body of her friend. She pulled at his arm. He did not respond. She realized he was either unconscious or dead; either way he would feel nothing. She pulled harder; at last the fourteen pound hammer came free. She was by now so weak she could barely lift it. She dragged it and herself over the heaving rubble, constantly being bombarded by shards of masonry. The oscillator was still secured to the main upright stanchion which was withstanding all that the heaving foundations did to it.

She lifted the hammer and aimed it at the machine. She missed completely. The weight of the hammer took her off balance, and she measured her length on the rubble, tearing her clothes and skin. She recovered the hammer and tried again. This time it was even more difficult to lift. She managed to get it above her head and with a last despairing lunge brought its full weight crashing into the oscillator. It destroyed Tesla's earthquake maker, but it did not stop the earthquake.

One segment of roof was left. Another surge of underground movement dislodged it. It collapsed inwards and struck the vertical girder a glancing blow, sufficient to shake it in its foundation, the trembling ground did the rest, and the conductor of the resonance that was wrecking Geneva toppled over, killing Ruth Coverdale.

The telephone survived. It rang, and rang.

CERN: 7.49 a.m.

The high speed transmitter consisted of a telex machine to which was attached a radio transmitter. The message had to be typed into the telex, transmitted to a buffer store, and then broadcast at very high speed, which to the ordinary ear would sound like a rapid gabble. At the receiving end, the message would be recorded at high speed and then played back slowed down, and printed out at normal word-processor pace. Its defences against detection were its speed – a few seconds, the near-impossibility of monitoring every wavelength, and the fact that it was transmitted in code; a formidable set of obstacles.

The computer operator finished typing the coded instructions. The buffer store was assimilating the information.

Lloyd burst through the door. Telinger fired at him. The

exploding grenades threw the KGB colonel off his feet, and his two revolver shots passed harmlessly into the ceiling. The buffer store continued digesting information.

Lloyd was the first to recover. He shot Telinger twice; once through the chest and the second time in the head.

Vilkov, Ashensky, Andrevich and the computer operator faced the attackers without a weapon between them.

Rakov's reactions were faster than Telinger's. He took quick careful aim at Tyson's head. Only the heaving floor responding to the continuing earthquake saved his life. Rakov aimed again, but Tyson was already diving for cover.

The printer stopped. The high speed transmitter was fully primed. He needed to press the transmit button and hold it down for three seconds. He took a quick shot at Lloyd. The bullet entered his thigh, just above the knee. It brought him down. As Rakov stood up to finish Lloyd, Tyson fired two quick shots; one grazed the Russian's left arm.

Rakov realized that he had only once chance, to fire quickly at each man and then stand to find and press the vital key. Nothing could then stop the message being transmitted; the prospect of his own death, which he knew was now inevitable, made him angry, and the more determined. His mistake was to fire first at Lloyd. Richard – whose reactions had been quickened by his weeks with the SAS – realized the ploy, quickly ducked, then stood up, putting his life in the hands of his instinct, and was rewarded with the sight of Rakov, having loosed his second shot at Tyson, looking at the transmitter. Lloyd shot first at the outstretched hand as it moved towards the button. Richard's luck held. There is no way anybody, however well-trained, can prevent the instinctive withdrawal of a hand shattered by a bullet. Strive as he did, to force his hand to continue its course to the keyboard, pain commanded the reflex action. Rakov knew, in that instant that he was dead and his mission a failure. His face contorted in rage, almost *risus sardonicus*, thought Lloyd, as his second bullet tore into the Russian's body.

Vilkov sprang to life and his hand snaked out to press the transmitting key. A three shot burst from Tyson's carbine took the professor full in the chest, lifting him off his feet. Tyson lowered his aim. The radio and recorder disintegrated under the impact of burst after burst of repeated fire.

Tyson stopped firing. Ashensky, Andrevich and the operator were like wax figures in a chamber of horrors; white-faced, rigid in fear. Tyson planted his feet wide apart to steady his aim. Lloyd had a similar stance, both hands gripping his .45 calibre pistol. Both weapons were aimed at the Soviet citizens. The Yank and the Brit knew they should kill them, but Lloyd hadn't been at Hereford long enough, and Tyson was no cold killer. They lowered their weapons.

The operator moved his hands towards the drawer. Lloyd and Tyson reacted in unison. Their weapons reared as they fired at the Russians until long after all three were dead. The reaction was instinctive, fear holding their fingers on the triggers, fear that the computer operator kept the means of death in the drawer of the console. He did; a packet of cigarettes.

CERN: 7.52 a.m.

The tremors lessened and ultimately stopped. A section of tunnel roof came away and crashed on to the bank of computers, starting a fire. Tyson and Lloyd tried to put it out, but failed; they tried to get past the flames to salvage the encoded message; they were beaten back by the flames.

Aftermath

CERN

The main control room was a mass of rubble, destroyed by the earthquake. A painstaking search of the wreckage failed to reveal the other two pieces of the Tesla Trinity.

London

The British and American Governments agreed to pay reparation to the Swiss. The Russian ambassador presented a note denouncing 'imperialist warmongers for an act of barbaric aggression on a small band of misguided patriots whose only crime was to seek the survival of their people.' It was decided that no useful purpose would be served by publishing the incontrovertible evidence that the USSR had invaded a neutral country with arms and men and held hundreds hostage.

Washington, DC

The earthquake was ascribed to unique seismic activity. The tabloids produced soothsayers who said it was an Act of God, foretelling the end of the world if the race for weapons of mass destruction was not halted.

The President of the United States did not attend the funeral of the wife of his Special Advisor. She, Roskill and Lubbock were described as 'among the many victims of all nationalities who perished in the worst European earthquake in living memory.'

Frederick Coverdale was a changed man. He had aged ten years in as many hours. The spring had gone from his step; he walked like an arthritic. 'I'm sorry to resign so soon into the job, Mr President, but . . . '

'There's no need for that, Freddie. Take a couple of weeks at my ranch. Grief passes, you know.'

'I've found out too much about myself these last weeks, and a lot of it I don't like. The last thing you need in this job is a man with an identity crisis.'

'As you wish. What will you do?'

'Ruth had a place at Malibu. I never really cared for it, but I think I'll go there now. It might help me find out a bit more about . . . my wife.'

Geneva

The Swiss government announced that any 'perpetrators of the murder and mayhem' still at large would be hunted down. All would be brought to justice and mercy was not on offer.

Kimitrov, Nr Varaslav, USSR

At 9.57 a.m. on 29th November 1981 Aleksandra Nikolayeuna Rakova shivered as a sense of foreboding overcame her.

She had had the experience before; it usually foretold an accident to one of her family. This time the sensation was so strong she had to sit to catch her breath. She knew it concerned her beloved Yuri.

A few days later written confirmation arrived. This would normally be factual and perfunctory, but the writer must have known Yuri the man, not Rakov the Chekist, and have taken some risk in writing of his 'daring and courage' and that he died a 'soldier's' death for Mother Rodina!

Yuri's father still hardened his proud face against news of his son, but alone, in the fields, tears flowed to relieve his grief. That night he silently consumed two bottles of vodka and the family knew forgiveness had begun.

* * *

Work continues, unabated, in both East and West, in search of the secret of the Tesla Shield. It has been given fresh impetus by President Reagan's Strategic Defense Initiative. Russian protests that this is a new escalation are not convincing; they have had their own 'star wars' programme for years. But one day, somebody in Sarychagan, Siberia, or Huntsville, Alabama, or Maidenhead, Berkshire, will make it work.

John Malcolm,
Wimbledon Common,
England.